DAW Books Presents GINI KOCH's
Alien Novels:

ALIEN
IN CHIEF

GINI KOCH

DAW BOOKS, INC.
DONALD A. WOLLHEIM, FOUNDER
375 Hudson Street, New York, NY 10014

**ELIZABETH R. WOLLHEIM
SHEILA E. GILBERT
PUBLISHERS**
www.dawbooks.com

First Printing, December 2015
1 2 3 4 5 6 7 8 9

This is dedicated to the ones I love. All of you.
You all know who you are.

ACKNOWLEDGMENTS

As always, love and thanks to my fantastic editor, Sheila Gilbert, my awesome agent, Cherry Weiner, my amazing crit partner, Lisa Dovichi, and the best beta reader in the West, Mary Fiore. Cannot do this without you guys. Okay, I can, but everything I do is better because of the four of you.

Love and thanks to all the good folks at DAW Books and Penguin Random House, to all my fans around the globe, my Hook Me Up! Gang, members of Team Gini new and old, all Alien Collective Members in Very Good Standing, Members of the Stampeding Herd, Twitter followers, Facebook fans and friends, Pinterest followers, the fabulous bookstores that support me, and all the wonderful fans who come to my various book signings and conference panels—you're all the best and I wouldn't want to do this without each and every one of you along for the ride.

My list of those I want to give special thanks to is normally pretty darned long, but time is tight (I'm late again, what *were* the odds?) and so I'm going with the time honored "If I thanked you before I'm thanking you again, even more so" approach. So, if your name is not listed, I still love you and thank you for all you do, I just ran out of time to shout your name from the rooftops again.

So, special love and extra shout-outs to: my awesome assistants, Joseph Gaxiola and Colette Chmiel for continuing to always keep me sane, on time, and efficient; Adrian & Lisa Payne, Hal & Dee Astell, and Duncan & Andrea Rittschof for continuing to always show up everywhere, with smiling faces and books (and Poofs) in hand, ensuring anywhere I'm at is always a warm, fun place to be; Scott

Johnson for being the nicest bed & breakfast spot and the oasis of calm in my book tours; Tom & Libby Thomas, Pat & Barbara Michel, Koren Cota, Chrysta Stuckless, Missy Katano, Christina Callahan, Amy Thacker, Jan Robinson, Mariann Asanuma, Koleta Parsley, Mikel Dornhecker, Carien Ubink, Terry Smith, Joan Du, James Du, Michael Shelton, Janet Armentani, Colette Chmiel, Anne Taylor, Heidi Berthiaume, and Shawn Sumrall for bestowing beautiful, supportive, wonderful, and delicious things upon me what seems like all the time; Robert Palsma for continuing to like everything I do; all the fans who travel from far away to see the me, like Missy Katano, Michele Ogle, and Paul Sparks; and for a ton of physical labor and emotional support during cons, special love to Duncan and Andrea Rittschof, Terry Smith, Missy Katano, Brad Jensen, Joseph Gaxiola, Edward Pulley, and Kathi Schreiber.

Always last in the list but never in my heart, thanks to my Husband in Chief, Steve, and our First (and only) Daughter, Veronica. You're the best in the world and I love you both more than words can say.

AH, TO SEE THE WORLD, travel to exotic locations, and meet interesting people. Sounds great, doesn't it?

Of course, most people get to plan their exotic trips and exciting vacations. I get yanked into mine, almost always against my will and often through literally being dragged there by powerful forces unknown to man. Well, okay, known to some men, and women, too. Hey, can't blame a girl for adding a little drama.

Anyway, vacations are a little different when you're seeing new solar systems, traveling to exotic planets, and meeting lots of interesting aliens, many of whom are trying to kill you. Well, of course, as I look at my life over the past six years or so, that just kind of sounds like business as usual.

Oh, it's not all negative, though. I've gotten to save the world so many times I've lost count. Saved the galaxy at least once. Saved other solar systems, too. I'm just that kind of can-do girl.

And though discovering aliens were living on Earth came as a shock six years ago, nowadays it's almost commonplace. Almost.

"My" aliens are all from Alpha Four in the Alpha Centauri solar system, and they're all drop-dead gorgeous, super brainy, and come loaded with a lot of special talents including hyperspeed, faster regeneration, super strength, and then some. They really are all that and a Bag of Super Deluxe Just Like the Justice League and the X-Men Chips.

Other aliens seem split between the Friends of Earth or Want To Destroy All Other Life Forms factions. So far, we and the Friends of Earth side have been doing okay, despite the fact that Earth itself has a plethora of cackling evil geniuses, multinational crime lords, and cuckoo megalomaniacs. We could export them, we have so many.

Not that I am for one minute suggesting we should. We have enough problems out there, why give our enemies a chance to gang up on us? I mean, more than they already do.

One of those evil geniuses in particular is the proverbial thorn in our sides: The Mastermind. Someone we all trusted. Someone we all wanted to eliminate with extreme prejudice. And someone who—until we can find all his strongholds, and all his plans, and all his cohorts, and make sure that he doesn't have some awful doomsday plot or three that will activate if he dies suddenly—we cannot touch.

I'd thought I'd have taken him down a year ago, but the cosmos had other plans and, instead, we got to avert a gigantic system-wide civil war over in Alpha Centauri while also stopping yet another huge invasion of Earth. We did get some cool parting gifts in the bargain, including two clones of former enemies who are now on our side, plus some alien pigdogs and foxcats. I'm in the minority in thinking these made everything else worthwhile, but some people just can't see the roses for the trees. Or some such.

We also made a lot of new alien friends. Many of whom want to visit Earth. Because, to them, Earth is that exotic tropical island way out in the middle of nowhere where a person can just relax and get away from it all.

Yeah, I know, right? They're thinking they're going to waste away in "Margaritaville," but we're a whole lot more like "Welcome to the Jungle." After all, there's a reason it took Axl Rose twenty years to write "Chinese Democracy." And a classified reason for why it had to suck. But I digress . . .

CHAPTER 1

"**M**OMMY, why is that car floating?"

For most mothers, the answer would be "special effects" or "just watch the movie, honey." For me, it required a different explanation.

"Ah, Jamie, well . . . I think it's because your little brother, um, wants it to. Charlie? Charlie, honey, put the car down, please. Now."

Thankfully, the car in question was one of the toy cars that my son was far too young to play with. That didn't stop him from wanting them, however. And, because he wanted them, well . . . Charlie took them. By making them come to him.

In the past years I've gone through so many changes that you'd think change would be commonplace, something I didn't even think twice about.

You'd be wrong.

Becoming an alien superbeing exterminator? Handled like a boss. Becoming the Ambassador for an alien principality? So four years ago. Being the wife of a still-unwilling but going to do his best for his people and country politician? Got it covered. Finding that the Mastermind of the majority of our problems on Earth was a good friend? Still plotting the revenge. Swapping places with another me and visiting another universe? Check. Averting a whole solar system's civil war? Double check.

But none of these changes prepared me for my biggest battle.

Being the mother of two.

Two alien hybrid children with, oh, shall we say, unusual abilities. Don't get me wrong—I love my kids. They're great and, frankly, I have tons of help, a super supportive husband, totally there parents and in-laws, and a plethora of Secret Service agents following us everywhere. I mean, I have no right to complain at all.

I just have to say that, sometimes it felt like averting an alien civil war was a lot easier than parenting. Times like right now, for instance.

My daughter Jamie of course knew why the toy car was floating. She was just asking so that she could point out that her little brother was doing something I didn't want him to in a way that might mean she wasn't a tattletale.

Of course, since Charlie's birth six months ago, we'd actually needed Jamie's tattling, because Charlie's very unusual talent had manifested at birth.

Being the family of the current Vice President of the United States meant that we were under microscopic scrutiny. Seeing as my husband, Jeff, was also an alien whose parents and family were originally from Alpha Four of the Alpha Centauri system meant we were under scrutiny at subatomic levels.

The A-Cs, as they called themselves on Earth, were religious refugees when they came in the 1960s. And they'd integrated into the world, sort of, and stayed hidden, almost completely, as citizens of the United States first and the world second. Now, thanks to a just-barely-foiled alien invasion from four years ago, the entire world knew that aliens were real, and that the best looking ones in the galaxy had chosen to live with us.

Perks aside, our A-Cs were here to protect and serve. Could not say the same for at least half of the alien races out there we'd encountered so far.

The A-Cs had two hearts and, as such, this gave them faster regeneration, hyperspeed, and super-strength. Some of them also had special talents, like Jeff, who was the strongest empath in, most likely, the galaxy. Besides the empaths, there were imageers, who could manipulate any images, static or live or whatever, dream readers, and troubadours, who were the actors and public speakers of the bunch.

All female hybrid children, of which we still didn't have all that many, were especially talented, with skills far surpassing the A-C norm. But before now, no hybrid boys had exhibited exceptional talent. They'd gotten normal talents, or none at all—the only exceptions were those children who were the progeny of Ronald Yates. For whatever reason, the newest crop of male hybrid kids were all talented in some ways, but nothing like Charlie. Because until now, telekinesis hadn't been an A-C trait.

I'd gotten pregnant on a world where telepathy and telekinesis were normal, though, which was the only explanation we had had for Charlie's abilities. Psychic osmosis? I'm at a point where nothing surprises me, so yeah, maybe.

You'd think that, with all the other things the A-Cs could do, Charlie being telekinetic would be no big to anyone in the A-C community.

And you would be wrong.

The car was still floating, and now it had company. "Charlie, put the cars down, please and thank you." He grinned at me—he totally had his father's smile—and yet the cars continued to fly away from the other kids in the American Centaurion Embassy School and Daycare Center and fly right to Charlie. "All the cars down, please, Charlie. Now."

Counted to ten. Listened to the music while I did so—my rule was that music needed to be happening as much as possible wherever I was, inside the Embassy and in whatever car I was in in particular.

Other people's rules were that the music in the daycare

center couldn't be hard rock or be loaded with suggestive lyrics because others were far more into censorship and keeping cool things from kids than I was.

But I still managed to get good music of all eras piped in for the little ones, because the term "hard rock" was subjective and complex lyrics helped young minds to grow and learn. Jethro Tull had just finished "War Child" and Paul McCartney and Wings were now singing "Children, Children." And cars were still flying. It was time to channel my mother.

"Charles Maxwell Martini, you return those cars and put them right down this instant, young man."

No more grinning from my son, but the cars zoomed back to the kids who'd been playing with them and landed nicely. One for the win column.

Denise Lewis, whose husband was my mother's right-hand man in the Presidential Terrorism Control Unit and our Embassy's Defense Attaché, smiled at me. "Good job, Kitty."

Managed not to say that Jamie hadn't been this much work. She had been, she'd just been different.

Was saved from having to respond in any way by Kyle Constantine and Len Parker sticking their heads in. I'd met them in Vegas when they were still playing football for USC and they'd helped me out in a big way. They could have both gone pro, but instead they joined the C.I.A. right after they graduated. Len had been assigned as my driver and Kyle as my bodyguard, and both had done a great job.

But right before some of us took a trip to the Alpha Centauri system to avert a variety of civil wars, evil plots, and yet another alien invasion, Kyle had been put in charge of the Second Best Lady's Cause.

Actually, I still had no idea what my official title was as the wife of the VP. No one around seemed to know, or care. I'd searched the papers for clues, but stories written about me tended to focus on all the madness that surrounded us on a daily basis, with adjectives tending more toward "outspoken," "blunt," and "trigger-happy."

Anyway, a politician who'd been aligned with all of our enemies during the presidential campaign that had put Senator Vincent Armstrong into the White House, dragging Jeff along kicking and screaming, had somehow managed to become our ally. The slipperiness of political bedfellows and changing alliances never ceased to amaze me. It truly made fighting alien invasions, mad super-geniuses, and crazed megalomaniacs seem like such clean work.

"Kitty, Gideon Cleary's here," Kyle said. Speaking of the devil I'd just been thinking about. "We need to brainstorm the next ad campaign."

Mommy Time was over. Time to get back in the saddle and handle grown-up things.

"And," Len added, "we have news, too. News you're not going to like."

CHAPTER 2

HUGGED AND KISSED JAMIE and Charlie, handed Charlie to Denise, petted all our animals — of which we had so many, both Earth and alien, we'd all lost count — grabbed my purse, and headed out.

Once we got out of the daycare center even better music was playing. I kept us tuned to the Aerosmith Channel, and while other bands were allowed and even encouraged, my rule was at least one song from my Bad Boys from Boston for every ten on the playlist.

"What's going on?" I asked as "Back in the Saddle" was, possibly prophetically, playing softly in the background and we got on the elevator and headed down for the meeting. "New issues with The Cause?"

The Cause was protecting campus co-eds from being attacked and raped. When we'd met, Kyle had been drunk and suggested that I might like to get to know half of the Trojan football team intimately. Len had stopped that — well, Len and Harlie.

Harlie was a Poof, aka the best wedding gift ever. Poofs were alien animals that looked a lot like tiny, fluffy kittens with no visible ears or tails, but with shiny black button eyes. They were fluffy balls on tiny legs and paws and I and everyone else loved them. They were also incredibly great protection because they could go Jeff-sized with tons of razor sharp teeth when danger threatened, so they were wonderful personal protection bundles of cuteness.

Supposedly they were pets for the Alpha Four Royal Family only—which I'd somehow married into—but the Poofs were androgynous and mated whenever a royal wedding loomed. Supposedly.

In reality, the Poofs were Black Hole Universe animals, and apparently our Poofs had decided to go forth and multiply. We had tons of Poofs, and more seemed to show up with a lot of regularity.

In the Poofs' world, if you named it, it was yours. And the Poofs made the call as to what they considered a name— and therefore who they considered their "owner"—so a lot of people had scored Poofs simply because they'd said something like, "Look at that, how adorable is that?" Which is how one of our friends, Representative Nathalie Gagnon-Brewer had gotten a Poof. She called hers Dora for short.

Harlie had gone large and in charge way back when and scared Kyle straight, and to prove it, totally without my even knowing, Kyle had started a Take Back the Night program while he and Len were still at USC, which created a service where anyone on campus could call to get a security escort back to wherever they called home, and led info sessions to teach girls how to avoid date rape situations and how to get out of them safely.

Many colleges had these programs, but Kyle's had been particularly effective, in part because he'd gotten all the jocks involved in a positive way. He'd been one of the representatives for USC's sports program's preventative counseling service, which worked with athletes to keep them from becoming the kind of men who thought women were playthings made to be dominated. He'd been, from all Len said, quite intense about it.

All this had made him the man for the job when Cleary had come to us asking for support with putting a similar program in place in all the colleges and universities in

Florida, where he was still governor. He'd also suggested it as my Cause, and I honestly had no objection.

Cleary had thought up The Cause, however, because he was intimately involved in a scandal that we had, so far, managed to keep under wraps.

"No, not an issue with The Cause," Kyle replied. "Though I'm sure that's the reason we'll all give for why he's here. We think we have a hit on Stephanie."

"Really?" Think of the scandal and it appeared. Or something like that. Maybe I still had some telepathic resonance from Operation Civil War. Or maybe Charlie had done a mother-and-child feedback with me like Jamie had and I just wasn't fully aware of it yet. "How confirmed of a hit?"

"We're not sure," Len said, as the elevator opened and we headed off for one of the smaller salons. "Governor Cleary didn't want to tell us a lot without you in the room."

"For a guy whose state isn't next to the Beltway, he's sure up here a lot."

"He's going to run for President again," Len said. "We all know it. He's keeping his ties tight. Can't blame him for that."

"I can guarantee he wants to activate Clarence, though," Kyle added. "So if you still want to tell him no, you'd better call Jeff."

"Why?"

"Because Mister Reynolds sounds like he's on Cleary's side," Len said. "Not sure why."

Speaking of one of my son's namesakes and my best friend since ninth grade. "Chuckie's here? When did he get here?" Normally I knew when he or Jeff were coming to or in the Embassy during the work day. I pulled my phone out and sent a "get home now, please and thank you" text to my husband. It sounded like the boys were right and we were going to need him here sooner as opposed to later.

Chuckie was the head of the C.I.A.'s Extra-Terrestrial Division and, thanks to what we brought back from

Operation Civil War, the Golden Boy of the Agency. Which meant that he had even more enemies within the Agency than he had had before.

Chuckie lived in the Embassy now, because his apartments kept getting trashed by people trying to kill him. And his emotional state hadn't been stable since we'd gotten back from Operation Civil War, because of the horrible things that had happened to him out there, and the fact that the guy he'd thought was his best friend had turned out to be the Mastermind and therefore the guy directly responsible for the death of his wife. Crap like that can affect a person for some reason.

"He came with the governor," Len answered as we reached the salon and the music changed to Mötley Crüe's "Chicks = Trouble." "And they came in with Mister Buchanan. And they were all vetted by the Secret Service."

We had a lot of Secret Service agents with us, more than the VP normally got. Because of me. Oh well, I was keeping people employed. Go me, creating jobs. We had less Secret Service tailing us inside the Embassy because we were in one of the most secure buildings we could be, and because we had other internal protection.

Malcolm Buchanan had been assigned by my mother to be my personal shadow and bodyguard when we'd first come to D.C. And there wasn't a day I wasn't grateful for Mom's prescience. I insisted Buchanan had Dr. Strange powers because he came and went like the wind and if the man didn't want you to see him, you didn't see him.

I saw him now, though. He was standing at the back of the room, clearly on guard, leaning against the wall in a way that I knew meant he could propel himself wherever he wanted, instantly. The boys moved to similar positions within the room.

Chuckie and Cleary were sitting, and they both looked rather stressed and grim. So, it was going to be that kind of meeting. Oh goody.

"Missus Chief," Buchanan said with a small smile. "In case you haven't already guessed . . . we have a problem."

"I took the leap, Malcolm. Chuckie, Gideon, why so serious?"

"Someone just tried to kill me," Cleary said, voice shaking. "And I'm pretty sure it was Stephanie."

CHAPTER 3

STEPHANIE WAS JEFF'S NIECE, his eldest sister's eldest daughter. Her father, Clarence Valentino, had been
an A-C traitor of the highest order. And I'd had to kill him.
But not before he'd turned Stephanie.

Understandably, she'd blamed us for her father's death
and joined the Mastermind's team with gusto. That had gotten her arrested at the end of Operation Defection Election. But that hadn't kept her down.

During the campaign she'd somehow been released into
Cleary's custody—partly because she'd only been nineteen,
partly because the case had been made for extenuating circumstances and insanity due to grief over her father's death
and all that jazz—meaning a lot of strings had been pulled,
undoubtedly by the Mastermind, who we all knew Cleary
had been working with.

And, because of that pull, her record had been wiped
clean, at least her record with the government. With us, not
so much, but the A-Cs were all willing to forgive if she
wasn't going to try to kill everyone again.

Stephanie had seemed semi-normal for a while and appeared to be toeing the legal line, though she'd avoided all
the A-Cs, even her mother and siblings. Cleary had seemed
to think he and his family had rehabilitated her, and they'd

treated her like family, though Cleary was still on the side of the Mastermind at the time.

But unfortunately, the best laid plans of mice and men and all that, she'd also started sleeping with the Mastermind. And then he'd had her kill eight of our Secret Service detail during Operation Bizarro World.

Stephanie had freaked out and disappeared, which we'd discovered right at the start of Operation Civil War. There were two theories about her disappearance. One was that she was faking us out, so that we'd come after her and walk into a trap. The other was that she was afraid of the Mastermind and hiding from him. The longer she was gone—and she'd been gone for over a year and a half now—the more credible the second theory seemed.

There was also the theory that said Stephanie was dead, killed by the Mastermind. While we never discounted that one, if she'd been sighted, that would be a good thing. Barring her once again trying to murder people.

"Are you sure it was her?" I asked as I sat down at the small conference table we had in this room.

"Fairly sure," Chuckie said.

"Very sure," Cleary said.

Looked to Buchanan. Who shrugged. "I didn't see any of it, Missus Chief. I was just near enough that when Reynolds called I could get to them the quickest."

Wondered why Buchanan had been near to Chuckie, versus near to me, for this particular situation. Chose to table the question for later. "What happened?"

"The governor was finishing a meeting with several lobbyists," Chuckie said. "I was . . . observing the meeting."

"He was spying on us, he means," Cleary said, without a lot of animosity. Chuckie just shrugged.

"What was the meeting about?"

"Whether or not to close NASA Base," Cleary replied.

Well, that was new. And now it made a lot of sense why

Chuckie had been "observing" this meeting. "Why would anyone want to close NASA Base?"

"I have no idea," Cleary said. "I certainly have no desire to do so."

"But you did, during your Presidential campaign," Chuckie pointed out, as the music changed to "A Letter to Both Sides" by the Fixx. "And the people who you met with are still pushing for it, even though you've dropped it to have a better chance of success in the next election, or the one after."

Cleary nodded. "That's very true. At any rate, we finished the meeting, and as we were leaving the restaurant, I saw Stephanie across the street. As soon as she saw me she disappeared. I thought she'd run away from me. But then someone took a shot at me."

"Excuse me? No one's mentioned that Florida's governor was attacked on our streets."

"The restaurant lets out into the back, where there's an alley and a small parking lot," Chuckie explained. "So that people can leave without being seen together, if needed."

"Gotcha. But still, shots tend to draw attention."

"Not," Chuckie said dryly, "when they're done with a bow and arrow."

"What, Stephanie's become Green Arrow or Huntress? I don't buy it."

Sure, Stephanie was a traitor and a murderer, but she was still a young woman, only twenty-one years old. Maybe she thought Cleary wanted to shut down the Base and so was trying to protect her family. Maybe not. But she was so young, there was a chance she could be salvaged, saved, redeemed. Again.

And we'd brought just the person to do it home from another solar system.

On Beta Eight we'd discovered a clone of Clarence. The Clarence Clone had been created quickly and without all the bells and whistles our Earth clones had. And he'd lived on a world where a large number of us—Jeff, Chuckie, and myself included—were somehow considered gods. And he still thought we were gods, even though we'd told him that we weren't.

He had some of the original Clarence's memories and mannerisms, but otherwise, he'd been a lonely, simple but not stupid, living Secret Sentry. He'd proved his worth and loyalty, and we'd brought him home with us.

Sylvia and their other children had been overjoyed. And, despite our explaining that this was a clone, they'd chosen to ignore us and act as though it was the original Clarence, who'd just had a terrible head trauma and memory loss.

The Clarence Clone had none of the mean or the evil that the original had developed in spades by the time Jamie was born. The Clone was more like the guy Sylvia had fallen in love with. So I could understand the desire to play pretend.

However, TCC, as we called him in shorthand, was the one person who could probably bring Stephanie in from the cold, and potentially even get her to confess. Because without her confessing to the fact that Clifford Goodman was the Mastermind, we had no solid proof that could convict him of anything in a court of law.

Of course, Cleary had been in the Mastermind's Inner Circle during Operation Defection Election. However, he hadn't known that Cliff was the Mastermind, or at least so he'd told us when he'd come fully over to our side after the events of Operations Bizarro World and Civil War and, frankly, we believed him. In part because Cliff hadn't launched whatever his Doomsday Plan might be against us, meaning Cleary hadn't told Cliff that we all knew who the Mastermind really was.

Cleary knew now, and had given us what intel he had, but because he *hadn't* known that Cliff was the Mastermind, he didn't have any information that worked as actual proof.

Cleary couldn't confirm that Cliff was the Mastermind, or that Cliff had done anything illegal, ever. It was all the "we were at this meeting together" or "he gave me a sealed letter" type of circumstantial evidence that would, at best, prove that Cliff had been one of the Mastermind's flunkies, but nothing more.

We had to take Cliff down definitively, and that meant we needed someone who'd seen him get his hands really dirty and who would also actually say so in a court of law. And that someone was Stephanie.

"No, I don't think she's become some amazing archer," Chuckie said. "But she was close enough when she shot—using a crossbow, so stick with your Huntress analogy—that if I hadn't seen Cleary react to something I wouldn't have been near enough to knock him out of the way."

"Are you okay?" I was asking Chuckie. I cared a hell of a lot more about him than I did Cleary. And, crap, I'd told Jeff to come home and that meant he could be in danger from whoever our Huntress actually was.

He smiled. "Yeah, I am. I alerted Jeff, by the way. He'll be coming home soon, alert and aware, and via a gate. Just in case. And yes, on my order." Gates were alien tech that looked like airport metal detectors but could transport you thousands of miles in seconds. They were great, but still made me nauseous to use.

However, I wasn't the one using the gate, and they were safe. I relaxed. Always nice to have the smartest guy anywhere on my side and thinking ahead. "Good. So, I'm going to guess the next questions. Do we bring in outside help or not?"

Chuckie shook his head. "That's not the question, but nice try. The question is, do we activate TCC or not? I feel it's time. He's acclimated, he's willing, and if the governor really did see Stephanie, then she's active in some way and we need to try to catch her before the Mastermind, other enemies, or even the police do."

We'd made it a point to refer to Cliff as the Mastermind so that we didn't give away that we knew who the Mastermind was to anyone we might not be able to trust. Sure, everyone in this room knew, but the concern was well-founded. We'd had a Secret Service agent working for the Mastermind who had been discovered just in time.

Sam Travis had been in C.I.A. custody for a long time now, with no access to anyone other than Mom and Chuckie. They'd made up some excuse that seemed to have appeased Cliff, in part because he'd been transferred out of Homeland Security around the same time. And apparently Dear Sam wasn't nearly as important as Stephanie, because no one had pulled any strings to get him out. Fine with me. I wasn't a fan of someone who'd been sleeping in my home while trying to destroy us, call me a Mean Girl.

"The police aren't going to catch an A-C, or at least not the human police." Heaved a sigh and sat down. "Look, I know you think TCC is ready. But . . ."

"But you don't want to risk him getting hurt because you care about him," Chuckie said gently. "However, he does understand the risks and, more than that, Stephanie and potentially many others are at even more risk of getting hurt."

"Couldn't we call in Nightcrawler and my 'uncles'?"

Benjamin Siler was the son of our first Mastermind, the Ronald Yates-Mephistopheles in-control superbeing, and one of our female Brains Behind the Throne biggies, Madeleine Cartwright. This probably made him our first hybrid. We hadn't discovered him until Operation Defection Election, but he was, until this generation, one of the only exceptionally talented male hybrids.

However, that hadn't been good enough for these people. His parents had done horrific experiments on him, turning him into someone who aged very slowly, among other things. One of those other things was his ability to "blend" — he kind of went chameleon and you couldn't see him, or anyone he was touching. He made no noise and didn't reek of sulfur, but Nightcrawler still fit as a nickname.

His uncle had rescued him and trained him in said uncle's profession—assassination. In a nice merging of situations, I'd been sort of adopted by the two best assassins in the business, Peter "The Dingo" Kasperoff and his cousin Victor. They considered themselves my uncles, and, due to a variety of favors I'd done for them, they worked with Siler to protect me and mine.

"They're advised," Buchanan said. I had a feeling he'd become an honorary member of Team Assassination during Operation Defection Election. "However, since we don't want her killed, I'm in agreement with the others—it's time to utilize the weapon you brought home from your trip to another solar system."

"Yeah, about that," Jeff said, coming into the room to "Hot" by Avril Lavigne. Considering he was tall, broad, the handsomest thing on two legs, with wavy brown hair, light brown eyes, and the sexiest smile in the galaxy along with the best naked body, the song was totally apt.

"Glad you're here, Jeff," Cleary said, as Jeff nodded to him and the others.

"Thanks. I realize you're thinking of TCC as a weapon. Hi, baby," he kissed my cheek as he sat down next to me and I did my best to wrench my mind from mentally undressing him and get it back onto business. "But the reason why Kitty's hesitant, and why I agree with that hesitation, is that, clone or not, Clarence is a real person. And he's a real person my sister and her kids are in love with and really can't emotionally handle losing again."

"Yeah, I'm honestly far more concerned about the potential closing of NASA Base than Stephanie."

Jeff nodded. "So is Vince. But on top of all this, we have another issue that is, I think, going to take precedence."

CHAPTER 4

"CAN'T WAIT," Chuckie said in a tone indicating that he really could.

"No, it can't." Jeff sighed and ran his hand through his hair. "We've received a message from Alpha Four. And by 'we' I mean me, the Office of the President, the Cabinet, and all the Joint Chiefs of Staff. Expect a call from Angela at any time."

"We're all always happy to hear from Mom and I know we all want her take on the latest fun and frolic. But since you're already here, Jeff, what's the good word? I mean, I doubt they were sending springtime greetings or asking if this was a good time to drop by and see the cherry trees in bloom."

Jeff laughed. "No, they weren't, at least as far as I know. And I don't know if I can call the word 'good,' baby. Apparently the new Planetary Council—which includes representatives from Beta Eight, Alpha Seven, and Beta Sixteen, as well as the usual suspects—wants to visit Earth."

"So," I said as Fountain of Wayne's "I Want an Alien for Christmas" came over our airwaves, "they *do* want to see the cherry trees."

"When?" Chuckie asked, expertly ignoring me. Decided to be a grown-up and not hum along with the song. Too loudly.

"Soon. From what we can tell, very soon. The request was in the usual overly formal vagueness that seems to be something the Alpha Four leadership loves to use."

"They're not declaring war, right?" Cleary asked.

"No." Jeff shot him a glare almost worthy of his cousin, Christopher White. Christopher was the unequivocal champion of glaring on this or any other world, but Jeff was really giving it a good shot for the silver medal. "They want to visit Earth. On a peace mission. At least as far as we can tell."

Chuckie's phone beeped, he took a look, and grunted. "Angela just sent me the text. Yeah, it does sound like all they want to do is visit." He looked up. "However, I'm not sure we should say yes."

"I'm not sure we should, or can, say no," Jeff countered. "I can't even begin to imagine the chaos another giant spaceship hovering overhead will cause, but it'll be worse if they use a warp gate of some kind and just show up on the steps of the Capitol building."

"Why not announce it to the general public?" As soon as the words were out of my mouth I put my hand up. "Never mind. I can think of all the reactions, and so many of them will be utter panic, with a lot of alien hating and alien worshipping thrown in."

"Right." Jeff sighed. "Even though everyone knows aliens are here and out there, it's been four years since the invasion. People have finally stopped jumping when they look up at the clouds."

Operation Destruction seemed both very far away and, if I let my memory wander even a little ways, as if it had happened yesterday. "And this will only give Club Fifty-One and all the rest of the anti-alien lunatics something new to get all fired up about."

Chuckie rubbed the back of his neck. "I'm honestly not sure how we get out of this. Insulting the Alpha Centauri system will never be in Earth's best interests."

"Can you read the message? Just so the rest of us can know what you and Jeff do and feel all special, too."

Chuckie barked a short laugh. "Sure. 'To our honored relative and those he holds in esteem, we request the opportunity to come and welcome Earth fully into our galactic community. The Planetary Council, which now includes members from all our sentient worlds, will arrive at your convenience, in the manner most appropriate to the comfort of your people. We await your formal invitation. Yours in solidarity, Emperor Alexander the First.'"

"Emperor?"

Jeff nodded slowly. "Technically, he's the king of Alpha Four and, since we managed to keep that solar system from destroying itself, he's the leader of all the planets. That would make him the emperor."

"They've never used that term before. The late and totally unlamented King Adolphus was the kind of dude to revel in the title of emperor, but he didn't use it, ever as far as I know. And he was far more controlling than Alexander is."

"I think the wording comes from Councilor Leonidas," Chuckie said. "And I'd imagine that wording is for us. Not 'us' us, but for Earth. As in, the guy who rules all these planets is dropping by to say hi to his relatives. Toe the line."

"Did Leonidas give you any secret Super Smart Guys Only message in this?" Probably sounded a little too hopeful, at least based on Buchanan's grin.

"Sadly, I don't think so." Chuckie rubbed his forehead as Tears for Fears' "Everybody Wants to Rule the World" came on. "I'll study it, though, just in case I'm missing something." All of a sudden, relatively soothing music or no, he looked like he was about to have a migraine.

In the olden days of about fourteen months ago, it would have taken a lot to get Chuckie headed for Migraine Land. After what had happened to him during Operation Civil War, however, his migraines hit fast and hard these days.

And he had mood swings that came right before or right after. Sometimes both.

I stood up. "Chuckie, I need to talk to you about something in private."

Everyone in the room, Cleary included, had experienced Chuckie's mood swings and migraines. So no one argued. It was a fiction—what I needed to talk to him about was getting him to lie down and take the medicine that our Embassy doctor, Tito Hernandez, had come up with to help ease the pain. But it was a fiction we all used.

Chuckie shook his head. "I'm fine."

"No," Jeff said gently, "you're not. Go with Kitty, Chuck. We'll focus on all the issues, and we'll consult you before we do anything, I promise."

Buchanan moved off the wall, and Chuckie saw him do it, presumably because Buchanan had wanted him to see him do it. Chuckie sighed. "Fine. You don't have to force me. Sure, Kitty, let's go talk about whatever."

I gave Jeff a quick kiss, then took Chuckie's arm and led him out of the conference room and to the nearest elevator.

"I'm okay," he muttered.

"You're not. The infirmary, or your room, which would you prefer?"

He sighed. "I'd prefer not to feel like a helpless detriment."

"You're neither. But you were hurt, badly, and all of us want to help you get better as fast as you're able." It had been fourteen months, so the term "fast" was kind of ridiculous but he didn't call me on it. "And none of us want to see you in pain, either."

We got into the elevator and he leaned against the back wall. "I know." He closed his eyes. "My room, I guess."

I hit the button for the third floor. Not that this meant anything. The infirmary and the general housing and guest quarters were all on that floor.

"You know, I know she's out there somewhere, Kitty."

"Who? Stephanie? I think we're thinking she's out there close by, aren't we?"

"Maybe, but that's not who I meant."

"Who did you mean?"

"Mimi."

CHAPTER 5

MIMI WAS THE NICKNAME he'd given to Naomi Gower, who was the half-human half-A-C he'd fallen in love with and married. And then she'd died, before they'd even been married six months.

The trouble was, I knew Chuckie was right. Naomi had taken so much Surcenthumain—what I called the Superpowers Drug—in order to protect the rest of us from the Mastermind, Chuckie and Jamie in particular, and to save ACE, that she'd become something very other than human. She'd become a superconsciousness. And she wasn't allowed back here, ever.

I'd never told Chuckie this. He didn't need to think his wife was out there somewhere where he could find her. "What do you mean?" I asked carefully, as the elevator doors opened.

"I mean I saw her, when I was strapped to that machine. She's out there, somewhere. And I know I can find her, if I just look in the right way and in the right place."

This was the very definition of "not good" for more reasons than I could count. The biggest ones were that Naomi wasn't allowed here by older and far more powerful superconsciousnesses, and they would hurt Earth if she came back. And they'd do it by hurting ACE, the benevolent superconsciousness that was now housed in my daughter. And they'd probably out Algar in the process, which would be bad for, potentially, our entire galaxy.

Algar was a Black Hole Universe being who had the biggest hard on in the multiverse for Free Will and was, therefore, on the run for crimes against his people's laws, which were more along the lines of not letting the lesser races destroy themselves. He'd taken a shine to the Alpha Four royal family thousands of years ago, and when Jeff's family had been exiled to Earth he'd come along for the ride. He was the entire Operations Team, which I'd nicknamed the Elves. There were only a handful of us who knew about Algar, and Chuckie wasn't one of them.

However, the very human reason why it was bad for Chuckie to think Naomi was alive and out in the universe somewhere was that he'd focus on trying to find her. Meaning he'd never move on and find someone else to love.

This wasn't idle speculation on my part. Chuckie had been in love with me for years—not that I'd been aware of it for most of the time, my romantic density being somewhat legendary by now—and it had taken him a long time to get over my choosing to marry Jeff. That he'd literally waste his life away searching for Naomi was a possibility that had real potential.

Time to be the worst and, at the same time, best best friend in the world and do the right thing: Lie.

I took his arm again and led him out of the elevator. "I think you saw what you wanted to see," I said gently.

"You don't believe I saw her?" He sounded confused. A mood swing was looming on the horizon.

"I believe that you believe you saw her, Chuckie. But that makes sense."

"It does?"

"Yes." We reached his room and I opened the door and led him inside. Because I wasn't a dictator, everyone was able to listen to whatever they wanted in their own rooms. Most of the staff didn't leave music going when they weren't in their living quarters, and Chuckie was no exception. But I wasn't certain silence was what he needed.

"How so?"

"You were being horrifically tortured, watching your friends being hurt, wondering if you were going to hold out or if your mind was going to be destroyed. No matter how brave a person you are—and, trust me, I know you're incredibly brave—that had to have been terrifying as well as horribly painful. When we're that hurt and scared, it's natural to see a person we love and hope that they're coming to save us."

"But . . . it was so *real*. As real as everything else I saw. Like—" He stopped speaking. Wasn't sure, but I had a feeling there was something else he wasn't telling me. But now wasn't the time to push him about whatever that might be.

"Dreams almost always feel real." I got his medicine and went to the small fridge in his room. "Water, please," I said to the fridge, aka the Elves, aka Algar. Opened it to find a bottle of Dasani waiting. Algar was always on the job. "Thank you." Algar appreciated that I was polite, and knowing that made me want to ensure I kept my record intact.

Chuckie closed his eyes. "Yeah." He swallowed hard and opened his eyes. "I don't want to take the pills."

"The medicine Tito's made for you helps you with the pain."

He shook his head. "I hate taking drugs, you know that."

"Yes, but it's non-addictive. Tito made sure."

"I just . . . what if the medicine is making me worse?"

Here it came. Paranoia was the first phase of his mood swings. It was normally followed by anger, then rage, then listlessness, remorse, and utter despair. All while he felt like his head was breaking apart.

"Why would I give it to you, if that was the case?"

He stared at me, and I could see the suspicion coming. But he didn't say anything.

I put the pills and water bottle on his nightstand. "Look,

this has been going on for months now. No one in this Embassy, heck, no one currently on Earth is responsible for what happened to you."

"*He* is," he snarled.

"Yes, in a way, Cliff is the one responsible. For so many bad things. However, he isn't the person who strapped you into that mind-expanding torture device. The people who did are dead."

"Some of them will be visiting." He sounded ready to go join Club 51. Normally when he was like this we tried to calm and soothe him. It rarely worked.

I was the one he responded to best, which made sense. I was also the one who'd spent the last many months insisting that we not rush his recovery in any way. Basically, I was willing to coddle him because I felt that he needed it.

Maybe it was the stress from him telling me he thought Naomi was alive. Maybe the worry about our impending visitations combined with the worry about everything else that was going on. But I just couldn't handle coddling him today. It hadn't been making any positive change in over a year, after all. So maybe it was time to try a new tactic.

"And I suppose you'd like us to kill them as soon as they step out of the spacecraft? Or maybe in the air?"

Chuckie stared at me. "What?"

"You're hurting, you're angry, and you're snarling. I'm all for killing Cliff Goodman. The problem with that is that we know he has clones of himself and LaRue the Clandestine Ancient Alien and Leventhal Reid all over the place. You're the first person to mention that he also probably has a doomsday plan in place if he's killed. So killing him right now is out."

"I know that, but—"

"*But* the Rapacians who put you into that machine are all dead, and the ones that will be coming to visit will be on the tightest leashes around because they'll either come that way or I'll be the one putting said leashes on. So, aside from the pain, I'm just wondering if you want us killing people, or if you're just actually enjoying wallowing in pain and sorrow somehow."

He stared at me again. "Why would you think that?"

"Because the medicine you don't want to take relieves your pain and calms your moods. I realize that this means you're not getting to be all natural. On the other hand, you're going to be more like you actually are. So unless you're really set on no longer being Batman but instead being the Incredible Hulk twenty-four-seven, I think taking your meds, lying down, and taking a nap is what a mature, intelligent adult would do."

"What . . . why are you mad at me?"

"I'm not. But, seriously, we need Normal Suave and On Top of Things Chuckie back, not Mister Emotions' Wild Ride Chuckie hanging around, moping, whining, threatening, and generally playing into all our enemies' hands."

He blinked. "I'm helping our enemies?"

I shoved him gently onto the bed. "Dude, think about it. If you're out of commission, then the best mind we have is out of commission. Why do you think Cliff centered all his evil crap on you? Sure, because of the insane rivalry, but it's there *because* you're smarter than he is."

He shook his head. "He's been three steps ahead of us for years."

"Because we didn't know who the hell the Mastermind was. We know now. Sure, we have some catching up to do, and we have to hide that we know he's a freaking backstabbing traitorous loon, but we *are* catching up. And our allies, such as the President, are aware of who and what Cliff really is, and he doesn't know that they know. But we need you, the real you, in order to catch up all the way. And that means we need you focused on getting better and on doing what you do best, which is thinking, not going off on a wild wife chase that will only end in heartbreak all around."

He was quiet for a few long moments. "Why are you saying this to me today?"

"Versus at any other time over the last fourteen months? Because you told me today that you think Naomi's still out there somewhere. I could be spitballing here, but I think that means you've been trying to find her all these months. And that's probably contributing to all your health issues in a big, nasty, negative way. And I'm telling you that you need to stop it. For you, for us, for Earth. And for the two people Naomi sacrificed herself to save—you and Jamie."

Chuckie stared at me for another few moments. "What if I can't?"

CHAPTER 6

HEAVED A SIGH AND asked the key question. "Can't or won't?"

Chuckie managed a wry smile. "Either." He heaved his own sigh and reached for his meds. "You're right, you know. I don't want to stop looking for her. And yes, I have been. Desperately. Which is pathetic."

"No, it's not. It's human." I turned on his iPod and selected the Soothing Songs playlist I'd created for him. Melissa Etheridge came on, softly singing "Sleep." "You loved her and she was taken from you. Why wouldn't you want to find her again?"

"Yeah." He took his pills and lay down. "But I think you're also right—I may have imagined it." He didn't sound convinced of this.

"Look, let's say you're right. What, exactly, can you do?" Hoped his answer wasn't going to be to take a lot of Surcenthumain and become a superconsciousness. Or die.

"Nothing. Because if she's still here, it isn't *here*, you know? I don't think she's anywhere on Earth. Or really on any planet. I just feel like she's out there, somewhere."

"That's how a lot of people feel when they lose someone—that the person's spirit is still out there, watching over them. And if that's true, then I know Naomi's watching over you. And I also know that she doesn't want you wasting your life away, allowing her family and friends, her goddaughter, and the husband she loved so much to be destroyed."

This I did know to be true, so I wasn't lying so much as protecting all of us, Naomi included, from the Superconsciousness Supreme Court.

Chuckie nodded and his eyes got droopy. Had to hand it to Tito, the medicines he created worked fast. And if Melissa Etheridge wanted you to go to sleep, you went to sleep. "You're right, Kitty." He reached for me and I took his hand in mine. "Thanks for always being there for me."

I kissed his forehead. "Always, and right back atcha. Now, get some rest and feel better—I'm going to go back to Stress Central and figure out our next moves."

He heaved one more sigh and then his hand went lax. He was asleep. I covered him up with a throw blanket, turned the music down a little more, then, as his Poof, Fluffy, and Naomi's Poof, Cutie-Pie, crawled out of his pockets and snuggled on either side of his neck, I quietly left.

Decided to take a quick look in at the kids, mostly because any time Chuckie was like this I had a strong suspicion Jamie knew somehow and was upset by it. So I used hyperspeed, which I had thanks to giving birth to Jamie, and headed upstairs one floor to the daycare center.

To find Seraphim's version of "Baby Face" on the airwaves and Amy Gaultier-White in da house, playing with the kids. A year ago this would have been odd—Amy loved all the kids, but she wasn't someone who was going to drop everything because a baby was nearby. Then.

But Amy and Christopher were finally pregnant and, since her second trimester, Amy had been spending more and more time with the kids, particularly in the daycare center. This was fine with Denise and all the rest of the parents, but since Amy was also still fighting off the rest of the Gaultier Enterprises board members—well, the evil ones, which I kind of assumed were all of them until we discovered differently—her attachment to the kids was kind of freaky.

It was definitely freaking Christopher out. But Jeff wasn't overly concerned about it, and since we were reasonably sure that we'd gotten rid of all the emotional blockers and overlays our enemies had planted everywhere, if he didn't feel Amy was off the deep end, then the rest of us didn't need to worry.

"Hey Ames, how goes it?"

She was holding Jamie in her lap. Unlike me—both times—Amy hadn't turned into Henrietta Hippo during pregnancy. She looked great, though there was definitely a baby on board. Also unlike me, her long red hair really looked more luxurious, her skin was clear and glowing, and she had a Madonna and Child look going with Jamie. She was one of my oldest and closest friends, so I chose not to hate her.

"Okay. Kitty, is Chuck okay?"

Well, that explained why Jamie was in her lap. "Migraine." Which was our code for Chuckie's Delicate Condition.

"We figured." Amy hugged Jamie. "I'll bet your mommy got your Uncle Charles all taken care of."

Trotted over and gave Jamie a kiss. "I did. He'll be fine."

"I miss Auntie Mimi, too," Jamie said.

Not good. I had no idea if she was reading Chuckie's mind, if they had some sort of mind-link due to what had happened during Operation Civil War, or if she just knew why Chuckie was always sad these days. But still, of all of us, the one most likely to be able to contact Naomi was Jamie—because she housed ACE inside of her.

ACE was a superconsciousness that had been created by those on Alpha Four who'd wanted to keep all their exiled people firmly on Earth. During Operation Drug Addict, when we'd discovered ACE and what he was supposed to be doing, I'd originally filtered ACE into Paul Gower,

Naomi's older brother and the current Supreme Pontifex of the Earth A-Cs.

ACE had always been our protector, and after Operation Destruction, Alexander had ensured that any imposed restraints ACE might still have were removed, essentially freeing ACE to protect Earth as he saw fit. But due to events that happened during Operation Defection Election and some other, extremely interfering superconsciousnesses, ACE had had to move into Jamie, for both his protection and hers.

I knew that ACE, like Algar, knew Naomi was still around, so to speak. Whether this meant Jamie knew for sure or not I didn't know. And I was afraid to ask.

"We all miss her, Jamie-Kat." I stroked her hair as "Mysterious Ways" by U2 came on. "Are you okay?"

She nodded. "Auntie Amy's here." She patted Amy's stomach. "And Becky's here, too."

"Excuse me?" This was a new one.

New to Amy, too. She looked confused. Well, not about the sex of the baby—since Jamie, the "no finding out the sex prior to birth" rule the A-Cs had had was struck from the rulebook. But to my knowledge, Amy and Christopher hadn't settled on a name.

"Ah, we haven't picked the name yet, sweetie," Amy said, right on cue.

"She likes Becky," Jamie said as if she was stating that water was wet.

Amy and I exchanged the "oh really?" look. "Ah, well," Amy said slowly, "that's one of the names we've been talking about—Rebecca Ann. But it's not the only one."

"It's the one she likes," Jamie said. "And she wants to be called Becky by her friends."

"Well, as I remember," I said carefully, "this generation all likes to be named early." Jamie had certainly responded to her name while in utero, and we'd had to assign names to some of the other hybrids during labor for their safety and the safety of their mothers. "Apparently you're having a talented girl."

Amy nodded. "But we knew that." True enough. All of our crop of hybrids had shown their talents early. Though none as much as my children, at least so far.

Speaking of which, Charlie crawled over, looking indignant for being ignored this long. I picked him up and hugged him while he cuddled into my neck. "I guess you need to tell Christopher that the name is set."

Amy managed a laugh. "I guess so." She hugged Jamie. "Thanks for letting me know."

Jamie hugged her back, beaming. "You're welcome, Auntie Amy." If I ignored Jamie's continuing ability to communicate with other children while they were still in the womb, some of which was probably due to ACE, everyone seemed fine, and I had a meeting I needed to get back to. Hugged Amy, kissed Jamie, kissed Charlie and handed him off to Amy, and headed off again.

Used hyperspeed to get back downstairs quickly. Christopher still worked with me regularly on my skills and control, and I almost never slammed myself into walls anymore. At least, not very often.

"... so, I think we're going to have to say yes," I heard Jeff say as I rejoined him and the others to Flo Rida's "Club Can't Handle Me."

"To visitors or to activating The Clarence Clone?" I asked as I seated myself to the beat.

"Both, honestly, baby." Jeff sighed. "By the way, I didn't want to say this while Chuck was in the room, but Cliff knows about the message from the Planetary Council."

"How so?"

"We were having a meeting with the Cabinet and their top people. Cliff's the head of FEMA now, he was there."

"Fantastic. What's his stance on the NASA Base situation?"

"Out loud? Total support for keeping the Base open."

"Is that the general viewpoint?"

"Most. Shocking no one, the Secretary of Transportation is against it. A few others. Some not for anti-alien reasons, at least out loud."

Cleary nodded. "I understand the issue, in that sense. The issue is that with you all out in the open, why have a special base at NASA just for A-Cs?"

"Because the majority of our tech comes from there?" I asked with only a hint of sarcasm.

Cleary shrugged. "Just as much comes from Dulce. However, I don't want to say yes to closing NASA Base."

"Then that's going to be on you, Gideon. Because you're the dude who started the whole 'shut it down' movement in the first place."

"Yes, I know, Ambassador."

"Why so formal? All of a sudden, I mean." Looked around. Nope, no one of importance had just arrived via Stealth Mode.

"He's trying to focus you on the fact that you're going to have to take an active role in preserving NASA Base," Jeff said. "And he's not wrong."

"What about the Stephanie the Huntress situation?"

"That we're leaving to me, Missus Chief," Buchanan said. "And the boys are going to make sure that happens," he added, nodding at Len and Kyle, who nodded right back with super-serious expressions. Apparently what had been discussed in my absence was me and my expected roles. And how to prevent me from doing anything too active.

"Fine, fine. Well, I guess that means some of us are heading to Florida." Meaning Jamie, Charlie, Len, Kyle, and I were definitely heading to Jeff's parent's house. That would make Alfred and Lucinda happy, so that was one for the win column. "Jeff, are you coming with us or do you have to stay up here?"

"It'll depend on what we determine we're doing about the Planetary Council."

"We're in a damned if we do and damned if we don't situation," Cleary said. He and Jeff started discussing the various options, with Buchanan and even the boys adding in. No one was thrilled.

Considered the option they hadn't. "You know, why don't we just kill two birds with one spaceship?"

CHAPTER 7

GOT THE ROOM'S ATTENTION with that one. All the men stared at me for a few long seconds.

"Excuse me?" Cleary asked finally.

"If we have the Planetary Council arrive at NASA Base, it would make a statement that the Base is necessary, plus keep the Planetary Council out of D.C."

"They want to chat with the President, I'm sure," Jeff said. "I don't think we want to drag Vince down to Florida for this."

"Why not?" Cleary asked. "I mean that seriously. It's his home state, too, and, frankly, I like the Ambassador's idea."

"And if things get dull, we can always take them to Disney World." The entire room ignored this statement. Always the way.

"I'm not sure about the logistics, Gideon," Jeff said, as if I hadn't spoken. "And a spaceship over Florida is no better than a spaceship over Washington."

"Have them show up via the Alpha Five Transport System." This one got the room's attention, go me. "They're all comfortable with that method, and as long as no one's trying to stop them their trip here should be relatively smooth."

"You just don't want to be away from the action," Jeff said. Accurately.

Not that I was going to admit that. "I think we solve

several problems by doing this all at NASA Base, and if
Gideon's with us, then he's away from Stephanie. And The
Clarence Clone is in Florida, too." "Road Runner" by Aerosmith came on, as if to solidify the rightness of my train of
thought. "Really, I think it's road trip time."

Jeff sighed and pulled his phone out. He looked at Kyle.
"Turn the music off. I don't want to talk to the President
with rock music screaming in the background."

"Spoilsport," I muttered.

Kyle grinned and sent a text, presumably because Jeff
was dialing and Kyle didn't want to use the intercom system
therefore. The music stopped. Did my best not to pout.
Failed, if Buchanan trying not to laugh was any indication.

"Hey Vince. Kitty's suggested we have the Planetary
Council arrive via phasing transport, meaning no space-
ships. Yeah, I agree. Also, she's suggested that they arrive at
NASA Base." He was quiet for a bit. "Yeah, that's her
thinking, too. It'll allow us to easily activate TCC at the
same time as well." He chuckled. "I'll tell her." He hung up
and turned to me. "Vince likes your plan."

"Really?"

"Yeah. He said that suggestions in these matters from
the woman who averted the total destruction of Earth at
least twice probably should be listened to."

"Vince is my favorite. But I think it's been more than
twice."

Jeff heaved a sigh. "You can argue with him about it on
Air Force One, baby. We're flying down there. Tonight."

Let that sit on the air for a bit. Then found the right
words. "No way in hell are we doing that."

Before Jeff or anyone else could argue, I quickly explained why it just wasn't that simple. In part because we
had a huge entourage if it was just going to be our family
unit going to Florida. And seeing that it was us, there was
no way that only Jeff, the kids, and I were going. Half the
Embassy was going to want to go and, once Jeff let Alpha

Team know what was going on, they were all going to want to come, too.

Most embassies didn't clear out half their personnel when the Ambassador was going on a short trip. But most embassies probably weren't packed to the gills with personnel and family members like ours was. And most embassies also didn't expect their ambassadors to get attacked merely by crossing state lines. We were just special that way.

"We could tell them all no," Jeff said finally, in the tone of voice of a man who already knows he's lost that battle.

"As if. We're going to have far too many people who have *legitimate* reasons to come along to fly them down unless we take not only Air Force One and Air Force Two but also Air Forces Three through Twelve as well. Which, even if they exist, would be okay, as long as we aren't racing down there like our parents are coming home from vacation a day earlier than we expected and we're desperately trying to clean up the house from the all university kegger we threw the night before."

"I'm not even going to ask why you used that as an example." Jeff heaved a sigh and dialed again, this time putting us on speakerphone.

Repeated my issues, kegger example included. Armstrong didn't seem to have any issues with it. Then again, I knew he'd been in a frat. "Vince, it's insane to drop everything and race down. And I doubt the Planetary Council expects it, either. Let's get ready, as in really ready, prepped to do double duty or more on the way there, and let's go in such a way that we don't appear to be running."

Heard a sneeze.

"Bless you. Are you getting a cold?"

"Maybe," Armstrong said. Was fairly sure I heard him trying to discreetly blow his nose. "If so, it just came on in the last hour. But anyway, you have a good point, Kitty. Several of them, really. Fine. As you say, we won't race like panicked maniacs. We'll plan an impromptu campaign trip down to Florida that will provide us a safe political reason for the trip and allow us all to be at NASA Base whenever we ask the Planetary Council to meet us there. Gideon, you'll get things set up on your end?"

"Yes. We'll be ready with whatever you need, whenever you need it."

"Excellent, my office will coordinate with yours."

"How are we going down?" Jeff asked.

"I don't recommend the plane," I said quickly. "In part because we're going to have so many in our entourage that the plane might not be able to get off the ground. And a lot of planes flying down sort of screams that the king is fleeing the palace. Plus, if you do have a cold, being up in the air isn't in your best interests."

Armstrong chuckled. "True enough, and I anticipated your entourage. And, happily, I have a solution that will do the double duty you're so fond of—we're going to take Rail Force One."

That the President has his own railroad version of Air Force One shouldn't have come as a shock to me when I first found out, but it had. However, it was extremely cool, too, and in ways far different from the mighty plane heralded in song and Harrison Ford movies.

"Awesome!" I loved the train. The Vice President had Air Force Two and Rail Force Two, and we'd used it a few times, but not often enough in my opinion.

"I assume we'll need Rail Force Two as well," Armstrong said.

We discussed logistics, and the plan was to hook both trains together, hopefully giving us enough space to bring along everyone who felt they had to join us or die trying.

In the olden days, before the A-Cs were outed as being on Earth, this never would have happened. Having the President and Vice President both traveling together was considered far too dangerous, because there had been people trying to kill leaders as long as humanity had had leaders. And, realistically, it still was pretty dangerous.

However, since the VP and most of his entourage were all A-Cs or, in my case, enhanced, the risks were different. It was actually safer for the President to be with us, since an A-C could, and definitely would, grab him and get him to safety faster than anyone else could have a hope of doing.

From a PR standpoint, Armstrong was all for making the "the A-Cs are our people now" statements as much as he could, and that included showing that he hadn't asked Jeff to be his running mate just for show. So we were gaining several advantages by traveling in this way, including potential stumping stops along the route, since winning office meant that whatever politician had won his or her office immediately had to start campaigning to win said office again.

I was all for the train. Not only did that mean we'd get to actually see some scenery, but the food was always far better than on the airplanes. And the added bonus of no one being able to blow us up while in the air was huge, too. Not that I didn't think that we weren't at risk from some lunatics trying to blow up the train tracks, but we would be on the ground, essentially, and that gave us far more of an advantage.

Calmer Plan B in place, we got off the line and went over what Cleary had to do. We needed him back in his home state to prep things for the imminent arrivals and be there to greet us when we disembarked in Orlando. Sadly, not to go to Disney World, despite my suggesting it again, but to head across to the Kennedy Space Center and NASA Base.

After reassuring Cleary that we weren't going to allow him to be assassinated, we sent him home via a gate. We also sent three Field teams with him. He was the easy one. We had a gigantic entourage coming along for the ride and we weren't taking gates.

But before we could discuss our team's logistics, my phone beeped. "Huh. Lillian Culver wants to grab me for a late lunch."

"Why?" Jeff asked. Rightly. Culver was the head lobbyist for the top defense contractors, most of whom were our enemies. However, due to a variety of things that had happened, my "uncles'" intervention being one of the biggest, she'd become an ally. However, she wasn't one to want Girl Time.

"She says she heard something that may or may not be significant, but if it is, then she wants me forewarned and herself advised. She's suggesting we go to the Teetotaler so that it looks like we're really having a fun time together, rather than her coming into the Embassy."

The Teetotaler was one of our favorite little restaurants near the Capitol and Rayburn House, where Jeff's offices had been when he'd been a Representative.

"She want me there, too?"

"She hasn't said, should I ask?"

"No. If she's coming to get you, I'll wait with you and take you to her car. If she wants me along, then it'll look like she was always getting both of us. If not, fine, I'll just go back inside."

"I'll be tailing you in a car," Buchanan said. "The boys are required to go with you. She's aware of that, I know, but has she figured on it?"

"No idea, but she'll be here in five minutes so we're going to find out together."

CHAPTER 8

CULVER DROVE A very nice Bentley, which pulled up in front of our Embassy exactly as promised.

I wasn't really Dressed for Bentley Success, seeing as I was in jeans, my red Converse, and one of my newer Aerosmith shirts that had just Steven Tyler and Joe Perry on the front. Normally I preferred to roll with all of my boys in the band on my chest, but I hadn't been expecting action. Hopefully the only action I'd have is the hard decision about what tea to have at the restaurant.

I'd had just enough time to run upstairs at hyperspeed and grab my purse, ensuring that it had my Glock, several clips, and anything else of vital importance in it, and get back down before Culver had arrived.

Jeff, Len, and Kyle all went down the walkway with me. Culver left the car running but got out. "Jeff, nice to see you. Gentlemen, I'll let you do what you do best."

She was dressed as I was used to—in red, which was "her" color. Her lipstick always matched. Culver was one of those women who, when you first looked at her, seemed very attractive. But, the longer you looked, the more you realized she was all bones and angles, and when she smiled widely, she always reminded me of the Joker after he'd pulled a particularly nasty stunt on the people of Gotham. I called her Joker Jaws to myself for this reason. However, not nearly as much these days as when we'd first met. Go D.C. politics.

Len grinned. "I like your style, Miz Culver."

She was married to Abner Schnekedy—who I'd had the "fun" of meeting in my Washington Wife class along with many other people who were now either still my enemies, dead or, somehow, my friends—but had wisely kept her maiden name for business.

Len got into the driver's seat while Kyle trotted around and opened the driver's side rear door for her.

"You want Jeff, too? Or is this just girls and bodyguards only?"

"I think just the four of us, if that won't offend you, Jeff."

"Not at all. Just make sure all four of you get back in one piece."

"Wow, optimistic much?" I leaned up and kissed him goodbye. "I'll text or call if we need you, I promise."

"I'll be monitoring you, baby, don't worry." He tucked me into the car as Kyle came around and took shotgun.

We waited to drive off until Jeff was back in the Embassy. Once we were rolling, Culver leaned back and sighed. "Having a driver is a wonderful thing."

"Yeah, the boys are great. Why are we hanging out?"

"To pretend that I haven't given you the information I'm about to give you." She looked behind us. "Is that your Mister Buchanan behind us?"

Looked as well. There was a taxicab behind us that seemed to be following us. "Yes," Len and I said in unison.

Culver laughed. "Good. I feel much safer."

"You normally don't feel unsafe, Lillian. What's up?"

"Several things. There's a new player in town. European, I think. I haven't met him yet. But Thomas is working a business deal, and from the little he's told me, it could give Titan Security the edge in the weaponized robotics field."

"You mean more of an edge than they, Gaultier Enterprises, and YatesCorp have already?"

"Yes. I have no idea if it's related to the supersoldier program, or the androids that you've told me about, but it's the first time I've heard of this player. His name is Gustav Drax."

"That has freaking got to be a made up name."

She shrugged. "Maybe. Maybe not. I haven't been able to find anything on him, so I can't say."

"Is he an arms dealer?"

"I'd assume so, until proven otherwise."

"Fabulous. Well, I guess it's good to be forewarned and all that." Heard what sounded like a really loud motorcycle. The Bentley's soundproofing was good, meaning that either its engine was about to die or we had the mother of all Harleys next to us.

"That's only one thing," Culver said, as I turned to look at what was indeed a Harley coming up fast. "The other is—"

She was interrupted because Kyle shouted a warning and Len swerved so fast and so hard that she and I were both tossed to the side and down. Which was a good thing, seeing as an arrow hit the seat rest her head had just been leaning against.

My reflexes were fast, and I was used to being under attack. Plus, I'd gotten a glance at the Harley's rider, so had seen it was a blonde chick. So while Len floored it, and Kyle continued to shout at us to get down, I was already on the floor, pulling Culver down there with me.

"Glad the glass is shatterproof. Lillian, are you okay?"

"Yes." She looked up. "That was intended for me, wasn't it?"

"I think so. Um, were you going to tell me that there's a rogue assassin in town who's a chick who's using a crossbow?"

"Yes, I was. She tried to kill Gideon Cleary earlier today."

"Yeah, Chuckie saved him."

"Don McMillan wasn't as lucky."

My body went cold. "Is he okay?" Senator McMillan was the senior senator from Arizona and someone we all considered one of the few honest politicians out there. And he was a good friend.

"Yes, but only because he still has a soldier's reflexes and intuition. She only winged him."

"So that's two of our allies, and you make number three."

"Count us as three through seven, Kitty," Kyle said. "Because she's following us."

"Where's Malcolm?"

"Not keeping up," Len said tightly, as he weaved us in and out of traffic. At least, that was what I assumed he was doing, since Culver and I were sliding back and forth on the floor, hearing a ton of people honking at us and the sound of screeching breaks. "This car's got a lot of power, thank God."

"Head for somewhere with a lot of security."

"I'm open to ideas," Len said.

"Andrews. Get us to the Air Force base."

"You got it, we're close to the Beltway."

I could tell when we hit the Beltway because apparently the Bentley had more power than Len had been using on the surface streets. We were going much faster, though still weaving, and I didn't hear nearly as many honking horns.

"She's still in pursuit," Kyle said. "Andrews is prepped for our arrival."

But before we could get there I heard a sound. I'd heard the sound before. And it was never a good sound when you were going really fast.

We'd blown a tire.

CHAPTER 9

"**SHE'S SHOT A TIRE OUT!**" Kyle shared, as we spun. Heard another explosion. "Two!"

Because Len was a great driver, we didn't flip and somehow we also didn't hit anything and no one hit us. But we did come to a stop, after a few dizzying seconds.

The Harley was nearby, I could hear it. And that meant the four of us were sitting ducks.

I didn't really think about it. I was the only one with hyperspeed in this car, and if Huntress was on a motorcycle, then she wasn't an A-C. A-C's had reflexes that were so good they couldn't handle human machinery because they'd destroy it. So whoever Huntress was, she was a human. Or, based on Culver's recent revelations, an android. And I'd fought androids before and won.

I put my purse over my neck. "Protect Lillian and call for backup!" I shouted as I leaped out and slammed the door behind me.

We were actually on the off-ramp, which was probably why we hadn't been hit by anyone else. And the Harley was coming right for us, its rider's crossbow aimed right for me.

The chick was in black leather, so totally into the whole look. She was definitely blonde. And she was also definitely wearing a mask that covered the top half of her face. Always the way.

She shot and I readied myself to catch the arrow. But something went past me and caught it instead. She shot again, the arrow was grabbed again.

"Don't just stand there," Christopher shouted at me. "Get her!"

Didn't have to tell me twice, especially since my own personal Flash was now on the scene. I went after the motorcycle on foot. And she gunned it and took off at top speed.

Christopher caught up to me, grabbed my hand, and then we took off at his Flash level. This would ensure that I threw up the moment we stopped, but I planned to throw up on our Huntress chick, so all was well.

We caught the Harley because A-Cs were fast enough to begin with, I'd been a sprinter and hurdler in high school and college and daily life ensured those skills remained sharp, and nothing was going to outrun Christopher, other than possibly a supersonic jet, but I'd still put money on Christopher, best two out of three.

As we reached her, I realized we had to stop the motorcycle on top of grabbing Huntress, because she was heading into a lot of traffic, and a bike this big and heavy going this fast would do serious damage to whatever it hit.

Jumped onto the back of the bike behind her. She hit at me, and I hit back. Neither one of us was landing anything that had any power. Android was starting to seem as unlikely as A-C.

Christopher leaped on behind me, meaning we had three people on a motorcycle built for two. Tried not to let the old song, "Daisy, Daisy" play in my mind, but without my iPod going, that particular earworm took hold. Oh well, it was a cheerful turn of the past century song my paternal grandparents had sung to me and there were worse songs to play on repeat in my head, after all.

I was revved up enough and we hadn't been at the Flash level for too long, so I was able to contain the nausea.

Which was good, because I wanted to barf on this chick's face as I ripped her freaking mask off.

However, what I wanted and what I was going to get were two different things. She was still hitting at me, but as she swerved us into the slow lane and we passed a clear area, she slammed her elbow into me, wrenched out of my hold, and jumped off the bike.

Reflexes took over and I grabbed the handlebars and slid forward. Managed to keep the throttle open, because if I hadn't, the bike would have gone down, with us under it.

"You weren't holding onto her?" Christopher shouted as he, too, slid forward.

"Jump off and go get her!"

"I don't know where she is now. Because you let her go."

"Blame and chastise later. It's been a while. Lean if I lean, don't if I don't. Dig through my purse and get my sunglasses — a bug in my eye means we're dead. And hold onto me."

On the plus side, I knew how to ride a motorcycle, mostly because of an ex-boyfriend in college, and also because Reader, Tim, the flyboys, and I had all gone riding several times. We normally rode crotch rockets when we indulged, but the principles were the same. And I'd had a ride on a supersonic cycle in Bizarro World, going so fast I could and did move around the insects. So I was good, bugs hitting me or not.

On the not plus side, this bike was going hella fast and even though I was easing up on the throttle, I had to slow us down, not come to a screeching halt, because Christopher and I weren't in gear, let alone helmets, and the last time I'd hit my head I'd ended up in Bizarro World. Going splat on the highway was not my preferred plan.

Thankfully, Christopher found my sunglasses in record time and put them on me, which was nice, and smart, since I wasn't ready to let go with one hand.

We had to maneuver through traffic until I could get the

bike slowed down enough that I felt safe trying to stop. To Christopher's credit, he leaned when he was supposed to.

"This is far too much like our first airplane ride," he said as we got around a trash truck.

Decided I didn't want to stop anywhere near something that big and we rode on, looking for the next exit. "Yeah? I'm ignoring you. Besides, it's not relevant. This isn't my first time on a motorcycle."

"Really? Based on how we're wobbling, you could have fooled me."

Decided stopping wasn't going to happen here. It was called the Beltway for a reason, and I was shifting, breaking, and accelerating like a pro. Revved the bike and zipped us through traffic. It was time to get back to the Bentley.

"If I apologize will you slow down and let me off?" Christopher shouted.

"No."

Other than my being slightly nervous that we weren't in gear, wishing there were no such things as flying insects, and being ever so thankful that Christopher had gotten my sunglasses onto my face, the ride was pretty fun.

We reached the Bentley and I was able to safely pull over next to it. Just in time to hear sirens.

As we got off the bike and I managed to get the kickstand down and not drop the bike to the ground, three police cars pulled up. Len, Kyle, and Culver all stood up—apparently they'd been hiding behind the Bentley which, since it was essentially off the highway, made some kind of sense. Not tons of sense, but some.

"Let me do the talking," I said to Christopher. "And definitely keep your hands where they can see them."

A squad car door opened, but no one got out. Well, no one human.

A giant German Shepherd bounded toward us, barking his head off. Then he jumped at me.

CHAPTER 10

I CAUGHT THE DOG and gave him a big hug while he licked my face. "Prince! Kitty's so glad to see you! How's my favorite officer of the law?"

Prince was great, thank you very much, and really happy to see me, too. He was also relieved I was okay. Prince was the greatest.

Two other dogs joined us for their lovies and praise. "Duke, Riley, good dogs! Where's Officers Moe, Larry, and Curly?" They were Larry's and Curly's dogs, respectively, so they should know where their handlers were.

Much barking ensued, to share that, naturally, their handlers were getting out of their squad cars.

When we'd first met the K-9 squad, during Operation Assassination, I'd nicknamed these dogs' owner-handlers after the Three Stooges. Moe's real name was Herman Melville, because he had literary parents who'd never been to a playground, apparently, and he didn't care for my calling him Moe. Since we'd become good friends, I'd stopped calling him that. To his face.

"I hate that nickname," Officer Melville said as he joined us.

"Your buddies are good with being Officers Larry and Curly."

"They like you better than I do."

Possibly true. At any rate, I had no idea what Larry and Curly's real names were. Possibly really Larry and Curly. No one had ever said and I'd never asked. And I wasn't going to break that streak today, either.

"Did anyone catch the woman who tried to kill us?" I asked now.

"No." Melville sounded pissed. "Your car chase and subsequent motorcycle joyride caused enough havoc that we lost her." He went over to Culver and the boys. "You three alright?"

Culver nodded. "Our driver was very good."

"And we were lucky," Len said.

"We need to pull the arrows." Kyle pointed to the tires that had arrows sticking out of what was left of them. "Just in case we can get evidence off of them."

"She's human. No A-C could ride a motorcycle, and she didn't hit like an A-C or an android."

"She's new," Melville said. "What with the attack on two politicians already, we've contacted all international law enforcement, including Interpol. There's no criminal footprint like this out there."

"She's making a hell of a splash," Officer Larry added. "It's been sheer luck that no one's ended up dead."

Christopher and I looked at each other. "I don't believe in luck like that," I said slowly. "Especially because we're talking someone trained enough to have taken out a car going at top speed. And then she jumped off a motorcycle going at top speed and she's not dead."

"We assume," Christopher added.

"We have cars at every off-ramp," Melville said. "And there's no body. Or any sign that anyone might have jumped off a motorcycle and landed somewhere."

Christopher made a call. "Yeah. Yeah, we're all okay. No, she got away. Yeah. Please. Send teams to search all the off-ramps. No, I don't think Kitty really knows where she jumped off at either."

I shook my head. Christopher nodded.

"Nope, she doesn't. It was just someplace she could land, versus fall. Yeah. Look for any trace evidence. Thanks, James." He hung up and turned back to Melville. "Our people will do a thorough search. We can do it faster than your teams and we'll let you know if we find anything."

Melville nodded. "I'd argue about procedure, but I know you're right. And we've found nothing, and I can't justify sending CSU to every off-ramp and area without a drop-off on the Beltway."

"Lillian's car is totaled. Is someone coming to tow that and take us back to the Embassy?" Clearly lunch was out at this point. Couldn't speak for Culver or the boys, but I could have eaten. However, it didn't seem appropriate under the circumstances.

As I asked this, a big black Lincoln Navigator pulled up. Buchanan got out, and he looked seriously pissed. "Why didn't you wait for me?"

Len and I looked at each other. "You were behind us in a cab," I said.

"No, I wasn't. I was, in fact, blocked from leaving the Embassy's garage by several cars."

"The driver looked like you," Len said. "I checked."

"I did, too, Malcolm. I mean, he wasn't close enough for us to make out details, but it looked like the cab you use and he looked like you."

"He wasn't, and that means this assassin isn't working alone."

We brought Buchanan up to speed on what had transpired. "This was coordinated," he said when we were done. "They knew to block me. Meaning they know how we work."

"Can we go back to the Embassy to discuss this? I mean that seriously. Lillian's being a total champ, but we were just attacked and in a crash, and I'd like our Embassy doctor to take a look at all of us."

I did want Tito to check us out. But I also wanted to discuss what Culver had told us, and I knew without asking she didn't want us sharing that with the D.C.P.D., even though Melville and his team were 100 percent on our side.

Melville nodded. "I'll escort you home. The others will stay with the vehicle. We know how to reach Miz Culver."

She smiled weakly, not her usual wide smile that always reminded me of the Joker's. "Thank you, officers. But I'd really like to see the doctor, if it's acceptable for us to leave the scene."

It was and we did. Prince insisted on riding in the car with us, which Melville allowed, mostly because I figured he didn't want to hear Prince whine for the entire trip back.

We brought Buchanan and Christopher up to speed as Buchanan drove home and I petted Prince, who was sitting in my lap.

"Think she's working with Drax?" Kyle asked when we were done. "I only ask that because she's new and he's new."

"I think that's a very good possibility," Buchanan said. "And I'll be checking out the options once we're home."

Knew he'd be calling Team Assassination. "Give them my love when you call."

"I will. Miz Culver, I think we need to keep you under protection. Do you want Centaurion Division personnel or D.C.P.D.?"

Culver managed a laugh. "A-Cs, please and thank you." Kyle nodded and made the call.

"So, if the assassin was after Lillian, does that mean they wanted to prevent her from telling us about Drax, prevent her from telling us about Huntress, or are these attacks about something else entirely?"

"That, Missus Chief, is the sixty-four-thousand-dollar question."

CHAPTER 11

WE GOT HOME without incident and immediately went to medical. The Secret Service harangued me the entire way, until Buchanan told them to shut it up and take the whining elsewhere. Literally.

Nurse Magdalena Carter—who we'd met during Operation Assassination and who had not only become our Embassy nurse but also Richard White's girlfriend and therefore potentially Christopher's stepmother one day—greeted us as if she'd been expecting us. No surprise, really.

"Doctor Hernandez is waiting for you," she said as she hugged Christopher tightly. He hugged her back, showing impressive personal growth in the acceptance that his father had found love again over twenty years after his mother's death. Amy had helped a lot with that.

"Nice to see you guys are up on current events."

"Jeff is, too, and he's on his way here," Nurse Carter said. She let go of Christopher and gave me a gentle hug. "Glad you're all okay."

"Us too."

Culver went into the examination room first. I waited another second and Jeff arrived. He didn't say anything, just picked me up and hugged me, gently, like Nurse Carter had.

"I'm okay. I'm not hurt. What little banging up I got has already gone away."

Jeff grunted, then pulled Christopher in. Group hugging was an A-C thing, but I didn't mind it. Even when Jeff then pulled Len and Kyle in, too.

"We're all okay," Len managed to get out. "Really, we were lucky."

"No," Jeff said as he let go. "You're a great driver, Christopher reached all of you in time, and Kitty chased off the lunatic and didn't crash that Harley."

"We made the news?"

"In this town, someone's always watching," Buchanan said.

"Too true." We brought Jeff, and Nurse Carter since she was right there, up on current events. "So, you think the Mastermind hired the Huntress, or are you on the side of it being this Gustav Drax?"

"No bet. But we sent teams over to check on Don. He's alright and already out of Walter Reed and back home. We have teams assigned to him. We also put them onto Lillian's husband."

"Good. So, I think Huntress is missing on purpose."

Buchanan, who'd been texting this entire time, nodded. "It seems likely. Our sources don't know of her. She seems remarkably new and unknown for someone with this high of a skill level."

"You're sure she's not an A-C or android?" Christopher asked. "And before you point out the fact that she was riding a motorcycle, for all we know a hybrid could do it."

"Paul can't," Jeff said. "Neither can Abigail. Chuck tested them years ago. They have the same issues full-blooded A-Cs have with human machinery."

"Did he test Serene?"

Everyone looked at me. "I don't know," Jeff said slowly. "I sort of assumed he did."

"You know how they teach you to spell assume, Jeff. I think we need to know."

Christopher nodded and started texting. Hyperspeed

being what it was on both sides of this conversation, he had an answer fast. "No, Serene hasn't been tested. It's not for a lack of Chuck asking, either, or her being unwilling. Brian objected."

"Why?" Brian Dwyer had been my boyfriend in high school, but, after the events of Operation Drug Addict, had seen the light and fallen in love with Serene. They were both a tad obsessive when it came to relationships, though.

"As far as I can tell and Serene knows, it's because he didn't trust that she wouldn't get hurt." Christopher shrugged. "It wasn't a vital thing before, so Chuck stopped pushing, since he'd tested Naomi and Michael, too. None of the Gowers have the ability to handle human machinery."

"But none of them are a direct Ronald Yates/Mephistopheles progeny, either. I think we need to test Serene, pronto."

Christopher nodded. "She agrees. She's going to do it in a controlled environment, without telling Brian. She wants to know if we want Chuck there."

"We do," Jeff said. "Stay here and make sure Tito checks every one of you, and that includes you, Christopher." With that, he zipped off, presumably to wake Chuckie up and share what had transpired while he'd been sleeping.

Culver came out and gave us a weak smile. "Doctor Hernandez recommends rest and some food."

"Once I get checked we'll get you something here."

She shook her head. "I feel fine, I've told you what I wanted you to know, and the need for secrecy is clearly gone. If it's alright with you, I'd really like to go home."

"We'll get your protection unit to take you back," Buchanan said. "I'll escort her to them," he said to me.

I nodded and they left. Sent Len then Kyle in to Tito before me. They didn't have faster regeneration. Both boys were declared the same as Culver—a little banged up, but otherwise okay.

My turn with Tito. He shook his head at me. "We can't leave you alone for a minute, can we?"

"This wasn't my fault."

He grinned. "It never is, Kitty, when you think about it." He did a fast check. "You seem fine. Any pain anywhere? Be truthful."

Did a body check. "No, honestly, I feel fine. Still a little pissed, but nothing hurts."

"Let me know immediately if that changes. And next time you go out, maybe you should have Rahmi and Rhee with you." They were sisters and princesses from Beta Twelve who'd come for Jamie's first birthday party and stayed. Beta Twelve had the best warriors in the entire Alpha Centauri system, and Tito, who'd been a UFC cage fighter in his spare time when we'd met, had been training them and Abigail on fighting techniques for several years now, so this suggestion was a good one.

"I'll keep it in mind."

He grinned again. "You know they won't cramp your style."

"Oh, true enough. But the question right now is going to be if Jeff will let me leave the building at all or not."

"My money's on not. But when you disobey him, like you always do, take one of the other gals with you. Abigail and Mahin are trained, too. And all the women fight nastier than all the men, other than Christopher."

"True dat. But what I think you're telling me is that all the girls are bored."

Tito laughed. "But you didn't hear it straight out from me."

Headed out of medical and went downstairs to Jeff's office. He was there with Chuckie, and they were both watching something on a video screen. Serene handling a car in the middle of Groom Lake, to be exact.

"Hey," Chuckie said, looking and sounding normal. "We're on a feed with Serene."

"Hey, Kitty," she said through gritted teeth. "This is hard but not impossible."

"Then you can stop now."

"No, I really think I need to learn how to drive."

"No you don't," Jeff and Chuckie said in unison. Decided not to worry about the unison thing—great minds were just thinking alike was all.

"As long as it's safe and you don't overdo it, Serene, go for it."

"Thanks! Jeff, Charles, I'm going to disconnect from you, then. I'm still on with Dulce and Area Fifty-One."

"Fine," Chuckie said with a sigh. "Please make sure I get a copy of all the results and transcript."

"I will do. Head of Imageering out." Our screen went blank.

"I love how she reminded us of her rank right before hanging up on us," Jeff said.

"I love more that she can do it. So, this means that the likelihood is that a Yates offspring with enough Yates in there can probably handle human machinery, doesn't it?"

"One test subject isn't enough to be anything close to conclusive," Chuckie said. "But I'm willing to hypothesize that the answer is yes."

"I thought Buchanan and the assassins got rid of all the Yates progeny out there," Jeff said.

"They got rid of all the Americans they could find and Nightcrawler knew about. But there could easily be Ronnie's Kids that they missed or that are in other parts of the world. Ronaldo Al Dejahl Prime was raised in Europe, remember, and so was Nightcrawler."

"We have the results from the Field teams' investigation," Chuckie said. "They indicate that no one jumped off of anything on the Beltway, other than Lillian Culver's car."

"Meaning Huntress has some kind of skills. I'm going to work under the assumption she's one of Ronnie's Kids until proven otherwise."

"What that means is that she's not Stephanie," Jeff said, sounding relieved.

Chuckie shook his head. "Actually, if one A-C can learn, even if that A-C is a hybrid child of the most powerful A-C we know of, that means a regular A-C can learn. Would it take a lot of time and training? Yes. Is it a doable thing? Absolutely yes."

Hugged Jeff's shoulders, which I could do since he was sitting down. "I know you'd like to believe Stephanie isn't involved. But I think we have to accept that even if we do everything we can, and even if TCC does everything he can, she may still not ever come back to our side of things. Or even Cleary's side of things."

Jeff heaved a sigh. "I know. I just want to believe that she will until I have proof positive that she's not redeemable."

"The truth is out there, Jeff. And I'm sure we'll find it."

CHAPTER 12

THE REST OF THE week was fairly uneventful, other than Tito calling it right and Jeff not allowing me to go anywhere, and the raging arguments for who was going with us down to Florida.

Fewer people were staying to keep things running than were coming along. Of course, other than Doreen and Irving Coleman-Weisman and their son, Ezra, pretty much the entire staff and extended friends and family who lived with us wanted to take the train. Possibly because I'd raved about it a little too much. My bad.

Doreen didn't want to go because her parents had been in the Diplomatic Corps all her life — well, before the Poofs ate them. But we were all okay with that, Doreen included, because Robert and Barbara Coleman had been traitors of the highest order and also not the most loving and supportive parents someone could want, especially when their only daughter had wanted to marry a human.

Doreen was our only truly trained diplomat on staff and also the only one who took the job seriously. Why she wasn't our ambassador I didn't know, but every time I mentioned this, Doreen was the loudest voice shooting down the option.

I'd bowed out of most of the passionate arguments for who should be allowed to cause us to have to add ten more cars to the train. But we were a day away from leaving and we weren't finalized in any way.

Finished my breakfast meeting with Embassy staff, which consisted of almost all of them sharing why they needed to go to Florida, then decided to head upstairs to see what the daycare set was going to demand, in part because Amy was up there again and in other part because I wanted to see what Denise thought about her and her kids coming along, too.

What Denise thought, it turned out, was that I was an idiot. Not only did she not want to go, she also specifically didn't want some others to go, and had apparently been waiting for the last minute to share this with me. Probably so I'd have to give in.

"Kitty, I think it's a terrible idea for you to take Jamie and Charlie on this trip," she said for, by my count, the fifteenth time, while Ben Kweller sang "Family Tree" as backup.

"Vince wants us to do a family dog and pony show."

"I don't care what the President wants. The last time you all went somewhere on a mission, you were dragged into another solar system. And considering what happened to Charles, and what almost happened to Jamie, there is no good reason to put not one but both of your children into similar danger."

"I don't think the Planetary Council is dropping by to try to kidnap my kids."

"Prove it." Denise rarely looked as stern as she did right now.

"Ah . . . can't."

"Exactly."

"They can steal the kids from here, you know. They stole us all that way for Operation Civil War."

"I realize that. However, Walter, William, and I have been working on the problem since all of you were taken." Walter Ward was the Head of Embassy Security and his

older brother, William, was the Head of Security Worldwide, based out of the main A-C facility, the Dulce Science
Center. That they were working on this issue wasn't a surprise. "In fact, we've been working with the Security heads
at all the Bases worldwide. I think Missy from Australia has
the best fix."

"Missy?" This was a new one.

"Melissa Gunnels. She handles Sydney Base. I know you
met her when you were there."

Oh, right. I had at least interacted with Melissa during
Operation Bizarro World. She hadn't liked me enough to
share her nickname with me. Oh well, I'd have to find the
will to go on somehow. "What's she come up with?"

"A new way to lock our bases back down, so that no one
can get in or get our people out unless we want them to."

In the olden days of just a couple years ago, this had
been a given. All the Bases and external A-C housing had
shields that prevented us from being blown up or from enemies entering once said shields were activated. Events had
shown that our enemies, and our friends as well, had found
ways around these safeguards.

Not that we all hadn't been concerned about beefing up
security, but after a few months of relative calm that issue
had moved to the back burner for most of us. Jeff and I had
been getting ready for Charlie's arrival, we were busy with
our day-to-day jobs, everyone else had lives they were enjoying, and all that jazz. But it was nice to know that some
of our folks hadn't given up the good fight, so to speak.

"Does it work?" I had to ask. A plan and an actionable
plan were two different things.

"So far, yes." Denise heaved a sigh. "And even if it didn't,
you should not be bringing the children into what could be
a coup, an attack, or worse."

As the music changed to Sugar Ray's "Fly," a car flew up
in the air, swooped around Denise's head, and landed on

my shoulder. Was pretty sure that Charlie was exercising his sense of humor.

She and I looked at each other. "And . . . there's also . . . that." I removed the car and looked around. Charlie was sitting on Amy's lap, grinning at me.

"We've managed to keep Charlie's talents hidden, but if you bring him along on this trip, I can only foresee a lot of negative press." Denise took the car from me, turned, and handed it back to Ezra. "Charlie, that will be enough of that. Stop showing off for your mother—she's very impressed by you already."

Charlie gurgled at her, but nothing else floated or flew.

"I'm looking forward to the trip," Amy said.

"No, you're not," Denise countered. "You shouldn't be going any more than the children." Amy opened her mouth to protest and Denise put her hand up. "You're eight months pregnant. That means that the baby can show up any time. And it is insane to head into what could be an action situation in your condition. I'll have Doctor Hernandez lock you down on bedrest if you try to go. And, trust me, he'll do it."

Amy closed her mouth and grimaced. "I hate it when someone makes a logical point that goes completely against what I want to do." She heaved a sigh. "But you're right. I don't want to do anything that puts . . . Becky at risk. I'll stay home, Denise. I promise."

Denise shot me a look that literally dared me to keep on arguing. However, I knew when I was beaten. I was rarely beaten, but in this case, I was ready to wave the white flag, preferably without Charlie's assistance.

"You win. I'll talk to Jeff about it. Ames, I'll wager that Christopher will be relieved that you're staying home."

"I think he will be, yeah."

"I've already explained to Kevin that the children will not be going," Denise added. "And neither will he."

"Wow, I get Amy and the kids being grounded, but why Kevin?"

"Because he's the Defense Attaché of this Embassy and in everyone else's absence we need the protection."

"Cannot argue with that logic. Mostly because I figure you'll just keep on giving me the Mother Superior look you've clearly been practicing and I'll lose."

Denise grinned. Like her husband and children, she had great teeth and a killer smile. "Just need to make sure you see reason."

"Fine, fine, you win." Realistically, Denise was right. Besides, with the kids safely at home, Jeff and I might be able to fit in some sexy times on the train. So a win-win all the way around.

Before I could say anything else, like ask her who else she wanted to stay at home, my phone beeped and I pulled it out of my back pocket. I had a text from an unknown number.

Meet me on the Embassy roof right now. Come alone.

CHAPTER 13

THERE WERE ONLY a handful of people who liked to hold meetings on my roof, and all of them were trained assassins. And when the trained assassins who've got your back tell you to go to the roof, you go to the roof.

"Denise, as I said, you win. I need to take care of some things, like starting to figure out how to tell Jeff you've won and how Kevin isn't going and all that, so I'm going to leave you, Amy, and the kids and get back to this business we call show."

"I'll give you that politics is a lot like acting," Denise said with a laugh, as Coldplay's "Trouble" came on. "I plan to have agents here while you're gone, so it won't be just Kevin, but he's staying, and if you can convince any of the others to stay, that would be good, too."

"Gotcha. I'll do what I can. Though I think that you're going to have the best success with that, Mother Superior, so feel free to give that look to whomever you think needs to stay and just keep me advised."

With that, I gave Jamie and Charlie quick kisses, then trotted out of the daycare center and to the stairs.

Used hyperspeed to get up onto the roof. Telling no one I was going up here wasn't a problem—Walter monitored all the public areas of the Embassy, and while the likelihood that he already knew we had rooftop visitors was slim because they were the best of the best, the chance that he'd see me go out onto the roof was high. And any time I could go somewhere without the Secret Service tagging along I went for it, and an anonymous text telling me to come alone was a good reason to continue ditching them. At least in my opinion.

Of course, with someone imitating Huntress on the loose, it wasn't the smartest move to come up here by myself, since the text could be from her. However, my experience was that the people really trying to kill me liked to call me and make it all really personal.

Not that I was worried, even if Walter wasn't paying attention to my whereabouts. Maybe I should have been, but when you get "adopted" by the best international assassins in the world, and then bond with the guy who was right up there with them, it takes a certain edge off.

Unsurprisingly, I appeared to be alone on the roof. Scanned the sky just in case there was a drone or something heading for me, but it was a beautiful May afternoon and the skies were clear.

Scanned the neighboring rooftops, as I searched all of ours. Wasn't positive, but had a feeling we had someone on the roof of the Zoo and across the street on top of the Romanian embassy. Found no one on our roof.

Would have figured I was being punked in some way, but my life didn't roll like that. "Come out, come out, wherever you are," I said softly, as I stood behind the doorway area that created a natural shield from most views.

"Well, if you insist," a familiar voice said from behind me.

As I jumped like a cat on a hot tin roof, Siler appeared or de-cloaked or whatever he called it. But he wasn't alone.

There was a young girl who I put at around fourteen or fifteen standing there with him. He was in black jeans and a turtleneck, she was in blue jeans, a vintage Ramones t-shirt, and had a messenger bag slung over her neck, with a jeans jacket folded over the bag. They were both in what looked like comfortable hiking boots. They were both also grinning at me.

"That blending thing of yours is a real pain, Night crawler."

He laughed. "We like to keep you on your toes. Your 'uncles' are very proud of you for checking the skies and the rooftops."

"Which one of them is on the Zoo and which one is covering Romania?"

"The Dingo always takes the higher ground."

"Nice to know he wants to visit the alien animals. So," I looked at the girl with him, "who's this?"

"My daughter."

I did a fast comparison. Siler was between Jeff and Christopher in height, so around six feet, reasonably attractive, with olive skin and dark hair and eyes. The girl, however, was fair skinned, with dirty blonde hair, gray eyes, and a slighter build. She was a cute girl, but didn't look a thing like Siler. Examined their features—none were alike.

If an A-C mated with a human, human genetics tended to rule the external while A-C genes ruled the internal. Siler had been enhanced in weird ways by his fab parental units, but even so, he was only half alien, meaning that if this girl was his daughter, there should be some resemblance. And, other than in confidence, I saw none.

"Pull the other one, it has bells on."

The girl's eyes narrowed. "She's adopted," he said. She sidled just a little closer to him.

My eyebrow raised. "Really? You just felt the paternal tug and couldn't let it go?"

He put his arm around her shoulders. "She had parents . . . something like mine."

"Oh. Wow. I'm really sorry to hear that. I'm not going to ask. Well, not right now. I'm sure I'm going to ask later. But for now, we'll pretend I'm going to let all the story that has to be behind that go. And instead, I'm going to say, it's nice to see you and your nameless daughter, but why are you both here? I know why *you're* here, Nightcrawler—Malcolm called you. But why is your teenaged daughter along for the ride? Training mission?"

The girl looked like she wasn't sure if she should laugh or hate me. Siler, however, hugged her, let go, and chuckled. "Lizzie, this is the friend I've been telling you about, Katherine Katt-Martini. Kitty, this is my adopted daughter, Elizabeth. She goes by Lizzie."

"Happy hellos later. Why is Lizzie here with you? Seriously, I think she's a little young to embrace the assassination lifestyle."

He sighed. "I normally have her in boarding school when I'm on assignment. However, there are some . . . issues . . ."

Lizzie rolled her eyes. "I kicked a couple of bullies' butts and Mister Dash thinks it's a good time for me to lie low in case their parents decide to try to enact revenge while he's not around to . . . handle that."

"What kind of bullies?"

"The kind that pick on kids littler, weaker, smarter, or different from them. Why?"

"Just wanted to enjoy the Full Kindred Spirit Experience. Okay, so you want to, what, leave Lizzie here for babysitting?" I asked Siler. "And, Mister Dash? Really?"

"All the women in my life like to give me weird nicknames, what can I say?"

"I'm flattered to make the cut. Anyway, I'm certain Malcolm told you what was going on."

"Yes. I'm also aware that the woman who handles Embassy Daycare rightly wants all your children to remain here. I'd like Lizzie to remain here, too. She can help out."

Lizzie's expression said that helping watch a bunch of little kids wasn't high on her Impromptu Spring Break To Do List. Honestly couldn't blame her.

"Are you cool with that plan?" I asked her, while I actively refrained from asking Siler just how he knew Denise didn't want the kids to go to NASA Base.

She shrugged. "Quick Girl does what Mister Dash needs.

So, right now he needs to know I'm safe, so, yeah, I'm good with the plan."

"How old are you, ah, Quick Girl?"

"Fourteen going on fifteen. Perfect babysitting age," she added, sarcasm knob at least an eight on a scale of ten. Had a feeling she was going to flip well past eleven without even trying. "And you don't need to call me Quick Girl. Since we're incognito here and all that."

"Oh, need has nothing to do with it. Okay, so, what else does your Mini-Me have going on that makes her someone you want to leave here, versus someone you want traveling with me?"

"She's fluent in eight languages and six forms of martial arts, competent in surveillance, and quite good at moving without being seen or heard," Siler said.

"I also get straight As, can do arts and crafts, know how to play a lot of sports and am particularly good at lacrosse, and know CPR," Lizzie added. "I normally charge twenty dollars an hour for babysitting services because I don't like doing it, but for you I'll make a special deal."

I managed to control the Inner Hyena and only snorted a laugh. "Got it. We weren't advertising for an au pair or nanny."

"I know. I want Lizzie here so I don't have to worry about her and so you have one more competent protector watching your home and children."

"And he's really afraid that there's going to be retaliation, but if they find out I'm here there's no way they're going to start something with American Centaurion," Lizzie added, sounding as if she'd have preferred to face the retaliation head on.

"Who is the 'they' whose offspring you taught lessons to?"

Siler and Lizzie exchanged a glance. "Ah," she said as she looked back at me, "It's classified."

CHAPTER 14

"I'LL BET IT IS. Here's the thing—I either know who might decide that they want to mess with American Centaurion based on what they apparently might feel is a really good reason or you go elsewhere."

Siler sighed. "Fine. The offspring of several prominent captains of industry, politicians, and heads of state."

"Names?"

He gave me a long look. "Classified."

Thought about it. And then considered what assassins did to those who threatened their families. There was probably a really good reason Siler didn't want to name names, starting with plausible deniability. Decided this would become Buchanan's problem, because I was all about delegating the hard stuff.

"Okey dokey. So, are we sharing that Lizzie is your daughter or are we playing pretend?"

"We're on the roof for a reason," Lizzie said, sarcasm meter definitely heading for eleven.

"Kiddo, in my experience, your dad and the men I presume you also get to think of as uncles meet on rooftops like other people meet in internet chat rooms. This location no more says 'introduce the kid in a clandestine fashion' than if you'd come in through the front door."

She grinned. "You've got a point."

"Introduce her as Elizabeth Vrabel," Siler said. "Because obviously I don't use my real name ninety-nine percent of the time, in part because I didn't want my parents to find me and still don't want their cronies able to hunt me down. All of Lizzie's paperwork says Vrabel, not Jackson."

"Because you don't want her parents or their cronies to find her, either, right?"

"Her parents can't find her anymore. I took care of that. Long ago."

"Three years, give or take," Lizzie added quietly. "They were—"

"Doing terrible things," Siler interrupted. Lizzie shut her mouth quickly. Interesting. Another story I'd have to get when Siler wasn't around, apparently. "Anyway, I'd appreciate you letting Lizzie stay here while I'm off on assignment."

"For us. Yeah, quid pro quo and all that Latin jazz. I'm sure Denise will appreciate the help. Lizzie, what's your status on following rules, staying inside the Embassy, things like that? As in, if someone isn't watching you twenty-four-seven are we going to have to worry about you disappearing, sneaking out, or similar?"

She gave me a long look. "Mister Dash wants me to stay in the Embassy. So I'm staying *in* the Embassy unless there's a compelling reason to leave it. And by compelling reason, I mean life or death, safety of others, and so forth."

Decided I'd tell Walter to keep a couple of extra eyes on Lizzie, just in case. She might not be lying to me, but since Jeff wasn't up here on the roof to tell me one way or the other, had to figure that she was going to be a typical teenager and try to get away with whatever she could the moment Siler wasn't around.

"Works for me. So, Nightcrawler, are my 'uncles' going to come by and say hi, or are we under attack and I just don't know about it?"

"They're on guard because you have a Huntress problem."

"See, this is why you're my favorite—you get with the program and I don't even have to ask you to or tell you the other code names, you just know." Meaning our Embassy was probably bugged by the Assassination Squad. I'd decide if I wanted us to try to find those bugs or not. Later. "Yeah, Cleary thinks it's Stephanie. Chuckie's not so sure, but we've done some tests and it could be. What does the Assassination Squad all think?"

"Maybe. Cleary could be right, but Reynolds could be as well. But Stephanie never showed any of those skills in the time I spent with her."

"She's had time to practice."

"True enough, which is why your 'uncles' are on the roofs. I'll tell them your feelings are hurt that they didn't come by for hugs."

"Please do, but try not to sound totally sarcastic like you do right now—I don't want you to hurt their feelings. So, are you seriously planning just having Lizzie walk down from the roof with me and get introduced as the Junior Member of the Assassination Squad, or did you have a smoother plan?"

"I think it will be a lot better if no one sees her go into the Embassy."

"Fantastic." Was about to ask how he thought no one could spot her on our roof, then remembered that where we were standing pretty much blocked us from view, particularly since we were the tallest building within normal eyesight, and no one was going to be able to spot us from the streets. "Are the rest of the staff and residents allowed to know she's here, or am I supposed to hide her like she's E.T. and only let Denise and the kids know?"

"I'd prefer Plan B but reality says that you'll have to let everyone know she's here. I'm sure your crew can roll with it."

"Yeah, me too. So, if it's not Stephanie, who *is* our Huntress?"

He gave me a slow smile. "That's what I'm here to find out."

"In other words, you guys have your suspicions but you're not sure. Let me just say that if it's that murderous bitch Annette Dier, kill her with extreme prejudice." Dier, like other prisoners from various lethal actions against us, was being held in the same place and in the same way that Dear Sam was. Didn't mean she wasn't out, though. Just might mean that no one knew she was out.

Siler nodded. "We don't believe she's escaped, but that's an avenue we're pursuing."

"Works for me. And keep me apprised."

"Always. At least, as you need to know."

"Blah, blah, blah. I'd like to know before I need to know."

He laughed. "I'll mention it to your 'uncles.'"

Siler and Lizzie had a very normal father and daughter goodbye, wherein he told her to be good and she whined about how she could go with him really, and he said no and told her that he wanted her to behave and make him proud, and then they hugged. Lizzie didn't want to let go, but Siler gently extracted himself, kissed her forehead, then disappeared.

She stared forlornly where he'd been.

"He's probably still standing here," I pointed out. He could be standing right in front of us—his blending talent meant we wouldn't know.

She shook her head. "No, he's already gone. I can tell."

Decided to trust her on it. "Okay, well, ready to go down and meet everyone else?"

"I guess."

"Where's your stuff?"

"I travel light." She had the messenger bag and that was it, and the bag didn't look packed to the gills. She might be the junior member of Team Assassination, but there was no teenaged girl on Earth who willingly traveled *this* light for a stay of indeterminate but likely extended time.

"Huh, yeah. So . . . before I take you downstairs, I want the truth."

"We told you the truth." She was looking right at me, and did look truthful. However, not only had I been trained by Mom, but I'd been a teenager and I'd known how to look totally innocent when I was lying like a wet rug, too.

"Not all of it." I locked eyes with her. "Who the hell did you piss off? To the point that your father had to swoop in and grab you with, literally, just the clothes on your back?"

Had to hand it to her, she gave it the old college try in terms of outstaring me. And she was good. But, she wasn't Mom or Chuckie good and, as expected, I won.

Lizzie dropped her eyes and mumbled something.

"Sorry, missed that. Try again. With actual volume and coherency."

She heaved a sigh and looked up at me. "The kids of the American ambassadors to about half of Europe and the Middle East. And their friends, who are all kids of people who run giant multinational corporations or are legit princes and princesses."

"Huh. How many did you take on?"

"About half of the Junior Skulls. So, like, ten of them."

Ten was impressive. Lizzie didn't look like she had a scratch on her. Meaning she was either exaggerating or really good. Considered who'd adopted her and who else were likely training her on her school vacations and chose to assume really good.

"Is that what they call themselves or what you call them?"

"It's what the rest of us call them. But, yeah, I started it."

I put my arm around her shoulders. "Lizzie? I believe this is the beginning of a beautiful friendship."

"You're not mad at me?" She sounded surprised.

"If you'd been the bully, heck yeah, I'd be mad. But I'm never going to be mad at someone who protects the underdogs and those weaker than they are."

"Mister Dash is worried about them contacting you to complain about me being here. That's why he wants you to sneak me in."

"Well, I'll do what he wants because he could have other reasons. But they can feel free to complain to me about you. But they won't."

"Why not?"

"I treat bullies the same way you do and always have."

She grinned. "Yeah? He said you were cool."

"Yeah? I'm going to bet cash money that wasn't the word he used."

CHAPTER 15

PROVING THAT WE as a group rolled with the weird punches naturally by now, no one was even remotely fazed that Lizzie was here, let alone had come in via the roof.

Denise was happy to have the extra help, Walter was apologetic for not knowing that Team Assassination had doctored the cameras to hide their arrivals, our Secret Service agents gave me their standard Why Do You Go Anywhere Without Us, Do You Hate Us? lecture, and Jeff merely muttered that we apparently needed to put a welcome mat up there, and that was it.

My Secret Service detail did search Lizzie and her messenger bag while they sent another part of our detail up onto the roof to search there. Nothing dangerous was found on Lizzie or the roof, but the agents seemed so happy to be doing something that I decided not to argue with them.

When we reached Pierre, our Embassy Majordomo and the Most Competent Man in the World, however, the casual attitude about Lizzie being here was over. Because Pierre took in the same things I had and made the leap that Lizzie was here without anything she might actually consider hers. Including a change of underwear.

"Our brave young lady needs her personal things," he said once he'd gotten the full story, or at least as much of it as I was willing to give him with the Secret Service standing there. They'd all proven they were trustworthy, but why mention that we had more assassins in town? That tended to make them twitchy. "May I send either the Operations Team or some agents to retrieve?"

"Operations Team, please and thank you." I'd prefer to have Algar snapping his fingers and making whatever so than risk sending any of our people into a trap or a situation they weren't prepared for.

"Excellent. Now, once that's taken care of, I'll get you settled into your room in the Ambassador's suite."

"Excuse me?" Lizzie and I coughed out in unison.

Pierre gave us both an arch look. "Where else would we be housing her? She's underage and therefore needs a guardian. While I could ask the Lewises, the Gaultier-Whites, or the Coleman-Weismans if they were willing, it seems to me that our brave Mister Siler put her into *your* care, Ambassador. Meaning she should be staying in *your* suite."

Ran through all the other options. All the single males were out, of course—not that any of them would do anything inappropriate with an underage girl, but still, I knew without asking that Siler didn't want his daughter sleeping in a room with a strange man.

Other than my Secret Service detail, which had women on it so that I didn't have to risk going to the bathroom by myself in public places, we didn't have a lot of single gals on staff anymore.

And after we'd gotten back from Operation Civil War, Abigail Gower had asked Mahin Sherazi to room with her. Mahin had been excited to have the bonding time, and the two of them had gotten close, which was great for both of them. They went to clubs and on double dates all the time, and why ask them to stop actually having a little fun in order to essentially babysit?

There were Rahmi and Rhee. She'd be incredibly safe with them, but having to take care of her could potentially throw them, because I had no idea how anyone on Beta Twelve treated teenagers. Plus they had other things going on that were getting the majority of their focus.

No, of the four families housing in the Embassy, Pierre was right—it made the most sense to have Lizzie with me and Jeff.

Plus Pierre was being extremely formal—he only called me Ambassador when we had people around he felt needed to have my status impressed upon them, or if he felt I wasn't acting up to that status. Meaning he potentially had other reasons for this plan.

Decided he was usually right, and nodded. "That makes sense, Pierre, thank you. Our suite is gigantic, Lizzie, so don't worry about us cramping your style."

The soundproofing was fantastic in the Embassy, so I wasn't terribly concerned about my waking her up when Jeff and I had sexy times. Plus, we were going to be on the train and in Florida for most of her stay anyway.

Interestingly, once I'd agreed to this, Lizzie seemed to relax. And Pierre clearly approved because he flashed his gracious smile at me then shooed me out of the kitchen. But not before giving me one of Jeff's mother's brownies which, because they were the best brownies in all the galaxy, I'd sort of passed an embassy law that we had to have on hand 24/7.

I left Lizzie ruining her appetite for dinner by happily scarfing brownies and drinking milk while Pierre gave instructions to the refrigerator, which was how we dealt with the Operations Team. That no one found this odd was proof, if I'd ever needed it, that Algar worked in mysterious and powerful ways. It also confirmed that he liked his little jokes just like the rest of us.

Was going to head upstairs when our doorbell rang. "I've got it," I called to Pierre and anyone else who might be listening. Went to the door and opened it up, to see the last person I'd expected.

Cliff Goodman.

CHAPTER 16

FORTUNATELY, my being shocked wasn't out of character—most people, Cliff included, called ahead to let us know they were coming. "Cliff! Are you okay?"

"Yes, sorry I'm dropping in like this, but I've been trying to reach Chuck and he hasn't picked up."

Chuckie never took Cliff's calls unless he felt emotionally able to play pretend, and this week he hadn't been. "Yeah, he's been having a lot of migraines recently. I mean, he's fine, but that's probably why. He's napping right now, for example."

"He's had to do that a lot this past year and a half." He looked sad. As if he wasn't the one who'd set things up to begin with. Then again, he probably was sad, since Chuckie's mind hadn't been destroyed.

"Yeah. It's been sucky, but we're getting him through it."

"Are you okay?" Cliff sounded totally concerned about my welfare. "I saw what happened to you and Lillian. That was awful."

"Yeah, it was weird, too. Lillian and I were trying to do a rare girl's lunch out. Guess that won't be happening again for ages now."

Cliff looked around. "Ah, can I come in?"

"Oh!" I did not want him inside. It was Sunday, so no one was at work, and therefore Chuckie was here. He was also wide awake and totally unprepared for this visit. And Cliff seeing him awake would be the epitome of not good. "Well, actually, I was just getting ready to go out. That's why I got the door."

"Without your purse?"

Crap. This man knew me well. I shrugged. "Yeah." I dropped my voice. "Jeff's been like a mother hen since that attack and I'm going a little stir crazy. I was only going to go across the street and visit the Romanian Embassy. But if I have my purse on me, then everyone would know I was planning to leave."

"Ah, gotcha." He seemed to be thinking. "Well, if you want, I can go with you. That way, you're not alone and you have someone to protect you."

"Sure, that sounds great." It didn't, but I was now committed to this course. Fortunately, I'd learned to play poker young, because I was now riding on the bluff.

I stepped out and closed the door quietly behind me.

Cliff offered me his arm. "Across the street, then?"

Took his arm as if he was really our buddy and someone who wanted to protect me. "Nah. Since you're here, I don't have to go. They aren't expecting me, I just figured it was a safe place to sneak to that Jeff couldn't bawl me out too much for visiting."

Cliff laughed. "Gotcha. So, a walk, sit at the park in Sheridan Circle, hit up the Teetotaler, what's your pleasure?"

I appeared to consider this. "While I'd love to head for the Teetotaler, let's just go for the park at the Circle. It's close, so Jeff hopefully won't be too mad if he catches us." And I certainly planned for him to catch us, since I was doing my best to send carefully tuned emotions and thoughts to him.

"Sounds good, and if you change your mind, it's always easy to grab a cab."

"I like where your head's at." Time to talk to Cliff as if he wasn't the Mastermind. And time to also see what he might let slip. He'd slipped before. Not a lot, but enough. "So, that weird assassin chick hasn't tried for anyone else, has she? I haven't heard it if she has."

"Assassins aren't my thing anymore, unless they cause disaster-level damage, but since she appears to be hitting allies of American Centaurion's, I've been extra careful."

Considered this, and what I'd say if this was a real ally of ours. "Maybe we shouldn't be sitting outside in the park. I mean, I don't want anything to happen to you."

I didn't. Cliff knew where the Leventhal Reid and LaRue Demorte Gaultier clones were, and how many more of them were being created. He knew where everything planned against us was hidden and he knew what was being created to be tossed at us. We were all sure he had a dooms-day plan or a kill switch that would cause the end of the world if he was killed out of hand. He was the Mastermind, and as much as I wanted him dead, I had to keep him alive.

"Well, I'm sure I'm okay. I took a cab here, and we're close to the Embassy."

"Yeah, but seriously, dude, I don't want anything to happen to you. Jeff will be even madder if I've snuck out and gotten you hurt or worse." I wanted to ask him if he'd heard from Stephanie, since he'd been dating her when she'd disappeared. But he'd been dating her on the down low, so my asking would give away that we knew about the relationship.

"I guess." Cliff put his free hand over mine and gave it a gentle squeeze. "I appreciate the concern, Kitty. I really do. If it's making you nervous, we can go to the Teetotaler, to the Romanian Embassy, or just back to your Embassy if you'll feel safer."

We were crossing the street to get to Sheridan Circle as he said this. And no sooner had the words left his mouth than I heard a sound I was becoming familiar with—the roar of a Harley going fast.

CHAPTER 17

I DIDN'T STOP TO THINK. I pulled my arm out from Cliff's, then grabbed his hand. Took a look around and saw the Harley coming toward us. It wasn't the same bike she'd been riding before, but it was big, fast, and loud, so wherever she was getting these bikes from was definitely working on a theme.

"We need to run," I told Cliff. I was about to take off when it dawned on me that if I did, I'd be going at hyperspeed. I couldn't remember if Cliff knew I was enhanced—because it was hard to remember who knew what these days—but if he didn't know, my taking us to hyperspeed would give away one of the only secret weapons we possessed.

"Yeah." He started running toward the park and dragging me with him. He wasn't going slowly, and he wasn't leaving me behind.

Ran at human speeds and checked his expression. He looked freaked out. "The park isn't going to give us much cover. We should go back to the Embassy."

"We can't."

He was right. Huntress had come to a stop, between us and the Zoo. If we couldn't make the Zoo—and without my using hyperspeed we couldn't—we certainly couldn't make the Embassy, any of them on the street, let alone our own.

Cliff dragged us behind a tree. "We need a plan."

True enough. The Harley started going again. This might be a ruse to get me to use hyperspeed. Then again, Cliff had wanted to get inside the Embassy. Me going out with him couldn't have been in his game plan, because normally Pierre or Rajnish Singh, our Public Relations Minister, answered the door. And Cliff hadn't done anything I'd seen to send a message in the short time we'd been together, and I *had* been looking for it.

He pulled me around the other side of the tree, meaning the arrow missed us and went into the tree's trunk. I pulled him toward the street. He pulled me back and down. Just in time, as yet another arrow just missed us.

"Kitty, seriously, she's going around in a circle and is faster than we are. We need a plan. Up into the trees, you think?"

It was a viable option, but one that would take time. "She'll be able to shoot one or both of us if we try," I said, as we scurried around to the other side of the tree again and I wondered where the hell Jeff was.

Huntress got tired of going in a circle and drove up onto the grass, blocking us between her motorcycle and the tree. She leveled the bow, but not at me. She was aiming for Cliff's heart.

I readied myself to pull him down, fast, when someone slammed into us and suddenly we were far away. I looked up expecting to see Jeff, but instead saw White. "Great timing," I said as we zipped up Massachusetts Avenue, aka Embassy Row.

"It's luck. I happened to look out the window at the right time. I'd inquire as to what the two of you were doing outside, but I'm sure it's a reason that makes no sense."

"Kitty was feeling stir crazy," Cliff gasped out. "I'd

dropped by and figured I could keep her safe and let her have a little time-out. I was wrong and I'll be the first one to admit that I'm an idiot."

"Hardly. But she must have followed you, Cliff. She was aiming for you." Of course, during Operation Sherlock, Cliff had had his own brand new car blown up for the sole purpose of making us think the bad guys were after him. It wasn't beyond him to have done the same now. Only . . . he'd looked terrified. Truly terrified. Ready to die and not wanting to terrified.

We turned left and followed Waterside Drive back toward our section of the Row. Got off the street behind our property. White and I could have scaled the fence, but there was no way Cliff could do it, and no way I could do it if I wanted to keep Cliff in the dark about my A-C abilities.

White stopped and I caught my breath while Cliff had the standard human reaction to hyperspeed—he threw up. Tried not to enjoy it a little. Failed.

"I think we need protection on Cliff."

"I think we need to get Mister Goodman somewhere safe," White agreed. "However I'm not convinced our Embassy is that place anymore."

"Not sure my place is safe, either," Cliff retched out.

"Protective custody? The police will absolutely do that for you."

Cliff stood up and shook his head. He was shaking. Did what I would have before I knew who he really was—took his hand and squeezed it. He squeezed back, and gave me a grateful smile. "Thanks, Kitty. I don't know how you guys do the action stuff all the time. It's not fun at all." He shuddered. "Neither is having someone pointing a deadly weapon at you with clear intent to kill. You guys are all a lot braver than I am, I guess."

"You get used to it."

"Really?"

"No, I'm lying. You really don't. Some of us have fight, some of us have flight, Cliff. That's all it is."

"I suppose." He heaved a sigh. "So, do we go to the Embassy and get bawled out, or do I go to the police?"

White looked thoughtful. "Honestly . . . if you feel safe enough, I'd say the police. They have no leads on this would-be killer, and you're a prominent person in town. You'll have top protection, and what you saw could help them."

"We have nothing, too, so it's not like we've got more than the police. But will Cliff be safe with just humans guarding him? If you hadn't come when you did, Richard, both of us might be dead."

"We'll assign some Field teams to protect you as well," White said. "If you'll allow it."

"I normally say no, but this time? This time I'll gladly take the protection, Richard, thank you."

"Then, prepare your stomach, Clifford—we're about to go fast again."

We zipped off and went to the D.C.P.D. location where the K-9 squad was based. Gave our stories, which didn't take all that long because there wasn't much to tell. More units were assigned to Embassy Row, Cliff was put under protection, and three Field teams arrived before we were ready to leave.

Hoped that the six agents and the cops wouldn't get hurt, either by Huntress or one of Cliff's people.

We were offered a ride home, but White and I passed. Instead, we used good ol' hyperspeed—this time with me providing the speed and White providing the navigation and steering—and headed back to the Embassy.

We got inside and I was prepared for questions and a lot of shouting. But no one was waiting for us.

"Where's Jeff?"

"I have no idea," White said. "Truly, I looked out the window at the right time."

"Huh. I was sending mental and emotional signals. Good ones, too. I was sure of it."

Heard the sound of running feet and all of a sudden Jeff was there, looking freaked out. "What's wrong? What happened? Why are you two so stressed?"

White and I looked at each other. "Mister Goodman must have been wearing a particularly strong emotional blocker," White said.

"Yeah, that's the only thing that makes sense." We filled Jeff in, fast, on what had just transpired.

When we were done he didn't bawl me out. "That was honestly good, quick thinking, baby. And Richard's right — Cliff must have been wearing a blocker of incredible power, because I got nothing from you at all." He hugged me. "And you could have been killed."

Hugged him back. "No. I'd have used hyperspeed before I let her kill me. Or, sadly, him. I'm just glad Richard was there."

"So, you really think he wasn't faking it?" Jeff asked.

"Well, without empathic confirmation, I have no way of being a hundred percent sure. But he looked and acted totally terrified. And I've seen him for a long time now — this is the first real fear I've ever seen Cliff show."

"We'll discuss it with Charles," White said. "And get his impressions. For now, however, I think we work under a new assumption — that whoever this Huntress is, she's after our allies. Because Cliff is identified as such."

"Maybe. But there's another possibility."

"What?" Jeff asked.

"She could be after us and our allies *and* after Cliff. For two entirely different revenge reasons."

"You think your Huntress is Stephanie?" Jeff asked sadly.

"More and more each day, yeah, I do. She's had time to learn to drive and the Yates blood is, let's face it, strong in your family, Jeff. But, as we say in Pueblo Caliente, that's a cactus spine for another day."

"Do you really say that where you come from?" White asked, sounding mildly surprised.

"Well, I do. As always, I can't speak for anyone else."

White chuckled. "You can, and do. But as *we* say, that's a fight I'm not willing to have right now."

"Wise man once again proves his wisdom."

CHAPTER 18

THE REST OF THE afternoon and early evening were uneventful, besides filling Chuckie in on what had transpired and then being forced to make him take his migraine meds and a nap.

Dinner was a group affair, because Pierre insisted that Lizzie needed to meet everyone and that would be the easiest way to ensure I hadn't missed any introductions. For whatever reason, Jeff had asked for Men At Work's "Cargo" album, so that was our background music. I liked it, so didn't argue.

Denise took the time during dinner to give me a list of who she felt should stay at the Embassy. "I already ran this by Doreen, and she agrees. I also ran it by the Secret Service, and they agree as well, though they'd like more names on the list."

"I'm sure they would, but we'll go with whatever you two want. But you two also get to be the ones who have the fights with everyone you want to keep here."

In addition to the kids and Amy, Denise and Doreen wanted to keep Pierre, Tito, and Nurse Carter home. Keeping our medical staff in the Embassy made sense, especially since Amy was in her eighth month of pregnancy with a hybrid baby.

Nurse Carter wasn't big on getting into the action, and

White rarely tried to take her along on missions anyway. White was definitely on our list of those going down to Florida, and not only because he'd been the former Supreme Pontifex—he was the best diplomat we had other than Doreen, though he constantly tried to deny it. He was also my unofficial partner whenever butt-kicking took place and, as earlier events had shown, quite good at it.

Also, as Christopher's father, Jeff and Gower's uncle, and someone both the A-Cs and the Planetary Council would listen to, he was vital to any political cause we had.

The problem with our not taking Tito along, however, was that this meant we wouldn't be taking Rahmi and Rhee. And I knew we'd need them, even if Tito hadn't already hinted that they were bored.

Tito and Rahmi had gotten engaged at the end of Operation Civil War. Based on the majority of our human-alien courtships, they should have been married by now. However, we did have some extremely long engagements— Ravi Gaekwad and Jennifer Barone, for example, who had had a two-year-plus engagement before finally getting married a few months ago in a lavish ceremony. Tito and Rahmi appeared to be trying to break Ravi and Jennifer's record.

Not because either one of them were dragging their feet, but because Beta Twelve had two marriage rituals— battlefield joinings, which were incredibly fast, and official matrimony, which wasn't. They'd foolishly not gotten married when we were on Beta Eight, meaning that they were on the long and winding ritualistic road to the altar.

That the Free Women from Beta Twelve reproduced via cloning and had done away with men thousands of years ago wasn't speeding things up, either. Rahmi was possibly the first Free Woman to want to marry a man in hundreds of years, plus she was the eldest of the two princesses, meaning that she technically would inherit the Queenship of

Beta Twelve. There were, therefore, alterations that had to be made to the rituals for both the potential for succession and the fact that one of the participants was the "wrong" gender.

Despite having typical sibling spats the princesses were already pretty inseparable, but some of the rituals were requiring Rhee to never be too far from Rahmi. And Rahmi never wanted to be too far from Tito unless we were in battle. Which meant that we wouldn't have the princesses with us, and that had a real potential to make the Planetary Council nervous at best.

Scanned the rest of the suggested Stay At Home list. Hacker International was on it, which wasn't a surprise. None of them liked to leave the Zoo, let alone the city, and after a short time around them they all bothered Jeff for various reasons. Them clamoring to take the train was unlikely, but they could fight with Denise and Jeff if they desperately wanted to go.

Decided that the needs of diplomacy were going to outweigh the medical risks. "Tito and the princesses are coming with us," I said as I handed the list back to Denise. "You can win on all the others, but I need the three of them. Nurse Carter is more than capable of handling the majority of our potential medical emergencies, and Tito can always take a floater gate home if he's needed urgently."

Denise grinned. "Okay, you win."

"You put Tito on the list just so I'd focus on him and you'd keep everyone else, didn't you?"

"As you like to say, Kitty, whatever works."

"I think you're all learning to be far sneakier than is good for me."

As I finished speaking, I got a text from Caroline Chase, my sorority roommate and one of my besties who also happened to work for Senator McMillan.

"Caro wants to go with us," I told Jeff. "The Senator can't

go, and not only because he was injured by Huntress, and he'd like her to represent him."

Jeff heaved a sigh. "You're sure it's Don's suggestion?"

"Seems like it. Besides, Caro's good in these situations. And she needs to get out anyway." Caroline had been engaged to Michael Gower. Prior to their engagement she'd been someone who'd had no issues playing the field, just like Michael, really. They'd matched up so well, and been so happy, but our enemies had cut that short. Since Michael's murder, however, Caroline had become far more quiet and withdrawn. Basically, Chuckie wasn't the only one still mourning the loss of their significant other. Unlike Chuckie, I hadn't been able to convince her to move into the Embassy.

I'd have been worried about her being outside of our immediate reach with our Mystery Huntress out there, especially since McMillan had been a target. But since my "uncles" were in town, I figured they were watching over her. The Dingo had actually dated her for a while—when he was first assigned to kill me, not that she'd known he was an assassin at the time—and he still seemed quite fond of her, so Caroline was probably safe. Well, as safe as any of us ever were.

Chuckie, who was looking much better after today's nap, took the list out of Denise's hands and scanned it. "I'm with Kitty—Tito and the princesses need to come. I'd also recommend we bring along Mister Joel Oliver, because I'm pretty sure we're going to want to ensure that, whatever happens, our side of the story is told."

"Makes sense to me," I said before anyone else could argue. Oliver was the best investigative reporter in the world, but until Operation Destruction he'd been considered a quack conspiracy theorist. He was also a very good friend and someone we could always rely on.

"That's good," Tito said. "Because Doctor Morin isn't feeling well, and he sent me a text a few minutes ago asking if I could function as the Presidential Physician for this trip. I already said yes, too."

Chuckie nodded. "You're the obvious choice for a variety of reasons. I also want Stryker with us. And Adriana. And, Kitty, if you can convince him, Vance Beaumont."

CHAPTER 19

ALL OF US WITHIN EARSHOT STARED AT HIM.
"Really?" I asked finally as Jeff groaned quietly and Men at Work's album ended and "Crazy" from Aerosmith started. Hey, Walter had orders from me and we'd definitely gone more than ten songs without an Aerosmith number.

Hacker International tended to eat in their computer lab at the Zoo, so none of them were in the dining room with us to whine one way or the other. So, one for the win column. Already had the feeling I'd need to try to frontload the wins as much as possible.

"Yes. In regard to Stryker, we can't take Chernobog with us for a variety of reasons, and I want someone with strong hacking abilities along. Just in case."

Jeff sighed and shrugged. "Whatever you say, Chuck." Figured Jeff was just placating Chuckie so that he didn't have another meltdown, so I didn't argue and merely nodded.

"I agree about Adriana," Len said. Kyle nodded.

"I do, too." Adriana was the granddaughter of the Romanian ambassador. The ambassador's wife, Olga, however, was former KGB. Olga had MS and was confined to a wheelchair, and Adriana was her helper.

In addition, Olga was literally the All-Seeing Oracle and had been training Adriana in the Old Ways. Adriana had saved my life during Operation Assassination, and she was always a huge asset to our team. Plus Len and Kyle really liked her, and she liked them.

"She's cleared," Joseph, who was the head of Jeff's Secret Service detail, said. "As is Stryker Dane. Vance Beaumont, however—"

"Is also cleared," Buchanan said, in a tone that indicated he had the higher authority, which, considering he was part of the P.T.C.U., he did. "And I agree—he's got a knowledge base of who's who, who's sleeping with whom, who's fighting with whom, and who is and isn't friendly to American Centaurion."

"Vance isn't wild about action," I pointed out.

"But he's willing to do it when he has to," Raj said in a soothing tone. Raj was a very powerful troubadour, so the entire room relaxed, because he wanted us to relax.

Raj was also part of our very secret A-C C.I.A. that Serene Dwyer, our current Head of Imageering, had started a few years ago. Other than the troubadours who reported to her and me, no one else knew about them. Which was fine— hard to be a secret agency if everyone knows your name. Come to think of it, I didn't know their official name. As always, my attention to the little things was nonexistent. Well, as with so many other things, I'd worry about that later.

"Then that's settled," Chuckie said.

"Yep, I'll call Vance after dinner."

Christopher took the list next as "Everybody's Gonna Be Happy" by the Kinks came on. "Why isn't my dad on this list?"

White, who was on the other side of Amy, and I exchanged a look. He was trying not to laugh. "Because I'm needed, son," he said gently.

"I wish you'd stop risking yourself constantly," Christopher muttered. "Our baby deserves to have at least one living grandparent."

"Your dad's the best agent we have, Christopher." I pointed out. "And you know we won't let him get hurt."

"And my parents will burst into tears if they hear you say that your child will only have one grandparent," Jeff added. "In a very dramatic way. Which I'd love to avoid."

Christopher looked embarrassed and Amy patted his hand. "It'll be fine. Our child will have the best extended family anyone could have."

Christopher managed a grimace I was fairly sure he thought was passing for a smile. Wondered if I could suggest that he be the one to stay home on this trip, but the reality was that we couldn't afford to have our own Flash far from where the action was most likely to happen.

Mahin and Abigail weren't on Denise's list, and those two were sitting and eating quietly, presumably so none of us would mention that they should stay home, too. Frankly, I wanted them both with us. Mahin was essentially an earth bender, and we were going to be on the ground. And Abigail had gotten all her powers back and her sister's to boot during Operation Civil War, meaning she was scary formidable.

The rest of dinner was spent with minor discussions of who was going, when we were going, and who else outside of the Embassy staff needed to come along. Unsurprisingly, our Secret Service staff had a lot of opinions on who should be staying at home. I stayed out of it—their arguments were fruitless because we'd all do what we wanted anyway, but it was nice to let them feel like they had input.

Then it was time to put Charlie and Jamie to bed and we figured we'd need to get Lizzie settled in, too, even though she wasn't going to be expected to go to bed at seven in the evening. Sure, Pierre had set up her room already, but that wasn't the same as seeing how a family group operated and figuring out how you were going to fit within it during your enforced vacation. Pierre approved of this plan, so that decided that.

Lizzie, presumably to show willing, carried Charlie while Jeff had Jamie. Jamie was chattering away at Lizzie, telling her all about the animals we had living with us and generously offering to let Lizzie sleep in her room with her should Lizzie be missing her daddy and mommy. To Lizzie's great credit, she didn't share her family situation with little children, but merely smiled and said that she was good in whatever room we offered to her.

As the five of us and four Secret Service agents got out of the elevator to the melodious sounds of Adam Ant's "Here Comes the Grump," my phone rang. Pulled it out and took a look. Not a number I recognized. This tended to mean I was getting what, by now, I considered a standard Crazed Lunatic Opening Gambit. But I answered because it could have been AeroForceOne telling me I'd won an all-expenses paid trip to see Aerosmith live and hang backstage with the band. A girl could dream, after all.

Besides, our phones were tapped by the Secret Service—at least our main phones that they knew about were tapped—and that meant that they'd be able to trace the call if need be. "Hello?"

"Ambassador Martini?" Male, didn't recognize the voice, though it was vaguely familiar. The chances of the caller being about to tell me I was going to hang out with Steven Tyler and Joe Perry in person dropped.

"That's me! Who is this?"

"One of your biggest admirers." This was hugely doubtful.

"Does said supposed admirer have a name or am I just supposed to guess?" Jeff's eyebrow rose at this, and I could tell he was now paying full attention.

So were Evalyne and Phoebe, the head and second-in-command of my personal Secret Service detail. Joseph, meanwhile, was fiddling with something on his phone, meaning he'd started a trace, just in case. Rob, the second-in-command of Jeff's detail, was texting, presumably alerting the rest of the troops that I had a Creepy Caller.

My Mystery Caller chuckled. "Of course. It's Ansom Somerall. I'm surprised you didn't recognize my voice." Somerall was the Chairman of the Board of Gaultier Enterprises, and one of what I referred to as the Land Sharks—a cabal of businesspeople who were definitely smarmy and almost certainly evil.

"Ansom Somerall, what a surprise." Jeff's eyes narrowed and this news created more Secret Service activity. "It's been so long since you ambushed me at breakfast, I'd managed to forget the dulcet tones of your voice." Happily, I hadn't had to interact with any of the Land Sharks in any real way since Operation Infiltration. Apparently those golden days were over now.

He chuckled again. "I'm flattered you find my voice attractive." Right, Somerall fancied himself a ladies' man.

Managed not to throw up a little in my mouth, but only just. "Oh yeah. So, what are you calling about?" I had a guess, and it started and ended with the Planetary Council coming by for a visit.

"Actually, I'm calling for a friend. I believe you're housing a person you undoubtedly don't realize is a juvenile delinquent and a danger to your personnel and home."

Well, that was unexpected. Though all things considered, it shouldn't have been.

Looked over at Lizzie. She hadn't reacted to Somerall's name, meaning that whoever's kids she had problems with, they weren't his. "I'm not sure who or what you're talking about."

She caught my looking at her, however, and her expression turned from mildly interested in what was going on around her to worried and confused. Put my arm around her shoulders and felt her visibly relax.

"I'm talking about a wanted criminal, Ambassador. As in someone with an outstanding warrant for her arrest."

"Oh goodness gracious me." Jeff managed not to laugh. We were outside our apartment, but due to said animals

Jamie had been chattering about, Jeff wasn't opening the door until I was off the phone. You tended to lose focus when a tide of fur and feathers descended upon you.

"You don't sound worried."

"Oh, I am worried. I'm worried about you thinking you know who is or isn't in my Embassy."

"Ambassador, I don't think you know the true story behind the juvenile recently put into your care. She murdered her parents before she went on the run."

Interesting. And doubtful, since I was fairly sure whoever had murdered them had been Siler. "Gosh. She sounds terribly dangerous." Joseph gave me the "keep 'em talking" sign as the music changed to "Teenage Rampage" by Sweet. Never a problem—keeping the bad guys monologuing was my go-to move. "If I knew who you were talking about, I might be panicked and all that."

"Elizabeth Jackson. She's about fifteen."

"Oh. What a relief. We have no one by that name here. If we run across her, I'll be sure to let the proper authorities know." Noted that Somerall was using Lizzie's real name. This probably boded.

"Ambassador, we know she's there."

"See, Ansom, here's my problem with all of this 'knowing' you claim you have. I have no idea *how* you think you know anything about who is or isn't in my Embassy. And, being the infinitely suspicious person that I am, I'm thinking you either have illegal surveillance in my Embassy—which, by the way, would be both an act of war against American Centaurion *and* an act of treason against the United States—or you're just guessing."

Jeff handed Jamie to Phoebe while he pulled his phone out and made a quiet call. I assumed it was to Dulce to get some Field teams over here searching for new and improved bugs.

"We have no illegal surveillance in your embassy."

"Ah, but what if you think you have legal surveillance?"

Jeff made another call, this time to Chuckie. As he did, the elevator opened and our hallway was flooded with Secret Service personnel. I saw a floater gate flicker into existence and a ton of A-Cs pour out of it and zip off, presumably to start doing yet another bug search.

"Ambassador, why aren't you concerned about what I'm telling you?" Somerall asked, nicely avoiding replying to my legal surveillance question.

"I'm far more concerned with why you think you know who is or isn't in my home." Chuckie, Buchanan, Len, Kyle, and Raj all arrived via the stairs, meaning Raj had used hyperspeed and they'd done a daisy chain. Always nice to be popular. "I have no idea why you're guessing, or why a fifteen-year-old would be a danger, but since we have no one by the name or age you gave me here, let's hope for your sake that you're just trying to scare me with a teenaged boogeyman. Now, let's get back to the relevant conundrum— what legal surveillance are you tapping into?"

He heaved a dramatic sigh. "Ambassador, I've called as a friend. If you need help, you have my number now. Please be cautious—we wouldn't want anything to happen to anyone in the American Centaurion embassy." Then he hung up.

I looked at Evalyne. "We need extra guards on Amy, right now."

CHAPTER 20

"A MY?" Evalyne sounded confused. "Why?"

"Because Amy is still fighting with the Gaultier board, and I think Somerall called to 'tell' me about Lizzie because he's going to have someone attack Amy and try to put the blame on Lizzie."

"It's very possible," Chuckie said. "Especially because all the earlier attacks were perpetrated by a woman."

"A much older woman," Jeff said.

"Honestly, Huntress is wearing a mask. She could be any age."

"I'm not here to kill anyone!" Lizzie sounded freaked out and scared, and I couldn't blame her.

I still had my arm around her and I hugged her again. "We know. But this is how our enemies work. And, under the circumstances, once we know what kind of surveillance that's in our home that we don't want, you're going to give me more of that story your father didn't want me to hear."

"Okay," she said quietly. "You can check my stuff that Pierre had picked up. There's nothing bad in it."

"I'm sure there isn't," Jeff said. "Because it was already searched before it was brought into our apartment."

"Speaking of which, I haven't heard the melodious sounds of animal howling, so I assume our apartment hasn't been searched yet."

Manfred, one of the A-C troubadours who was a part of my extended security detail whenever we left the Embassy, zipped over. "You're right, Ambassador. The Embassy has been searched, and Dulce has done scans, but due to the animals, we've saved your apartment for last. So far, we haven't found anything untoward."

"Then, barring us finding all the bugs in the main apartment suite, how did Somerall know she's here," Phoebe asked, nodding her head toward Lizzie.

"Saw us on the roof maybe?"

Evalyne shook her head. "I know why they want you to meet up there—unless someone's watching with a high-powered scope or in aircraft overhead, your roof is a good hiding place."

Buchanan grunted. "Sheridan Circle."

"You think there's someone in the trees?" I asked him.

"There was when the assassins weren't on your side, Missus Chief. More than once."

"Operation Assassination was exciting, wasn't it? But could someone really see on top of our roof from the treetops?"

Buchanan looked at Manfred, who nodded. "We'll go check it out right now, Mister Buchanan."

"Taking me with you," he said. "Everyone else needs to stay put. And have Walter put the shields on, Missus Chief."

"Already done," Rob said. "So we'll advise him that you're going out."

Buchanan nodded then he and Manfred disappeared, literally, thanks to hyperspeed. Hyperspeed was hard on humans, but Tito had created a Super Dramamine that controlled the effects. Every human on staff in the Embassy took it daily, as did most of our human agents worldwide. So Buchanan wouldn't be barfing his guts out in two seconds when they reached Sheridan Circle across the street from the Zoo. Unless he wanted to, of course.

Thinking about this reminded me of Cliff tossing his

cookies earlier. "I wonder if he was coming to see if Lizzie was here."

"Who?" Jeff asked, while Rob talked quietly to Walter. Rob could have used the internal communications system but the Secret Service really seemed to enjoy their phones, earpieces, and lapel and wrist mics, and who was I to steal all their fun?

"Cliff," Chuckie said, without snarling, which was impressive. "Maybe. We certainly can't rule it out, especially considering she'd only been here a short while when he arrived."

"Yeah, and we need to make sure that Siler knows that Somerall and whoever his 'friends' are know Lizzie's real name."

"They do?" She sounded freaked out, not that I could blame her.

"Yes, Somerall told me our murderous juvenile delinquent was named Elizabeth Jackson."

"Can I send my dad a text?" she asked.

"Only if we see it," Chuckie said. "I'd really suggest you wait. This information is unlikely to be an issue for your father, and you're safe for the time being. We have other things we need to focus on."

"Okay." Lizzie didn't sound like she thought it was really okay. I hugged her again.

"So, now what?" Jeff asked Chuckie.

"Now we wait for what Buchanan finds."

"I say we go in and get our apartment searched while we wait." Everyone looked at me and I shrugged. "Either we find bugs or we find none. But I have two Junior Ambassadors who need to get to bed."

"I agree with Kitty," Jeff said, possibly because Charlie was yawning.

"Let us go in first, please, Mister Vice President," Joseph said, as "Keep It Together" from Puddle of Mudd hit our airwaves.

"You know, I thought we'd broken all of you from the formality."

"Not when danger's around," Evalyne said with a quick smile. Phoebe was still holding Jamie and Lizzie had Charlie. And Jeff and I had hyperspeed, meaning that if someone was lurking somehow in our apartment, then we could avoid them or just take them out like we did in the good old days of not all that long ago.

While the animals were used to A-Cs and other Embassy personnel coming in regularly to walk them and ensure that they had what they needed food- and water-wise, they had to know a bunch of us were right outside in the hallway, and that meant they were probably worked up and ready for action of some kind, even if that action was just bowling over everyone who came through the door with love and demands for attention.

Jeff took my hand, so I knew he'd read what I thought we should do. "Nope." Then he kicked up the hyperspeed and got us into our apartment in less than a second. We did a fast room check. Lots of fur and feathers—though not all the fur that we'd be getting shortly—no untoward humanoids. While I greeted our First Line of Animal Defense, Jeff went to the front door and opened it. "Come on in and check whatever."

We had four dogs—Dudley the Great Dane, Duke the Labrador, Duchess the Pit Bull, and Dottie the Dalmatian—and they all wanted pets and praise for having guarded things so very well.

And, as Lizzie walked in, all four dog heads turned toward her. She was still holding Charlie and I worried for a moment that the dogs wouldn't like this.

Duchess bounded over and Lizzie froze. Duchess sniffed her all over, then jumped up and licked Lizzie right on the face. Charlie laughed and Duchess licked him, too. Then the other three dogs raced over to do their own versions of sniff and lick.

Jeff retrieved Charlie from Lizzie. "Feel free to go wash up," he said. "All the dog licking can take some getting used to."

"It just means they like her," I pointed out.

"Good," she said with feeling. "I wouldn't want the four of them mad at me."

"Oh, you haven't seen anything yet. Trust me."

"You have more pets?" Lizzie asked as she headed for a room one down from Jamie's, which was where I presumed Pierre had assigned her. "Jamie wasn't just talking about her stuffed animals?"

"You have no idea," Jeff said as the others came in and the A-Cs started their standard hyperspeed searches.

Lizzie stopped in her doorway and backed slowly toward the living room. "I don't think they want me in here."

Went to her room to see which animals were in there. Because we had lots of animals in the apartment with us. And when I say "lots," I mean "more than you could easily count." And all the animals I'd been expecting to be brought up from the Zoo not sixty seconds ago were in here, too, somehow. Though I had a good guess for the "how"— hyperspeed or temporal warps—as well as the "some"— Poofs or Peregrines.

Other than some people's assigned Peregrines, the Alpha Four Royal Protector Birds that looked like peacocks and peahens on steroids but could, like Siler, go chameleon, all the other Peregrines roomed with us.

We'd worried, way back when, that the Peregrines weren't going to go forth and multiply. As Jeff put it now, how silly we were to think their moratorium on reproduction would last. While we didn't have as many Peregrines as we had Poofs, there were plenty of them now. Thankfully, they used the toilet, literally, as opposed to messing up the Embassy or the Zoo.

We also had my parents' cats in addition to their dogs and all the Poofs that were ours and any that were

unattached. And we now also had ocellars and chochos,
Beta Eight animals that had come home with us. And those
were the animals that were normally delivered to our rooms
at bedtime and by A-Cs assigned to the task.

Ocellars looked like a caracal-fox combo, and chochos
were essentially pigdogs. The ocellar Ginger and chocho Wil-
bur had attached to me during Operation Civil War and they,
along with a set of their fellow breeds, had come home with
us. They did make the animal exhibit portion of the Zoo
more interesting, so there was that. And they, like the other
animals, were good protection. However, none of the animals
slept in the Zoo. When not "on exhibit" they were with us.
Literally.

And they were all in Lizzie's room.

CHAPTER 21

FORTUNATELY, the rooms in the Embassy were large, but even so, there was a lot of concentrated Animal Kingdom in here.

"Huh. Who brought you all in from the Zoo?" Got a shot of the Sea of Animal Innocence look from all of them. "So, was it Poofs or Peregrines who brought the chochos and ocellars over? And stop trying to lie to Kitty, it's not appreciated in the least."

Now I got some chagrined animal looks and the acknowledgment that, yes, since we had someone new living with us, they all wanted to pass judgment.

And I knew this, just as I'd known what the K-9 dogs were thinking, because, among the many weird and wonderful things that had happened to me over the past few years, I'd become Dr. Doolittle and could talk to the animals. All the animals. And all the animals had wanted to be here, just in case.

"And, your thoughts?" No one other than Lizzie was looking at me like I was crazy because they were all used to it, even the A-C Field agents I could see using the slow version of hyperspeed—that always sounded like an oxymoron but wasn't—in order to get around the animals safely and still do their search and seizure stuff.

One of the unattached Poofs bounded over and jumped

onto Lizzie's shoulder. "Ah, is this little *fofo* dangerous?" she asked.

The Poof purred. Loudly.

"Um, Lizzie? What does '*fofo*' mean?" I had a guess, of course, that it indicated something cute in some way.

"Fluffy. In Portuguese. Why?"

"She's okay, I see," Jeff said with a sigh.

"Yep. You're Poof Approved, Lizzie. And, meet your new Poof, now named Fofo."

Lizzie's eyes opened wide. "Really? It's mine?" She looked excited for a moment, then her face fell. "I can't have pets. Mister Dash says we can't have a living creature dependent upon us who can be hurt, used against us, or who we'll have to dump off somewhere in case we have to—" She stopped herself and looked down.

"Run," Jeff gently finished for her. "But you're in luck. Poofs are . . . different."

"And once you name it, and the Poofs tend to choose their own names, it's yours for life. Trust me, it'll be a great pet, and possibly the only pet you can have that can disappear whenever needed, find you pretty much anywhere, and protect you, too, when necessary." And now I had a good guess as to what country Lizzie's School for Gifted and Wealthy Minors was in.

"It's okay, Lizzie," Jamie said reassuringly. "Fofo wants to be your Poof. That's why the animals are here—they wanted to welcome you home."

We all looked at Jamie. "Ah, home?" Jeff asked.

Jamie nodded. "Isn't Lizzie going to live here forever?"

There was something in how Jamie was asking this that made me really think about my reply. "We haven't really discussed it, Jamie-Kat. But we will, okay?"

"Okay. Lizzie, you can have some of the animals sleep with you if you'll feel better." This was a generous offer— Jamie normally insisted on all the animals who weren't on duty elsewhere or who hadn't taken up residence with others in the Embassy all sleep with her. Ergo, there were a lot of animals in her room every night. Not as many as before Charlie's arrival, but thankfully Jamie had been willing to share.

Well, she'd been grudgingly willing to share after Jeff and I had explained that Charlie was allowed to have his own Poof and other animals who favored him. That Jamie was offering animals to Lizzie without prompting said a lot about how much Jamie liked Lizzie already.

We used this as a segue to getting Jamie and Charlie into bed. Charlie was in the nursery attached to our bedroom and Jamie was in the room next door, otherwise known as the Shrine to Pink, which was her favorite color in the world. Charlie hadn't indicated any color preferences yet, but I figured that was just a matter of time.

While Jamie got ready for bed—being a *big* girl and not a *baby* like her little brother, at least as she'd announced a couple of months ago—Jeff and I tucked Charlie in and did with him as we'd done with Jamie. We sang songs and made sure that he was happily asleep before we left his room, baby monitor on.

Of course, he had animals in the room with him, a sampling of all we had. The dogs and chochos had doggie beds, the cats and Poofs had cat trees I called Poof Condos and we'd gotten some bigger ones to make into Ocellar Condos, and the Peregrines had bird hammocks. Charlie had one set of Peregrines, one Poof Condo where his Poof, so far unnamed as far as anyone other than Charlie knew, Sugarfoot the cat, and an assortment of other Poofs slept, plus Duchess, two chochos, and two ocellars, who mixed it up and shared a doggie bed in between the chochos and the pit bull.

Well, they slept there when Charlie wasn't in the room. When he was, it was Snuggle Fest Time on his bed.

That anyone could walk in the nursery was a miracle, and Jamie's room was even worse. She had most of the rest of the unattached Poofs as well as her own Poof, Mous-Mous, and the cats Candy and Kane, all hanging out in several Poof Condos, a variety of ocellars in their Condos, the rest of the dogs and four chochos, all in doggie beds, and at least six Peregrines snoozing in hammocks.

Fortunately, all Embassy rooms were huge. Even so, we'd had to expand Jamie's room by breaking out a wall and combining two bedrooms into one. This was handled by the Operations team, meaning Algar, and had taken about five minutes. Leaving us with merely something like half a dozen other bedrooms of large size.

Once our room was, like the rest of the Embassy, declared free of bugs and surveillance we didn't want, we did our regular nighttime ritual with Jamie, which happily still consisted of singing songs to her, also now included the reading of a couple of bedtime stories, and definitely included the Parade of Animal Love. However, there were a few animals missing.

Once Jeff and I had finished up and kissed Jamie goodnight several times, I checked on Lizzie's room. Sure enough, there were a couple of Peregrines already in their hammocks, a chocho in a dog bed, and a Poof Condo with several Poofs and an ocellar in it.

"I'd ask when I started living in a real zoo," Jeff said as we headed back to the living room, "but I already know."

"They're loyal and they love us."

"Oh, I'm not complaining, baby. Much."

In addition to Lizzie—who was petting the Poof in her lap—Chuckie, Len, Kyle, Raj, Joseph, Rob, Evalyne, and Phoebe were waiting for us. "It's still a party. Yay." Looked around. "Where's Malcolm and Manfred and the others?"

"Following a lead." Chuckie was texting on his phone. "They found signs of surveillance exactly where he says he'd found it before."

"You mean Operation Assassination before?"

"I do." He looked up from his phone. "Do you think it was Huntress?"

"Honestly? Doesn't seem like her style, though she has to hang out somewhere. And, it could be." After all, her father had lurked in Sheridan Circle, too, during Operation Sherlock. Maybe it was a family move. If, of course, Stephanie was our Huntress.

"If not her, then who?" Jeff asked.

"The list is so long. For all we know we were being watched to see if Lizzie came to the Embassy. But, you know, Nightcrawler knew what was going on today, including that Denise didn't want the kids and others going on the train trip. As in, he knew that Denise, specifically, didn't want to go. If there aren't any bugs, was he inside the Embassy somehow earlier?"

"Not to my knowledge," Chuckie said. "But Buchanan doesn't tell me, or anyone else, everything."

"No," Lizzie said. "We weren't in here. We were visiting the nice lady across the street."

"Olga?" I asked to be sure. "You were in the Romanian Embassy?"

She nodded. "Yeah. She told us what was going on. And gave us a lot of food and stuff. Though your mom's brownies are better," she said to Jeff, which might have been her sucking up or her being honest, based on how great Lucinda's brownies actually were.

Jeff groaned. "What does Olga know that she wants us to know but won't actually come out and say?"

Chuckie rubbed the back of his neck. "I have no guess, and I also don't know if we should be happy she's friends with the assassins or not."

The adults all shared commiserating looks, but Lizzie giggled. "She said you'd say that. And she said to tell you that she knows you'll figure it out and that everyone should always do their best to have a lot of friends."

"She *is* the All-Seeing Oracle. So, Lizzie, was there anyone else with you while you were having this visit? I mean aside from you, your father, and my two 'uncles.'"

"Adriana. She's nice."

"She is. Anyone else? Anyone at all?"

Lizzie shook her head, then gave a start. "Oh!" She dug into her messenger bag. "Sorry, I totes forgot—she asked me to give you a letter."

Took the envelope and examined it. There was no name on the outside. Not that weird, Olga was having it hand delivered after all. Opened it up and pulled out a piece of paper.

It was blank.

CHAPTER 22

I STARED AT THE blank piece of paper. Then I turned it over, just in case. Nope, still blank on both sides. "Um, Lizzie? Are you sure this is what Olga wanted you to give to me?"

"Yeah. I watched her write something and fold the paper up and everything."

Chuckie put his hand out and I gave the paper to him. He sniffed it. "I'm not sure, but I think she's using invisible ink."

"Why's Olga going all *National Treasure* when this was just going across the street?"

"I'd assume it's because she wasn't sure that Lizzie would arrive here safely," Raj said.

"She was with the top two assassins in the world and Nightcrawler. How much freaking safer can you get?"

"Ansom Somerall just called to try to get you to give her up to him," Evalyne pointed out. "And he knew her real name. Apparently Mister Siler wasn't exaggerating the need for her to remain inside the Embassy."

She turned to Lizzie and put on her Extreme Protector of Important Politicians Face. It was a scary face if she wanted it to be, and she did. "I'm sure Kitty wants this in-formation. I'm now asking officially, as part of the Secret

Service—just what did you do that required you to take asylum on American Centaurion soil?"

Lizzie clutched Fofo and sort of shrank back into the couch. "I already told Kitty," she said, sounding scared but defiant. "I beat up some bullies."

"They're the kids of a lot of rich, important bigwigs and I'm sure at least a couple of their parents are best buds forever with Ansom Somerall and probably a host of our other enemies. And I'd like to ask everyone to relax while I point out that Lizzie is holding a Poof which willingly bounded over to get attached to her."

In some circles, this statement would have earned me a big "so what?" from the peanut gallery. However, everyone, Secret Service included, had learned that the Poofs were good judges of character. How they knew who they could trust I had no idea, but they hadn't been wrong yet.

So the room relaxed a bit, and heads nodded. However, there were still some suspicious looks being shot Lizzie's way.

Of course, I knew that Alexander was using Poofs as his spy network in the Alpha Centaurion system. However, it felt like a stretch to assume that Fofo had decided to get attached to Lizzie to spy on her. The Poofs could have done that without one of them making their Poofy Love Connection.

Jeff grunted. "I agree, baby."

I knew he wasn't getting an emotional signal from me this time, but a mental one. Due to the Surcenthumain our enemies had given him during Operation Drug Addict Jeff had mutated and was not only the strongest empath in the galaxy, but he was also able to read minds. Mine mostly, but he was working on reading the kids and, due to what had gone on during Operation Civil War, Chuckie.

"We need the names of those you attacked," Joseph said.

"And we'd like them now," Evalyne added.

"No," Jeff said calmly, but with his Commander Voice on.

"Lizzie will share that with me and Kitty when she's feeling safe enough to do so. I'd like everyone to stop making a fourteen-year-old girl feel threatened in the very place where she's been taken to be protected. And that's a Vice Presidential order, in case no one's clear."

The Secret Service agents all nodded, and while they all didn't actually take a giant step back, they looked like they'd done so in their minds.

"Thanks," Lizzie said in a small voice. "I'm not trying to withhold information. It's just . . ."

"That your father plainly didn't want you sharing. I have a feeling he knew we'd get it out of you, though. I think he didn't want to give me a chance to say no, that's all."

"What if you want to say no when I tell you all the names and stuff?"

I shrugged. "Like I told you before, as long as you're not the bully, I'm always going to back the person protecting the underdogs."

Chuckie gave me a fond smile. "True enough." He looked at the Secret Service agents. "We're all good here. Why don't you make sure that the extra guard on Amy is in place? We'll let you know who we think might be getting ready to be upset with us in a little while."

The four of them nodded and headed out of the room. Lizzie didn't seem any more relaxed. Shot a look at Raj, who grinned at me, then turned to her.

"So, Lizzie, what country is your school in?" he asked, Troubadour Tones set to Extra Soothe.

"Portugal."

"Really?" Raj asked, still working his troubadour magic.

"Yeah. I know, it's kind of a weird choice, but my dad went there, too, and the school is totes great. Well, mostly."

"Beautiful location, I'm sure," Raj said.

Lizzie nodded and seemed normal now. "Yeah. It's got everything. Even horses so we all learn to ride."

"We have Poofs, Peregrines, chochos, ocellars, dogs, and

cats, so we're competitive. So basically your school's great other than for the Junior Skulls?" I asked her. Chuckie straightened up.

"Yeah," Lizzie said with a little grin. "They make everything suck as much as they can."

"Is that what they call themselves?" Chuckie asked.

"No, that's the nickname I gave them. I already told Kitty," she added, sounding worried.

"I'm not objecting to the nickname, I'm sure it's apt." Chuckie seemed intent, but not in a threatening way. "Why did you pick that name, though?"

She shrugged. "Seemed obvious. I mean, we do get to see movies and stuff. Their parents are ambassadors and lobbyists and tycoons and kings and queens. Literally. The American kids are the ringleaders, but it's not like any of them are cool to anyone who isn't 'at their level'. And a couple of them love bragging about how their fathers are world leaders and are in the Skull and Bones and crap like that."

"I'm just going to spitball it and say that they're the kids of people who hate us, because that's just how our luck rolls."

Chuckie nodded. "Yeah. Lizzie, I'm sorry, but we really need the names of the kids, the Junior Skulls. Can you write them down so we have the list?"

"Sure." She rummaged in her messenger bag, seeming unperturbed now, pulled out a pad of paper and a pen, flipped a few pages in, and started to scribble quickly.

"What are you thinking?" Jeff asked Chuckie quietly while Lizzie wrote away.

"I'm thinking exactly what Kitty said—that we're going to recognize several of the last names."

"You know, during Operation Defection Election, I asked Vance about the full roster of the Dealers of Death. I wonder how many of their names are going to show up."

"Speaking of which," Raj said, "you need to get Mister Beaumont on board with going down to Florida with us."

"I'll call him now." Pulled out my phone and hit his speed dial. That Vance and I had actually become close enough friends that he *had* a speed dial on my phone was one of the many things I'd have said never would have happened in a million years during Operation Assassination. Many things were so different now from when we'd first gotten to D.C. that it would easily take me a month to list them all.

"Hey, Kitty," Vance said as he answered. "What's up?"

I gave him the *Reader's Digest* version of the various situations. "So, we were wondering if you'd be up for a rail trip."

"Oh my God, are you kidding me? You're offering me a chance to be on Rail Force One and Two and you think there's even the slightest chance I'll say no?"

"Hey, it's possible."

"How soon do you need me to be ready?"

"Well, as to that . . . honestly, I think we could use you right now. Can you pack while I send a couple agents to bring you over?"

"Trouble's brewing, huh? Well, I'm your man, Kitty, you know that."

"Yeah, you do always come through for me. So, pack, say goodbye to Guy for a while, and I'll send some agents over to collect you."

"Gotcha. See you shortly."

Raj was already assigning a couple of Field teams to pick Vance up as I got off the phone. "Wow, you're Mister Efficiency, aren't you?"

He chuckled. "I just believe we'll need Mister Beaumont's help as quickly as we can get it and, under the circumstances, sooner is better than later."

"You mean you don't want anyone to get a chance to shoot him with a bullet or an arrow, get him on their side instead of ours, or give Guy Gadoire a chance to ask to come along."

"Especially what's behind door number three."

"Cannot argue." Guy Gadoire was Vance's husband and the head lobbyist for the tobacco industry. He spoke in a French accent we all felt was faked, and always seemed to be channeling Pepé Le Pew. Guy and Vance were both bi, meaning they viewed literally anyone as fair game.

Jeff grunted. "One of them here is bad enough."

"Oh, they're alright once you get to know them."

"Ha. Ha ha ha. I laugh about the two men with the most voracious sexual appetites out there being 'alright.'"

"They haven't done anything untoward since you all embarrassed the hell out of them while simultaneously scaring the crap out of them during Operation Assassination."

"They haven't *done* anything, no. What they'd *like* to do, on the other hand? I'm fully aware, as is every other empath within a fifty-mile radius."

"Ah, are they going to be creepers?" Lizzie asked, sounding worried and grossed out.

"Not to a girl your age, thank God," Chuckie said.

"Not if they want to live," Jeff added.

"If they look at you wrong or try to touch you, you let us know," Kyle growled, as he indicated himself and Len.

"That goes for anyone," Len added.

Lizzie shot them both a grateful look.

"Boys, I'm glad you're ready to treat Lizzie like part of the family and your new little sister. That's awesome. However, you're all kind of maligning Guy and Vance. They have standards, and they're not into underage anything, or forcing anyone to do what they don't want to do. And, I might add, you guys are the ones bringing up the potential sexy times. Vance didn't mention anything like that."

"Out loud," Jeff muttered.

Lizzie giggled. "You sound like my dad any time there's a school dance."

"Good to know he's a good father," Jeff said.

"Let's look at your list," Chuckie said, possibly to change

the subject. Lizzie handed it to him. Chuckie stared at it, and heaved a sigh.

"How bad is it?" I asked finally, since he wasn't sharing.

"On what scale?"

"One to ten. Ten being worst for this scenario."

Chuckie shot me a rueful grin. "Eleven."

CHAPTER 23

"**F**ANTASTIC. Truly, I cannot wait to hear the names Lizzie's given us."

"Before we all get to that," Len said, "shouldn't we figure out what Olga wanted us to know?"

"And get Adriana ready to go, too," Kyle added. "I don't think anyone's called her to get her on board with the latest activity."

"We might as well wait for Vance to go over the list," I said as I stood up. "He'll know the nuances and details and we can all learn what fun we're going to be having together."

Jeff sighed. "If we must."

"We must. In the meantime, hang on."

Trotted into my bedroom. I wanted to get a blow-dryer, but it occurred to me that now might also be a good time to check in with the King of the Elves and see what, if anything, he might want to share.

Went to our huge walk-in closet and looked at our hamper, which was, as far as I'd been able to figure out, one of Algar's portals. "So, any words of wisdom, warning, or advice you want to share with me before we head for Florida?"

A rakishly handsome dwarf with tousled, dark, wavy

hair and eyes that were unnaturally bright green appeared, sitting cross-legged on top of the hamper. Well, Algar was a dwarf by human standards. What he was by Black Hole Universe standards I, so far, hadn't asked.

"I suggest you stop stalling."

"I'm not stalling. I'm asking you for any guidance your free will allows you to share with me."

He sighed. "You know I won't tell you anything."

This was a gigantic whopper of a lie. Algar told me things all the time. Sure, they were in a form of code, usually via music on my iPod or vague hints disguised as verbal sparring, but he still told me things frequently. And during Operation Civil War he'd been practically throwing help my way. Which I'd needed, of course.

But he was a Free Will Fanatic of the highest order, and so he didn't want to *admit* that he was helping me. It was our little fiction, but since ACE had taken up residence in Jamie's mind, I'd become more demanding that Algar toss a few bread crumbs my way.

Decided to go with something easier. "Any suggestions for how to read Olga's invisible letter?"

"Lemon juice and heat, just like you're thinking. See? You don't need to ask me for help."

"I know, but I enjoy the verbal sparring so very much. Want to give me a hint about what's coming?"

Algar cocked his head at me. "Why are you asking me this right now?"

"Because we have people from your favorite solar system about to drop by, assassins all over the place, a teenager who appears to need protection probably from a host of our mutual enemies, and we're about to take the train down to Florida to attempt to keep NASA Base open, among other things."

"Sounds like business as usual for you."

"Aren't you hilarious? Are we taking the right team

members? Are there others we should leave at home, so to speak, or bring along?"

He shrugged. "I think you've chosen well, if that's what you're asking."

"It's not, and you know it. You're really testy. Did I disturb you from a chess game with Death or making your bed or something?"

"Nothing that interesting. You left a far more interesting discussion to come into your closet and harangue me."

"See, that discussion's going to happen in a couple of minutes. I'm delaying the gratification. You should be all proud of me. And I decided to spend my delayed waiting time with my favorite non-helpful Operations Team Member for the fun and reassurance you're not giving me."

"What possible reassurance would you need? Everyone's following your plan."

"I'm going to let both of us contemplate just how often my plans don't go as I envision. Sure, they work out in the end. But it's the excitement and twists, turns, and horrific surprises along the way to the end that I'd like to get a handle on."

"Talk to Chuckie if you want to discuss time, the past, or the future, not me."

"Huh?"

"Seriously, why are you so worried about this? Just been out of action too long?"

"I'm going to seriously resent that comment, especially coming from you. I'm worried because I'm leaving my children here. Is that a wise thing to do?"

"I try not to tell any of you how to parent. And you should be happy about it—if I'd meddled like that, none of the A-Cs would be on Earth."

Managed not to ask if he'd interfered that way in another universe though. My experience over the past years said that, with the infinity of the multiverse, he'd done so at least once. Though, of course, while managing to pretend that whatever he'd influenced was achieved through everyone's free will.

"I'm not asking you if time-outs work on a child of Charlie's age or when to give up trying to make Jamie take a nap. I'm asking if my children will be safer here than with me and Jeff."

"Ah. Safer here for certain." Algar gave me a bright smile I felt was totally faked.

"So, you're saying they won't be safe here, either. Should I send everyone to Dulce?"

"If it makes you feel better."

"Will it, in point of fact, make my children and the other children safer?"

Algar sighed again. "No. Look, you need to get back to things. All I can tell you is that while you'll handle everything you need to, the real threat isn't anything you're used to dealing with." With that he snapped his fingers and disappeared.

Managed not to mention that he was a real jerk because I was sure he knew and I also didn't want to make him not want to toss those inscrutable bread crumbs to me whenever he felt I actually needed them. Heaved my own sigh. "Thanks."

As I turned to leave the closet, something caught my eye. A pair of what looked like night vision goggles. We definitely didn't have these hanging around in our closet. Picked them up. Yep, goggles. "Um, thanks again. I'll just . . . put these in my purse for later. I guess."

Waited. Nothing happened. Presumably these were for later. Or Algar was amusing himself. Possibly both.

My purse was on our dresser and I dropped the goggles into it on my way to the bathroom to retrieve my blow-dryer. Flushed the toilet while I was in there, just in case. The soundproofing was good enough that it was unlikely anyone would hear the flush, but that way I wouldn't be lying at all if I had to tell the others that I'd been gone so long because I'd had to go.

Rejoined the others, blow-dryer in hand. Chuckie grinned. "Going full *National Treasure*, are we?"

"Yeah, we are." Took the blank paper from him and went into our kitchen and to the fridge. "Some lemon juice. And a Coke." Opened the fridge to find a small bowl of lemon juice and an ice-cold bottle of the really good Coke up from Mexico, the one with real sugar in it. Clearly Algar wanted to kiss and make up. "Thank you very much!"

Grabbed the juice and the Coke. Got the bottle cap off and had a nice, long drink. Thusly fortified, plugged the blow-dryer in, got a couple of tissues, laid the paper on the sink, and started to lightly brush it with the lemon juice.

Chuckie joined me. "Mountain Dew," he said to the fridge. Got his soda and joined me. "Want me to do the drying?"

"Sure, if you want the thrill of helping."

The others trooped in. Jeff explained to Lizzie how to work the fridge. She asked for a Dr. Pepper, was thrilled when it appeared, then wanted to get everyone else's drinks. Couldn't blame her—that had pretty much been my reaction to how the Elves worked, too.

So, while Lizzie acted like the most enthusiastic waitress ever and got everyone's nonalcoholic beverage of choice—and had it explained to her that no one in the entire Embassy was allowed to drink alcohol, her especially, so she shouldn't bother asking for it when the adults weren't around—Chuckie and I worked on my Secret Letter.

Somewhat to my surprise, this method worked. But what we got as a result of it working didn't make things any clearer.

"Can you read it?" I asked Chuckie as we stared at letters that made no sense.

"No. I want to say it's in code, but I don't think it is." He studied it more closely. "I think it's in a form of Cyrillic."

liked th... Romania used the same alphabet that we do."
learned Cyrillic. And have for well over a hundred and
manian or not, since the ...what I think it is."
to bet she missed the action. ...st having fun at our expense?"
...I knew about Olga. Olga
...as a good chance she'd
...eeded to know it, Ro-
...sed it. And I had

Took the leap. "She wants to come along."

"Excuse me?" Raj said.

"I think Olga wants to come along with Adriana. And so she sent us a super-secret spy letter written in a language only she could translate. Meaning we need to ask her if we can come over to have her translate the letter she wrote. And then she'll suggest, to make it easy for us, that she and Adriana come over here."

Len started to laugh. "What?" Jeff asked him.

"I called Adriana while Kitty was in your bedroom. She said that her grandmother won't let her come over right now. That has literally never happened before, and I know they aren't mad at us for some reason. I think Kitty's right. Shall I call back and share that we need translation services?"

"Please and thank you. And, of course, offer for you and Kyle to help them over here when they insist that we shouldn't go there."

Lizzie cocked her head. "Why wouldn't Olga have just asked to go along? Why all the James Bond stuff?"

"She likes to have her fun."

Chuckie stared at the paper. "Len, wait."

"Okay." He stopped dialing. "Why?"

"I don't know if we're right. Because Chernobog could translate this, too." He looked at me. "So why was our first thought to call Olga?"

"Because it's not written in binary code."

Raj jerked. "What if this letter is ... ot doing get Olga over here, but, in fact, ... eeds us to do. give to Chernobog? And, if th ... ms."
whatever it is Olga either ...
And that could cause ...

CHAPTER 24

WE ALL LOOKED at each other. "I hate it when Kitty's right about things like this," Jeff said. "And I'm learning to hate it when you're right, too, Raj."

Len's phone beeped. "Huh. Kitty, Adriana just sent me a text asking me if our new houseguest gave you her grandmother's message. What do I tell her?"

"Tell her yes, a few minutes ago. This means we're behind schedule. We need to see what Chernobog can make of this letter."

"I'll get her," Raj said, then disappeared. Well, not really, but he went to hyperspeed and that was about the same thing.

"I'm sorry I forgot about it until now," Lizzie said, sounding miserable.

"It's okay," Jeff said. "There was a lot going on, including you being left with total strangers." He shot a strong look at Chuckie.

Who sighed. "No one's mad at you, Lizzie. And don't beat yourself up."

"Should we go over to the Romanian embassy?" Kyle asked. "Especially if they don't really want to come over here?"

"No," Chuckie said. "Not yet. Let's see what Chernobog makes of this first. The fact that Adriana didn't say anything about this before but wasn't allowed to come over could mean that Olga fears we have non-friendly assassins on our street."

"Amazing how we can use the term 'non-friendly assassins,' isn't it? But yeah, after all, Malcolm and the others are still out there searching for non-friendly assassins and such. Possibly searching with our friendly assassins, too. The less of us outside the better, I guess."

"Based on your foray earlier today, I'd say no one out is the way to go," Chuckie mentioned. "And I think we should work under the assumption that Huntress is out there, lurking and waiting for us."

"It'll be interesting to see if that's what Olga's telling us." Then again, Huntress was old news, something we definitely knew about. Olga tended to prefer to give clues to the long game and about things we weren't clear were coming.

"Why can't our allies make it easy on us, ever?" Jeff asked.

"It would make life too calm?" Kyle suggested.

"They want to ensure we stay on our toes?" was Len's shot.

"They think it's funny to make you work for it?" Lizzie asked. Sadly, had a feeling her guess was the closest to the mark.

There was a knock at our door. I went to open it to find Vance and four Field agents there. And a whole lot of Gucci luggage. "Wow, you do realize we're going down to Florida for, probably, a couple of days? We're not heading to the Himalayas and expecting to be gone for six months."

"I want to be prepared," Vance replied, with almost no signs of embarrassment.

"For what?" Jeff asked as he joined us and motioned for the agents to bring what looked like all of Vance's belongings inside. "Moving in?"

"I'll never say no," Vance said merrily.

"Wouldn't Guy miss you?" Could tell Jeff was waiting for

him to suggest they both move in, in part because I could see Jeff's lips forming the words "not just no, but hell no."

"Oh, eventually. He came home with some weird cold, though, so I'm happy to be nowhere near him. I don't need to catch it."

"Yeah, we'll run you through a contamination filter later."

Vance laughed. "Trust me, I didn't get near his sniffling self. So, what room am I in?"

Jeff grunted. "Farthest." I was impressed that he didn't say more than this, but got the impression he was both relieved and really controlling himself.

"Fair enough." The agents trotted off, presumably to drop off Vance's luggage. He started to follow them, then Vance noticed Lizzie. "Oh, hi there. You must be Lizzie. I'm Vance."

She sort of shrugged. "Hey."

Vance shook his head. "I'd complain about the youth of today but I'm sure hanging out with all the old people isn't your idea of fun. What's your Poof's name?"

"Ah, um, Fofo. I just got him."

"They're androgynous," Vance shared. "But amazing. You'll love it."

Everyone stared at him. "Excuse me?" Jeff said finally.

Vance gave him an arch look. "I kind of think I should be offended right now." He made a soft, clucking sound. "Because it's not like I don't have one."

Sure enough, a Poof I recognized as an unattached one I hadn't seen for a while crawled onto his shoulder. Well, a formerly unattached one. "So, that's where you went," I said, in part because I was thinking it and in other part because I wanted to distract Vance from the looks of utter shock on Jeff's and Chuckie's faces.

Lizzie perked up, though. "How long have you had yours?"

"Oh, gosh, a couple of years now."

"Really? Wow, what have I been doing?" I didn't remember the Poof not being around for that long.

"Oh, saving solar systems and having a second child," Vance said. "Seriously, you didn't realize I had Sophi all this time?"

"Ah, no. Sophi?"

"Short for Sophisticated. Which all the Poofs are, of course."

"Of course," Jeff said weakly.

"Does Guy have a Poof, too?"

"Yep, his is named Dove. For you, honestly."

Amazing. Maybe everyone in the entire country had a Poof and I just didn't know about it. Maybe the Poof Population Explosion was getting out of hand. On the other hand, this meant that Vance and Guy were indeed fully on our side. The idea that a variety of other people who'd started out as our enemies and were now our friends also had Poofs occurred to me. Decided to table the worry about this for later. We had so many other things to focus the worry on, after all.

Realized Vance expected me to comment on Guy's choice of Poof name. "Oh, how sweet."

"Fantastic," Jeff said in a way that indicated it really wasn't.

Vance rolled his eyes. "He knows she's off limits, Jeff. So, before you do your jealousy thing—which is always impressive, don't get me wrong—do you want me to unpack or go over the list of names Lizzie has for us?"

"Names," Chuckie replied quickly. "Definitely the names."

"I thought so."

"You don't need to unpack," Jeff said quickly. "We're going to Florida tomorrow."

Vance shot Jeff a "really?" look as he put his hand out and Chuckie put the list into it. Vance took a glance and gave a low whistle. "You're at quite the school, aren't you?" he asked Lizzie.

"Apparently," she replied. "You know all those kids?"

"No. I know or know of their parents." He shook his head. "Well, it'll make it easy and, Kitty, you'll enjoy getting bingo."

Took the leap. "Lots of the Dealers of Death on this list?"

"Among others."

Before Vance could say anything else there was a knock on our door. Jeff heaved a sigh and went to get it. To find my parents there, chatting with the Secret Service folks who had the thrilling job of guarding our particular portal.

Dad trotted inside while Mom continued her chat with—as I got up to give my father a hug and then immediately go eavesdrop—Evalyne and Joseph. Oh, good. They were tattling on us.

Well, that was probably not true. They were telling the person who had the most influence over us and to whom they dotted-line reported to, now that Cliff Goodman had been moved to a new job, what was going on from their perspective. Which was the grown-up way of saying they were tattling. Maybe Jamie was learning how to do it from our Secret Service detail.

Mom noted me noting this conversation, of course. My mother was nothing if not on top of everything. She was the only non-Israeli non-Jew to ever be in the Mossad, and since we had good friends who were currently active in Israeli Intelligence, Mom's status as a living legend had been confirmed many times over.

She'd been the head of the P.T.C.U. for years, an agency I hadn't even known existed until I'd met Jeff and the rest of the gang from Alpha Four. I hadn't known that my father wasn't just a history professor at Arizona State but also a cryptologist for NASA or that Chuckie was in the C.I.A., either. The lies my nearest and dearest had told me for years were so numerous that I could count them instead of sheep if I was having trouble getting to sleep.

"Keep me posted," Mom said to Evalyne as she stepped through our threshold and closed the door behind her. "So, you have a new houseguest?"

"Nice to see you, too, Mom."

Mom chuckled and gave me a hug and a peck on the cheek. "Sorry, kitten. It's good to see you."

I hugged her back. "You, too." Considered why my parents might be here and decided to make the educated guess. "You're leaving Dad here to watch over the kids and you're coming with us down to Florida, aren't you?"

Mom nodded. "It's always so nice to know that you're on top of things."

"Well then, you're just in time to find out what we're not yet on top of but plan to be just as soon as Vance and Chuckie tell us just how bad our situation is."

"First, I want to meet the girl."

"Lizzie," Jeff said, as he joined us. "Her name is Lizzie."

Mom raised her eyebrow.

"She has a Poof," I offered, lest Mom and Jeff get into some kind of spat. Jeff rarely if ever upset my parents, in part because he could tell *when* they were upset—far more often with me than him, and of course, never with the kids—and almost always did whatever was necessary to smooth things over.

"I'm not mad at your mother, baby, and I don't think she's upset with me. However we have a fourteen-year-old girl now under our protective care who far too many adults in high levels of authority have been intimidating."

"Trying to intimidate," I pointed out. "Lizzie hasn't really been intimidated, emphasis on the 'ed.'"

"That *you* can tell," Jeff said patiently. "However, I can tell you that she's a child, and a child whose adoptive father left her with total strangers, and she's faking being calm and collected really well. But she *is* faking it."

"So, you know, Mom, be nice to her, like you always were to Brian. Not how you were to me, Amy, Sheila, or Chuckie."

Mom gave me a look that said she was seriously considering the benefits of grounding me. Sadly, my mother still had enough authority in both the world and my life to make a grounding threat a reality. "I'd like to meet her, and then we'll decide if I coddle her or not."

"I don't need coddling," Lizzie said from behind Jeff, who stepped out of the way so she and Mom could be face to face. "I totes get why everyone's freaked. My dad told me you'd come to check me out. Peter said to tell you that if I was a threat I wouldn't be inside."

Mom looked her up and down. "What else did they tell you, young lady?"

"That, other than them, the person who had the best skills to kill anyone she wanted to was you, and that I should mind my manners and be a good girl so you didn't ground me. And, seriously, that's a verbatim quote." Mom raised her eyebrow. Lizzie shrugged. "I'm at a good school. I know what verbatim means."

"That's not what I'm questioning," Mom said. "I'm questioning my reputation."

"You're saying you're not able to kill anyone just using your pinky or something?" This was disappointing news. I kind of thought Mom could kill someone with a stare, let alone any other way.

Mom rolled her eyes at me. "That level of intelligence indicates that they understand our movements and that, therefore, we're being far too predictable."

"My dad and the uncles aren't going to hurt you or anyone else here."

"The uncles?" Mom asked. "As in the Dingo and his cousin? That's the Peter you mean?"

"Yep," I replied, before Lizzie could. "We're just one big happy family, Mom."

"Wonderful," she said in a tone that indicated clearly that it wasn't. "I'm concerned about our enemies knowing exactly what we'll do in any situation."

"They know our playbook," Chuckie said quietly as he joined us in the hallway. "They helped us create the playbook, remember?"

"Magneto helped Professor X build Cerebro, dude. It happens. So, can we all go rejoin Vance or are we just going to do our meeting in the foyer?"

Before anyone could reply, the door opened again and Raj returned with Chernobog in tow. She didn't look happy.

CHAPTER 25

"AND, ONCE AGAIN, it's a party." Sometimes I wondered if it was just my lot in life to end up cramming a million people into a room at any given time. Probably.

Headed back to the living room where Vance was sitting chatting with Dad about totally inconsequential things. Lucky them.

Everyone else sat, but Chernobog didn't. Like Olga, she was former KGB. She was also the computer hacker that the best hackers in the world had considered a myth because she was that good. She'd gone rogue decades prior, but had been hired by our enemies and caused us and everyone else a lot of problems, especially during Operation Infiltration. However, we'd tracked her down during Operation Defection Election, and, due to a mutually beneficial arrangement, she was now our willing prisoner.

When we'd found her, Chernobog was calling herself Zoya Darnell and working for the U.S. government. However, we'd determined that her real name was Bogdana. She looked like Everyone's Grandma, particularly tonight, because she was in a nightgown, robe, and slippers. No curlers in her hair, though, so we had that going for us.

"What took you so long to get back here?" Jeff asked Raj.

"She wouldn't let me use hyperspeed."

"I'm an old woman and I refuse to take those drugs."

"Hey, Boggy, just say no and all that. Anyway, sorry Raj had to drag you out of bed."

"I'm still waiting for that nickname to grow on me. And I wasn't in bed. You're disturbing our movie night at the Zoo."

Let that one sit on the air for a few seconds. "Ah, do you mean that you and the rest of Hacker International, and all the other A-Cs and such who live and work at the Zoo, are all in their jammies watching the gigantic big screen TV?" That Stryker had demanded a few months ago.

"Yes. We're doing a double feature — *Big Trouble in Little China* and *Galaxy Quest*. And I'm now missing it."

"Add in *Mortal Kombat* and that's a three picture deal I'll take any day. However, I'm sure you've seen the movies many times before or can demand that they rewind when you get back."

"It's not the same thing. The popcorn will be cold."

"Our deepest sympathies," Jeff said, sarcasm meter definitely heading toward eleven, "but we need you to translate this message." He handed her the paper.

"Invisible ink?" She didn't sound impressed. Honestly couldn't blame her.

"Could be a joke," Chuckie said.

"Huh. I don't think so."

"What does it say," I asked finally, after a few long moments of Chernobogian silence.

"No matter what they say, what you hear, or what you want, stay home." She looked up. "What's going on that Olga's suddenly so concerned for my welfare?"

When we'd brought Chernobog in from the cold, this would have been asked with the sarcasm knob turned to at least eleven, possibly even fifteen. Chernobog and Olga had *not* been friends. But, as Chernobog had just pointed out, they were old now, and, frankly, had more in common with each other than most other people around them. So, over the past couple of years, they'd gotten close. But Olga had never indicated concern about Chernobog's welfare before.

"Why would she even think you'd want to go?" I asked.

"Or that we'd let you?" Chuckie added.

Mom's phone beeped and she took a look. Her expression changed—she'd been interested and alert, but now Mom looked angry and determined. Got the proverbial bad feeling about this.

"What is it?" Jeff asked softly.

"We have a prison break," Mom said. "From the best supermax prison we have."

Chuckie went white. "I'd say that's impossible, but ... who's your intel from?"

"Malcolm."

Meaning said intel was accurate and up to the minute. Took the leap. The only supermax prison I knew of was underneath the Pentagon. And it housed a variety of our enemies. All of whom wanted to destroy us in very personal and varied ways.

"How could anyone get out from there? I mean other than by being released by the powers that be." As soon as I asked the answer waved at me. "We have another enemy A-C or A-C hybrid out there, don't we?"

"Most likely," Mom said, looking grim. "And now Olga's message becomes clear." She shot a glance at Raj, who stepped nearer to Chernobog. "Among those who've escaped is Russell Kozlow." Also known as Chernobog's son.

Chernobog blinked. "He's out? But how?"

"Maybe he figured out how to use his A-C talents," Chuckie suggested.

She shook her head. "He doesn't have any."

"So everyone claims," Mom said, in a way that indicated she didn't believe everyone was truthful. Couldn't blame her.

"And what does this mean to you?" Raj asked Chernobog carefully. She'd helped us originally because we had her son—whose father was the late and totally unlamented

Ronald Yates/Mephistopheles in-control superbeing—in
custody. She'd stayed with us because I'd convinced the
Dingo to pretend he'd killed her, even though he knew she
was still alive.

"It means terrible things." Chernobog swallowed. "Russell was safe. Not much of a life, but a life, nonetheless. If
he's out, they can do whatever it is they do to those they're
using or no longer have a use for."

"You think the Mastermind would turn him into an android?" Chuckie asked.

"I have no idea, I just know they have no scruples and
no limits. Despite what you want to insinuate," she shot a
glare at Mom, "Russell has none of his father's talents. He
has no idea where I am, but I'm sure he thinks I'm dead
since that was the plan and there's been no chatter anywhere about my still being around, either as myself or as the
Ultimate. So, he has nowhere to go."

Chernobog didn't seem like she was lying about Kozlow's abilities. However, it was unlikely that any of the
Yates Kids were untalented. But there was a possibility that
Chernobog didn't know what talents her son had, either because said talents were weak or because he'd hidden said
talents from her. "Think he'll come here?"

"I'm sure he will," Chuckie said dryly. "Along with the
others."

"I meant to take refuge."

"No," Jeff said flatly. "We are not going to try to make
another enemy of ours into our friend. So don't ask."

"His mother is with us," I pointed out. Needlessly, based
on the "really?" looks everyone, even Lizzie, shot at me.

Jeff shot me a look I was familiar with—his "why me?"
look. "Baby, I know you want to find the good in everyone,
but he's someone our allies don't like."

"True." The Israelis weren't fans of Kozlow in any way,
shape, or form. And there were others lining up to hate him,
too. I'd never really interacted with him. During Operation

Infiltration I was far more focused on people who were more immediate threats, like Annette Dier the Murdering Psycho-Bitch.

And that made another thought occur. "Did Malcolm say when they got out? As in, have they been out a while, and therefore that bitch Annette Dier is our Huntress, or did they just escape?"

"Just escaped," Mom said. "As for who the main suspect is for how they got out, you get one guess."

"Stephanie," Jeff said sadly. "She's the only A-C we know of who's got the skills and the motivation to do it."

"And she knows the place, having been there for, apparently, far too short a stay."

Once again, had to hand it to the Mastermind—he was really good at making lemonade when we gave him lemons. Someone killed your A-C flunky? Recruit his daughter. She gets arrested? Make sure she's cased the joint, then get her out. She freaks out after killing people? Work with her to get everyone else out, too.

Or else she was doing this on her own. Always a possibility. Especially if I considered that I still didn't think Cliff had been faking his terror. After all, there was no fury like a woman scorned, and perhaps Stephanie felt scorned by him in some way.

"This makes the 'Stephanie's trying to lure us into a vulnerable position' theory look more likely," Raj pointed out.

"It makes the Stephanie is the Huntress Theory look more likely, too," I pointed out.

"Yes, but right now any A-C is a suspect in regard to the breakout," Chuckie said calmly. "Anyone with hyperspeed is a suspect, honestly."

"It wasn't me. Just in case anyone wasn't sure. Or me and Richard."

Got a full blast of the "really?" looks. "Thank you for clearing that up," Mom said, sarcasm meter on eleven and rising.

"Did Olga's note say anything else?" Raj asked.

Chernobog looked at it again. "Yes. Give me a moment, this is in code."

"You mean the original wasn't?" I asked.

"No, just in the old language." She grunted. "Interesting. 'A catastrophic event is being planned. Remain at your post at all costs.' And that's it."

"That doesn't sound good," Jeff said. "Why didn't Olga warn us directly?"

"Warn us about what?" Chuckie asked. "The term 'catastrophic event' is vague. In less than a minute I could list at least a dozen events that could be catastrophic, none of them the same or even related to each other."

"Maybe she means the Planetary Council coming, or the prisoners escaping," I suggested. "I mean, it's possible she knows about both."

But again, this was old news. Sure, it wouldn't have been old news when she'd given Lizzie her note, but at the same time, aliens coming to visit and prisoners escaping were things we'd find out about quickly. Olga tended to know the things we weren't going to discover without a lot of help.

Chernobog shook her head slowly. "What you should all focus on is the phrase 'remain at your post'. It indicates a reason for me to leave my post. And I don't believe Russell is that reason."

Vance cleared his throat. Once everyone looked at him he gave us all a polite smile. "Not that this isn't thrilling in a totally par for the course you guys always play way, but how does this affect tomorrow's trip?"

"You really want to take the train, don't you?"

"Hells to the yeah."

Mom shrugged. "Too bad. The trip is cancelled."

Took a deep breath. "No, it's not."

CHAPTER 26

EVERYONE STARED AT ME. I shrugged, but kept eye contact with Mom.

"The President cannot spend his time hiding because of potential threats. We have a far bigger issue than some hired wacko killers and escaped enemies of the state going on. If we don't meet with the Planetary Council, we're putting our planet and potentially the Alpha Centauri system at risk."

"As far as we've guessed," Mom pointed out. "This could merely be a state visit, meaning it can be put off."

"Maybe yes, maybe no. We don't know, and until we do, we have to assume that it's a visit that cannot be put off." The last times Alexander and Leonidas had sent us messages we'd been invaded or were about to be under attack.

"We haven't asked to put the visit off, and it should be an option." Mom didn't sound angry. Couldn't tell if she really didn't want us doing this or if she was just testing my resolve. Gave it even odds for both.

"That should be our Plan D, E, or F. The President and Vice President are already under protection. We'll just make that protection more stringent and pervasive. But we have an intergalactic political issue going on, and that has to take precedence over a few loons with guns running around."

"The risk factor just went up exponentially due to who's out," Mom said calmly.

"Let me guess. In addition to Kozlow the Swarthy Slapper, we have Insane Assassin Chick Annette Dier, Secret Service Traitor Sam Travis, Air Bender Darryl Lowe, and the guy whose name I never got, the one Gladys tossed out of the chopper during Operation Infiltration who's likely also one of the last living Yates offspring."

"His name is Rudolph Wruck," Chuckie said. "He's a German, and his talent appears to be the ability to be sneaky."

"Seriously?"

"Think slip around in shadows unseen sneaky."

"Dude, you and I do that all the time. Team Assassination does that in the same way that they breathe. How is that a talent? He's a Yates progeny, isn't he?"

"He is. It's at a higher level than what we do or even the Dingo does. If there was no outside help, then look to Wruck to be the one who engineered and achieved the prison break. We also have Nerida Alfero, the female Yates offspring who you called the water bender. And Nigel Kellogg, the assassin who attacked Missus Maurer and tried to kill Jeff during the election."

"Nigel? Really?"

"Nothing wrong with the name," Chuckie said mildly. "Though there's a lot wrong with him."

"True enough. So, it's the Unmagnificent Seven or the Crazy Eights, depending on if Stephanie's around. Could even be the Abnormal Nine if our Huntress chick isn't Stephanie."

"We'll worry about naming their team later," Chuckie said quickly, presumably before Mom could ground me. "But, Angela . . . Kitty's right. Seven, eight, or even nine dangerous criminals out is still not a good enough reason to put off meeting with the Planetary Council. Presidents have always faced dangers."

"And some of them have died," Mom said quietly. "But not on my watch. And I want to keep it that way."

"So does everyone in this Embassy, at Dulce, and everywhere else." Hugged Mom. "We'll be on top guard and I promise we won't let Vince, or Jeff, or anyone else get hurt."

Mom hugged me back, her breath-stopping bear hug. "That's not a promise you can make, kitten." She let me go and heaved a sigh. "But, I know you. And you're right—ultimately, galactic politics has to take precedence." She looked at Lizzie. "So, where's this list of names of the next set of juvenile delinquents who are going to grow up and try to wreck the world because they think they have the right?"

Lizzie grinned. "Vance has it."

He waved it at Mom. "I can guarantee you know the parents of every kid on this list. You probably have them on a watch list."

Mom put her hand out. Vance got up and gave her the list. "Huh. No exaggeration. You've made quite the enemies, young lady."

"Sorry?" Lizzie said, sounding unsure if she was in trouble or not.

"Do I have more?"

"Yes, yes, kitten. You have more. It's always a competition with you." Mom shook her head and winked at Lizzie, who giggled. "Though, right now, you both have plenty."

"Is anyone going to let me and Kitty see the list?" Jeff asked. "Since it seems like half the room knows who our new boogiemen are and we don't."

"I don't either," Raj said.

"I don't care," Chernobog said. "I'm still focused on what the catastrophic event is that Olga's warning us about. But," she took the list out of Mom's hands, "if you want to ensure they never bother you again, we have ways."

"All of them illegal," Mom said dryly. "So, let's pretend that you didn't say that."

Raj took the list from Chernobog and whistled. "Wow."

Looked at Jeff. "You know, it's going to end up being totally anticlimactic by the time we ever get to see this list."

"I don't even care about the list," Jeff said, sounding annoyed. "I just want to know who's coming after Lizzie and how they're going to use her situation against us."

"Oh, so, routine."

He chuckled. "Exactly."

Raj handed the list back to Vance. I was certain he'd done it for a private laugh. Vance shrugged. "We know how to avoid these people. You guys deal with them all the time. I think we should focus on the fact that Ansom was the one to call Kitty. I think that indicates a deal of some sort forming."

"Or a coup," Raj suggested. Vance nodded.

"In my experience it just means someone's coming after us," Jeff said, rightly. "Usually with explosives."

"Oh, that was so Operation Drug Addict ago."

As Jeff shot me a look that shared he still hated that particular Operation Nickname, everyone else other than Lizzie snorted.

"I think you could count every operation as having explosions of some kind," Chuckie pointed out. "And, Lizzie, don't worry. The Embassy is extremely safe."

"My dad didn't exaggerate, did he? You guys see a lot of action."

"We do," Jeff said, as he took the list from Vance and showed it to me. Sure enough, it was a list of names of people I didn't know, or didn't know well, but who Vance had told me about in relation to our enemies.

Titan Security, Gaultier Enterprises, and YatesCorp were run by people we didn't trust. Sure, all of these people had been put in place after we'd taken care of the original people in charge of those corporations, but that was merely a changing of the Anti Us guard. Sure, we'd eliminated the First Wave of Evil Corporate Heads, but it was as if we'd cut the heads off the hydra—the replacements popped right up and they were more in number.

Amos Tobin now ran YatesCorp, Somerall along with Janelle Gardiner and Quinton Cross were fighting Amy for control of the Gaultier Board of Directors—and it was a testament to the skill and tenacity on both sides that this fight was still going on with no clear winner—and Thomas Kendrick was in charge of Titan Security. Each of them had special cronies in the Lobbyist League, though Kendrick, having come out of the military, still had more pals in the Department of Defense and other military branches than otherwise.

Faded memory nudged. "You know, Vance, way back when we were talking about the Dealers of Death the first time, right after you'd told me that Berkowitz was tight with Somerall, you wanted to tell me to consider something about Somerall, but we got interrupted. Do you remember what that was?"

Vance's brow furrowed. "I should, but that was a long time ago now. Gimme a minute to think about it."

While Vance thought, I perused the list. In addition to a couple Saudi princes, a Malaysian sultana, and a Japanese princess—none of whom registered names-wise and who I knew nothing about—there were certainly last names I recognized.

Some were indeed the children of ambassadors, and those names didn't really raise any red flags for me or anyone else, other than that, for the most part, they were people who we couldn't count on for support.

However, there were plenty of names that raised a multitude of flags.

Confirmed relationships with Lizzie, with Vance adding in even though he was supposedly trying to remember a key point from our past.

Elsa Van Dyke was Myron Van Dyke's granddaughter,

meaning we probably had other Van Dykes running around who weren't awesome like Dick Van Dyke but were, instead, mortal enemies of ours we merely hadn't met yet.

"Kingman? Who names their kid after a town in Arizona?"

"That's Kingsley Teague's son," Vance shared. "His father likes the 'king' moniker, I think I mentioned before."

Lizzie snorted. "Like father like son. Kingman acts like he's royalty and makes everyone call him King."

Showing amazing personal growth, I refrained from additional comments. About the Teagues and their naming choices, anyway. Connor Lee was Talia Lee's son and Delilah, Leanne, and Remy were her nieces and nephew. "The Lees are really clogging up the system, aren't they?"

Lizzie shrugged. "They claim to be descendants of Robert E. Lee."

Filed that one away—we'd had a Lee descendent try to kill us all during Operation Drug Addict. Curtis Lee had been part of Club 51, and while it was a common name, as were those claiming Robert E. kinship, Chuckie had trained me to never believe in coincidence. But the connection was something to follow up on later—Curtis Lee hadn't been any kind of mover or shaker; he'd been a patsy for Club 51. But then, every family had its black sheep.

Continued my perusal and confirmations. Violet Carr was Luxx Carr's daughter, and Skylar and Stewart Hopkins were the daughter and son of Simon Hopkins.

"I'm amazed how many of these people are educating their kids outside of the country."

"It's a good school and they're making international connections they'll need as they grow up and take their places in the world," Lizzie said, in a tone of voice that indicated this was the school's motto and was repeated daily, if not hourly. "The School Abroad is where all future leaders of wealth, power, and discernment learn all they'll need to know."

"They'll go to U.S. colleges," Vance added. "The
good ones. And they won't have any worries about how
they did on their SATs, either."

"Hopefully not USC," Len said with a growl.

"They don't seem like Trojan material," Kyle added.

Chuckie looked like he was controlling himself from
laughing or sharing that we all knew that USC's nickname
was The University of Spoiled Children. However, if Len
and Kyle were good examples of the Trojan system—and
they definitely were—then they were right. Besides, movers
and shakers like these families liked to cluster in the Ivy
Leagues so as to be much closer to D.C. and New York.

"Chuckie and I both scored great on the SATs and had
excellent GPAs and could have gone anywhere. We chose
Arizona State because we wanted to go there."

He grinned. "I don't think anyone was slamming our
alma mater, Kitty."

"Go Sun Devils and all that."

It said a lot about how well international assassination
paid that not only Lizzie but Siler before her had gone here.
Wondered if Siler had made enemies just as Lizzie had,
then decided it wasn't relevant. Sure, my bet was no, but he
had talents she never would—hyperspeed and the ability to
blend would mean, knowing him, he'd have had blackmail
material on every kid in that school within a week.

"Got it," Vance said, interrupting my defense of my college education. "I remember what I'd wanted to tell you."

CHAPTER 27

WE ALL STARED at Vance politely. "Yes?" I asked finally, since he appeared to be waiting for a reaction of some kind.

"Sorry, just wanted to be sure you were focused and I also seriously expected someone to call or evacuate us or something so that I'd forget again."

"And yet," Jeff said, "here we are, all breathlessly hanging on your every word."

"Kitty's really rubbed off on you. Anyway, I'd thought that you needed to add in one more Dealer. Ansom Somerall is also tight with Susan Howells, who is the head lobbyist for the insurance industry. Her husband, John, is also an insurance lobbyist, it's how they met, but he's not nearly as powerful as she is. And because it may matter, her maiden name is Pearson."

"And we have bingo again, because I'm looking at Nick Pearson, interestingly using his mother's maiden name as his last name, who I'd guess is their son?"

Vance nodded. Lizzie glared. "He's the leader of the Junior Skulls, too. Well, him and Noah and Sophie Berkowitz. They're twins, so they share a 'special bond.'" She made a gagging face. It was official—I loved this kid.

"So both of Ansom's buddies' kids are pissed with you, which explains why he's involved."

"Okay," Jeff said. "But I don't see any connection to this incident and the high-security breakout. Or our Huntress situation. Or the Planetary Council's impending visit, for that matter."

"There's always a connection," Chuckie and I said in unison. I'd worry about the unison thing later, since we were, I was sure, right.

"So, do we get Adriana or not?" Kyle asked.

Len waved his phone. "She says that she'll be over tomorrow morning. Apparently Olga wanted to be sure that we got her message before giving permission."

"That's kind of weird, isn't it?" Jeff asked. "I mean that seriously."

Chernobog shrugged. "You told her I'd gotten her message?" she asked Len, who nodded. "Then it makes sense. We're warned, so she's not sending her granddaughter into a situation where she's the only prepared person."

"I still don't understand why she wanted to do the invisible ink and secret message crap," Jeff muttered.

Chernobog looked at Lizzie. "Perhaps as a test."

Lizzie looked embarrassed. "I'm sorry I forgot about it until after dinner. There was just a lot going on."

Chernobog smiled slowly. "But you did deliver the message. A message you couldn't have read even if you'd wanted to. And a message you couldn't have created on your own."

Lizzie cocked her head. "They said it was written in Cyrillic. The uncles know that alphabet. They could have taught me. They haven't yet, but they could have."

"But they could not have written the coded portion. And Olga would know this." Chernobog nodded and seemed to make up her mind. "If you get bored while you're here, feel free to come over to the computer lab."

Everyone else looked shocked, but Lizzie looked interested. "Really?"

"Really. I rarely make idle offers." Chernobog turned

back to the letter from Olga. "We still need to determine if the escape is the event Olga refers to. I truly doubt it."

"It could be the start of something bigger," Chuckie pointed out. "Wouldn't be the first time, after all."

My phone rang. "Aw, Vance, sorry, the interruption was just a few minutes late." Took a look at who was calling and answered quickly. "Malcolm, what's up?"

"Missus Chief, I assume you know about the breakout?"

"We do and we're all thrilled to pieces over here. What are your thoughts about who let them out?"

"The smart money's on Stephanie, no matter how much anyone would like it otherwise."

"Yeah, not a shocker. We have some interesting things going on here, too." Filled him in on Lizzie's list and Olga's note. "So should we avoid going out onto the street or near the windows?"

"I had bulletproof glass installed years ago and I test it regularly, so look at the street as much as you want."

"Really? You had all the windows replaced?"

"I'm full service."

"Apparently so."

"But stay inside unless you have to exit. Not that this warning stopped you earlier today, but I like to live optimistically. The shields need to stay up, though I'm sure Walter's already on top of that. I'll get Adriana tomorrow—she's safer in her own embassy tonight."

"Vance is here. Does that mean he's less safe?" Chose not to look at Vance's expression, but Jeff and Chuckie clearly trying not to laugh again indicated that Vance's expression was probably pretty priceless.

"No, he's fine with all of you. We have guards on his husband, in case he cares."

"I'm sure he does. And thanks. Guarding anyone else?"

"Reader's assigned a lot of Field teams out, at my request, in addition to all the other teams out based on a variety of requests, so yes. Your allies are all under protection.

Bases are all on full alert, Dulce is scanning the Embassy regularly."

"Good. Why hasn't James called us to tell us that? Or William?" Shot a look at Jeff, who shook his head. So no one had called or texted any news to him I didn't know about.

"Because, despite how the two of you think, how things *actually* are is that you're not in active combat positions anymore. I realize it's been this way for the past four years, but I expect the two of you to adjust in another decade or so."

"Wow, bitter much?"

"Yes, because I just had a similar conversation with Paul Gower, wherein I had to explain to the Supreme Pontifex that, despite his desires to kick butt, he's going to be under as much security as the President and Mister Chief are tomorrow."

"So, you called me second?"

"Yes. I like to keep you guessing and not allow you to get too complacent with our relationship."

"Thanks for keeping it spicy." Noted the look Jeff shot me and decided getting off the phone was going to be in my best interests. "See you tomorrow, barring the end of the world."

"The world doesn't get to end on my watch. And you'll only see me if I want you to."

"True enough, Doctor Strange." We got off the phone and I filled in the others on Buchanan's half of the conversation.

Chuckie rubbed the back of his neck. "I wonder who else is activated either before or because of the breakout."

Mom sighed. "Could be no one. Could be a long list."

Thought about things, Operation Bizarro World in particular. "We need to alert James and Malcolm and Team Assassination that if there are assassins named Luis Sanchez or Julio Lopez, most likely out of Cuba, that there's a good chance they're both out to kill us. Too, I mean."

Mom and Chuckie both stared at me. "Where did you get those names from?" Mom asked.

"When I was, ah, away." In another universe, but since Lizzie was probably already seriously considering running away to join the circus, figured sharing that wasn't in her best mental interest.

"My dad said you changed universes," Lizzie said, without missing a beat. "So don't worry about freaking me out. I think that's totes the coolest. He said that it could mean that in other universes my parents weren't total traitors working with Harvey Gutermuth."

Our turn to stare at her. "Your parents were traitors?" Mom asked slowly.

"Working with the head of Club Fifty-One?" Chuckie added.

"Yeah. They were working on a drug that would kill all the A-Cs. It would kill humans, too."

We were all quiet for a few long moments. "Well," I said finally, "now we know what the catastrophic event is going to be."

CHAPTER 28

WE GOT THE FULL details of Lizzie's family history but it was pretty much what she'd told us, with one addition—her parents had been "Old World" Russian spies, which explained why the Dingo and Surly Vic were okay with adding her into the Family von Assassination. They were many things, but Old World they were not.

Her father's cover had been being a professor at ASU, meaning Dad knew him, but only tangentially since they weren't in the same department. Her mother had supposedly been an author, but a quick perusal of the interwebs had shown that she'd never really published anything—her bibliography was as faked as her U.S. citizenship.

"Mister Dash destroyed my father's notes, and my parents are both dead," Lizzie said, for what was probably the tenth time. "So they can't really have created the drug, right?" Got the impression she was hoping that we'd give her a different answer than the last nine.

"No," Chuckie said for the tenth time, consistent to the core. "Because your father wasn't working alone, I'm sure, and there are always backups."

"I'm more concerned about how you know about some of the worst assassins out there," Mom said to me.

"Seriously?" Jeff asked. "When you know who's essentially adopted her?"

Mom shook her head. "The Dingo is one thing. He has a code and a price. These two? They enjoy killing."

"Then I can guarantee they know Annette Dier and are probably on the Mastermind's payroll. And we took them out in the other world. But where are they in this world, Mom? That's my question."

"Cuba," Chernobog replied before Mom could. "At least the last time I checked on them. And yes, I check on them because your mother is correct—they're crazy in all the wrong ways."

"They won't be coming up here," Chuckie said. "We're going to Florida. They'll be there."

"I may never sleep again," Vance muttered.

"You get used to it," Lizzie said reassuringly. We all looked at her and she shrugged. "There are different cartels. Peter says to think of them as guilds. These guys aren't in the same guild as my dad and the uncles are. That could make them business rivals, but it can also make them enemies."

"The Dingo has a strict code, and I don't think he's a fan of any assassins who don't follow it," I pointed out.

Mom rubbed her forehead. "Yes, yes, kitten. The Dingo and his cronies good, all other assassins bad. Got it."

"Hey, it works for us," I indicated Lizzie and myself.

"Until it doesn't," Mom said. But Dad shot her a look I recognized—his "not in front of the kids" look—and she dropped this discussion.

We discussed things we had no answers to or plans for for a while longer, but finally everyone went to bed or, in Chernobog's case, back to Movie Night with a new tub of hot popcorn courtesy of the Elves. Mom, Dad, Vance, Lizzie, Jeff, and I all had hot chocolates and then we sent Lizzie to bed, Jeff ordered Vance to go to his room and sleep, and Mom and Dad turned in, too.

Once everyone had gone to their respective rooms I went to what I now called the Viewing Room—where the three-way mirror we'd had installed after Operation Bizarro World resided.

In order to see the other universes you had to sit at the right spot, where you could see yourself clearly reflected in all three mirrors, look straight ahead at yourself, and then wait for the other universes to come into your peripheral vision. Looking to the right or left made you lose the images. I'd gotten good at this over the past year and a half, so I got into the zone quickly.

I'd promised the Jamie in the other universe that I'd look into this mirror regularly to see what might be going wrong in the other universes where "we" existed. It was our bargain—I'd do the regular looking and she'd focus on her family in her world. She was allowed to look occasionally, but not all the time as she'd been doing before. As far as I'd seen, she'd kept her promise.

Sometimes Bizarro World Jamie and I were looking into the mirrors at the same time, and this was one of those times. She waved to me and I blew her a kiss, both of us still looking forward into our personal mirrors.

She left the mirror, but I could see her still, and she was drawing or writing something. I perused the other myriad universes—despite there being more universes than I could count, and what seemed like more forming every time I looked, I was able to take them all in quickly. Figured that the various Powers That Be out there on our side were giving me the assist and chose not to question or argue.

Finished the Tour of Everything. Nothing stood out as being wrong for those worlds, which was nice, because we had enough going on in this one right now.

Jamie came back and held up a piece of paper. It took some concentration, but I finally made out what she'd written: yek eht m'I.

It didn't take much to realize I was reading it backward and to translate to "I'm the key." I had to figure she meant the Jamie in my world.

But this wasn't news, really. Since she'd been born Jamie had been the focus of all the bad guy plans. They wanted to get my daughter and use her in all the ways imaginable to further their own ends. And I'd never, ever let them.

Jamie held up another piece of paper: niart eht no luferac eB. "Be careful on the train." Okay, I was going to be anyway, but Jamie sometimes saw what was coming, and when she did it was always bad. So, forewarned was forearmed and all that. I hoped.

One more piece of paper: swonk eH. "He knows."

There were a lot of he's out there who could know a lot of things. A part of me wanted to ask for more information. But she was a little girl, and—all space-time continuum and such aside—my daughter. And I didn't want her reverting back to watching the mirrors 24/7 and losing herself to the Jamie Channel.

I nodded, blew her another kiss, and did a little pantomime that indicated it was time for her to go outside and play. She grinned at me, turned, picked up something, and turned back. It was Stripes, the kick-butt cat we'd adopted. She waved his paw at me, waved again herself, then she put the cat around her shoulders, got up, and left.

"Jamie's a lot more help than you are, my King of the Elves," I said under my breath, while I allowed myself to miss everyone in that universe for a few moments.

Algar appeared behind me in the mirror. "You know there's that thing called free will still, right?"

"Right. I'd like to ensure that our enemies' free will doesn't harm the people I care about, let alone a lot of other innocent people. Call me a demanding whiner."

"You're asking for a lot of help." He cocked his head at me. "That's not like you. Are you alright?"

Heaved a sigh. "I'm just trying to get ahead of all the bad things coming to ensure that we protect everyone we possibly can, my children in particular."

He shook his head. "You're at war. Wars have casualties."

"I know that all too well. I don't have to like the casualties, and I also don't have to just blithely accept the casualties. I want to lose no one on my side. Sorry if that's a bad leadership attitude to have."

"Your enemy doesn't have that mindset. Remember that—it's his strength. And he knows you don't want to lose anyone, and that's your weakness."

"And his weakness is that he doesn't care. And I'll never apologize for not considering anyone to be cannon fodder. Are you suddenly suggesting I need to become a heartless bitch in order to win whatever's coming? Because I refuse to become like them. Any of the thems out there who are against us."

Algar smiled. "No. It's the right attitude to have. And you're right—strengths can be weaknesses and vice versa. Just remember that you can be as prepared as possible and still not be ready for what's coming."

"Thanks for the comforting pep talk."

He laughed. "Just remember that your real strengths are that you always think outside the box and nothing actually throws you. Metaphorically."

"Yeah, I've gotten thrown a lot literally."

The door opened and Algar disappeared, without even snapping his fingers. Jeff came in. "Viewing time's over, baby. We need to get some sleep before our trip."

I let him help me up. "Well, I was hoping to relax before we slept."

Jeff grinned. "Sucks to be me as always, I see."

CHAPTER 29

WE MADE SURE everyone was honestly asleep, Jamie and Charlie in particular. Then we zipped into the closet and got out of our clothes as fast as possible.

In the good old days, we could have taken a while to get undressed, with Jeff having me at the edge of orgasm, or better, the entire time. Two children and an apartment full of people and animals meant that we needed to hurry up and get to the good stuff as fast as possible, before someone woke up.

Jeff had finally adapted to having sexy times with a bunch of animals around, mostly because the majority of the animals didn't sleep with us anymore and those who did had picked up that he preferred them to be discreet and at least pretend they were sleeping.

I had a second iPod that mirrored my main one, and it was permanently in a dock in our bedroom. Jeff liked to create playlists to surprise me, usually in bed, and tonight was no exception.

After listening at the baby monitor and ensuring that Charlie's breathing was still rhythmic, Jeff hit play and the sounds of the Mamas and the Papas "Dedicated to the One I Love" hit our airwaves.

"Aww, a new playlist?"

He grinned. "Just for you, baby." He pulled the covers back, picked me up, and placed me onto the bed.

"Just like old times."

"Hopefully." And with that, Jeff kissed me.

He had been and remained the best kisser on any planet, and, as always, his lips owned mine and his tongue made my entire body shiver with anticipation. We kissed for a good long time, and then he moved his mouth to my main erogenous zone—my neck.

Jeff knew all the spots to lick, nibble, and rub to get my hips shaking like I was Shakira. Whose "Hips Don't Lie" came on right on cue. Found myself wondering if Jeff was timing himself to the musical selections, but then he nipped in the right spot in just the right way and I was too busy howling to worry about that anymore.

Thankfully the soundproofing was great here, because while I'd managed to occasionally be silent during sex, it was a rarity and not something I could manage on any kind of a regular schedule. Especially because Jeff moved his mouth to my breasts next. He had a pattern, but I didn't care because it was a great pattern that ensured my sexual happiness.

He'd brought me to orgasm at second base the very first time we'd slept together, and tonight was no exception. As Big Mountain's version of "Baby, I Love Your Way" came on, so did I. Loudly, as was my pattern.

Felt Jeff smile against my skin. "Nice to know the old ways still work."

"Oh ... yeah ..." I managed to gasp out. "They do."

He slid down, tracing my skin with his tongue, until he was between my legs and I was on Auto-Purr and Constant Yowl Modes. Lit's "Too Fast for a U-Turn" came on and Jeff kept time to the beat, proving once again that he was a sexual impresario for the ages. The song built and so did I, until I climaxed right along with the song.

Jeff flipped me onto my stomach and stroked my back with his hands and mouth. "What's this about you thinking other men are spicy?" he breathed into my ear.

"I like . . . to keep you . . . on your . . . toes." It took a lot of effort to talk since Jeff's hands were stroking various parts of my already quivering body and he was back to nibbling my neck.

"As to that . . ." He shifted me onto my hands and knees as "Sexy" by the Black Eyed Peas started up. "Let's talk about what kind of spice I want to sprinkle all over you right now."

"Cinnamon and sugar?"

He laughed as he slid into me and my head went back. "For starters. And honey." He thrust deeply into me and I slammed my hips back to get him even deeper inside.

"Love . . . honey . . ." My hands clenched the pillows. I'd already climaxed several times, so technically it should have taken me a while to be ready again. But Jeff's technique ensured I was already at the edge by thrust number three, when the Aerosmith's "Love XXX" hit the airwaves.

As always, we were like this for longer than I could really comprehend. The beauty of being with an empathic man was that I didn't have to spend a lot of focus or effort in screaming that he should keep on doing it longer, faster, and harder, because he already knew and was doing what I wanted literally the moment I wanted it.

"Mmm, I think I'm going to pour honey on you and lick it all off," he growled as I got closer and closer. "Three times a day. Just like the song says."

"Only if . . . I get . . . to do the same, ahhh, to you."

"I can arrange that."

"Promises, promises." The last word ended in a wail as I crashed over the edge and Jeff erupted into me.

I collapsed onto the bed, but he wasn't done with me yet. Jeff flipped me over again and as Mötley Crüe's "Sticky Sweet" came on he dove between my legs again. Conveniently, he was placed in such a way that I could reciprocate, which I did because, you know, I was a really great wife that way.

Tommy Lee's drumming was a great beat to work with and didn't take all that long before another rewarding me and my... finally quieted, "Love" by Elefant started I ran my fingers th... snuggled up with Jeff's arm around

"Think we're going to b... chest. He stroked my arm and I asked.   on his chest.
                        ...in sex on the train?"

Jeff laughed softly. "God, it just *sucks* to be m... No idea, baby. I'd love to say yes, but we're not going to be alone."

"There's always the bathroom." Hey, they weren't huge but they kept them really clean on the Presidential and Vice Presidential travel options. The perks of leadership and all that.

"There is. As always I'll keep your needs and requirements foremost in my mind."

"As it should be."

Jeff hugged me. "And, speaking of those needs, I sense that you're not sleepy enough to actually go to sleep yet."

"Not quite."

He rolled on top of me as the Kinks' "All Day and All of the Night" came on. "Then, let me do my best to exhaust you in the best ways possible."

"Darn. Well, if you insist and all."

"I do. In that really Vice Presidential way of mine."

"Oooh, sounds like it's time for me to play Secretary to the Big Man."

Jeff grinned. "And it's job review time."

I ran my hands over his chest, around to his back, and then down to his truly awesome butt. "And just wait until you see what I've added onto my resume. Some really impressive job advancement stuff."

"I'll be the judge of that."

"Challenge accepted."

CHAPTE...

HOURS LATER AND promotions all the way up to Second Vice President secured for me, we fell asleep, wrapped around each other. I slept heavily and, thankfully, if I had dreams I didn't remember any of them.

The next day dawned without a lot of eventfulness, other than waking up to the Kinks' "State of Confusion," which either meant Algar was giving me a hint, Jeff's playlist had some weird non-sexy songs on it, or neither one of us had paid any attention to my iPod after sexy times and it was now on some sort of random play option. Had to give not paying attention the edge.

Algar might have been a jerk about many things, but when it came to being the Operations Team he was spot on. When we finished showering, and having some fast clean up sex, just because who knew when we'd get to do the deed next, our rolling bags were packed and ready and waiting for us in our large walk-in closet.

Our clothes were also laid out. In Jeff's case, this merely meant that one of his many black Armani suits, crisp white dress shirts, black ties, and shined black shoes were waiting for him. No fedora, which was a disappointment, but I decided not to argue with the Elves.

For me, it was an iced blue suit with a cream blouse and cream pumps. I winced just looking at the outfit. The

chances were so very high that I'd ruin it in some way, po
tentially before we even left the Embassy.

However, there was also a small leather duffel bag I
didn't recognize next to my shoes. Checked inside. A pair of
Converse, jeans, an Aerosmith shirt with all the boys pic-
tured, and a Fall Out Boy hoodie were inside. "You are totally the best," I said quietly. Put the duffel next to my purse
on the way out of the closet.

We had breakfast in our dining room, since we had Mom,
Dad, Vance, and Lizzie added in, and Jeff had had me call
Chuckie up to join us, too. Normally for this many we'd
have gone downstairs and left it all to Pierre, but Jeff
wanted to cook so I didn't argue. He was great at it, I hated
cooking, and the Elves provided whatever he needed for
ingredients and performed all the cleanup, so why not let
him enjoy himself?

Jamie sat on Chuckie's lap next to Lizzie and prattled on
about all the pets with her during breakfast. Charlie did me
a solid and didn't try to float anything this morning, possibly
because he was sitting with Dad and having fun getting fed
by his Papa Sol while petting the dogs and cats, who were
living it up having my parents around for a while.

The rest of us did our best to discuss potential strategies
in a way I hoped the kids weren't picking up.

We finished breakfast rather quickly, all things considered, and then it was time to get moving.

Went in and grabbed our rolling bags while Jeff and
Chuckie discussed how they wanted us divided up to drive
to the rail station. "Any Poofs who aren't staying home to
guard and who want an adventure, now's the time to get
into Kitty's purse. Everyone else be good and guard the
manse and everyone we care about in it. Bruno, my bird,
time to chameleon it up, grab whoever you want along, and
hit the road."

Bruno was the Head Peregrine and the one most attached to me. All the other Peregrines answered to him and

his mate, Lola. Lola always remained on child care duty, since that was part of what these birds had been bred for on Alpha Four—protecting the Royal Children. And having seen the Peregrines in action more than once, they were impressive and good at their jobs.

They also, like Siler, were able to blend in with their surroundings, so that no one saw them. Bruno also had Keen Animal Senses and was pretty good at letting me know when someone was a threat. Sure, he hadn't done so with Cliff, but Cliff had been in the Circle of Trust before Bruno had arrived. Animals being animals, the Peregrines had watched and waited. And now they knew they weren't allowed to rend Cliff unless it was absolutely necessary, since we were trying to remain stealth and not let him know we knew he was the Mastermind or, more importantly, have him die and his Doomsday Plans go into effect.

Made sure my purse had anything and everything I could think of that I might need in it, including the Poofs who planned on taking a trip. The goggles were still in it, and I shoved them down a bit, lest Jeff notice them and ask me why I had them.

Plenty of Poofs On Board, or at least in my purse, and Bruno trotting along at my side, I left our bedroom, dragging the suitcases behind me. This didn't last long, since the Secret Service had arrived and they took the cases from me immediately.

It was time to head out. We kissed the kids goodbye and hugged Lizzie. "You have our numbers, just like my dad does," I reminded her, since we'd programmed her phone and ours with all our relevant digits during breakfast. "So don't hesitate to call or text if you think something's up or if anything happens."

"I will, I promise."

"And remember that there are Secret Service agents here, protecting all of you," Jeff said. "So don't hesitate to go to them for help."

"Got it." Lizzie shot Dad a worried look.

He smiled reassuringly. "We'll be fine. This is the most secure building on the eastern seaboard."

With that we headed downstairs to our underground garage. A-C facilities were odd in that the elevators never seemed to go all the way down. Presumably because, with hyperspeed, there was no elevator faster than an A-C. Or some other reason. Aliens Were Weird was a statement I still repeated daily, though usually in my mind or under my breath.

We had a lot of people going, and half of our team were staging from the Embassy, so we also had quite the number of cars waiting for us. Conveniently, the underground garage was big enough to accommodate our vehicular needs.

We had several gray limos but we weren't taking them this time. In the past year we'd been sent back to the future, in that sense. Centaurion Division used a variety of upgraded and extended Lincoln Navigators, and we'd been assigned our own fleet for use during times when we needed to ensure the Vice President and his entourage arrived in a style that said Heavy Duty Security On Board.

In addition to our gaggle of Secret Service folks and our standard A-C protection details, Buchanan was waiting for us downstairs, along with Len and Kyle and Burton Falk, a human agent who reported directly to Buchanan. Normally Len was my driver and Kyle rode shotgun as bodyguard, but today Buchanan wanted Falk driving us and he was taking the shotgun seat.

The boys might have been hurt or pissed, or both, but if they were they kept it to themselves. Or else I missed it, because I was busy greeting everyone else who was already in the garage.

I'd expected to see Caroline and Mr. Joel Oliver, who were chatting with White, Mahin, and Abigail. But happily Alpha Team was here as well. Because, as it turned out,

Buchanan wanted to ensure that Gower was under control sooner as opposed to later.

Reader gave me a hug. "You look great, girlfriend. Runway ready." Reader had taken over as the Head of Field when Jeff and I had been shoved into the political lifestyle. Before then he'd been a Captain in Centaurion Division. And before that he'd been the world's top international male model. And there wasn't a day that he didn't look as if he could step right back into that life without missing a beat.

"Thanks, James. You're still a great liar. And I don't expect my look to last."

"Oh, don't sell yourself short," Tim Crawford, who was the Head of Airborne, said. "Sometimes you make it whole days at a time without dropping something on your blouse."

"I'll hurt you later. Where are the flyboys? And Serene?"

"The flyboys are ready to go in the air once we take off," Tim replied. "We want aerial cover, just in case."

"Serene's off wrangling Stryker," Reader said. "He responds best to her after Reynolds, and Reynolds was with you and Jeff."

This was true. And I was sure that Stryker was putting up quite a fuss, though hopefully Chernobog was helping Serene get him moving.

Lorraine and Claudia, who were still my closest A-C girlfriends and were now filling the Captain roles Reader and Tim had vacated, both zipped into the garage from the Embassy. "Kids are all taken care of," Lorraine said as she gave me a hug.

"Daycare's in your apartment right now," Claudia added. "Your dad insisted."

"He just wants easy access to snacks."

"He said you'd say that," Lorraine said with a laugh.

"And he said to tell you he wants the couches more," Claudia added. "He said he's planning a Disney film fest, regardless of what Denise wants."

"Oh, I'm sure she'll roll with it."

"I'm sure we could just send everyone down via gates and have absolutely no security issues," Gower said, as he came over and gave me a hug. Gower was big, black, bald, and beautiful, so getting hugs from him was never a bad thing. I rarely suggested it out loud anymore, but if Reader and Gower had been willing to add me into the marriage, Jeff might have had some real romantic worries.

"While I like where your head's at, you can't stump for reelection if you're taking a gate," I reminded him. "Not you, of course, Mister Supreme Pontifex for Life or until you pass it off to your groomed right-hand man." This is what had happened when White had retired and handed the religious reins to Gower, after all. "But as far as I can tell, politicians start campaigning for reelection the day after they're sworn into office."

He grunted. "Not every situation demands double duty."

Before I could argue or support this mindset, Serene and Stryker came down. Somehow she'd gotten him dressed in a suit just like those the other men wore. I managed not to gape, because this was the first time I'd ever seen Stryker in a suit, let alone in the Armani Fatigues. The Elves were amazing, considering Stryker didn't care overmuch about his appearance and had never met an exercise he was willing to perform.

But, you know, I was a politician's wife now. "Hey, Stryker, you look great." Lying came with the territory. And he did look better dressed like this than in the Hacker International Standard Uniform, which was khaki shorts, some sort of comfy yet ugly foot covering, and whatever science fiction or fantasy TV show or movie T-shirts were on the day's rota.

He shrugged. "Maybe. I feel like an idiot." He had a duffel over his shoulder.

"What's in the bag?"

He looked at my matching duffel. "I'll show you mine if you show me yours."

"That one never worked on me and still doesn't."

"Can't blame a guy for trying, and I wasn't trying at all in case Jeff and Chuck are listening. But anyway, Kitty, I think you need to get the gang rounded up."

"Why?"

"Because," Serene said, voice tight, "Stryker and I need to tell everyone what we just saw on the news."

CHAPTER 31

CONVENIENTLY, A-Cs had better hearing than humans, and all the humans were trained to listen well, so Serene and Stryker had everyone's immediate attention.

"What's going on?" Reader asked, Commander Voice on Full.

"Every major network is carrying the story about the breakout," Serene replied. "There's nothing our people can do about it—it's too prevalent."

In the good old days, before Operation Infiltration, the imageers would have made this all go away, because that was their talent—the reading and manipulation of images, any images.

But our people had been infected with something that harmed Imageering abilities, which had ground Imageering down to a halt. Christopher and Serene, who were the first and second most powerful imageers, still had most of their abilities. But even so, nothing to what they'd had before.

Imageering was building back, and with Serene as the Head it had become a far more political section, albeit still media-centric. She dealt with all the news media and then some—which was how she'd have stopped the story if it had been possible—so it was a good thing that she was a Secret Troubadour. Literally only her A-C C.I.A. personnel and I

knew about her troubadour talents. Though I had a strong
suspicion that Team Assassination had their suspicions.

"That's a PR problem for the Pentagon," Reader said.
"Not us."

"It's a problem for us when those escaped prisoners
have said that they'll negotiate their return to custody,"
Stryker said with a grimace. "But only if Farley Pecker and
Harvey Gutermuth do the negotiations. With the President."

We all stared at each other. "So," I said finally, "the
leader of the Church of Hate and Intolerance and the head
of Club Fifty-One have finally recovered from their media
humiliation and are back, bigger and better than ever.
Lucky us."

"Aside from the fact that there's no way any of those
people actually want to return to custody, what possible re-
assurances could those two dunderheads provide?" Mom
sounded annoyed, as she always did when things like this
caught her unaware.

"No idea," Serene said. "But I'm not going down to Florida now. I'm going to stay here and work with Kevin and
Doreen to ensure that we have a prepared response for any
and all of the calls that are going to be coming in just a few
minutes."

We all looked at Raj. Whose turn it was to grimace. "I
need to stay, too, don't I?"

"You're our Public Relations Minister," Jeff said, sounding unhappy. Couldn't blame him—Raj was good at fixing
the things we messed up. And by we I meant me.

"I should as well," Oliver said, looking at his phone. "Because my editor just told me that he expects me to find out
just what the American Centaurion response to all of this is
going to be."

Raj's phone beeped. "Right on cue. That's Bruce Jenkins." Another reporter we'd become friends with mostly by
saving his life. We were good that way. "He'd like to come

over, same reasons as Mister Joel Oliver. And we're going to need all the positive press we can get, I'm sure."

"Why?"

Everyone looked at me. "Because it's bad?" Kyle suggested.

"Yes, it is. But why are *we* the focus? Why does anyone in their right mind think that we're responsible for these wacked-out killers? I'm not asking in terms of reality—I know they all hate us and most of them want us all dead. I'm asking in terms of media spin."

"Because they say they're going to start killing people in the name of getting the aliens off this planet if their demands aren't met," Stryker said.

"Ah. Nice of you to mention that at the start."

He shrugged. "I thought it was self-evident, considering who's involved."

Chuckie's eyes were narrowed. "The timing is interesting, don't you think?"

"You mean that this is going on right when the Planetary Council is about to visit, thereby making the anti-alien contingent freak out even more than normal?"

"Yes, that's exactly what I mean." He rubbed the back of his neck. "We have a mole."

I snorted. "No mole. We have names. If it's somehow not Cliff Goodman, then it's Langston Whitmore, the Secretary of Transportation. The President has to advise the Joint Chiefs and the Cabinet of what's going on and what he's doing. And despite our strongly urging him to dump Whitmore, that asshat is still sitting pretty."

"How would Cliff know?"

"Ah, he was there when the information came in," Jeff said. "Sorry, Chuck. I forgot to tell you."

"You mean you didn't want me to freak out and make my migraine worse." Chuckie sighed. "Doesn't matter, because Kitty's right. It could easily be Whitmore. He hates everything associated with American Centaurion. Cliff wouldn't even need to activate him—Whitmore's capable of this leak all on his own."

"I'd always thought Vince was smarter than this," Mom said. "It's rarely a good thing to keep someone else's people in place once you take over. But he insists on keeping Whitmore and a few others around."

"He does a good job with the role. It's why Vince kept him, and the others, on," Jeff said with a sigh to match Chuckie's. "But you're right—if it's not Cliff, then I'm sure Whitmore is the leak, so to speak."

"Do you think they've made this announcement right now to keep Raj and Mister Joel Oliver and the others here?" Vance asked.

His turn to get everyone staring at him.

"Why would they want to keep me, or Serene, or anyone else Embassy-bound?" Raj asked.

"Why do they do anything they do?" Vance countered. "I'd guess because you guys can affect things in a positive way. Or they think you can."

"So . . . does that mean we think that we should all go as planned?" Serene asked. She didn't sound like she felt this was the right course of action.

Thought about it. "No. They've set it up so that you guys really do have to stay here. So, let them win this portion of the round. We're already on high alert."

"I don't like it," Chuckie muttered. Probably presciently. "But I agree with Kitty—we need you handling the PR stuff here, not on the train."

Remembered that Bizarro World Jamie had warned me to be careful on the train. Maybe she'd meant from a PR standpoint, rather than an action standpoint. And maybe pigs were flying in some other alternate universe, too.

"Speaking of which," Reader said, "we need to get moving or we'll delay everything and that won't spin well, either."

We divided up. The SUVs seated eight, including the

all in o… dition to Falk, Buchanan, Jeff, and me with

Len and K… om, Chuckie, Stryker, and Vance were
White, and Christop… Adriana, Tito, Rahmi, Rhee,
gail, Mahin, Claudia, Lorra… and Tim had Gower, Abi-

Those A-C reflexes meant tha… roline.
teams were in their own SUVs, they ha… ough the Field
drivers. The three were, like Falk, all part of Bu… have human
human team, though only Falk was coming along w… h us
down to Florida.

The rest were going to get all the SUVs back then take
an A-C jet and fly down to meet us in Orlando. And, in fact,
Buchanan had several other humans in their own SUV, who
were each going to drive one of the Cars O' Doom back.
Whether they were all joining us in Florida or not I didn't
know and chose not to care—that was Buchanan's bailiwick, thankfully, not mine.

The Secret Service wanted Gower, Jeff, and me in a car
with them, but settled for having only Secret Service in the
Secret Service cars after much protesting, whining, Jeff putting his Vice Presidential foot down, and then Mom saying
make it so. Unsurprisingly, it was Mom's vote that got the
Secret Service to comply.

Not that we didn't think our Secret Service agents were
great, but Reader was the best at anything he did, and driving was certainly one of those things. Len had passed the
C.I.A.'s driving tests with the highest scores in years and
he'd spent all his time with us having to increase his skill set
up to Reader's level, which he'd definitely managed or Culver, Kyle, Len, and I wouldn't be alive today. And if Buchanan felt Falk was a better driver than either Reader or
Len, and he did, then Falk was a damned amazing driver.

So, bundled into our mighty, reinforced with extra steel,
bulletproof glass, and all the A-C bells and whistles like laser shields and cloaking Cars O' Doom, we trundled off.

Unsurprisingly, we had protestors... ...They ...nt was smaller ...not just in the U.S. but ...y'd learned to stop throw- ...very driver had the laser shields were out of the garage and the shields ...whatever was thrown right back onto the thrower... were such a natural part of our registered them. The anti-al... than it had been, but still around the world. Ho... ing things at us, be... activated befo... tended to...

"...here were no protestors out yesterday. I just realized that."

"So, were they not there because Goodman was coming by, or for another reason?" Buchanan asked.

"No idea. But . . . they weren't around when Lillian came to get me last week, either." And again, it hadn't registered until right now.

"That would seem to indicate more that whoever Huntress is, she's got pull with Club Fifty-One and Pecker's people," Chuckie said.

"Just assume they're all working together in some way and you'll be safer," Mom said. Couldn't argue with that mindset.

We didn't talk about much otherwise, because going over the notes Raj had given us before we left kept us busy. As always, his notes on what to do and how to handle a variety of situations were top-notch and extremely detailed. Still had the bad feeling that we should have ensured we had a troubadour of some kind with us, but calling in some of our Troubadours in Reserve might have highlighted Serene's clandestine operations, and I knew without asking we didn't want that.

Bruno snuggled up to me, and I realized my stress must have been obvious, at least to his Keen Animal Senses. I petted him and did my best to relax. No need to stress Jeff out any more than he probably already was.

Rail Force One and its related Two were almost secrets.

Even though everyone saw pictures of presidents on rail-cars, no one seemed to realize there were assigned trains just as there were assigned airplanes. And while Air Force One and Two housed at Andrews Air Force Base, the trains did not.

The trains were leased to the government, and because of that, they weren't held in any one place. When the President or Vice President needed to travel by rail, the cars were called back from wherever they were, and sent to the train station that made the most sense for the top officials to leave from, depending on where they were heading.

Because we were heading south and weren't going to be making any stumping stops in the D.C. area, we headed for the Arlington station.

There were a variety of routes we could have chosen, which would have also affected where we boarded the train. If we'd been focused solely on getting down to Florida quickly, or if we'd needed these particular SUVs when we arrived, we'd have gone to Lorton and used the Auto Train route. But since campaign stumping was being included in the journey and we had more SUVs that would meet us coming from NASA Base, the Silver Meteor route was the big winner.

Happily, despite how obvious we looked with something like a dozen giant black SUVs driving in formation, no one seemed to pay us any mind once we'd gotten away from Embassy Row. Uneventful trips were rarities for us, but we never complained about them.

We parked in a small secured parking section that I doubted anyone who wasn't high up in the government even knew existed, and then were hustled down to the loading area. I let Bruno fly on over on his own.

"Wow," Vance said when we reached the platform. "It's damned impressive from the outside."

I laughed. "Just wait until you see the inside. There are reasons I love the train."

CHAPTER 32

RAIL FORCE ONE was normally six cars long, not counting the engine and the caboose. With Rail Force Two added on we had thirteen. Chose not to think of this as an unlucky fact.

"Thirteen cars," Tim said. "Not good." Many heads nodded. Though apparently I was the only one trying to not think of it as unlucky.

"Is it too late to add another car?" Joseph asked. When the head of a Secret Service detail asks about the dangers of the number thirteen, you have to consider just how widespread that superstition is.

"Consider it a lucky number for gamblers," Chuckie, the Voice of No Superstitions Allowed, said. "And let's get rolling."

Mom nodded her agreement, and everyone else stopped whining. At least out loud. I was pretty sure some were still whining on the inside.

After the engine, there was a car for Secret Service and other personnel, then the President's car, the War Room car, the Private Dining Car for the executive families and anyone else they felt like eating with, then the Vice President's car, another Secret Service and other personnel car, followed by two guest cars, the General Dining Car, yet another guest car, a last car for Secret Service and related personnel, and finally the caboose. All the cars were rather sleek, painted white with a pretty blue that matched my suit. Go me, color coordinating with our transportation.

"If you don't count the engine, it's twelve cars," I said to Joseph as we headed for the official Rail Force Two car, or Car Number 6.

"It's important to count the engine. And if you note, the engine is Car Number One."

"Just trying to help."

"I have a bad feeling about this," Joseph muttered under his breath. Chose not to tell him that this just showed he was aware of how our luck rolled, mostly because I didn't think he'd appreciate it.

The Secret Service and our A-C agents fanned out, two to a person, to get everyone onto the train, into the right cars, and otherwise organized. Besides Joseph, Rob, Evalyne, and Phoebe, Buchanan, Len, and Kyle were with us, though because they were part of our protection detail they didn't drag along extra Secret Service agents.

Though the agents would be sleeping in the nearest personnel car down, Buchanan and the boys would be sleeping in Rail Force Two with us. Which would put a major crimp in my plans to do the deed on the train, but I was confident I could find a workaround. My plan had a shot of succeeding, since at least Mom was sleeping in Rail Force One, and there was no way I could do a workaround if she was in the car with us—the soundproofing was nowhere near good enough.

The interior of the cars was extremely plush, kind of like a rolling luxury hotel. Lots of rich woods, brass fixtures, and an air of understated opulence. The Presidential Seal was the overriding motif, and there was a reliance on a lot of red, white, and blue, too, in terms of decorations, but it was worth it.

The President's and VP's private cars were similar— sleeping areas near the front, with a private room for the

POTUS or the VPOTUS, living room/lounge/dining table, kitchen near the back, a small double bunk for the steward and porter, with two bathrooms, one for the sleeping quarters, one for the rest.

The dining cars were typical in that on one side there were tables that seated four and on the other the tables only seated two. The kitchens in each of these cars took up less than a quarter of the car, but it was amazing what came out of them. I couldn't have made anything decent in them, but the stewards and porters insisted that the kitchens were set up for maximum efficiency and I wasn't going to argue with them. I could smell food being prepared already, and my mouth started watering.

The guest cars were typically nice sleepers, with a small lounge and seating area in addition to the sleeping bunks. The cars for personnel were similar, with less niceties and a lot more easy access to everyone they needed to protect and care for.

The War Room car was just that—a car filled with a long conference table, comfy chairs, and all the electronic bells and whistles that allowed the President to stay in touch with everyone he might need to. It had a smaller kitchen, if such could be believed, and a small lounge in it as well, to keep everyone fed and hydrated.

The caboose was one of my favorite cars, in part because this was where all the PR took place. Whenever the stumping was going on, as it would be, frequently, on this journey, the caboose was where the President and whoever else stood, entered and exited, and so forth. Ergo, the caboose was also decorated more than any of the other cars, mostly with American flags and some Armstrong-Martini posters.

The interior of the caboose reminded me of newsrooms in the movies—lots of electronics, lots of people frantically working, writing position papers, altering speeches, and so forth. The Press Secretary and, when he was with us, Raj,

tended to spend most of their time here when not in the
War Room.

Ariel Hillel was Armstrong's Press Secretary. He was a
nice guy around our age. I didn't interact with him all that
much, but I knew that Raj liked him and vice versa.

"Where's Raj?" Ariel asked me with a sniffle as he joined
us in our car, trailed by his requisite two Secret Service
agents. It was a credit to the car's design that having twelve
people in here didn't make it feel crowded. "I've been looking for him."

"You crying because he's not here?" I asked.

"No. The President has a cold and I've caught it, I guess."

"Ugh, condolences, and please don't share that around."

We brought him up to speed on why Raj and others
weren't with us. Ariel didn't look happy. He also didn't look
like he felt all that great.

"I realize why he stayed home, but we're going to get hit
with the same questions while on this trip, and none of you
are prepared with answers. And while your answers can and
should match the President's, you're going to be asked different questions than he is."

"Do you want us to call him in?" Jeff asked. "He can get
here in less than five minutes."

"I'm not sure. I thought you were bringing Oliver along,
too."

"He stayed home for the same reason as Raj," I shared.

Ariel grimaced. "I wonder if that was their plan all
along."

"Welcome to Team Megalomaniac. Yeah, that's what
we're thinking. But everyone felt that we needed Raj at
home."

"Let me discuss it with the President," Ariel said, as he
bustled off, his agents trailing him.

Before Jeff and I could discuss this, our steward came in.
"Good to have you back," he said with a beaming smile.

Happily, he didn't look like he'd caught the Presidential Cold yet.

"Javier, always great to see you." Jeff gave him a hearty handshake.

"Even better to smell your cooking," I said as I gave him a big hug.

Javier did quadruple duty—he was the steward, porter, chef, and waiter. It was nice for us because it meant only one extra person in the car, and he said he both enjoyed all the duties and made more money because of them, so it was a win-win all the way around. The President had his own All-In-One dude, too.

Javier laughed. "It's always my pleasure when you two are taking the train. I went over menus with Raj last night." He looked around. "Where is he?"

"That's the question of the hour." Time to fill Javier in on what was going on, which we did.

He looked worried once we were done. "So, Raj, Mister Joel Oliver, and Missus Dwyer all aren't here? I'm not going to try tell you guys policy, but it really seems like your enemies wanted to be sure some of your key personnel weren't around."

Had to think for a moment who he meant, then realized that Mrs. Dwyer was Serene. "Well, we have other key personnel still with us, so we should be okay."

"And for all we know, Ariel is going to ask us to have Raj come anyway," Jeff added.

"And the kids aren't along?" Javier asked, this time looking disappointed.

"No, they stayed home. Under the circumstances it seemed wiser." At least per Denise, and who was I to argue?

"Well, it won't be as fun without them, but that means I'll have even more time to pamper the two of you."

"You're my favorite, just sayin'."

Javier laughed. "Glad to be of service. Truly. I'll get your things unpacked." He nodded to Len and Kyle. "You two want to do the standard observations?"

"Yes, sir," Len said.

Javier grinned. "You know she likes us all informal."

"I say it again, Javier is my favorite."

"I'll get jealous later," Jeff said. "We need to make sure everyone else is settled and check in with Vince."

Joseph had his head slightly cocked, which he did when he was listening to his earpiece in a non-stress situation. He nodded. "The President wants everyone to meet in the War Room once they're settled in and their porters are handling their luggage."

"You want us in there before or after the train leaves the station?" Jeff asked.

Joseph relayed the question. "The President says he defers to what the Ambassador thinks."

"Wow. Vince is totally my favorite. Um, I honestly think I want to defer that decision to Malcolm, though."

Buchanan chuckled while everyone other than Javier shot surreptitious glares at him. "It's nice to be appreciated, Missus Chief. She'd prefer to ask her mother," he said to Jeff, "but since I'm here, I'm the best stand-in."

"Traitor." Buchanan knew me far too well, apparently. My phone beeped and I took a look. "Apparently Raj is on his way. With, huh, Mister Joel Oliver in tow."

No sooner had I finished speaking than Raj and MJO appeared. Several people jumped, but fortunately no one drew weapons. MJO also had Ginger in his arms.

"Why is that cat here?" Jeff asked, earning a snide look from Ginger, who leaped out of MJO's arms into mine.

"She wanted to come," Raj said. "Insisted really. It was bring her or risk her clawing up the entire Embassy."

"Good call then." Hey, I liked to be supportive. Besides, Ginger was great to roll with and would give me an extra snuggle buddy if Jeff was stumping and I was napping, which I hoped to have happen somewhere along the line.

"Thanks, and sorry we're late," Raj said. "We decided that Serene, Kevin, and Bruce Jenkins would handle things at the Embassy and Mister Joel Oliver and I would do what we'd planned to on the train."

"Hopefully thwarting what our enemies wanted." Put Ginger down next to Bruno, who de-cloaked, presumably so that he, too, could make people jump. They nuzzled each other in a form of Animal High Five. "So, Malcolm, back to you."

"Get these two settled," he indicated Raj and MJO, not Ginger and Bruno, "then have all the Secret Service and A-C agents check in with me. Once we know everyone's in place, then the train starts off. Once we're rolling, then everyone key goes to the War Room."

"Why do you want to wait?" Jeff asked.

Buchanan shrugged. "Because I don't trust anyone. Not even the people here."

CHAPTER 33

IT'S ONE OF your better qualities, yeah," I said as Jeff glared at him. "And Jeff, he's protecting us, let's remember."

I took for granted that Buchanan didn't trust me and Jeff, but not in a traitorous way. He didn't trust us to behave and follow his or anyone else's orders. Rightly.

"I am. That I'm not trusting should not be a surprise to anyone, you in particular, Mister Chief. And I want to make sure that everyone we want is on board and no one we don't is removed before we start off."

Evalyne tapped on her phone. "I've asked Manfred to take an A-C team and search all the cars once everyone's checked in."

"Good." Buchanan looked at Len and Kyle. "You two take these two," he jerked his head at Raj and MJO, "to their cars and hand them off to their protection details."

The boys nodded, everyone linked hands, and then Raj kicked up the hyperspeed and they disappeared.

"So, do we think that this circumvents whatever our enemies wanted?" I asked the room in general.

"Too early to tell," Buchanan replied. "But I'm sure we'll find out. Sooner as opposed to later."

Our Secret Service people spent a lot of time talking and tapping, then Len and Kyle returned to our car, the

confirmation that the A-Cs had done a triple search—
including scanning for all the things we routinely scanned
for—came through, and the go signal was finally given.

There were enough seats for all of us in our car to sit
comfortably, which we did, Ginger and Bruno at my feet.
There were no windows in the President's car, ours, or the
War Room car for security reasons, so we didn't get to
watch as we pulled out of the station. That was the down-
side. The upside was that Javier brought everyone delicious
fruit drinks that were refreshing and didn't even make you
miss the alcohol that wasn't in them. He also had a nice
cheese plate ready. And some water and food for the animals, too, because he was just that kind of awesome.

So we sipped and munched while the train worked up
speed. Once the cheese plate and our glasses were emptied,
Joseph declared us underway enough to head for the War
Room.

Told the animals to stay put, which they did by flying and
leaping onto our bed and snuggling down for a nap.

Walking on the train was always interesting because
even the smoothest ride was still somewhat bumpy, though
the only real issues were the changes between cars. However, from what I'd been told, the couplings between cars
were a lot closer together than they'd been in the old days,
so there was less risk of falling off.

Still, Jeff kept a firm hold on me, and I kept a firm hold
on my purse and the duffel bag I hadn't let Javier put away.
Had to figure that if Algar had specifically given the duffel
to me, then I should keep it nearby.

To get to the War Room car we had to walk through the
dining car that was for us and the President and whomever
else we might grace with the joys of eating with us and taking bets on how often I spilled what on myself.

I stopped to say hi to and get hugs from Isaiah, who was
the chef for Rail Force One and had been for several decades now, Brandon, his apprentice, who was much younger

and had only been working with Isaiah for five years, and Eleanor, who was the pastry chef and considered quite the phenom, since she'd been on Rail Force One since she graduated from culinary school.

Also got to greet and hug Nathan, the headwaiter, and Lincoln, the other waiter for the car. They'd both been working for the Office of the President for twenty years.

Greetings to some of my favorite people who made riding the train the awesome experience that it was over, I allowed myself to be dragged into the War Room, in part because everyone else on the train who wasn't with the President and First Lady were coming up behind us and I was clogging the transit artery.

Fortunately the War Room was set up to have a lot of people present, because we did, and I for one wasn't willing to stand in an impressive manner, especially since the Secret Service and A-C Field teams had all the good standing places claimed already. Frankly, if our enemies wanted to take us out, all they'd have to do was hit this one car.

"We shouldn't all be in here together," Chuckie muttered as he sat down next to me.

"Dude, I was thinking the same thing," I whispered back.

"We're fine," Jeff said to both of us. "Chuck, relax."

"Don't worry, we've got this," Reader said, as Gower sat on Chuckie's other side. Reader stayed standing behind both of them, possibly because he was betting on us not having enough chairs. "Planes are in the air."

By key people, Armstrong meant Jeff, me, Alpha Team, and Raj. I'd insisted on Christopher and White being here, too, and Chuckie had insisted on Oliver and Stryker. Caroline had done the insisting on her own, on behalf of Senator McMillan.

Tim, Claudia, and Lorraine brought up the rear. Our people definitely outnumbered those Armstrong had brought with him. Then again, our people were the ones the Planetary Council was likely coming to visit.

Armstrong's wife Elaine was in the car, but only to leave it once the rest of us had come in. Which was a pity, because I really liked her. On the other hand, I couldn't blame her for scampering off to hang out with everyone else and have food and drinks. I could envy her, and I did, but I couldn't blame her.

Sadly, in addition to Ariel, Armstrong had his Secretary of State with us as well. I'd personally had no opinion of her when she'd first taken the job, but Other Me from Bizarro World had hated her, and told Buchanan to be sure to tell me to keep an eye on Strauss at all times.

That intel had been helpful, and by now I was fairly sure that Strauss was anti-alien, though she was hiding it really well. It was something that I couldn't bring up with Armstrong—he thought Strauss was doing a bang-up job and she was indeed loyal to him. But she took any chance to discredit Jeff or American Centaurion with gusto, though always in a way that appeared to be coming from a place of concern. If we had a leak, mole, or internal enemy who wasn't Langston Whitmore or Cliff Goodman, I was certain Monica Strauss was it.

Once we were gathered, instead of discussing what to do in Florida, or in case of an attack while we were going down to Florida, or even discussing the escaped assassins and such, it was all talk of what we were campaigning about at each stop. In between Armstrong, Ariel, and Strauss all sniffling and looking like they didn't feel all that great. We were apparently going to be bringing the common cold with us as a defensive measure. Well, it had worked in *War of the Worlds*.

I heard the campaigning words, but my mind closed the Ear Windows and wouldn't let any of the boring inside. Instead, since no one else appeared to be worrying about this, I contemplated all the myriad ways our enemies were going to try to attack us. There were so many possibilities that I was completely occupied. At least until I heard my name.

"Sorry?" was all I could come up with.

"I asked your opinion," Armstrong said nicely. Clearly he'd thought I'd been paying attention. Go me for my college Totally Paying Attention Face still being good.

Christopher was in the room, however, and I knew he knew that I hadn't been, because he shot me an award-winning Patented Glare #5. This, of course, told me nothing other than the fact that Christopher felt I'd blown it. Hey, not my fault all the blah, blah, blah was getting to me.

Thankfully, though, Reader, who'd been walking around the room once everyone had started talking and was now opposite me, was the one who shared what was going on. "I know you want Vince to make up his own mind, Kitty, but I think it's important that you share your opinion on whether or not we discuss the Planetary Council's impending arrival at any or all of the various stops we're going to make."

Interesting. I hadn't caught any of this. Clearly my brain needed to open my Ear Windows at least a crack. However, my father had always taught me that if you didn't want to answer, or didn't have an answer, it was always acceptable to answer a question with another question.

"I think the issue is—how much of the Planetary Council's visit are we planning to share with the general population?"

Reader shot me a "good one" look, as Armstrong, Ariel, and Strauss all nodded in that way political types seem to learn quickly—the nod that made you think they were giving whatever you'd said some serious thought.

Strauss was the one who took the question, though. "You've made a good point, Ambassador. We honestly have no idea what the Planetary Council will expect. That's why all of you are along for this particular journey—because we expect you to anticipate their expectations so we can plan accordingly. After all, your first career *was* in marketing. We're asking you for your recommendations for how we spin this."

It was official—Other Me had pegged this woman correctly. Pity she'd had no suggestions for how to deal with her. And it was also a pity that, realistically, Strauss was right—I was probably the one who should be coming up with the right spin.

Raj cleared his throat. "I'm sorry, Ambassador. Due to the circumstances that delayed my arrival, I wasn't able to give you our finalized position papers on this. However, if you'd like me to share them with everyone, I'd be happy to do so."

"Carry on, Raj. That's your bailiwick." Made a mental note that, whatever Raj's salary was, it needed to be doubled the moment we were home.

He turned and gave Strauss a beaming troubadour smile. "American Centaurion is, of course, excited that beings from our original solar system are choosing to come to further strengthen relations with Earth. However, considering this was an impromptu trip on both sides, and since we have the same intelligence as you do, meaning we have no more information about why the Planetary Council has chosen now to visit, we don't want to push any particular agenda."

"Though we're fairly sure that they've picked up the discussions to close NASA Base," White said. "And I'm certain they're concerned about that."

I was certain that White was going to make sure the Planetary Council expressed concerns about the potential closing, whether they knew about it already or were going to find out once White told them about it in such a way that they would insist it remain open and viable.

"Add on the fact that we have prisoners out of supermax," Reader added, "and we're probably better off not giving anyone any ideas."

I was certainly on the side of not giving wacked out assassins and surviving Yates progeny any ideas at all, but I had a feeling they were full of ideas regardless of my thoughts on the matter.

All four of the men now looked at me. Clearly it was time for me to cough up the definitive reply. "Hence, I suggest that we focus on campaigning until we're at NASA Base."

"Is that your recommendation?" Strauss asked. A tad too eagerly for my liking.

Considered options. Decided that, barring Strauss, we were among friends and this was supposed to be the War Room, not the Position Papers Room. And I was already tired of having to act like a politician. Plus, despite the snack from earlier, I was hungry.

"No."

CHAPTER 34

EVERYONE STARED AT ME. "Excuse me?" Strauss said finally.

"I hate campaigning. I think us doing it constantly is a hell of a way to earn a living. I realize that it's par for the political course, but it's not a game I enjoy."

"So you're saying that you think we should, what, share that the Planetary Council is coming?" Strauss seemed thrown by someone speaking honestly. Good.

"I think that you and Ariel and many others spent the last week and definitely the last twenty-four hours getting every possible position for Vince ready. I think you have them. Why you're not sharing them with us is the question."

"We want to know what you've formulated first."

"Why? So you can tell us we're wrong, tell us we're right, or just to keep things interesting on a long journey?"

"Ah, no to all of those, Ambassador. We want to work together. We want to know what you think are the right courses of action. Isn't that what you'd recommend?"

"You want to really know what I think, what I recommend? I think we're wasting a hell of a lot of time. I think we've got escaped murderers out there who are absolutely after everyone on this train. I think we have allies who want to visit us for reasons we don't know. I think three of you are sick, in part because you've probably spent so much time on all this crap. And I recommend we disband and relax until we have to do the ridiculous dog and pony show that's our cover for why we're going down to Florida in the first place."

Strauss had recovered and was trying not to smirk. She wasn't succeeding, but points to her for trying. "Ambassador, you're sounding a bit like a loose cannon."

"That's because I *am* the loose cannon. And what a freaking surprise that totally isn't to everyone in this car. Look, Monica, it's going to be a good two hours until our first stop in Richmond. We can spend that time suggesting and recommending and pussyfooting around. Or you can come right damn out and tell us what you think we should do, and we can agree or disagree."

"We wanted your thoughts—"

"Oh, bullpookey. Let's face it—the moment the first person asks a question about the escaped killers, we're going to be busy sharing how we're ever so confident that law enforcement of all kinds will track them down that we won't have time to mention that we're headed to a reunion party at NASA Base. And what's *your* position on that, Monica?"

She shot a look at Mom. "We regret that our security was breached."

"See, I don't like your tone, or your insinuation. If there was a breach, it was in the Pentagon. Where, frankly, you're supposed to have guards. You, the Secretary of State, along with Secretary of Defense, are who has the responsibility for the supermax, under the Pentagon. Meaning we should be asking you, specifically, Monica, what you're going to do about it. So, what's your plan?"

"Ah . . . I have none. That's not really my area—"

"Bullpookey again. And, let's also face it, you're trying to get us to recommend or suggest, or whatever the hell weasel word you're hoping we'll use, a course of action so that if things go wrong, you'll be able to blame us for it. Just like you're hoping to blame us for the supermax escapees.

You want to set it up so you can blame us if things go wrong, anything and everything."

I leaned across the table toward her. "But, get this straight, right here and right now. You're not 'allowing' us on this trip—*we're* generously allowing *you* to come along. The only people who are friends with and have any influence over the Planetary Council and the rest of the folks in the Alpha Centauri solar system are us. So don't think that you're going to run this show—this is our area of expertise."

This time she did smirk. "So you're accepting responsibility for their actions?"

"Hardly, any more than I'd accept responsibility for your actions, Monica. Because influence doesn't mean we tell them what to do, any more than they tell us what to do. It means we can hope to keep them happy about Earth, or ask them for help, and vice versa. However, I can guarantee that they're coming here right now for a reason. Richard may be right—that reason may be that they're concerned about the status of NASA Base. It *is* the place that's been receiving and, presumably, replying to their messages for decades, after all."

"Gideon Cleary is meeting us in Orlando and will be doing what he can to support keeping that Base open."

"Yes, he is. He's also got influence with all those people trying to close the Base. And yet, for our current example, he can't make them change their minds just because he wants them to, can he?"

I wasn't asking rhetorically. So I waited, keeping eye contact with Strauss and also keeping my mouth shut. Thankfully, I'd trained everyone we worked with in this particular sales technique—once the offer or, in this case, the question was out there, the first person to speak was the loser.

Strauss tried, but, unlike me, her boss was sitting next to her, also not speaking. She gave in. "No. He can't make people change their minds just because he's changed his."

"Exactly. But there may be a whole lot more going on than we know about. There usually is. We can spend the trip guessing wildly, prepping plans for all possibilities, and you and I can literally and figuratively have a cat fight the entire time. Or we can accept that we have a whole lot of smart, competent people on this train, and decide that we'll roll with the punches as they come. I realize that's not the Political Weasel Word of the Day Way, but it's our way, and I strongly *suggest* you try our way for a while."

"We're on the same side, Ambassador."

"No, we're not. Vince is on our side. Ariel is on our side. You? You I'm not convinced are on our side." Felt Jeff and Chuckie both stiffen next to me.

"I'm on the side of what's best for this country and her people," Strauss said firmly. "All her people, and that includes those who have come here from other countries or other planets."

"Nice to hear." I didn't believe it, but the lip service was a pleasant change. "However, when things go wrong, as they always do, if you so much as try to blame American Centaurion for anything up to and including the escaped prisoners or any issues with the visiting aliens from far, far away, then you're going to find yourself on the wrong side of our good will. And that might not be a place you'll like to be."

I leaned back. "Or maybe that's exactly where you want to be. But you will not be making American Centaurion your fall guy for anything."

"American Centaurion is our ally and are our people," Armstrong added.

Strauss nodded. "That's not my intent, Ambassador, and I agree with the President. We are all on the same side here." She picked up the papers in front of her and tapped them on the table. Then she put them face down. "We'll focus on standard campaign discussions, lots of smiling, hand shaking, and waving. This is impromptu, so we're likely to hit very few stops where it's packed. Due to the breakout, however, we can and should expect press, probably more as we get closer to Orlando."

"See?" I asked. "Was that so hard? I agree. I'd suggest we have Raj and Ariel do most of the talking, with Vince and Jeff doing most of the smiling and waving."

"I agree," Strauss said. "And I think that while we want to show that you and the First Lady are along, we don't necessarily want the two of you speaking."

"I wouldn't want the loose cannon speaking either, so no worries there."

Strauss laughed and, for whatever reason, I felt like we'd just crossed some line together. Whether it was a good, bad, or indifferent line I didn't know. "Good point. So, since we're just going to hang out and chat, what are your thoughts about the escaped criminals? Do we have enough security?"

"You can never have enough security, as the escape just amply proved. And my thoughts about the escapees are pretty simple—shoot them on sight, and shoot to kill."

CHAPTER 35

STRAUSS AND ARIEL looked shocked, Armstrong looked concerned. "You're sure?" he asked me.

"Vince, I'm sure they're going to shoot to kill *us*. These are people we've been dealing with since before Operation Destruction. They want us and all of our allies killed. You're an ally and the most powerful man in the world right now. I'd have to figure you and Jeff both have the same targets on your heads."

"I don't know how we add more security than we have without making the population panic," Armstrong said.

"I think we're good with who we have with us." Why mention that I was fairly sure that at least part of Team Assassination was on their way down to Florida to provide backup? Or point out how many of our people were prepared to fight, which was, realistically, everyone other than Vance.

"It's security at each stop that's the issue," Mom said. "We have Secret Service, A-C Field, and P.T.C.U. agents assigned to each station. However, all it takes is one bullet that hits the mark."

"We'll be fine," Jeff said. "Vince, I honestly suggest everyone just relax for this part of the trip. We'll probably all be better off if we're less stressed."

"You'd know, Jeff," Armstrong said. "Let's do what the Vice President suggests."

The meeting broke up with everyone, the President included, heading out toward the dining car. We continued on through our car, and Jeff indicated the others should keep going and we'd catch up. But he kept a hold of Chuckie and Mom both in a surreptitious manner I was pretty sure no one had caught but me.

However, that meant it was going to be obvious that they were hanging back, and I had to figure Jeff didn't want that. "Hey, Mom, Chuckie, can you two hang here for a minute? I have a clothing question."

"Sure, kitten," Mom said. Chuckie nodded.

Armstrong grinned. "Whatever you wear will be fine, Kitty."

"Oh, you say that now, but I guarantee it's not so." We all chuckled and Armstrong and the others kept moving.

Once everyone else was through and it was back to the standard personnel for our car, Jeff turned to me. "You don't like Monica. I know it's because the other version of you didn't like her. Chuck, what's your impression of her?"

"I think she's a political animal of the highest order and has her eyes on your job and then Vince's," Chuckie replied immediately. "But I'm not sure that Kitty should have called her out in this way at this time."

"She should have," Jeff said, voice tight. "Because I didn't pick up any animosity or hatred from Monica, and the stress level was also very low."

"Meaning she's wearing an emotional blocker or overlay," Buchanan said.

Mom's eyes flashed. "You think she was responsible for the breakout?"

"I think the Secretary of State is four heartbeats away from the Presidency, and if you consider that two of those heartbeats are on this train, a third heartbeat was attacked, and the last one, despite current events, is probably not under the highest guard possible, I'd say the odds go up to at least even."

Evalyne and Joseph were both talking into their head-pieces and tapping on their phones. Buchanan was on his phone, too. Evalyne finished first. "We've increased the guard around the Speaker of the House and the President Pro Tempore of the Senate."

"Good," Mom said. "Hopefully it's enough. Good call keeping us back, Jeff, Kitty."

"Thanks. I'm a little attached to Senator McMillan, let's recall. And the Speaker of the House is always nice to us, too."

McMillan had been elected President Pro Tempore a year ago, and he was a huge supporter, meaning Huntress attack or no, his head was definitely in our enemies' sights. Whether or not the Speaker was with us, with our enemies, or neutral I had no idea, but it was probably best to figure neutral and needing protection.

"I don't care if you loathe them," Mom said. "They're not going to be assassinated on my watch if I can help it at all."

"Point taken and agreed with. And, not to point my fingers any more than I already am, but there was that assassination attempt on Senator McMillan last week. Ergo, Strauss moves to the head of the line in terms of suspicion. I do actually have a clothing question, though, Mom."

"Really? What is it?"

I held up my duffel bag. "Is it going to cause a lot of problems if I dress for what I expect to happen?"

"What is it you expect?" Len asked.

I snorted. "Dude, I expect us to be attacked. And I fight better in casual clothes. And before anyone tells me that I'm not supposed to get involved and, instead, stay all safe and protected, I want all of you to consider how often I get that option. Take your time, I'll wait."

The heads in the room collectively nodded and there were several sighs, heaviest from Jeff, Mom, and Chuckie, with the Secret Service's sighs echoing on cue.

"She's right," Chuckie said. "But Kitty, if you're expecting trouble, won't you changing just indicate that and tip off everyone?"

"Oh, you underestimate me. Trust me, I have a plan that will work. Besides, Strauss already knows we're expecting trouble, so if she's in on whatever's going on, her compatriots already know that we know."

Jeff laughed. "No one here underestimates you, baby."

"Awesome. So, let's head for the main dining car and rejoin everyone. I'm starving."

"You just ate," Mom pointed out. "For at least the second time this morning."

"Just accept that I'm part hobbit, Mom. Action and boredom both make me hungry, what can I say?"

We headed for the dining car, but I left my duffel bag in the room. I'd be back for it shortly.

Jeff had everyone else go ahead of us, though of course the Secret Service were trailing to ensure we didn't stop to have sexy times. Haters.

"I know what you're planning," he said quietly to me. "Just try not to affect anyone else. Not even Monica, though I know you'd love to."

"Fine, Stealer of All My Joy."

The main dining car's personnel had also been with the Office of the President for years. Shawn, who was the chef, Janet, who was the cook, and Kenton, the headwaiter, had all been in service for a couple of decades, Kenton for thirty years, the two women over twenty years each. Andrea, the pastry chef, and Wade and Duncan, the other two waiters for the car, had been around for seven years each.

Got my hugs from all of them, then headed in to find a place to sit and eat. Armstrong and Elaine were at a table for four, but they had no one else with them. Clearly the other two seats were for us, based on Armstrong waving us over.

We sat and gave Duncan our food and drink orders. In

deference to the A-Cs' deathly allergy to alcohol, Armstrong had declared Rail Force One as well as Rail Force Two alcohol-free zones.

While we sipped our drinks, it occurred to me that we'd been really lucky so far in one aspect. "You know, I hate to jinx us, but why do you think our enemies haven't just tried slipping vodka into every A-C's drink?"

Armstrong looked concerned. "I thought all A-Cs wore something to determine alcohol content."

"We do." Our scientists had created a sensor that every A-C wore. It attached to any kind of jewelry, and most of them wore the sensor attached to watches, bracelets, and even a few rings. Jeff's was in his watch. They'd been created after Operation Fugly, and everyone wore one, as soon as they were old enough to safely wear jewelry. I wore one in my watch, too, because we weren't sure if alcohol would affect me or not.

A lot of our human personnel wore them, too. Not to protect themselves, but as a catchall for the A-Cs they worked with. But still, mistakes could and did happen, and all it would take was the wrong sip at the wrong time.

"I'd assume our enemies know that's not a way to get to us, baby," Jeff said. "Why are you worried about this all of a sudden?"

"No idea."

Now Jeff looked worried. "Feminine intuition acting up?"

Jeff felt that what my mother called my gut and what I called my Megalomaniac Girl skills was my form of feminine intuition. And he trusted that in me as a gauge of what to worry about, listen to, prepare for, etc.

"I honestly have no idea. I guess it's just because I'm jumpy."

"We have food testers," Armstrong said. "Because there are plenty of poisons. As you well know." As he said this, Duncan brought our meals, though he didn't say anything about poisoning them one way or the other.

"Yeah." A friend of ours had been poisoned at a dinner party we'd thrown, at the start of Operation Sherlock. "As long as they're on the case, and not dying, I think I'm just trying to anticipate the moves. Especially because of Lizzie."

"Lizzie?" Elaine asked. "Who's that?"

"Oh. Right. We haven't caught you guys up on the other things going on." Which Jeff and I proceeded to do, leaving out some key Team Assassination facts.

When we were done, Armstrong's eyes were narrowed. "If Ansom Somerall is involved, I'm with Kitty—we need to be prepared for anything. Her parents creating a super-drug indicates Gaultier, too."

"But until we handle the Planetary Council, NASA Base, and whoever's trying to kill Gideon," Jeff said, "not to mention the escaped prisoners, illnesses and poisonings seem very low on the list of concerns."

Armstrong smiled. "Good point. Jeff, I realize we're hoping we'll get a second term. But when my time as President is done, you need to accept the party's request for you to run."

Jeff groaned. "Vince, I'm not happy being a politician."

"No, but you're happy helping the people of this country, and the world. You're one of the few whose heart, head, and actions are always in the right place. And while you're willing to compromise, you won't give in on the wrong things. And I know Don's told you the same things."

"He has," Jeff admitted. This was true. I'd heard McMillan telling Jeff things like this for years now.

"Well," Elaine said, patting Armstrong's hand, "Jeff will have plenty of time to worry about this, Vince. For now, let's just enjoy our meal and relax until the real action starts."

No sooner did she say this, than the train lurched. And I took my opportunity.

CHAPTER 36

"**C**RAP!" I spilled my drink, which was a brightly multi-colored fruit slushie, onto myself. It looked accidental, but the proof that it wasn't was that I didn't get it onto anyone else at the table.

Of course, those who'd been with me when I'd made this plan were less surprised than they could have been, but they all faked it well enough. Everyone else grabbed their drinks and looked freaked out.

"It's okay, folks," Kenton said reassuringly, as Duncan raced over with a towel to try to help me clean off. "Just hit a bump on the track."

A quick survey of the Secret Service agents on board told me and everyone else this was true. Other tables relaxed and went back to eating.

"I think my clothes need the Operations Team to have a hope of recovery," I said, after Duncan and I had done our best to clean me up, with not a lot of success.

"Did you bring a change?" Elaine asked worriedly.

"Yeah, but not enough to have options if this happens again. And, seeing as it's me, and seeing as trains remain bumpy and I remain klutzy, do you think it's the end of the world if I just change into jeans?"

Armstrong looked at Elaine. Who pursed her lips. "Well . . . we're on a campaigning mission, at least partially, so you won't be dressed appropriately for that. However, you do have a reputation as being laid back and a rebel. So it could work to our advantage, showing that you're going to be you no matter what."

"Then it's settled," Armstrong said. "Do you want to change now or finish your food first?"

"If you don't mind if I use hyperspeed, I'll finish." Why waste any of the great food was my motto.

Armstrong nodded to indicate I could go ahead, which I did. Then I excused myself and headed back to our car, Evalyne and Phoebe coming with me.

"Smooth," Evalyne said once we were in our car. "I honestly don't think anyone who wasn't in on the fact that you were going to do something realized the spill was intentional."

"We're not going to let you leap into anything, you know," Phoebe added.

"As if leaping in is my first choice? And I don't mean that sarcastically. But, we all know the escaped prisoners are going to be coming after us. I'm a lot safer dressed like this." I pulled the Aerosmith shirt on and heaved a contented sigh. I was always better with my boys on my chest.

Considered the Fall Out Boy hoodie. "Think I'm going to need this?"

"If it rains," Phoebe said. "And I checked the humidity index before we left. We'll be heading into some potential showers, though hopefully not at any of our stops."

"I'd leave it here until you need it, though," Evalyne said. "Unless you're chilly from the air conditioning."

Contemplated. "I was hotter in the nice clothes. So, yeah, I'll put it on. Why risk getting a cold?"

"It's a low risk," Evalyne said drily, "but good for you setting the good example for your children, even if they're not here."

"Blah, blah, blah. Everyone's a critic. And since Vince,

Ariel, and Strauss are all sniffling and look crappy, I think the risk of getting a cold is up significantly. Vince has had that cold for at least a week."

Gave Bruno some scritchy-scratches and Ginger some pets, then headed back and got to have dessert with everyone. I'd made it a point to not miss any food of any kind on the train, and Andrea's pastries didn't disappoint.

When we were done, Jeff, Armstrong, Mom, Strauss, Ariel, Raj, and their gaggle of Secret Service and A-C agents went back to the War Room. Mercifully, I was told I wasn't needed, possibly so I wouldn't get into another fight with Strauss.

Regardless of the reason, I was happy to have the downtime. However, hanging out at a table alone was no fun. Moved to join Vance, Claudia, and Lorraine, who were at a table between the one with Reader, Gower, Tim, and Caroline, and the one with Tito, Rahmi, Rhee, and Adriana. Oliver and Stryker were at the two-seater across the aisle, White and Christopher were at the two-seater across from Reader, and Mahin and Abigail were at the two-seater across from Tito.

Buchanan, Len, Kyle, and Falk, who'd been eating at the table behind mine originally, followed me, though they stayed standing around all of us, as did Evalyne and Phoebe.

"Nice of you guys to join the party," Reader said, as I sat down. "The one thing we're lacking is a place that's not called the War Room to hang out with this number of people. The guest cars are great, but they're designed to sit those who are sleeping in each car, not to bring in a party."

"I'm glad we're here," Tim said. "Since I expect an attack at any time."

"They'll wait until we're farther away from D.C.," Lorraine said.

Claudia nodded. "Or try at NASA Base."

"I'm expecting attacks constantly, but that's just me."

"Yeah, speaking of which," Tito said, "what's this we hear about you and the Secretary of State going at it? What happened?"

"It's Kitty," Christopher said. "Why ask why?"

"I don't like her. And I don't trust her, either."

"Think she's on the Mastermind's side?" Gower asked.

"Not sure. I'm certain she's on her own side, though. And that side isn't looking at any of us, Jeff in particular, in a helpful and friendly way."

"That's just politics," Reader said. "Unfortunately."

"Yeah. She was wearing an emotional blocker or overlay, too. Which is business as usual for us. Speaking of which, have we heard anything from anyone regarding all the things going on that we're hoping to prevent?"

Everyone shook their heads. "We've only really been gone around three or four hours, and only about ninety minutes on the train," Reader pointed out. "We'll be hitting Richmond soon, though. You ready?"

"As ready as I'll ever be."

"I'm worried that the President isn't going to be up to this," Tito said. "He looks terrible."

"He doesn't look all that bad, I don't think. He's got some weeklong cold, and I guess he's given it to Ariel and Strauss, but otherwise he looks fine."

"He's in makeup," Tito said flatly. "It's a very good makeup job, but it's still makeup. To hide that he looks ill."

"Really? I hadn't noticed."

"That's not a surprise, and I don't mean that as an insult," Tito added quickly. "But the makeup is good enough that you're not supposed to notice it. I did because I'm a doctor, and I was paying attention to how he looked the moment I heard him sniffle."

"Does that mean he has a makeup person with us?" Tim asked. "Because I didn't spot their name if so, and I went over the passenger list."

Looked to Evalyne who spoke into her wristcom. "Need

verification of who's handling Slick's hair and makeup on this trip. Huh, you're sure Sophistication is handling those duties? Really? Okay, thanks. Yes, reassure Playboy that Cyclone is contained. For now."

"I resent that. And tell them to say hi to Cosmos for me."

The Secret Service assigned code names to their charges, as shorthand and a form of protection. They used those names when they were talking to each other about us, but when we were just having normal person conversations they managed to use our real names. Names were also assigned by letter, so if your main person's nickname started with a B, anyone and everyone under their protection detail got B names as well.

Armstrong had landed his family a set of S names, and Jeff had gotten his C names. Jamie was Cutiepie and Charlie was Challenger. Chuckie, because of who he was to us and what his cover was for the C.I.A., had gotten the Playboy moniker.

Evalyne shook her head. "You two have been apart for less than five minutes."

"Jeff and I like spending time together. Anyway, so the word is that Elaine is doing Vince's hair and makeup? Isn't that hella unusual?"

"It is," Phoebe replied. "Almost as unusual as you being contained."

"Ha ha ha, this is me laughing uproariously. Seriously, though, doesn't that seem odd, especially because we're stumping *and* meeting alien dignitaries?"

Tito looked more worried. "I think it signifies that the President has more than a cold."

Reader and Gower exchanged a look, and both of them looked at White, who nodded. "I'll see what I can learn from the First Lady when we have a moment." As I'd slowly learned, White was a ladies' man of the highest order. If anyone was going to get state or family secrets out of Elaine, it'd be him.

"Good," Gower said. "I'll speak to the President when there's an opportune time, as well."

The train jerked a little, and Wade called to us from the kitchen area. "We're pulling into Richmond, folks. Think you might want to get to wherever you need to be for this stop."

Phoebe checked her watch. "We're a little early."

"Is that good, bad, or indifferent?"

She shrugged. "That all depends on what's waiting there for us."

"Ah," Gower said. "So, routine."

CHAPTER 37

THE THING ABOUT campaign stumping was that you weren't using the train like normal people did, to get from one location to another. Using the train to campaign meant stopping where you could be seen, preferably out in the open.

The special thing about how we were doing it was that we hadn't done a lot of publicity leading up to this particular dog and pony show. The reasons for this lack were good, but it meant that, at least at the first few stops, there might be no reason *to* stop.

Both of these things meant that we weren't going into the train station so much as pulling up, getting out, and stretching our legs, while casually looking around for people to impress and being shocked, just shocked, if there were people there to press the flesh in an impromptu manner.

Richmond had a nice station, and, thankfully, an area where we could indeed stop and get out that left us outside but not overwhelmingly exposed.

We exited from the cars we were in—the crowd, such as it was, wasn't large enough to have Armstrong and Jeff bother to campaign from the caboose.

The weather was pleasant, but I felt the humidity in the

air. Hoped I wouldn't be sweating like a pig shortly — I was
a desert dweller by birth and preference and I liked my heat
dry, thank you. Humidity and I weren't pals, and I could
already feel my hair starting to go limp.

We didn't have a large crowd but there were people mill-
ing about, some of whom seemed very excited to see us, or
at least Armstrong and Jeff. Those two started shaking
hands, giving out hugs, and taking selfies with various people almost immediately.

No one seemed to spot me, and Elaine wasn't being
bothered either, so I figured we weren't going to be doing
the Wives' Show Of Support Bit right now.

Spent the time, therefore, looking around. Not only to
see the station, but to see if there was anyone lurking somewhere. A group of assassins out of prison made me nervous
for some strange reason.

But, look though I did, I didn't spot anyone who looked
familiar, threatening, or was where they shouldn't be.

Got dragged over to shake some paws, which I did. No
one asked why I was dressed casually and I didn't offer any
explanations, either. Just figured that someone would take
a picture, post it, and then all the social media outlets would
have a field day. It kept them occupied and off the streets,
so whatever.

There were a couple reporters there, but they seemed far
more excited that the President and VP both were there
than anything else. Lots of pictures, professional and otherwise, were taken, but this wasn't a surprise — Jeff sort of
drew the camera's attention naturally. Being the hottest
thing on two legs tended to garner that response.

I wasn't the only one keeping an eye on things, of course.
The Secret Service were doing a good showing of standing
around looking quietly menacing. Plus Alpha Team was
here and, though Gower and White were both still on the
train, Reader, Tim, Lorraine, and Claudia were all out and

keeping an eye on things. Several of the A-C agents were zipping around at hyperspeed checking everything in the vicinity.

Christopher was also out and ready. He'd done a perimeter search before the others, and was waiting for any projectile of any kind to get tossed toward any of us, himself included.

We were all dressed up with nothing to fight, though. Didn't know whether to be relieved or let down. Tried for relieved.

Didn't spot any of the agents Mom had said would be here, but presumably that was because they were hidden or hiding in plain sight. Did spot the light rain when it started, which gave us all a reason to end things here.

Uneventful stop at Richmond over, it was back on the train and off to Petersburg. No one bothered with the War Room this time—we all congregated in the dining car or the caboose, depending. We barely had time to sit and sip a beverage and then we were there.

Petersburg's station was much plainer, though still nice. And, as with Richmond, while there were some people there, there weren't a lot of them, and no one was lurking about.

Once again we got out, did some waving, took some pictures, talked to some people, shook some paws, got slightly wet, and got back into the train. So far, no one had cared how I was dressed.

With two stops in the win column, we were feeling pretty good when we got back into the train cars. Well, most of us were feeling pretty good. Armstrong, Ariel, and Strauss were all feeling crappy. Felt bad for Armstrong and Ariel.

Tito waited until everyone was back inside, then he cornered the three of them. "You're all sick, and you're all trying to pretend you're not. I'm watching you get sicker by the minute. All of you need to go back to your quarters and get some rest, you especially, Mister President."

They started to argue, but Elaine stepped in. "Doctor Hernandez is right. Vince, you look ready to drop, and Monica, you're not doing much better. Ariel, let's not let you get as bad as these two, okay? All of you, let's head for our car and let the doctor do his work. Rocky Mount is our next stop and that gives everyone a good two hours or so of rest."

Strauss and Ariel looked like they were going to continue to protest, but Armstrong nodded. "You're both right." He gave the other two a weak smile. "Let's get that rest."

Everyone in the President's car headed off and Tito went with them. Told Manfred and the rest of my A-C detail to go with Mom, which they did. Some others wandered toward their cars, but most of us stayed in the main dining car. Chuckie watched them go, eyes narrowed.

"What?" I asked him quietly.

"Could be nothing."

"It usually isn't."

He rubbed the back of his neck. "I'm just wondering who else is sick." He shook himself. "I'm going to make some calls, Kitty. I'll be back." Chuckie strode off toward the front of the train.

Jeff and Raj were having a quiet discussion and I joined them. It turned out they were discussing policy. I kissed Jeff and quickly left them alone.

For whatever reason, I didn't feel like chatting with anyone, so headed for the more private dining car, where I found White and Gower with the requisite Secret Service and A-C guards. Couldn't complain—my shadows were with me, too.

Joined them for drinks and snacks, while I indicated that Len, Kyle, Evalyne, and Phoebe should all take a load off, too, which they did, albeit unwillingly. Lincoln bustled over to get our orders. I did love the food options on the train.

"Guys, slavish devotion to duty is great, but if there's one thing I've learned from hanging with these guys," indicated White and Gower, "it's to take the rest times when you find them."

White chuckled. "Good to know you've picked something up, Missus Martini."

"You thinking it's going to be action time soon?"

Gower sighed. "No guess, honestly. I'm relieved nothing's happened so far. However, the smart money says that's not going to last."

We had a light tea service, which was very nice. You'd never have known that I'd eaten not too long ago. I was hungry again. Oh well, I didn't want anyone working on the train to think I wasn't appreciative of their efforts, after all.

"You pregnant again?" Gower asked me as I ate my third scone.

"Not that I know of, why?"

"You're eating a lot."

"She always does when action looms," White pointed out. "I believe it's due to her enhanced metabolism."

"Aren't you sweet? No, it's because I really like food. But, yeah, I expect to work this off somewhere in the near future, Paul, thanks for the concern."

He grinned. "Just wanted to make sure we shouldn't be sidelining you for an important reason."

Raj came through on his way to see if Ariel was awake or not, and he stopped to chat with us about the likelihood that there was some new danger looming that the Alpha Centauri system wanted our help with.

More stress we couldn't do anything about done, Raj headed off for Rail Force One and I decided all the talk of naps along with tea and scones had made me sleepy, so I excused myself and headed for our car, Len, Kyle, Evalyne and Phoebe naturally going with me. Of course, the idea of napping with four people watching over me like I was the oldest kid in daycare wasn't that appealing.

Make that six people. Got into my car to find Buchanan and Chuckie there. They both looked a little stressed, but as soon as we arrived Chuckie took off, after telling me to have a good nap.

So, I settled into one of the comfy chairs we had and sort of dozed. For about five minutes.

Pulled out my earbuds and my iPod. Sure, my phone had all my music in it, too, and my earphones were able to answer calls, too, but I was still emotionally attached to my iPod. But I might not hear my phone if it rang, and considering my children were basically home alone without me, I didn't think that was a good idea.

Kyle came over. "Hey, I made a playlist for you," he said, sounding a little embarrassed. Kyle ran my iPod whenever I wasn't in charge of the sound system, and he controlled the music in the limos and the Embassy for the most part, too, since he was clear on what I liked.

"Really? That's very sweet of you."

He grinned. "Just seemed like you were going to need something special." He took my phone and fiddled with it along with his. "There, it's sent, and set up."

"Modern technology is the greatest. By the way, are you insinuating I should be listening to tunes now?"

He shrugged. "It relaxes you and you can still pay attention even if you have earbuds in. So, yeah."

"And this is why you're my favorite."

Did as Kyle suggested, dropped my iPod back into my purse, and plugged my earbuds into my phone. Sure, it wasn't my normal thing, but I could adapt and get with the new ways. And this way, I wasn't going to be a terrible mother and miss any important calls or texts while I, hopefully, fell asleep so as to dream through the boredom that this trip was becoming.

Kyle had created a Trains, Planes, and Automobiles

playlist for me. Made sure the volume was low, hit play, and let the music start.

Heard exactly six bars of UB40's "She Caught the Train" when my phone rang. Always the way.

And, in keeping with how my life rolled, the number was blocked.

CHAPTER 38

APPARENTLY USING the phone instead of the iPod had been the way to go. Answered, using my nifty earbuds' call answer thingy, which I was sure was the technical term. "Hello?"

There was no sound on the other end.

Gave it another go, just in case this was a telemarketer. "Hello? We probably don't want any, whatever it is."

Still no sound.

Contemplated the options. Hung up. And the music started right back up. I was impressed—the music had put itself on hold, so I wasn't missing a thing sonically. One for the win column. Sure, it was a small, almost insignificant one, but I'd learned a long time ago to take whatever wins I could get and treasure them.

Stood up and turned to Buchanan and the boys, who were all looking at me while I slid my phone into my front pocket and put my purse over my neck. "Expect imminent attack imminently." Sent a mental message to Bruno and Ginger and any Poofs who might be listening in on the Kitty Channel.

"From whom and where?" Buchanan asked.

"Blocked number just called with no one on the other end. The last time that happened I almost died." The last time that had happened, frankly, had been at the end of

Operation Drug Addict, and the person on the other end of the line had been Leventhal Reid, using GPS to find where I was.

Sure, the Ronald Yates/Mephistopheles in-control superbeing had been bad. Sure LaRue Demorte Gaultier was, as it turned out, an Ancient, a shape-shifting alien bent on working with her own race's mortal enemies, and ours, the Z'porrah. And sure, Cliff Goodman was the Mastermind. And there was a long list of other evil baddies we'd faced and some we'd face again.

But there was no one, on any planet so far, who personified evil in the way that Leventhal Reid did. He was like a human snake, the venomous kind, and I was terrified of snakes.

"I have no idea from whom, but I have a guess. As for where, wherever my phone signal is, is my best guess."

The door opened and Jeff came running in. "Whatever blocker Monica has on, it isn't blocking anyone other than her. What's wrong? Where is he?"

"He who?" Evalyne asked.

"Leventhal Reid," Jeff snarled.

"He's dead," Phoebe reminded him as Joseph and Rob ran in. Clearly Jeff had used hyperspeed to get to me and they'd just taken good guesses at to where he'd gone. "I realize you feel there's at least one clone of him around, but from what you've told us, that clone would still be an adolescent."

"No. Those clones were on the fast-aging plan. Reid could be my age now. Frankly, he could even be older. And that might not have been him. But I think it was someone trying to get a position on where we are."

No sooner said than I heard the distinct thump of something—or, more likely, someone—landing on our roof. And then another. And another.

Jeff and I looked at each other. Then took off running. At hyperspeed, of course.

The War Room car doubled as the safe house for the train. But Armstrong and Elaine, and my mother, were in Rail Force One, not in the War Room.

Jeff and I were headed for the same car, and we slammed through the War Room like it wasn't even there and were in the President's car in less than a second. Which was good, because I heard more thumps on the roof. Had a really good guess for who was hitching a ride on this train, and it wasn't hobos.

We got there in time to hear Evalyne shouting over the walkie-talkie. "Get Slick and Sophistication into the War Room, STAT!"

Oh, sure, this wasn't really direction being given to me and Jeff, but since we were there already, we grabbed them and anyone around them—which meant Jeff had Armstrong and Tito, who had the presence of mind to grab both his medical bag and Ariel, and I had Elaine and Mom, who grabbed Strauss—and took off.

Heard Raj shout to have everyone link hands, and he and the rest of the A-Cs were right behind us with the rest who's been in or around the President, including Grady, who was the President's steward.

Raj slammed the forward door shut and hit the special locking mechanism. No one was getting in from that side without a blowtorch and several months of time or a gigantic bomb. Sadly, I figured our enemies had Plan B on their persons.

As he did so, those who'd been in our car came running in, Len dragging Javier behind him, Kyle shooing the private dining car's staff ahead of him.

Knew what was going to happen if we let it. The Secret Service, the boys, and Buchanan were all going to try to keep me and Jeff in this car. But there were people on this train, all of them included, who didn't have the skills, the talents, the experience, and most importantly, the fast healing regeneration that Jeff and I did.

We might be able to get all of the civilians in here in time—we had enough A-Cs here to do it. But, when it came down to it, in this situation, we really only had one goal—to keep the President safe.

"You're both staying here now," Buchanan said to me and Jeff, right on cue. "Lock it down," he told Joseph, who was nearest to the door. And Joseph leaped to do just that.

Jeff grabbed my hand and we took off, though we stopped at the edge of the dining car. The door slammed behind us and the locking mechanism clicked in. "Boy, are they going to be pissed at us."

Jeff grinned. "Let's ensure that we stay alive and unharmed then, baby."

"Thanks for not trying to make me stay there, by the way."

"And the same to you. I just know you too well and I didn't want to have to hear about it for the rest of my life."

"Freedom Train" by Lenny Kravitz came on and I realized we'd really moved fast, which was the idea. "Figure it's the Crazy Eights on the roofs." Paused the music and listened. Didn't hear any more footsteps. Started the music up again. "They're going to spread out some of them, concentrate some of them on the War Room, and someone's going to go to the front of the train. All of them are killers and most of them are hybrids."

"It's never easy, is it, baby?"

"Or, as we call it, routine."

CHAPTER 39

"WE NEED TO GET the civilians into some form of safety," I told Jeff as we headed for our car. I had an ocellar and a Peregrine to pick up.

Only the animals weren't in our car. Before I could fret about this, though, we had something else to occupy our attention—one of the Crazy Eights was coming in from the back of the car, impressive gun at the ready.

It was Nerida Alfero, the water-bending chick. There wasn't a lot of water around. Felt fairly confident I could take her.

Did my best to send Jeff a mental message that we had to get the civilians protected in some way, keep Gower safe, and the rest of our people mobilized, and he'd be better at doing that than I would. Plus Jeff might have some issues hitting a woman, and I had less than none.

Of course, I had to clear the path for him. So, you know, I charged. And as I did, my music changed to "Prize Fighter" by the Killers. Had to guess this wasn't on the playlist Kyle had created, meaning I was now on the Algar Channel. Worked for me.

She started shooting, but I was, by now, seriously pissed, and the skills always worked better when I was channeling She-Hulk. Dodged the bullets that looked like very slow-moving pebbles, slammed into her, and wrenched the gun away from her. Tossed it to Jeff as he took off as mentally requested. We were a well-oiled politically incorrect team.

You'd think that someone who'd been rotting in the deepest supermax prison the government had would be out of shape. Apparently she was on the Thug Life Workout Plan, because chick had learned some moves.

We were doing some impressive hand-to-hand fighting. But it didn't stop her from talking. "We're here to end you murdering scum." She threw a right, I blocked it, and punched her in the stomach.

"Hypocrite much? You're all about being murdering scum." Hey, if it was a Talk While You Kick Ass fight, I was damned well going to represent. Tried to sweep her legs but she jumped out of the way.

"You killed my family." She landed and tried for a groin shot. I did a backward somersault.

"This again? No, I didn't, and anyway, they're no more or less your family than other people on this train." She was charging but I stayed down and did an upward kick as she got near. She flew back but landed on her feet. "And we had this discussion before. As I recall, you lost. Big time."

She smirked. "There's losing that's not really losing, you know." She did a rather impressive leaping scissors-kick. But I could tell she'd only done this in practice, never in real combat, because all I did was step out of the way, so all she crashed into was the dining table in our car.

Time to keep her talking, apparently, especially while she was struggling out of the table wreckage. Decided to play it smart and not charge in, in case she grabbed a table leg or something. "Sure there is. And then there's losing and really losing, like you and the other Crazy Eights are going to experience. Again, I might add."

Heard the sounds of gunfire nearby as the music changed to "Crossfire" by Brandon Flowers. Apparently Algar was in a Killers mood. I was certainly one with Brandon's band's name right now. Just hoped that my side would be the one doing the killing.

Based on noises and musical cues, had to figure I was needed elsewhere. But also had to figure I needed to make sure Nerida wasn't an issue.

She heard the gunfire, too, and smirked again as, sure enough, she came up with a table leg. Sometimes I was psychic, really. "It's hard to lose when you have insider information." She came out swinging, I backed up ducking.

"Tell that to Martha Stewart. Anyway, what information could you losers possibly have?"

Guns blazing elsewhere or not, this info I probably needed to get out of her. Ducked another swing, trapped her arm between mine and my body while I gave her a roundhouse elbow to the face, stomped on her foot, and, as I backed away, wrenched the table leg out of her hand. As always when the skills were totally impressive, there was no one I cared about impressing around to see it.

"We know how to get into the car you think is all locked up nice and safely." She grabbed décor and started throwing it at me. At not quite hyperspeed. Not at the slow version of it, just really fast. And yet, not *that* fast. There was something going on with these hybrids, something that hadn't been there before.

Thankfully, Algar didn't play "Something There" from the *Beauty and the Beast* soundtrack, but it was now singing harmony in my head along with Brandon.

Fortunately, Nerida tossing crap at me brought me back to the moment. Dodged glasses, batted a vase back at her, and backhanded a lamp in her general direction. I was a switch hitter, just like I was a switch hurdler. Not, again, that anyone was around to draft me for the Diamondbacks.

"You mean you have a traitor Secret Service agent and he has some intel that's giving all of you a very false sense of security." I sincerely hoped.

She smirked again as she threw more stuff at me. Apparently this was her fave facial expression ever. "No. Sam's given us a very real look into how the security around all of you is managed."

"When he was on our detail, sure. You seriously think we didn't mix it up to keep the bad guys guessing after he was incarcerated?" I again sincerely hoped.

We'd changed up how we did things, but whether the Secret Service had or not wasn't something I'd paid attention to. Added it onto the list of all the important things I didn't pay attention to until well after the fact and carried on by landing a great front ball kick to her stomach combined with my slamming the table leg against her head.

She flew back into a chair. Happily the force of my kick flipped her and the chair over, just as someone else arrived and "Jumping Someone Else's Train" by the Cure came on. It was White, and he grabbed my hand without comment and zoomed us out of there.

"Nice to see you, too, Mister White. I hadn't finished that fight." We went through the dining car. No one inside it, which was another tiny one for the win column.

"She looked down and hopefully out and, if not, I just assume you'll finish it later, Missus Martini, and in style. However, we're needed and there's no one who does what we're going to have to better than the two of us."

"I see the future by looking at the past. We're going on top of the train, aren't we?" We'd reached the War Room but didn't try to get in. The sound of gunfire was much louder and closer.

"We are. Mister Falk is trying to get to the engine to protect the engineer and crew from our enemies and he's in need of assistance."

"How did he get past me? You're the only one who's come through."

"He was in the forward personnel car and called back to us to alert us that we were under attack."

"How?"

"We have these amazing devices called cellular phones. Perhaps you've heard of them?" White's sarcasm knob definitely went to eleven. "Burton has all our numbers programmed in. And, unlike some people, he used his ability to dial."

"Oh, right. And bitter much? Jeff and I were busy getting people to safety."

"Yes, so he explained when he reached us. While we were talking to Burton on speakerphone."

"Gotcha. Sorry, I've just gotten so used to everyone talking into the air or at their wrists and lapels that someone using the phone to do something other than determine my position via GPS seems totally old fashioned."

"Duly noted. In case you're wondering, we're under attack at the rear of the train as well as up here, we're trying to protect the civilians who aren't in the safe room car, and Jeffrey and Christopher may not yet be aware that I'm not there anymore."

"Wise man is the sneakiest, I've always said it. Totally off topic, in that sense, but have you seen Ginger or Bruno?"

"No, I have not, nor have any Poofs made an appearance."

"I'd complain about this, but when they're AWOL they're usually off doing something else key, so I'll just assume that's the case and find the will to go on."

"That's the spirit." White took hold of the ladder.

"You know . . ." Rummaged around in my purse and grabbed the goggles. "I have these in here sort of randomly. Now seems like it might be a good time to wear them."

"Yes, probably."

Slipped them on. They might have been night vision or something else vision, but I could see well through them, so that was all that mattered. They were holding my earbuds in place, so that was another one for the win column.

Noted White trying not to laugh. "How do I look?"

"I don't want a pair, if you have extras along."

"I don't. It's really that bad a look?"

"If it's a choice between those or a catsuit, always choose catsuit. Don't risk a glance in a mirror and you'll be fine. I'm going up first. Please be prepared to pull me down quickly." With that, he started up the ladder on the outside of the car.

I was right behind him, and I was ready to grab and pull. But he was looking forward and I figured one of us had better be looking behind, especially when "Back, Back Train" by Aerosmith came on my airwaves. Either that or Algar wasn't helping anymore and I was back on the playlist Kyle had made for me. Gave it even odds for either option.

So, Algar helping or not, I wasn't all that surprised when I saw someone coming up on the roof of the car we'd just left.

CHAPTER 40

JUMPED FROM THE ladder on the War Room car to the corresponding ladder on the dining car. The gaps weren't bad and it didn't even feel scary. Much. Climbed up and flipped onto the roof in time to use my body to sweep the guy's legs out from under him.

Happily, this wasn't Falk. Happily also, this appeared to be Russell Kozlow, at least as far as I could tell from a brief glance, since he'd gone flat on his face.

Unhappily, he still had hold of his big gun, and also unhappily, hold of my left ankle.

Decided that if he died I'd find a way to apologize to Chernobog and kicked his head hard with my right foot. He didn't let go but his hold loosened. Kicked again using hyperspeed, so I was doing it a lot and very fast, while taking in what I could see.

There were two people behind Kozlow and, as I looked up and over, two people ahead of White. However, they weren't all that far ahead. And they were pointing very large guns down at the roof of the car and shooting, which was where the sound of gunfire had come from.

The War Room car was incredibly reinforced, but nothing was invincible. And far too many people I cared about were inside of it.

As the music changed to "Boys Wanna Fight" by Garbage, I kicked super hard and Kozlow let go. Scrambled to my feet as Kozlow slid down and toward the side.

Amazingly enough, there appeared to be no bridges or low overhangs coming that I could see. Was shocked to my core that the universe was doing me and White such a solid, but chose not to argue about it, lest said solid be whisked away with a low tunnel made of sharp rocks and rusty iron.

However, what we were lacking in bridges and such was more than made up for by an incredible amount of foliage on the sides, nothing that looked soft to land on should we fall off, and the big, nasty-looking helicopter that was above us.

It was clearly a stealth chopper, because it really wasn't making a racket. And while it did kick up wind, it didn't kick up nearly as much as I'd experienced in other circumstances.

Figured Wruck was the pilot—couldn't really see who was up there, but we'd now proved that hybrids with enough of the Yates Super Gene in them could handle human machinery if they worked at it, and my gut said that Wruck had the stick.

Ran and leaped across the gap in my best sprinter's hurdling stance. Landed and was able to grab White and take him down just as one of the people shooting at the roof turned and shot toward us.

Naturally we didn't luck out and the bullets didn't hit Kozlow. I could see this because White and I slid into the gunmen and, due to the speed I'd been going and the fact that while the roofs of the cars weren't soaked, they were a bit slick from the rain we'd gone through, flipped over and around. So I was now looking at the back of the train. We had a lot of people on the roof.

On the plus side, my smooth move had made both

gunmen lose hold of their weapons. Neither White nor I were able to grab the guns, though I tried, which was a mistake.

The grab shifted me on an already slick surface and I was now sliding off our roof and so lost interest in everyone and everything else. Unlike the nice train in France that White and I had apparently used as a practice run for right now, these train cars didn't have railings on top or much of anything to grab onto.

Belayed nostalgia for Operation Confusion and instead tried to get a hand- or foothold on anything, with limited success. Was able to see that the bullets had made some inroads into the roof's surface, too. Not a lot—certainly not enough for me to get a good hold while I was sliding around—but enough to indicate that the roof was penetrable with enough firepower focused on it.

Just as I was about to go off the side, White managed to grab my arm and I grabbed the leg of one of the shooters. Who, as he slid toward me, I realized was Kellogg, the guy who'd tried to kill both Mrs. Maurer and Jeff during Operation Defection Election.

Kellogg kicked at me. Unlike Kozlow, I let go instantly, which meant that Kellogg actually shoved himself closer to the edge. Worked for me.

What didn't work for me was the math I was seeing. We had a lot more than the people I'd been expecting to attack us up here. We had a full-on raiding party on the roof, and that wasn't counting our people who were also on the roof.

Ours were easy to spot, since I was literally the only one in jeans. Everyone else, humans included, was in the Armani Fatigues, looking spiffy while fighting crime and hopefully not falling off a moving train.

Who I couldn't spot were Jeff, Christopher, Gower, or Chuckie. This might mean that they were staying safely inside, protecting the Supreme Pontifex and Vice President.

to ~~ted it. Inside, yes. Being protected, no. Protecting
made it ~ho weren't in the safe room car, on the other
~y possible. Maybe Chuckie had managed

White drag~ compromise. Maybe I'd find out if I
gunman had run o~ticular gauntlet.
thought that he was pro~ middle of the car. The other

The majority of those ridi~ ~he front. Wasn't positive, but
the back six cars. There were so ~air bender, Darryl Lowe.
dered how the roofs weren't caving in. ~of rails were on top of
was that the only people on our side who we~ ~hat that meant
cars were me, White, and, as I looked forward, Falk. But he
was fighting someone on the car closest to the engine, and
Lowe was headed right for them.

"We have to get to Falk," I shouted to White. I was hella
glad I had the goggles on, because the wind was unpleasant
and White was wincing. That'd teach him to diss my fashion-
forward look.

White nodded, pointed, then shoved me behind him. Because, of course, Kozlow had recovered, was on this car with
us, and had helped keep Kellogg from sliding off. And Kozlow still had his gun.

Grabbed White's hand, yanked him hard, and ran for the
next car. We could destroy Rail Force One inside or out if
necessary, but we needed to get them away from the War
Room.

We jumped and landed well, go team. My music changed
to Public Enemy's "Party For Your Right To Fight." Which
worked, since Kozlow and Kellogg were also up and had
jumped onto this car with us. But that meant no one was
shooting at the car the President was in anymore, and that
was definitely one for the win column.

Decided to keep on running and try to get to Falk. We
used the time-honored serpentine move that worked in that
no bullets hit us, but that was probably because Kozlow

232

Gini Koch

wasn't able to aim well since whatever pa... ...alk was were on was really bumpy. ... ...Service spy.

Leaped and landed on the oth..., though. fighting Dear Sam Travis, aka ...uch worse.

Lowe wasn't actually engaged ...

What Lowe was doing w...

CHAPTER 41

LOWE WAS AHEAD of Falk and Dear Sam, and I could tell by his posture—arms out and hands curved in—that he was starting up his air bending. And if he could get a big enough gust of wind going—and experience said that he could—then he could derail the train.

Would have loved to have tackled him, but we had Dear Sam, Kellogg, and Kozlow to handle first. And they were definitely interested in keeping us away from Lowe.

Did my best to send an emotional message to whatever empaths, Jeff included, who might be able to pay attention. Focused a lot of longing on Mahin and Christopher. She'd been able to counter what Lowe had done during Operation Infiltration, and Christopher was the one who trained both her and me. Plus the fastest man alive was always useful.

However, I couldn't spend a ton of time on this because, as my music changed to "Fight" by Motörhead, Kellogg lunged for me while Kozlow went for White. Apparently they'd decided to switch it up and keep us guessing.

Fighting on a moving train was both exactly as it looked in the movies and nothing like how it looked in the movies at the same time. The danger, wind, slipperiness, and all-around disorientation of this situation was pretty much as the movies showed it to be. But the inability to really practice the "sweet science" or any form of martial arts didn't line up with what Hollywood had always told me.

Pop culture betrayal aside, the biggest positive was that no one else up here had spent time prepping by fighting on the tops of moving trains, and I could say this with some certainty since the bad guys were having as much trouble as White, Falk, and I were.

We hit at each other, then the force of the hits knocked us off balance and we spent some hilarious yet terrifying time trying to stay on the train or clawing to get back onto the top of the train, assisted by our allies. Those with guns had given up trying to shoot them—the risk was too high that we'd hit someone on our side.

"This is ridiculous," I shouted to White as he and I each managed to grab Falk's arms before he fell over the edge. "We need a new plan." Rod Stewart's "Street Fighting Man" came on. Resisted the desire to tell Algar that he wasn't helping.

"I'm open to ideas," Falk said, as we dragged him over and White landed an impressive upward kick into Kozlow's stomach, which caused Kozlow to knock into Kellogg and White to slip toward the train's side.

"I'd like us to figure out how to fight like Jackie Chan or Tom Cruise do on the tops of these things, and I'd love us to do it right now." Managed to sweep Dear Sam's feet out from under him right before he gave it a go anyway and tried to shoot us.

Happily he lost hold of his gun and that went off the side. Unhappily it was now my turn to, once again, start sliding off. And, so far, we had no cavalry showing up to save the day. Meaning it was all going to be up to us. Always the way.

We were now in some foliage that made what we'd been through already look tame. Something dropped onto the roof between us and Kellogg and Kozlow.

"Holy Mary Mother of God . . . is that a *snake*?" I

screamed this at the top of my lungs because it damn well was a snake and I was terrified of snakes.

"Jesus!" This was from Kellogg. "It's a copperhead!" He started screaming just like I was. How nice. A bonding moment.

"Calm down, it's just a snake," Kozlow said, earning my lifelong enmity.

Heard another scream from behind me. Turned to see Dear Sam freaking out because, lucky us, more snakes had landed on the other side of us, between us and him.

"Stay calm," Falk said to me and White. "They're probably falling out of the trees from the rains. They won't attack unless they're provoked."

"They fell out of the freaking *trees*! They are venomous attack snakes bent on murdering us all and I am officially not having any of it! Do you hear me? I did not sign up for this!"

White squeezed my hand. "We're faster than them, Missus Martini. I promise."

"I'd like to keep on screaming, okay? I'll run away much faster that way. Promise." A horrible thought occurred. "You realize that if we fall off there are snakes lurking in the trees and on the ground, waiting to finish us off."

"I'm more worried about the train and the people on it killing us," Falk said. "We can deal with the snakes."

"I can't. At all."

Dear Sam was backing up, doing his own form of freaking out. So he didn't realize that he was backing up into Lowe. Decided not to warn him, just to show that, terrified or not, I could still focus on the mission.

Kozlow really wasn't afraid of the snakes, and I could prove this by the fact that he kicked the one between him and us toward us. Showing that it was truly an evil murderer snake, it didn't strike at him but slithered closer to us. Decided Kozlow had to die, and die ugly.

As my screams reached the register that only dogs could hear, Dear Sam knocked into Lowe. Lowe fell forward and Dear Sam fell backward. They disappeared. Either they were between this car and the engine or they were dead. Had to figure that our luck indicated they'd both survive somehow.

"Try to talk to it," White suggested.

"I can't. Seriously. I cannot do that." During Operation Civil War I'd been able to sort of feel the snakipede's minds on Planet Colorful. But I hadn't been able to influence them in any way. There was no way I was going to be able to get the concentration going that I'd need to have.

Opened my mouth to scream again, only something else screamed for me. Looked up to see Bruno flying overhead, carrying Ginger in his claws. He dropped her and she landed near me.

Ginger snarled like I'd never heard her do before, and then she attacked the snake Kozlow had kicked toward us.

Was about to panic when Bruno cawed again, reminding me that a cat that had been trained from birth to fight and kill giant snakipedes that were venomous and could fly was not going to have a problem with a copperhead, no matter how dedicated the snake might be to survival.

Sure enough, Ginger moved in the way all cats can and do—murderously fast. She had the snake ripped to shreds in seconds. Then she spun and headed for the other snakes. And my music changed to "Bang, Bang," by K'naan, with Adam Levine helping out on the high notes.

Forced myself to dig into my purse and get my Glock out at hyperspeed, which wasn't hard since I was so revved up on Snake Terror Adrenaline. Got my gun out in time to see Kozlow aiming his gun for Ginger.

Aimed and did the rapid-fire technique Mom had taught me. Sadly, due to the movement of the train I missed him completely, but I hit the gun. The force of ten bullets hitting it knocked the gun from his hands and it skittered off and fell over the edge.

Aimed for him again. "No one shoots at my animals you bastard!"

Kozlow put his hands up and backed up. Thought he was going to jump or run, but apparently this was a signal and the chopper lowered and dropped a rope ladder. He grabbed onto it and Kellogg, now that Ginger had killed the snakes, managed to lurch into action and caught the ladder just before it was out of his reach. The chopper raised up.

I pointed my gun at them all anyway, but White gently pushed my hand down. "Save the ammunition. We have more to deal with here."

"Where are the flyboys? I thought Tim said they'd be in the air."

Falk nodded. "They were scrambled when we got onto the train. I heard Crawford give the order myself."

"I'd like to know where the hell all these other people attacking us came from, too. It would be nice to get some help up here."

White and Falk stared at me as Ginger came over to re-assure me that she was on the snake case and Bruno landed next to us. "What other people?" Falk asked finally.

"On the roof. Fighting our people."

They both stared behind us. "I see only our people and one other, Missus Martini. I think it's Annette Dier, but I can't be positive."

"Are you kidding me? There are a ton of people on the top of this train."

Falk shook his head. "Maybe your goggles are faulty."

Or maybe they weren't for wind, or night vision, or anything else. Maybe they were a very special gift from Algar that allowed me to see either ghosts or people who were cloaked. Gave it even odds for both. My music changed to

"Invisible Touch" by Genesis, so perhaps the odds were better for cloaking.

But there was one way to find out. "Get forward and make sure Dear Sam and our air bender aren't doing something terrible to the engineer or something. I'm going to see what the hell it is I'm really seeing."

I was essentially in a crouch, so I took off just as I had for every race, Ginger running next to me, Bruno flying beside us. It wasn't as bad running with the wind at my back, and I hurdled the spaces between cars and any little puddles of water, of which there thankfully were not many. Due to my time with the gang from Alpha Four, I still had a perfect four step, so nothing was slowing me down.

Due to the situation, I ran at human normal. This was not the time to overshoot anything, especially if there were copperheads lurking around every rock and leaf in this area.

Still made it to the nearest car with a bunch of people on it pretty quickly. Reader and Tim were on this car and now that I was near them, I could see that they weren't fighting normally. They were back-to-back, which wasn't unusual, but they were using techniques I knew they only did when they had to deal with A-Cs using hyperspeed.

But none of the people around them were moving fast. However, they were attacking my guys, and that confirmed them as my enemies.

"Ginger, Bruno, use those keen animal senses of smell and such and help me stop the bad people." So saying I body-slammed the nearest person to me.

Who made the "oof!" sound, stumbled, and fell off the side of the train with a scream. Go me. At least hopefully.

Of the other eight people on this car, six of them turned to focus on me. They weren't turned Secret Service or Field agents, and definitely not A-Cs—they weren't good looking enough by far. However, there was something about them that I recognized. Two things, really. They were all, to a man, wearing goggles that looked a lot like mine. And they were all dressed just like the commandos I'd had the displeasure of serving with in Bizarro World.

"James, Tim, you're surrounded by invisible commandos," I called to them. "Humans, not A-Cs."

Then I was too busy being attacked by six hulking guys to give them any more tips.

CHAPTER 42

OF COURSE, I had Ginger and Bruno and the six guys attacking me did not.

Bruno attacked one near to me and Ginger took another one. Both of them were screaming really nasty things in Peregrine and ocellar. I agreed with their sentiments.

Decided to go for what kung fu I could manage and slid into a crouch while sweeping the legs of the guy in front of me. The two dudes next to him were too busy being mauled by my Attack Pets to help out, but the three guys behind them weren't.

One grabbed the guy I'd knocked over and they both headed for me. The other two went to help their pals and tried to club Ginger and Bruno.

This pissed me off to no end, and while I was doing my kung fu moves like a champ, they weren't enough. These guys were trained. On the plus side, none of them had guns, which made sense, since they were clearly here to be stealthy, and nothing shows where an invisible person is quite like a gunshot and the related smoke that comes with it.

On the not plus side, they had knives, nasty looking ones, too. Though most of them weren't using them. Most. Two of the guys coming for me pulled their knives out—apparently they were sporting when their adversary couldn't see them, but not when said adversary could. Lucky me.

I landed a hit that should have knocked one guy into the other but merely made him gasp and stagger a little. Either he'd taken Surcenthumain—always a possibility—or he'd been training for how to handle a punch from someone with extra strength.

Got the proverbial bad feeling. We were all outnumbered and apparently they were far more prepped for us than we were for them. And as I dodged and leaped and did my best to keep from getting cut or worse, I realized that these guys looked more than generally familiar—I was pretty sure some of them were the same guys I'd dealt with in Bizarro World.

That should have given me confidence, but in that world I'd been Wonder Woman, and I'd had Cox, Alfred and all his toys, and even Esteban Cantu to help me. Here, while I had more people, none of them could see who we really needed to be fighting.

My music changed to "Battle Born" from the Killers. "Thanks, Algar," I said under my breath. He was right—I'd fought like this plenty before Jamie had been born. It was just time to use all the human skills instead of relying only on brute force and hyperspeed.

Focused some on what Christopher had taught me, but more on what I'd learned from my human kung fu teachers: Use your opponent's strength against them.

Hyperspeed or no, I was a sprinter, and that meant I was faster than these guys. Plus I'd brought a gun to a knife fight.

I hit another crouch—it gave me less wind resistance and a lower center of gravity. Then I aimed for the nearest guy to me with a knife out and shot at his leg.

He shouted and collapsed. I ripped his goggles off him, feeling rather nostalgic for Operation Civil War all of a sudden, then hit him with a side kick to the gunshot area.

He was writhing and a set of hyperspeed kicks shoved him and his knife over the side. Nice blending of all my skills, go me.

One of them grabbed at me but I did a somersault and then, since I was heading toward Reader, kept rolling and knocked the guy he was fighting away.

Shoved the goggles at Reader. "Put these on!" Then I flipped into the sprinter's blocks position and took off, running at the guys who were fighting with Ginger.

Slammed into the one holding her. He lost his grip and she went flying. Tried to get into a position where I could catch her, but the other guy grabbed me. However, Bruno gave a gigantic squawk, broke free, and flew to catch her.

He got her just in time and they landed at the far end of the car, so behind Reader and Tim.

Which was great for them. Of course, I was in some guy's arms, my back to his chest, he had my feet off the ground, and he was squeezing me at least as tightly as Jeff could when he was having an adrenaline reaction. Well, at least he wasn't trying to slit my throat, this moment's definition of damning with faint praise.

"Battle Born" was on repeat and I still had my Glock, so I did my best to shoot down to hit his foot. Missed, but I caused him to have to jump around a lot and I was able to slip out of his grip.

That clip was out, so I tossed the gun back into my purse as he grabbed me again. This time he didn't try to hold me. Instead he tossed me toward the side, with clear intent to throw me off the train. Couldn't blame him—that was certainly my game plan.

Managed to grab his arm as he was letting go, meaning he was sailing off the side with me. Against logic and clearly due to panic, he grabbed at me, meaning we were going to romantically go splat together. This was nowhere on my Top Ten Ways To Die list.

"Kitty needs help!" I shouted as we flew off and things moved in slow motion the way they do when you're really sure you're going to die.

Reader had goggles on, but Tim didn't, and they were

back to fighting six guys bigger than them. Bruno and Ginger were too far away to do anything, and they were even farther than White and Falk, who were running toward us.

The guy I was flying off into what might have been farmland but probably wasn't was screaming. Grabbed at his goggles, mostly so that if anyone on my side found my body they'd catch on and look through the goggles. There was no guarantee that Reader wasn't going to be flying off the train in a minute, too, after all.

Got the goggles and this separated us for whatever reason, though him flailing around in panic probably had something to do with it, as well. All this had taken roughly two seconds.

But I recognized him. He was definitely one of the commandos I'd known in Bizarro World. Good to know he was still open to the highest bidder. Just wished I knew which one had paid him. But not nearly as much as I wished not to hit the ground. And not even close to as much as I wished to not land on or even near any snakes.

He hit the ground with exactly the horrible splat sound I'd expected. But I didn't. Oh, I hit something, but it wasn't ground. Or, thank the good lord, a snake. It was big and fluffy and growling.

"Poofikins!" Hugged the Poof as I started to slide off. But my Poof didn't let me. Instead, it bounced, as if it was one of those big inflatable rubber balls that kids used to hop around on when I was really little.

I had no handle to grip, so I grabbed fur. Poofikins didn't seem to mind. The Poof bounced and bounded and then tossed me onto the train.

I slammed into two of the guys fighting with Tim. The force sent them sliding, but Tim managed to grab me before I flew off again.

"Thanks, Tim, nice catch. Put on these goggles. Grab goggles from the bad guys before you shove them off the train if you can."

"I'll worry about finesse when I don't think we're all go-ing to die." He put the goggles on as instructed. And jumped in time to avoid being body-slammed. I grabbed the guy's ankle and he lost his balance and fell on his face. Used his body to pull myself more firmly onto the middle of the roof. Slammed my elbow into the back of his head, which slammed his face hard into the roof. He stopped moving.

Falk and White were over by us now, but a few more snakes dropped onto the roof and I was far too busy screaming to welcome them politely to this part of the party. On the plus side, that seemed to freak out some of the commandos. A few of the commandos even broke their in-visibility cover and screamed along with me. Almost felt bad for them when White and Falk tossed them off the train. Into what I was sure was more snakes. That'd teach them to Side With Evil.

Thankfully Ginger handled all of the snakes, Bruno han-dled Ginger Relocation Services and Peregrine In Yo Face-ness, and the rest of us were too busy fighting and grabbing goggles for me to worry about any snakes that weren't in my immediate vicinity.

Finally our car roof was cleared of human and slithery adversaries and we all had goggles on. "As you can now see, we have a lot of people on top of this train who are cloaked in some way. Let's get their goggles, toss them off, and help the rest of the gang, shall we?"

"This is new," Reader said, sounding worried. "No one has cloaking tech for individual humans."

"That we know of," Tim amended.

"Dudes, trust me and your eyes now that you have the special goggles on—someone has this tech and is using us as their case study."

"Let's get this situation locked down," Falk said. "Then we'll worry about what's going on."

"Party pooper. Tim, where are the flyboys, by the way? I thought they'd be here."

"I have no idea," Tim admitted. "We've been too busy for me to make any calls."

"And, Mister White, why are you and Burton here instead of up front?"

"Because the helicopter lowered and those two got away, just as the first two did, Missus Martini."

"Where's Nerida?" I asked.

Right as water hit me in the back.

CHAPTER 43

TURNED AROUND. "Oh, there she is." We were near water—dirty, probably snake-filled water, but water, nonetheless—and she had clearly recovered.

Nerida was doing the bending thing where she was waving her hands around, meaning she was gathering more water from somewhere. "You guys help the others. Ginger and Bruno, that includes you. I'll handle the water witch. I'd love Mahin's backup, though, if it's at all available."

Then I charged.

Slammed into her just like last time, and, just like last time, I knocked her down and onto her back. All her hand waving ceased. Go me.

Slammed her head against the metal. "Where the hell did you get all the grunts from? Minions Unlimited?"

She flipped me off of her, but fortunately I was able to stay roughly in the middle of the roof. She also looked around. And then looked puzzled. "You all like fighting with nothing, don't you?"

"We're fighting all the people you brought along to help you on your latest insane quest." Got to my feet and debated if I should charge again or not. My music changed to "Long Train Runnin'" by the Doobie Brothers. Had a feeling this meant I was supposed to either get to the engine or the caboose. White had thought he'd seen Annette Dier at

the back of the train. The hell with Nerida and the engine—
I was probably needed in the rear.

Nerida looked confused, and even more confused as I
backed away then spun around. Didn't bother to see if she
was still staring at me or not—it was time to stop whatever
Dier had going on.

White, Falk, Reader, and Tim were assisting Lorraine,
Claudia, and Abigail, who were on the next car over. Spotted Mahin one car away, fighting back-to-back with Adriana. Decided they needed my help with the nine commandos
they were holding off more than those on this car who were
now evenly matched.

As I ran past and through the fighting, noted Reader
breaking one of the bad guy's necks, Falk and Tim two-
manning one of the larger minions and flinging him over
the side, and White getting goggles to the girls, who were
managing to land hits even though they couldn't see who or
what they were hitting. They were all good.

Didn't see Bruno and Ginger. Had a moment's worry
that they'd been hurt, but then reminded myself that they'd
been gone earlier and had returned. Besides, I had more
fighting I needed to focus on.

Hurdled onto the next car and did my by now patented
slamming into the nearest person move. Happily, it was still
working for me and I knocked the guy away from Mahin.
Kept moving and ripped his goggles off, shoved them at her,
and slammed into the next guy. I was going to ache all over
when this was done, but at least I now knew I had an alternate career in the WWE's Ladies' Division.

Unsurprisingly, Adriana was the most effective "blind"
fighter I'd seen so far. She seemed unperturbed to be fighting people she couldn't see, and she had bodies down.
Grabbed the goggles off their heads and got a pair to her.

While she put them on and Metallica's "Fight Fire with
Fire" came on my personal airwaves, I enjoyed some nostalgia and used several of my favorite kung fu forms, including

my beloved Crane Opens a Can O' Whupass. It was amazing how fun that one was to do at hyperspeed.

"Interesting," she said the moment the goggles were on. "Let's finish this." So saying, she and I did what we'd done before—we ganged up on the nearest minion. She went high, I went low, and he went off the side, his goggles in Adriana's hand.

Mahin wasn't using any of her bending that I could tell. However, she was kicking butt anyway, so maybe she just didn't want to expend the effort. In what seemed like a short time, we had this car's minions down or out, depending.

"Mahin, are you able to counter Nerida, the water bending chick. She's—"

"Getting off." Mahin pointed up. The helicopter was back, and Nerida was on its rope ladder.

"Why are they leaving?" I asked no one in particular. "Technically, they're still winning."

"No idea," Adriana said. "However, from what I can now see, we're still outnumbered."

Looked at the remaining cars. The next two had Field and Secret Service agents on both. And a lot of commandos.

But the caboose had Rahmi and Rhee—and Annette Dier.

"Well, let's lower those opposing numbers, then. You guys need to help the agents on the next cars. And I need to help Rahmi and Rhee. Just try to keep a couple of them around—we need to figure out how they're using the cloaking tech."

As I said this the others joined us. Nodded to Adriana, who nodded back. Then I took off again.

It was a credit to their training and skills that the princesses had Dier blocked and were keeping her essentially in one place. It was a credit to Dier's skills that she was neither down nor out.

The three of them were doing some impressive moves—leaping, jumping, staff hits, staff avoidance moves—but it was clear they were in a standoff. Which shouldn't have been possible, since Dier was human. I suspected that— whether the commandos had dosed or not—she'd had a Surcenthumain cocktail.

There were commando bodies on this roof. The staffs the princesses used glowed at the ends, and those ends could slice through bone, let alone flesh. There was a lot of blood and such up here, too, but not nearly as much as you'd expect. The staff's lasers or whatever they were cauterized while slicing and dicing.

Dier didn't have a scratch on her, more was the definite pity. The princesses didn't either. But all three of them were fighting furiously, so it wasn't from lack of trying on anyone's part.

Pulled my Glock out, put in a new clip, and then aimed at Dier's head. "Stop fighting or I'll do what I've wanted to for a long time."

She glared at me, but she stopped. The princesses blocked her with their staffs, so that she couldn't make an easy escape. "You can try. But your chances of hitting them are high."

"Maybe. Your pals have all taken off."

"I'll be taking off soon, too. And you'll let me go."

"Why will I do that?"

She looked up. Humored her and looked up as well. To see the helicopter hovering up above us. Kellogg, Kozlow, Dear Sam, and Lowe were strapped and leaning out. All of them had big guns. Aimed at me and everyone else on top.

"Because you don't have a choice," Dier said smugly.

Looked back at her. "They're just going to shoot us anyway. I might as well get some revenge for my friends and family and kill you now."

"Ah, but if you do that, then they'll certainly kill some if not all of your remaining friends and family on this train, and possibly you, too." She shrugged. "But, if you let me go, we'll let you call it a draw for this round. You have my word. And I don't give that lightly."

Contemplated my options. They sucked. I lowered my gun. "Fine. Girls, let the murderous bitch go."

The princesses moved off. Unwillingly, but they did it. Dier nodded to me. "You're showing a great deal of maturity and wisdom."

"Don't mistake it for personal growth."

She waved and the helicopter lowered. "Oh, I don't, never fear."

"So what was this all about? You do all this to set up that meet and greet with us and the heads of the Church of Hate and Intolerance and Club Fifty-One?"

She shot me a derisive look. "Hardly. We didn't give that message to the media. We couldn't care less about those idiots, and we have no intention of turning ourselves in. Ever."

As the rope ladder dropped down, I quickly tossed out another question. "What about Huntress and the rest of your minions on the train?"

She looked at me and this time her expression was confused. "I have no idea who Huntress is, and whoever all of you were fighting, I have no idea who they are, *if* they are, or if you're all not just crazy."

"What, you thought we were all having a rave up here or trying to bring back vogueing?"

"I put nothing past you people." She grabbed the rope ladder.

"Where's Stephanie?"

She rolled her eyes. "Who knows? Who cares?" And with that, the helicopter rose up and flew off.

CHAPTER 44

WAITED FOR A MINUTE, but they didn't come back around to shoot at us. "Okay, I'm shocked, but apparently Dier's word is semi-good." Handed goggles to the princesses while quickly explaining the invisible people issue.

The others joined us as they put their headgear on. We'd had a lot of commandos attacking—everyone had goggles on and White and Falk were holding many spares. We looked like a steampunk convention.

"Have to figure we still have issues inside," Reader said. "Since the others aren't up here."

"There are more invisible commandos inside?" As soon as I asked I knew the answer. Queen's "Fight from the Inside" coming on my music mix was also something of a "duh" clue.

"Yeah. Since we couldn't see them and all that, we had to leave people inside to fight whatever was attacking us," Tim said, sarcasm knob heading toward eleven.

"Hey, I was busy defending the front of the train."

"Let's now go in and defend the interior," White said. "And give the rest of our people the ability to see what they're fighting."

"Divide up, we have thirteen cars, and we have no idea

who's where," Reader said. He assigned us out—I had
Rahmi, Rhee, Mahin, White, and Adriana and we were
starting from the back.

Half of the Field agents paired with all the Secret Service
agents went up to the forward cars. The rest stayed on the
roof, determining which commandos were alive or dead and
ensuring the living ones were severely restrained. We didn't
have anyone down on our side, but we had plenty who were
hurt, though the A-Cs were, of course, healing up quickly.
Alpha Team and Abigail took the last car they'd seen Jeff
and the others in, which was the second dining car.

Wanted to ask to switch targets, but Reader didn't look
like he was in the mood for me to question his authority, so
I decided that discretion was going to remain the better
part of not making one of my two best guy friends mad at
me.

The teams split up and, on mine, the princesses insisted
on going down first. Considering they and Adriana were the
only ones who'd killed or even discomfited the invisible attackers, I chose not to argue.

Amazingly enough, there were no commandos in the caboose. We forged on. The next car had four Field and two
Secret Service agents. They were all hurt, but they were also
all alive and were in here under orders, to ensure that no
one got past them. Gave them some goggles, then told them
to hold down this part of the fort, just in case the Crazy
Eights or the Invisible Commando Force brought in
reinforcements.

"Assume we'll be fighting the moment we get into the
next car," I told Rahmi, as I took over the lead. "Let them
see me first—I'm always presumed to be less threatening."

Rahmi snorted. "They don't know you too well, do they?"
She stepped to the side and slid the door open quickly.

It was always nice to be right, and I was definitely right.
There were a lot of people in here, though most of them

were commandos. And they had prisoners, which was just peachy.

Caroline, Stryker, and Vance were all backed into a corner. They weren't fighting, though they all looked like they'd been hit, even Caroline. It was clear they'd been herded into this corner and they weren't trying to leave it because of the pain that had happened when they'd tried. Vance and Stryker looked frightened out of their minds. Caroline looked pissed.

She saw me and her eyes opened wider. She shook her head just a little. That was sweet, she was warning me. Needed to get my girl some goggles.

Algar did me another solid and Elton John's "Saturday Night's Alright For Fighting" came on. I enjoyed kicking butt to Sir Elton's tunes. Maybe it was the catchy piano riffs, but whatever the reason, I was primed and ready.

So, as the first commando turned around, I did a move that would make Jean-Claude Van Damme and Johnny Cage both proud—I dropped into the splits and slammed my fist up into his groin.

Rolled out of the splits as he was crumbling around his own personal pain and swung into a low sweep that knocked another commando on his butt.

Rahmi, Rhee, and Adriana were in the car now, and they were all kicking butts with the intent to not bother taking names later.

White and Mahin were in and they focused on getting to our three prisoners. Oh, sure, they had to knock a few heads and such to get there, but all in the line of duty.

It was a lot easier to fight inside the train than it had been on the roof, and it felt even easier by contrast, as if the roof had been a grueling 10K and this was just a quick warm-up sprint.

From the way the others were tossing hulking men trained in the ways of war down and aside, they felt the same way. We had a lot of unconscious or dead commandos by the time Sir Elton finished and "Ain't No Rest For the Wicked" by Cage the Elephant came on. As we removed their goggles I recognized the one whose groin I'd done my best to destroy—another one of my old "pals" from Bizarro World.

While I brought Caroline, Vance, and Stryker up to speed, Mahin went back and got the A-Cs from the other car. Since we had prisoners now, someone needed to guard them. White went up to the roof to let the A-Cs up there know where to bring their prisoners.

"And to think I was looking forward to this trip," Vance said when I was done.

"It could be worse," Adriana said.

"How?" Stryker asked.

"You could be dead," Rhee answered. She sniffed. "So few here are like the Great Tito."

Couldn't blame her for comparing her future brother-in-law far more favorably than Vance or Stryker. But in their defense, we hadn't brought them with us for their ability to kick butt. Fortunately.

"Oh, not everyone's a fighter. Some are lovers. And Vance, before you say the words I can literally see forming in your mouth, I'd suggest you reconsider and remember that silence remains golden."

White rejoined us as Vance slammed his mouth shut. "Things are under control upstairs. But from what I can tell, not so much next door."

"Lead on, Macduff."

"A literary reference? How refreshing."

"I do read, Mister White. More than comic books."

"You're a woman of well-hidden depths, aren't you, Missus Martini?"

"I'll hurt you later, Mister White. Shall we get our Avengers on?"

"I believe we shall."

"I really need to get you a bowler hat and an umbrella gun."

White laughed as "The Fight Song!" from Megadeth started. Algar was clearly enjoying himself, as was White. Nice to have them in sync. "And I demand that you get your catsuit. It's well past time."

And with that, we stepped onto the next platform, ready for the next round.

CHAPTER 45

WHITE MADE SURE the others were right behind us, then slid the door open for me with a flourish.

Fortunately, I was prepared for anything, because the main dining car reminded me of how pundits usually liked to describe Detroit—a devastated wreck surrounded by nice stuff and things that used to be nice.

There was no surrender going on in this car, but our guys who were fighting—Jeff, Christopher, Gower, Chuckie, and Oliver—definitely looked worse for wear.

That Oliver was fighting instead of cowering didn't surprise me. Nor was I surprised to find Shawn, Janet, Kenton, Duncan, Wade, and Andrea all hiding in the kitchen. Nor was seeing an absolute tonnage of commandos in here surprising in any way.

No, what was kind of a shocker was that Ginger and Bruno were in here, using their keen animal senses—meaning flying into and clawing the faces of the commandos in Bruno's case, and clawing the legs or biting down on the arms of other commandos in Ginger's case—to help the guys identify where a commando was and Reader and his team were not.

How the animals had gotten in was answered in that at least half of the windows of this car were smashed out. Where Reader's team was, however, was a mystery. One I was going to have to solve after we kicked some invisible butt.

We rolled into action. The only hindrance was that there were a lot of people in here, so the princesses couldn't really use their staffs. That was okay. What they lacked in battle-staff ability they more than made up for in Channeling Our Ancestors The Pissed Off Amazons ability. Some of the commandos they were destroying might survive, but I could guarantee they wouldn't want to.

Mahin again performed Goggle Distribution Duty but White was busy fighting with me and Adriana. I'd fought with each of them separately but never the three of us together. However, as I went low, Adriana took the middle, and White went high, it was clear we were a Super Team.

"Mister White, you remain the best we have."

"I agree," Adriana said we took down three big commandos in a row. "You're as good as Mister Buchanan."

"High praise indeed," White said, as he slammed a back kick into a commando behind him without even looking. "I'm flattered."

"I'm still wondering why we have any other agents, present company excluded and no offence meant."

"Oh," Jeff said, sarcasm meter well past eleven, as he picked up a commando he could now see and slammed the man repeatedly onto the floor, "absolutely none taken. At all."

"I'm going to be in therapy for the rest of my life due to your borderline creepy hero worship of my dad," Christopher added as he zoomed around us and tied up any still-breathing commandos.

"I'm just glad Bruno and Ginger showed up when they did," Chuckie said, as he twisted the neck of the commando he was fighting. "It was too loud to spot them via their breathing."

"It's been nice," Gower said, as he and Oliver slammed the last two commandos together and then against the wall in a move that looked practiced but I knew wasn't, "to get to do something active. Richard, I can see why you teamed up with Kitty with such gusto now."

"Where are the others?" Jeff asked as I checked him over to make sure he wasn't too hurt. Adriana did the same for Chuckie, White did the same for his son, Mahin had Oliver, and the princesses took the "honor" of verifying that Supreme Pontifex Gower was still intact.

"That's the question of the minute." Quickly brought them up to speed while I gave Bruno lots of scritchy-scratches between his wings and Ginger lots of pets. "We expected to see James and his team in here by the time we got in."

Chuckie and Adriana went to check the forward door. "It's sealed shut," he announced as they got back. "Welded as near as I can tell. So that explains why they couldn't get in."

"Why not come in through the other door?" Christopher asked. "Or through the broken windows like the animals did?"

"No clue, but my questions are—where are they now, and who sealed this door and why?"

"Why is easy," Adriana said. "To keep Jeff and the others trapped in here."

"We *were* trapped," Jeff admitted. "It's a lot harder than it sounds to fight someone invisible."

"Who is the big question. Was it more commandos? If so, that might explain what James' team is up to."

Megadeth's song ended and so did my music. Considered what Algar might be telling me. Pulled my phone out.

Apparently there weren't any songs entitled "Duh." It was a phone. I could, therefore, solve the mystery of where the others were easily. "Giving myself a huge duh right now. Hang on." Called Reader. He answered after several rings, right before I was ready to panic.

"Hey Kitty, good of you to check in. You guys okay?"

"Yeah, where the heck are you?"

"The front door to the car we're thinking Jeff's in was welded shut." Nice to know that Chuckie's Never Wrong status remained solid. "We were going to go in the back way, but Falk said he was concerned about the other agents, so we worked our way forward. He was right, by the way— they needed our help, so I'm glad we listened to him. Did you get to them?" He sounded a little worried. He'd left his husband in here, after all.

"Yeah, and they're fine, Paul included. Well, banged up like the rest of us, but no one's dead or maimed or anything. Are you guys still fighting?"

"No, we cleared the rest of the train." He sighed. "Not much of it's going to be usable."

"Well, we'll worry about refurbishing once we get somewhere safely. I think this means we need to cancel the further stops until Orlando, though."

"Yeah. I was on with Raj when you called. If you're all right back there, come join us if you can—we're in Rail Force One and the private dining cars. The President and the others are still in the War Room. Communications to the engine was destroyed, though."

"Okay, has anyone checked on the engineer, and we have prisoners."

"Yes, the conductor called the War Room a little while ago to make sure that the President wanted to go on. He said yes because he figured we needed to get to safety. And we have prisoners, too. Ours are in the dining car. It took the least damage."

"Okay, we'll move ours up there."

"Can you? If that door is still shut you're going to have to take them on the roof, and that will give them an opportunity to escape."

"We'll figure it out. Here or there, whichever we think makes the most sense."

"Sounds good. I need to get back to Raj, so . . ."

"Hey, James . . . before you go . . . did you find any more

Crazy Eights? I mean people who we would know or weren't invisible?"

"No. We didn't find welding equipment, either, by the way. I have no idea who welded that door shut, but it wasn't one of the commandos."

"Who do you think did it?"

He was quiet for a moment. "Honestly, with the way things are going, if you told me it was a ghost, I'd half believe it."

CHAPTER 46

READER AND I got off and "Keep This Train a Rollin'" from the Doobie Brothers started right up. Apparently Algar agreed with no more stops.

I shared the news with the others. "The Crazy Eights were here, only I only counted seven of them and James didn't find Huntress, Stephanie, or anyone else who wasn't an invisible commando. When I asked Annette Dier about Huntress she appeared to have no idea what or who I was talking about."

"And when you mentioned Stephanie it sounded as if they haven't seen or heard from her for quite a while," Adriana added. "She could have been lying, of course, she's done it before."

"Effectively, yeah. Only I'm with you—it didn't feel fake."

"Which doesn't mean that she was telling the truth," Chuckie reminded us. "These are killers who infiltrated us in any number of ways."

"Darryl did not," Mahin said thoughtfully. "And, neither did Russell. We were recruited but never for infiltration."

"Yeah, Dier came in as a reporter and such, but that was when Cliff was covering for her. And Kellogg wasn't an infiltration so much as a lurking shadow. And Wruck was the same as Lowe and Kozlow—recruited."

"Travis infiltrated," Christopher said.

"Yes, but again, he was put in by Cliff, and in a position we wouldn't question. So, realistically, none of these people have a lot of experience lying to us."

"She kept her word about not shooting us from the air," Rhee added.

"Yeah. So, let's take Dier telling the truth as a working hypothesis. What does that mean?"

"That you're going to make us call them the Unmagnificent Seven," Chuckie said. "Why does this matter right now? Especially with prisoners we need to deal with and civilians we need to get up to the forward cars?"

"I can't tell you, I just know that it does."

Jeff got more alert. "Feminine intuition?"

"I guess. More like curiosity not killing the cat. This attack wasn't coordinated."

"What do you mean?" Christopher asked huffily. "This was incredibly coordinated."

"No," Rahmi said. "I know what Kitty means. There were two distinct groups. When we were fighting Dier, she seemed unclear as to why Rhee and I were striking out around us, versus only at herself."

"The invisible guys were here to make it easy for the Crazy Whatever Numbers," Jeff said.

"Rahmi's right, though, Jeff. None of the Crazy Possibly Eights knew what I was talking about, either. For a good portion of the fight on the roof I was the only non-commando who could see the invisible guys. And when I mentioned them to Nerida and Dier they had no idea what I was talking about."

"Our enemies tend to hit us from more than one side," Gower agreed. "And they don't always coordinate. I mean, look at that time in Florida."

"Ah, Operation Drug Addict. Good times, good times. But yeah. Serene was out of her mind and being used, but her actions weren't coordinated with the other attacks."

"You think whoever sent the commandos isn't who activated the Crazy Whatever Numbers," Chuckie said. "Okay. I can see that. So, why was each group sent now?"

"We're in a long portion between stops," Adriana said. "We have to cross the river before we get to Rocky Mount."

"So it's a good place to hit us because we have nowhere to stop. And let's not forget the snakes in the trees." Thought about it. "Lillian came to warn me about a new player and, due to everything that's happened, we've let that one sit on the back burner. But, Gustav Drax is an arms dealer. And, I swear to you that name has to be made up."

"Harvey Gutermuth, Farley Pecker, Casey Jones, Howard Taft," Chuckie said dryly. "I could go on. However, I see what you mean. What better way to show off your new individualized cloaking tech than to attack Rail Force One? While it's loaded with A-Cs, I might add."

"That makes sense," Jeff agreed. "So why did the Crazies attack us?"

"And who sealed the door?" Adriana added.

"No clue. Yet. James suggested ghosts." This earned me a full set of "really?" looks. "Hey, I didn't say he was serious. At least not a hundred percent."

Adriana cocked her head. "But that might be where to look. Not at the dead, but at old enemies you're not thinking of. People who have been incarcerated, off grid, or off your radars for a while."

"The list is so long," Jeff groaned.

"Yeah, but I think Adriana's on to something."

"It's not anyone who was in the supermax," Chuckie said. "It was only the seven who got out."

"And then there's Stephanie," Christopher said quietly.

"Who doesn't appear to be a Crazy Eight after all. But who I sincerely think is Huntress."

"Meaning we think she's working for Drax," Chuckie said. "Since the attack on Lillian Culver happened when she was trying to warn you about Drax. And there's nothing like an assassin trying to kill all those politicians to make invisible security guards sound good."

"Yeah." I could see that Jeff, Christopher, White, and Gower were still hoping Stephanie could be salvaged. I wasn't as optimistic, but it was still worth hoping for. Heaved a sigh. "Okay, I know we need to get moving. We have a few prisoners and people who need protecting. Do we move them back with the others?"

"I think we open this door," Jeff said. "Because right now all the cars from here back are cut off from the rest of the train, and if someone wanted to disconnect us, we couldn't stop them easily."

"Oh, it's not that bad on the roof," White said. "But I do agree that it's an issue. Not that I believe anyone will want to use these cars until they're refurbished."

"True enough," Adriana said. "However, Kitty's right. And Jeff is, too. And so is James. We need to move the prisoners to a more secure car but taking them on the roof is risky. We need to get the former and still potential hostages to a safer location than what we have now, and I can say without asking that only Caroline will be game for the roof."

"The caboose isn't damaged at all," Mahin said. "We could put everyone there."

Chuckie shook his head. "That's the easiest car to get off of, and therefore onto. I'd like to put prisoners into a room like the War Room. Barring that, with the other prisoners so at least they're all in one place and we don't have to divide security forces."

"They need to be strip searched, too." Everyone stared at me. "Really? I'm not looking for cheap thrills. Somewhere these guys all have cloaking devices on them. We need to find those and get them to Dulce to be analyzed far faster than pronto."

"I'm tempted to just get floater gates to get everyone out of here," Jeff said.

"Let's get this situation locked down first," Chuckie said.

"I don't want us sending the wrong people or things to the wrong places."

"I agree," Gower said. "There's far too much distraction going on right now. The last thing we want to do is send any of it to the Science Center. Or to NASA Base, for that matter."

"We'll cross that floater bridge when we come to it . . ." Stopped talking because a reason for why the Crazy Eights had come waved at me.

"What?" Jeff asked.

"Crap. We need to remember that ninety percent of the time whatever our enemies are doing is to distract us from what they're *really* doing." Confirmation in the form of B.o.B.'s "Bombs Away" came onto my airwaves.

"I don't follow you, baby."

"Few ever do, Jeff. Rahmi, Rhee, MJO—handle the prisoners and hostages. Right now, everyone else, Jeff, Christopher, and Mahin especially, need to follow me. Fast."

I grabbed White's hand and took off.

CHAPTER 47

WE WERE OUT the door and climbing up the ladder in no time. White went up first, hauled me up, and we took off again. "I've learned not to question. But what are we trying to prevent?" We leaped onto the next car and kept on going.

"None of us ever made it to the engine, remember? You and Falk were supposed to go, but you came back to help the rest of us." Another leap, another roof. "Meaning that we have no idea who's actually running the train. Or that the person who called Armstrong was actually the conductor." Onto the roof of the personnel car nearest Rail Force Two.

"That's not the only reason you're panicked. Nor why you're keeping us on the roofs."

"It's faster." We leaped onto Rail Force Two. Looked over my shoulder. The others were coming after us. Good.

"What do you expect? I realize you enjoy keeping the air of mystery that drives us all wild, but I'd appreciate some clue."

"Know what the best way to kill us all is?" Onto the roof of the forward dining car, aka Prisoner Containment. We were still lucking out into no bridges or overhangs, and we were snake free, too, for the moment, though we were heading into more heavy foliage so I didn't expect that to last.

"There are so many ways, Missus Martini. Humor me. Which one are you referring to this time?"

"Blowing up the train tracks when we're over water. While everyone in the War Room car is locked in their impregnable car that's had enough damage to potentially leak. And drown them all."

We jumped onto said Impregnable Fortress of Potential Drowning Doom in silence. "It's also an excellent terrorist attack," White said, as we landed on Rail Force One. "Though I don't know if the river is deep enough."

"I don't want to find out. And, if successful, we have all those commandos who will be found along with all of us. Giving your terrorist attack theory real legs with the media."

"If we don't survive, that is. And, frankly, that's betting against people who have consistently managed to circumvent these kinds of plans." We jumped onto the last car before the engine and White slowed us down.

"Yeah, but I'm betting the Crazy Eights don't care. And we're sticking with that number, because even if Stephanie and Huntress are two different people, and even if she or they aren't with the old prison gang any more, there's an eighth who sealed the door and who is either off setting explosives or controlling the engineer."

"Possibly. Explosives were probably set prior. And they could have been set by the Invisible Commando Team, too, you know."

"Mister White, I just love having you on Team Megalomaniac. I agree. But the bottom line is that we probably have the last Crazy Eight still around or watching. And I think someone's going to try to blow the tracks really soon, because based on my extremely limited awareness of this area, I think we're getting to that river."

The leap from the last car onto the engine was harder just based on the slight differences between the engine's design and the passenger cars', the biggest one being that the engine was higher than the cars.

We decided to jump for the ladder, as opposed to the roof. White was fairly sure he could make the roof, but I wasn't sure at all that I could, especially since I'd need far more of a running start.

White, of course, made the leap without effort. I did my best, but I didn't make my most smooth jump ever and missed the ladder and railings. Okay, call it one of my worst jumps ever. The train had gone over something bumpy was going to be my excuse and I was going to stick with it forever, or for one second, depending.

Fortunately, White was prepared for me to not make it and he grabbed me before I went splat. Presumably my face would recover. Thankfully, the engine had more railings than the other cars, so I could grab on, too, though I wasn't in the greatest spot to get up.

Happily, Jeff made the leap and hauled me up. Christopher also made the jump and helped his dad up.

"You okay, baby?" Jeff asked worriedly.

"As long as my nose is in the same place and I've got all my teeth, yes."

He managed a grin. "You're still the sexiest girl in the galaxy."

"I'll take it. And I just want to defend Richard's jumping skills. Normally he'd have made it but he was trying to make it easy on me."

By the time we were done with that, my music had changed to The Killers' "The River is Wild," which boded.

Mahin and Adriana arrived now. They jumped and Christopher and White caught them and pulled them up.

"Where's Chuckie?"

"He went down with Alpha Team, to make sure things were secured and to tell them that you think someone's either got control of the engine or is going to blow the train tracks, or both," Adriana said. Jeff, Christopher, and Mahin stared at her.

"Really?" Christopher asked me.

"Really, those are my guesses and why I was in such a hurry. That I'm still in."

"How did he figure that out?" Jeff asked as we went back to moving along, him keeping a tight hold on my hand. White had Adriana and Christopher had Mahin in the same way.

It was somehow more disconcerting seeing clearly what was coming ahead of us than just being on the top of the other cars, don't ask me why, so it was harder to move safely. I was also once again happy I, and now all the others, had goggles, particularly as we were splatted with what seemed like a zillion flying bugs. We were getting very close to water, I was prepared to bet on it.

"He's the smartest guy on the Death Train and he knows how I think. I'm more concerned that you didn't pick it up."

"I have my blocks on high, baby. The panic on the train is more than I think is safe for me."

"Sorry, that should have occurred to me."

He squeezed my hand. "It's okay. We've been a little distracted."

"True enough."

"We're coming up on the Roanoke River," Adriana said. "The train will go over part of it, then through more forest, then another part of the river, and then we'll be in a less wooded area."

"So we know where they're going to hit us." One for the win column, such as it was.

"And soon," she added.

Got to the front only to discover that, shockingly, there wasn't an actually easy way down from the top. Older trains would have had platforms and railings along the side, but this puppy was a sleek, self-contained unit that didn't adhere to old-fashioned ways. Meaning we were kind of screwed.

Or, rather, I was. We had a short, fast, discussion that was more like an argument and finally it was agreed that I'd be lowered down, Jeff and White holding onto my ankles, and the others holding onto them, so that I could look in through the windshield and try to signal the engineer that there was trouble.

"Lonely Train" by Black Stone Cherry started as I was being lowered. So, as I took in the upside down view, I wasn't all that surprised at what I saw.

No one.

CHAPTER 48

WE HADN'T REALLY thought through what signal I'd give to get pulled back up. Which was a problem. Getting into the cabin of this engine was going to be a bigger problem since there was no one inside to open the door for us and offer a helping hand. But I'd worry about that once I was upright. When I was upright.

No worries. I had big strong A-Cs with me, burning to be men of action. I sincerely hoped. Of course, the first action I was hoping for was to be pulled back up before all the blood rushed to my head and it exploded.

Wiggled my feet a bit. Didn't want to somehow pull out of their grips. This didn't have the desired effect. Was about to start screaming when someone else did it for me—Bruno was on the case.

I was pulled up quickly and, once upright and no longer dizzy, gave Bruno a big hug. "Thanks for the save."

"We figured you were communicating with the engineer," Jeff said by way of apology.

"I would have been but there is no engineer in there. There is no one in there."

"How is the train still going?" Christopher asked.

"Autopilot or something, I assume. As if I know how to tell upside down and not in there?"

"The more important question is how are we getting

inside?" Mahin asked. "We have to be able to stop the train, regardless of what our enemies might have planned for us."

"There's a door on the side, Jeff," Christopher said. "I found it while you were dangling Kitty. We should be able to pull it open."

He and Jeff went into what I knew was an old pattern they were familiar with — they'd been teamed together as Field agents since they were twenty and had been running Centaurion Division in less than ten years. They flipped into Agent Mode.

Agent Mode I hadn't really seen for a while, but it was a nice nostalgic moment. With Christopher holding onto his wrists, Jeff slid down the side into the only open slot on this train, which appeared to be the doorway. Heard him grunt as he was pulling, meaning he was grunting really loudly.

"It's going to take both of us," he called up, which wasn't a surprise after the grunting.

So, White held Christopher while he slid down. Then we all lay on our stomachs and watched them strain. "One . . ." Jeff shouted. "Two . . . now!"

They pulled together and the door apparently opened. At least I took Christopher flying back and off of the train to mean they'd opened it and he'd lost his grip. Jeff just managed to grab him and pull him back as we got to discover exactly what our enemies had planned.

There was a gap in the trees ahead of us, indicating the river Adriana had told us was coming, then more trees. And then, what looked like another gap, just as she'd described.

And in that second gap, there was a huge billowing of flames and dust and such. And then we heard the explosion.

It was big and the noise was loud. Thankfully the four of us were lying down because the shockwaves hit. Managed to grab and hold Bruno, and White held onto me and Adriana, and Adriana and Mahin held onto each other.

Even so, we slid a bit, but were still on the roof, so that was something.

"Down and in, now!" Jeff bellowed. No one could bellow like my man. I was sure that Reader and all those with him had probably heard this directive.

White slid Adriana down first, and as Jeff got her I handed Bruno down as well. However, before Jeff could take him, Bruno squawked and flew off as "Fix Me Now" by Garbage hit my airwaves.

The train started to slow. "Who's doing that?" I shouted to Jeff, as Bruno surged ahead of us, using Peregrine Hyperspeed.

"Adriana, thank God. What?" He looked back inside. "She says she can slow us but can't stop us in time. We need to evacuate or figure out how to recreate train tracks."

We were quiet for a moment, then I looked over at Mahin. Algar was being, I felt, quite clear with his musical hints. "You can do this. Metal came from earth."

"But it's destroyed," she said.

Shook my head. "That makes it easier. It's little fragments now that you can pull together."

"We've got this," White called down. "Stay down there in case we need you." With that he stood and helped us to our feet. "Missus Martini is correct, Mahin. Now is your time."

She looked panicked "But I don't know if I can . . ."

I took her shoulders and gave her a little shake. "Since we met you, you've managed to save the day when it mattered. It matters again. Let's do this, okay?"

She took a deep breath and nodded. "Okay." She faced front, hands out in that bending way those that did it had.

Christopher was who'd been training me and Mahin both in use of powers and such. So, I tried to channel what he'd say here. "See the tracks in your mind. Find the particles and recreate them. Pull them together as part of the whole." I didn't have to add "and do it quickly" because that was a given.

And all of a sudden, I could see the damage. Bruno was there and he was reporting back.

"They've blown the track over the river. Pieces are floating everywhere—in the water, on the ground, in the air. Search for rusty iron or anything that you can form into tracks. There will be shattered wood, too, and shards of spikes."

Heard the sound of running feet and looked behind me. Abigail was following Ginger. "The cat indicated I was needed," she said by way of hello, as Ginger jumped up into White's arms. Abigail grabbed one of Mahin's hands and one of mine. "Show me, Kitty."

"Wonder Triplets Powers Activate." We'd done this before, first during Operation Confusion and then at other times. I showed Abigail what Bruno saw, and she sent her power through to Mahin, who started forming the tracks, while Abigail also encased the train in a protective shield. Yeah, she'd gotten all her powers back, her sister's powers, and then some, during Operation Civil War.

It was interesting to observe, in the weird way I was able to observe. I "saw" things from Bruno, which was weird in that birds and humans saw things differently. And then I "saw" what Abigail was telling Mahin, which was all mental influence and images.

Then I "saw" what Mahin saw, which was the entire earth covered with different colored specks.

First, she adjusted the broken parts of the tracks that were still attached, making them smooth and straight again. This didn't take her much time, so presumed this was the easy portion of the festivities.

Mahin then identified the base metal she wanted and the wood and other things that had been with that base metal only recently. Once identified, all those related specks sparkled in her mind, and she gathered them together and sent them down to form what they'd been before. They still retained the memory of their former shape, at least, as Mahin saw it, since the explosion was so new, making it slightly easier to get the pieces back.

We sailed through the trees. Some snakes dropped onto

the shield and promptly slid off. Go Gower Power. More happily, as we went over the first portion of the river, the tracks were reforming. Wasn't sure if they'd hold or not, but they were there, connected to the end of the tracks closest to us.

We passed this portion of the river and were back in trees. More snakes, more snakes sliding off, more tracks reforming, train still slowing but in no way stopping. About three quarters of the damaged track was recreated. But if we didn't have 100 percent we had utter failure.

"Faster," I said quietly. Abigail nodded. Mahin didn't say anything, but particles were flying through the air faster than before.

And then we were on it, the last portion of reformed track. With about a foot of track left to fix.

CHAPTER 49

FELT A HUGE surge of power from Abigail sent to Mahin, and the rest of the track reformed as Abigail collapsed.

Fortunately White was there and even though he still had Ginger, he was able to catch Abigail and keep her upright. My music changed to "Hold On" by Wilson Phillips.

The engine crossed the water and entered more trees. Of course more snakes dropped onto the shield because apparently we were just that kind of lucky. I ignored them and turned to watch the rest of the train as I felt us speed up as well. Meaning Adriana and I were on the same wavelength as Algar—get the train across before the A-C Magic ran out.

Bruno wasn't flying along with us. He couldn't get to me due to the shielding and he was staying to watch to make sure all the cars made it across.

"Hold on just a little while more," I said to the other girls. "We can do this." Felt an energy drain, meaning that Abigail was pulling from me, and probably White, in order to keep feeding her power to Mahin.

I gently tugged and pulled us all onto our knees. Experience said that falling right now would be a really bad idea, and when we were all drained we'd all fall—that was a given.

Bruno shared that the caboose was almost across as Mahin passed out. Abigail and White were both close, I could tell. I concentrated, focusing on the tracks.

It wasn't much, but it was enough. Abigail passed out as Bruno told me we'd made it. Then the shield disappeared and White and I sort of collapsed against each other.

In time for the one damn snake that had managed to hang on and not slide off the shield to land right by us. No one had hyperspeed enough to get away from it.

But Ginger was here and she wasn't drained. She made short work of the snake, then snuggled up to me for well-earned praise. "You are the best ocellar ever, you know that?" I said as I petted her head and scratched behind her ears.

Bruno flew up and caught up to us and landed next to me for his well-deserved scritchy-scratches as well.

We stayed up on top for a while. None of us were up to trying to get into the engine or anywhere else. My music mix went back to Kyle's playlist. At least I assumed "Going Nowhere" by Oasis was on Kyle's playlist, since the chorus lyrics were "going nowhere on a train." Hit repeat—I liked the song and it was soothing, and I figured we all needed soothing.

After a little while Gower and Reader crawled up and worked their way to us. "Jeff called and said it's too hard to get up here from the engine," Reader shared as they reached us. "So, he wanted us to help you all get down. Who's going where?"

"I'll go into the engine with Jeff. But I think everyone else should go down into the cars with you guys, James."

Gower nodded as he helped his sister up. "I think that's best, too, Kitty." He lifted Abigail up into his arms and zipped off using the slow form of hyperspeed.

"You're next," Reader said to Mahin, giving her a shot of the cover boy smile. "Paul's going to carry you, too. Richard, do you want help?"

"Yes, because my dignity isn't affronted by it. But let's get Missus Martini down first."

Gower returned and carried Mahin off as he'd done with Abigail.

"Someone needs to alert the train people that the track was blown." Bruno picked Ginger up and flew over the side, hopefully to Jeff.

"Chuck's doing that," Reader said. "We've sort of got it handled."

"How are we getting down to Orlando? I presume we're stopping at the next station, if Adriana knows how."

"Jeff said that she does. Apparently her grandmother trained her for everything."

"Thank God."

"And we'll worry about next steps once we get to Rocky Mount. Now, let's toss you over the side, girlfriend."

"You're a prince, James."

Gower was back and he did the tossing, so to speak. Mostly it was just what we'd done to get Jeff, Christopher, and Adriana down there—Gower held my wrists and lowered me down and Reader and White held onto him.

Jeff grabbed me, Gower let go, and then I was inside the engineer's area. Then Jeff hugged me tightly for a little while and I hugged him just as tightly back.

We finally separated, mostly because we weren't anything like safe yet. "Thanks. Cozy."

"Yeah, a little too cozy," Jeff said. "And I'm not complaining about the four of us being in here with the two animals, either. I'm worried about what happened to the engineer, the conductor, and their crew. Christopher and I have searched what we can—there's no sign of anyone."

"That bodes. As does everything else. So, what's the plan?"

Jeff shook his head. "We haven't made one yet. Figured we'd need to see if we survived before we planned any farther ahead."

"Can't argue with that logic." There were two high-backed seats. Adriana was in one, the one with the most levers, buttons, and such, which I was fairly sure was the engineer's chair. Christopher was in the other, which had a laptop computer and far fewer buttons, so presumably the conductor's chair. He was busy with the computer, and I decided not to ask what he was doing. Wasn't in the mood for any Patented Glares at the moment.

"The question is," Adriana said, "do we stop at Rocky Mount or do we power through to Orlando?"

"I don't know how bad it is back there. Hang on." Paused my music and took out the headphones. Contemplated who to call, then decided I'd go with the one most likely to make the right decision.

"Kitty, you're inside?" Chuckie asked without preamble.

"Yeah. And you're on speaker. Are James, Richard, and Paul back?"

"Yeah, we're all accounted for."

"Not really. We're missing all the engineering staff, however many people that would be. As in, gone like ghosts, not dead. Well, not dead that we know of."

"You want to know what to do next, right?"

"Wow, it's like you read my mind. Yeah, Engineer Adriana would like to know if we're going to stop in Rocky Mount or if we're going to power through to Orlando."

"That's the question of the hour. Hang on, I'm going to conference the War Room in."

While we waited, I decided I'd risk a Patented Glare. "Christopher, what are you doing?"

"I'm connected with Imageering Main. They'll connect us to whoever we need—Dulce, the Embassy, the White House, the main Amtrak hubs—and that way we'll be communicating in real time."

"Awesome, you're the man."

He shot me a quick smile. "Thanks, Kitty. Good work up there with Mahin."

"Oh, it was mostly your training, trust me."

He turned back to the computer and Jeff grinned at me as Chuckie came back on. "Okay, we're on with the War Room, as well as prisoner holding in the back. We don't have those in the dining car on just in case, since it's mid-train prisoner holding and I want to ensure that they don't hear anything so we can confirm any intel we might get from the prisoners in the rear."

"Fast status updates. We'll start with us in the engine. Adriana is currently our engineer and Christopher is our conductor. I don't know what Jeff and I are supposed to be doing up here, but the people who were here are gone without a trace."

"Succinct," Mom said with a sniff. "War Room car is secure, thank you to everyone for your hard work under dangerous circumstances." She ended this with a sneeze.

"Mom, are you okay?"

"I think I've caught Vince's cold is all, kitten, but thanks for the concern. Charles, your status?"

"Prisoners contained and searched. We can't tell where they're hiding their cloaking devices. We've tested—even if they're naked, if we take off the goggles, we can't see them. We have a couple dead bodies that we're holding to send to Dulce for examination, along with a set of goggles for duplication. Mister Joel Oliver, how are things in the back?"

"Stable, and we tested just as you did. They're invisible to the naked eye—either human, A-C, or Beta Twelve—without the goggles."

"Cloaking tech for certain," Reader said. "And it sounds like our cloaking tech, too."

"They infiltrated us and stole all our data," I was forced to remind everyone. "So them having our tech and then using it against us isn't a surprise."

"Who's likely doing it is, however," Mom said. "Charles

shared your thoughts about the so-called Huntress and Gustav Drax. Whoever Drax is, he's not on any radars, which usually indicates a fake name."

"Told you!"

"Or," Mom went on as if I hadn't spoken, "protection from far higher up. The last president and this one are not suspect, meaning we have someone else in government who might be. Won't bc the first time and, sadly, it won't be the last, either."

"Or they're from another planet, and before you pretend I didn't talk, Mom, that's me being serious."

There was silence on the other sides. Reader broke it. "You think Drax showing up as the Planetary Council is coming for a visit isn't a coincidence?"

"Someone very smart has always told me not to believe in coincidence. We get a real coincidence occasionally, but I'm not willing to bet that we have one right now."

"It would makes sense for why Stephanie would be working with him," Jeff said quietly. "You think he's an A-C?"

"I think he could be anything. I just want that theory out there, so that we don't ignore obvious clues. This could be someone high up in the government protecting Drax, it could be the fake name I think it is, or he could be an alien we don't know about. But that's honestly a discussion for another minute. This minute, we need to know if we're stopping at Rocky Mount and then going on as if this train isn't trashed, stopping at Rocky Mount and taking a nice, big floater gate to our destination, or powering through to Orlando."

"We can make it to Orlando without refueling," Adriana said. "As long as there was no damage to fuel tanks."

"None we've found so far," Reader said. "But none of us are locomotive experts. Other than you, apparently, Adriana."

"How do you know how to drive a train?" Buchanan asked. He sounded impressed. I certainly was.

"I have a classical education."

"I love you and your grandmother so much I almost can't find the words. At any rate, decision time, gang. What, literally, do we do next?"

CHAPTER 50

"I WANT THE PRESIDENT off this train and somewhere safe as soon as possible," Reader said. "I think that needs to be our first concern."

Could hear Armstrong protesting in the background. "Vince, stop for a minute. Think about it. This was a terrorist attack on the President, the VP, and the Secretary of State. I realize we foiled it, but still, if we were in Washington, you'd be in the bunker right now."

"We are in the bunker, in that sense," Mom pointed out. "But you're right, Kitty and James both—we need the President in a safer situation than he's in right now."

"That means stopping at Rocky Mount and getting this car safely unloaded," Buchanan added. "I agree with the Ambassador—we need to use a floater gate to get the President to NASA Base." Buchanan only used my title when we were being official or when he, like Pierre and everyone else, wanted to focus me on the business at hand. Chose to assume official was the word of the moment, since I felt I was laser focused on our current situation.

"We have a schedule already in place," someone who sounded like a very sick female said.

"Monica, that's not as important as your safety and Vince's," Mom said, clearing up the mystery.

"Frankly, it sounds like a bunch of you need to go to bed

and drink plenty of fluids. Which could be done far more quickly and with a lot less stress via our Gate It To NASA Base plan."

"But what about the train?" This was from Vance, representing in the rear. "And I'm not asking this because I want to ride in air conditioned luxury for the next several hundreds of miles. I'm asking because we can't just leave it sitting at Rocky Mount."

Looked to Jeff, who shook his head. "Dulce doesn't have the capability to transport a train. It's never been necessary."

"Before we worry about that, I'd like to ask Doctor Hernandez a question," Chuckie said.

"I'm here."

"In your professional opinion, who in the car with you needs to get to medical and rest, as opposed to continuing any form of campaigning?"

"The President, the Secretary of State, the Press Secretary, the Head of the P.T.C.U., and the First Lady."

"Oh, I'm fine," Elaine said. Only she sniffled right after she said this.

"Then that settles it," Chuckie imitated Mom and went on as if Elaine hadn't spoken. Would have given her a Solidarity Nudge if we'd been next to each other, but instead chose to enjoy that it happened to other people, too, for a moment. "I think it's imperative to get those five people, and any others Doctor Hernandez feels need observation or rest or medicines, to NASA Base's medical center."

"NASA Base has a medical center?" I asked Jeff in a very low voice.

He nodded. "You've never had any reason to see it, but yeah, it's good. Not as good as the Science Center or Walter Reed, but still top quality."

"Fine," Mom said with a resigned sigh.

"And I recommend that we use the gate at the train station," Jeff added.

This was new. I knew that the gates were in every airport in the world—and that included some of the tiniest, scariest airstrips around—and I knew there were gates in major train stations like the Metro in Paris, but that they were in smaller train stations like Rocky Mount was news to me.

Christopher didn't look away from his laptop and whatever he was doing on it, but he sighed. "Yes, Kitty, we have gates in all the train stations, too, not just the major ones. We put them in when Jeff became the Vice President, just in case. They're now in every station around the world. We're considering putting them in bus stations, too."

"No one tells me anything."

"It was sent out in a briefing packet."

"I read those!"

Christopher snorted. "Sure you do."

Couldn't help it—I had to ask. "Why bus stations?"

Christopher now deigned to look at me over his shoulder. "Because we never know what you're going to do, when you're going to do it, or where you're going to be." He shrugged and turned back to the laptop. "Just taking the necessary precautions to protect our high-ranking personnel."

"*Anyway*," Mom said, "I believe Vance has a point. What are we doing with the train?"

"I think the question is—what do we want our enemies to think we're doing?"

There was a lot of silence when I said this. Jeff broke it. "Ah, what do you mean?"

Heaved a sigh. "Look, they attacked us, three times, really. We're still alive and still chugging along. Sure, some of the cars are pretty wrecked, but we aren't, in that sense. So, do we want our enemies to know that we're taking the President and the others off the train?"

"Why would that matter?" Strauss asked.

"Because they're trying to kill some or all of us. If they're after the President, and if they know he's not on the train, then they know to hit NASA Base."

"Maybe," Chuckie agreed. "But there are far more protections for the President at the base than on this train."

"Ah, I wonder if I can break in," Oliver said. The back of the train continued to represent. "The princesses and I have been . . . chatting with some of our prisoners."

Decided not to ask how much actual talking the princesses had done. They'd learned a lot over the time they'd been with us. Threatening and hurting, that I assumed had happened. Friendly chats, not so much.

"And?" Chuckie said.

"And I believe that subterfuge might be important. As we've agreed, there seem to have been two teams who attacked at roughly the same time—the Crazy Eights, as the Ambassador has named them—and the Invisible Commandos. Our new friends insist that the Invisible Commandos have no idea who the Crazy Eights are, or why they were here. The first assumption was that they were an additional team sent by the Commandos' employer to test them. That theory has been discarded, and was discarded prior to their captures, when the Crazy Eights not only couldn't see the Invisible Commandos but clearly had no idea they were here."

"Confirmation of Kitty's theories is nice," Tim said, "but is there something more?"

"Yes, there is. First off, in case you're wondering where your team is, the Invisible Commandos have an invisible helicarrier, and it was sent up specifically to capture the planes you scrambled to protect this train."

"Are they alright?" Tim, Lorraine, Claudia, and I all asked in unison. I'd worry about that once we had the flyboys back safely.

"To my knowledge, yes, but assume they're prisoners of war. Our new friends expect their employer to bargain for their release by offering us our captured pilots and planes."

"Is their employer named Gustav Drax by any chance?"

"Why yes, Ambassador. Your megalomania skills are in top form."

"Always so nice to be right and all that. So, how many other attacks does Drax have planned?"

"None. And the train tracks being blown up was not courtesy of Mister Drax. The Invisible Commandos were to hit the train, take prisoners, and then advise their employer, who would then reveal to the President and the other hostages that his tech made their capture easy."

"Oh my God. It's all a freaking sales pitch? People have died because of this!"

"Yes, Ambassador, it *is* a sales pitch. One that's gone quite wrong. Our Invisible Commandos took tremendous damage, as we all know, and they were not expecting to. Their loyalty, shall we say, is a little tenuous at the moment."

Wasn't sure I cared. I knew some of them from Bizarro World, after all. And in Bizarro World they'd been world-class jerks who'd had real issues with listening to women.

Of course, while some people were the same in both worlds, enough were different that I had to admit that I probably needed to give the Invisible Commandos a chance. A very small chance during which I'd be watching them like a hawk, but a chance nonetheless.

"Hang on," Chuckie said. "Falk and I are going to go back to the dining car. Hooking Reader in first. I'm hanging up—I'll rejoin after we confirm if the story from our set of prisoners concurs with the story Mister Joel Oliver got."

"I'm on," Reader said a few moments later. "Reynolds and Falk are on with Tim, just in case. He'll relay until they're back or rejoin us on the group conference call."

"Okay, so do we think that the Crazy Eights blew up the tracks, then?"

"No," Raj said. "We do not. We actually have a group claiming responsibility. They're claiming it on the national news right now, by the way."

"Claiming that they blew up the train tracks or claiming that they've derailed Rail Force One?"

"The latter." Could tell Raj was trying not to laugh.

There was only one group who were this stupid and poorly run while also managing to be somewhat effective.

"Oh, I have three guesses for who's so claiming, then, and the first two don't count. Club Fifty-One is revved up for action again, aren't they?"

CHAPTER 51

"YES, AMBASSADOR," Raj said. "Club Fifty-One is claiming that they've derailed the train and are blaming the A-Cs for their need to destroy."

"How can they not be aware that we survived intact? We did warn someone to stop other trains from going through just now, didn't we?"

"We did," Tim confirmed. "Reynolds made the calls and I heard him do it. And as for how they're unaware, he says that his assumption would be that they didn't actually leave anyone behind to ensure that the bombs worked."

"That's just moronic."

"Reynolds says that this shouldn't really surprise you, all things considered. And I have to agree with him, Kitty. The Club Fifty-One grunts aren't usually the brightest."

"I agree as well," Oliver said. "As do the Invisible Commandos. There is no device they have or have ingested that causes the invisibility, by the way. They were irradiated."

"Holy crap, are you kidding me? Who willingly signs up for something like that? Are they all former Club Fifty-One people or something?"

"Not that they've told me, no. The promise of a rich reward and increased commando skills seemed to be enough incentive."

"So, if I've got this right, we have the usual three

different plans going against us. How nostalgic. It's always nice to have some continuity from Bad Guy Land. So, we might as well stop at Rocky Mount because we now have to actually show that we are *at* Rocky Mount instead of dead in the Roanoke River, right?"

"That seems to be the case," Mom said. "But that also means that this could be a trap. The information given to the press could have been done in order to make us stop and put the President in another vulnerable situation."

"If I may," White said, "I believe the simplest solution has been overlooked."

"Which is?" Mom asked.

"Floater gates can calibrate to a moving object. Missus Martini and I have utilized such several times before. I recommend we remove all those Doctor Hernandez feels should be in medical, all civilians, and anyone else who just wants to get off this train, and the rest of us will disembark at Rocky Mount. By then, you'll be able to tell us if we continue by train and have the Vice President make the planned stops, or if we merely use the gate at the station to get to NASA Base as well."

"He's so good," I said.

"I suggested that earlier and was ignored," Jeff said quietly to me.

"Now you know how most women in the working world feel."

"I know how everyone feels, all the time, baby. And I still want to know what I have to do to get that kind of hero worship out of you."

"Tell you later. In bed."

Jeff grinned. "Richard's right," he said to the phone chain at large. "And before anyone suggests it, no, I'm not going to NASA Base via the floater gate. At least not yet. We can still make this excursion work if we need to, and that's my job."

"We'll need more than one floater," Reader said. "One

has to go into the War Room, two others for the two mid-cars, ours and the one Reynolds is in now, and one for the rear."

"That's not a problem," White said. "I've hooked William into our call—he's getting it set up."

"Mister Reynolds joining group call," William said, presumably through White's phone.

"Well, that was fast," Chuckie said. "In addition to others, we have three unharmed empaths on guard duty in here. All reactions from prisoners confirm what we've already heard from the rear. They're also offering to surrender, switch sides, or whatever in order to reduce sentences."

"Do you believe them?" Jeff asked.

"Your empaths do."

"Works for me. Prisoners going to Dulce's containment?" I asked.

"No," Chuckie said firmly. "Going to Gitmo."

"Oh, give my regards to Guantanamo and my Uncle Mort."

"What about my team?" Tim asked. "We can't have these guys unavailable to us if we need them to get the flyboys back."

"They'll be available if necessary," Chuckie said in a tone that indicated that the Invisible Commandos might not be conscious, but they'd be around.

"Our commando representatives would rather go to Gitmo than back to their employer," Oliver shared. "They apparently trust us more than they trust Drax."

"Mine, too," Chuckie said. "Empath approved."

"Are we sure they don't have emotional overlays on?" Jeff asked.

"Yes," Reader said. "We strip searched all of them looking for what made them invisible. Unless the irradiation they underwent also made them able to alter or hide their emotions from empaths, they have nothing like that on them."

"Or they're supposed to take over Guantanamo Bay.

After all, they're invisible unless you're wearing the special goggles." At this point, nothing was going to surprise me, and our enemies thinking ahead wasn't unusual.

"Floater gates ready to activate," William said. "Suggest that a pair of goggles be sent through along with those going to NASA Base, so we can create duplicates quickly."

"We'll also send some with the dead bodies going to Dulce," Chuckie said. "Falk is going to escort said dead bodies."

"Lucky him." And better him than me, but I managed not to say that aloud.

"I think we should evacuate everyone in the War Room car," Tito said. "But none of us have the goggles."

"I've got the extras," Vance said. "And as much as I want to be the one to take them, we're sending Caroline through instead."

"What about the rest of you?" Jeff asked.

"Waiting for Guantanamo," Oliver replied. "I believe that the princesses will be the most effective at controlling the Invisible Commandos, and the A-Cs with us, of course. Plus our Secret Service agents will be helpful at the Base as well."

"No argument. Vance, are you going to Guantanamo with Mister Joel Oliver?"

"No, Kitty, I'm staying on the train with all of you." He didn't sound enthused.

"Not that I mind, but why?"

"Because I heard everything that Mister Joel Oliver, Rahmi, and Rhee got out of the commandos, just like Caroline did, so that means that each group will have someone with them who's aware of the interactions."

"Can't argue with the logic."

"And it makes sense," Chuckie added. "Falk and I didn't have the time to do in-depth interrogations. Stryker, what about you?"

"I'm choosing the lesser of two evils and staying on the

train, too, Chuck. I can't tell you how much you owe me for this nightmare."

"He owes you absolutely nothing," Jeff growled. "You and your cronies live in our facility rent-free. You have every need catered to. Whine about Chuck wanting your expertise with us again and I'll send you to Guantanamo myself. But I'll punch you through the gate."

"Geez, Jeff, way to kick a guy when he's down."

"It's okay, Jeff. Eddy just likes to whine, don't you Eddy?"

"You like getting into these situations, Kitty," Stryker muttered. "I don't, call me crazy."

"Oh, Eddy, I've called you crazy since the day we met."

"Pulling into the station in ten minutes," Adriana called, interrupting our familiar bickering rhythms. I could feel the train slowing down. "If you want people off, they need to go now."

"Gate going live in the War Room, calibrated for multiples passing through. Live in three . . . two . . . one . . ." William said. "Please begin stepping through now. Raj, please go last to advise."

Heard a variety of grumbling that got progressively less so quickly. "I'm about to step through," Raj said. "I'm the last one in the car, barring there being an Invisible Commando in here."

"Not that we know of," Oliver said.

"Singh out." There were a few seconds of silence. "Am I still on?" Raj asked.

"Man, am I impressed with A-C technology."

"I'll take Kitty's reaction as a yes. We're all here and accounted for, and patients are being admitted."

"Gate in War Room is removed. Gate going to NASA Base going live in the rear car," William said. "Calibrated for one, only."

"See some of you on the other side," Caroline said.

"She's through," Oliver said.

"We have Caroline here," Raj confirmed. "Goggles being taken to Science now."

"Floater gates prepping for the car where Mister Reynolds is. First gate is for Guantanamo prisoners only, prepped for multiples."

Heard Chuckie telling the prisoners to walk through. They seemed unable to see the gate, which wasn't a surprise since floaters were just a blur to human eyes. However, it also confirmed that the irradiation hadn't given them the ability to see like an A-C, which was, all things considered, a huge relief.

"They're through," Chuckie said finally. "And they're whiners, in case anyone needs to know. Worse than Stryker."

"I heard that, Chuck."

"Have advised Gitmo personnel, Mister Reynolds. Prisoners confirmed received. Gate for Guantanamo for the back car calibrated for multiples. Will be landing in a large containment cell where the other prisoners are already incarcerated. Mortimer Katt is on hand and will remove American Centaurion and United States personnel," William said. "Gate going live . . . now."

Another few seconds of silence. "Everyone's through but me," Oliver said. "Neither Vance's nor Stryker's phones are hooked in, by the way."

"Vance and Stryker, I'm coming to get you," Gower said. "Sit tight."

"I have no other choice," Vance said.

"What he said," Stryker added.

"Going through now," Oliver said. Again with the silence. "I'm through. Nice cell. Glad the Major General is here and removing most of us. The princesses are remaining inside with the Invisible Commandos, by the way."

"What if the commandos try something?" Reader asked.

Oliver chuckled. "Then I expect the princesses to truly enjoy themselves. The Major General wants his briefing.

Signing off from Guantanamo Bay, I respectfully remain your loyal correspondent."

"He's got style, you have to give him that," Jeff said.

"Do we?" Christopher muttered.

"Rear car gate is removed. Gate is ready for cadaver transfer to Dulce, Mister Reynolds," William said.

"Falk and I need to literally toss these bodies through. Please warn whoever's waiting, William. And give us a minute or so."

"Yes, Mister Reynolds. Floater gate prepping for middle car, Commander Reader, calibrated for multiples and NASA Base."

"We're only sending civilians through, William," Reader said. "The rest of us are staying on the train."

"Gate is live, Commander."

Another few moments where I heard the staff thanking Reader for getting them off their own personal *Terror Train*, then Reader heaved a sigh. "Civilians all off. Vance and Mahin are back with us."

"Civilians confirmed at NASA Base," Raj said. "Should I sign off?"

"Wait until we hear from Chuckie."

"I'm back." Chuckie sounded out of breath. "Falk is also through and has goggles with him as well as seven dead bodies."

"Ick."

"You have no idea. Raj, does Tito want you under observation?" Chuckie asked.

"Tito wants everyone under observation."

"Then yes, sign off," Chuckie said. "Advise us as necessary."

"Roger that, Singh out. Again."

"White House advised of the President's location, as well as that of the Vice President and the Rail Force One and Two staff," William said. "All gates are removed."

Heaved a sigh. "Everyone who makes taking the train epic is at NASA Base now."

"True," Gower said. "We checked the other cars on our way back. All empty."

"That was possibly worse than being attacked by invisible commandos," Stryker said.

"I'd like to mention that I checked them against my will," Vance chimed in. "But Paul's right—it's just the ten of us here. Well, and however many Poofs may or may not be around."

"There are times he's far too much like you," Jeff said quietly.

Ignored him. "Where's Chuckie?"

"Checking the other cars. Hang on, I have to climb outside on the War Room car."

"Charles, I'm joining you," White said. "Wait for me."

"Just the four of us here, along with Bruno and Ginger, still. Before Poof Head Count, that is. But if there's someone between you and us, we don't know."

"We do now," White said. "Charles and I have verified that all cars are devoid of anyone visible or invisible. We're all clear."

"No Secret Service, no A-C Field agents, just us against whatever's coming." I leaned against Jeff. "Just like the good old days all over again."

"Reaching the station," Adriana said. "The fifteen of us and all animal companions need to prepare for anything. Including crashing."

Jeff snorted a laugh. "That pretty much sums up our entire lives."

CHAPTER 52

WE PREPPED FOR impact as much as we could, but as we did I took a good look out the windshield.

The station was a red three-story building that looked more like a nice old-fashioned apartment building than a train station. There wasn't a lot else here—lots of concrete, some of which had cars parked on it, concrete benches dotted under the long free-standing awnings that lined the ground level platform area. The pathway to the station was covered as well.

The only real vantage point for any kind of long-range attack was the top of the station, and the sloping rooftops made that unlikely.

However, it wasn't long-range attack that was on the agenda.

"Adriana, floor it! Or whatever you do with a train!"

While Jeff and Christopher, and those on the phone chain, started to ask me why, Adriana did what I'd told her to and made the train go faster.

Not that this was simple, since we'd been slowing down. But fortunately we hadn't stopped. Because while the train station was loaded with regular people who looked like they were here to greet us—the competing Armstrong-Martini and anti-alien signs were something of a clue—they weren't alone. There were people I recognized standing a little too close to the tracks. Eight of them, really.

The Crazy Eights were all wearing long trench coats and, as we got closer, they pulled out the big guns they'd been concealing. And, naturally, aimed those guns at us.

Jeff had finally seen what I'd spotted. "Everybody down!" he bellowed. No one could bellow like my man. Assumed that the others would have heard him even if we weren't on the phone together. The Crazy Eights probably heard him. Hopefully the civilians did, too.

Whether they'd heard him or we were just near enough, the Crazy Eights started shooting. They had some seriously impressive guns on them, too. No rocket launchers, so we had that going for us.

It was all eight of them, and as we pulled into the station and kept going, albeit not nearly as fast as I'd have liked, I spotted the helicopter down in the parking lot. It had been hidden by the station when we'd been pulling in.

The civilians were, to a person, screaming and running away. Couldn't blame them and really hoped the Crazy Eights wouldn't turn the guns on them just because they couldn't hit us. Also really hoped they couldn't hit us.

Christopher had grabbed the laptop and hit the ground, but Adriana only ducked, since she had to keep the train going. Jeff kept pulling me down and I kept on getting up. "I need to see who number eight is," I said as I scrambled to my feet again.

He got up, pulled me behind Adriana, where there was a lot of metal and no window, near the door we'd come in that had a small window in it. We both peeked out. In time to see Dier jumping onto the platform that would let her into the engine.

Didn't hesitate. The door wasn't closed well since Jeff and Christopher had wrenched it open. So I kicked it open using all my enhanced strength.

Had the satisfaction of watching Dier fly off and land on

her butt on the concrete. Had hopes she'd at least bruised her tailbone. She was a pain in my butt, so it was fitting that she'd have pain in her own.

This also meant that the door, which had been holding by its version of a thread, also went flying. Karma did me a solid and the door flew into Lowe and knocked him back and down. Not only did we have two of the eight down, but the air bender was knocked out. Go team.

Speaking of team, saw the shimmer that meant we had a protective bubble around us, meaning that Abigail was feeling well enough to get back in the game. And dirt started flying at the remaining Crazy Eights, showing that Mahin was representing, too.

The train was doing its best to get moving fast again, but this many tons of steel neither slowed nor sped up quickly. Despite the dirt covering their bodies, Kozlow and Dear Sam tried to get onto the train, but were repelled by the shield.

As the engine passed the end of the station, I spotted Crazy Number Eight. It was a woman, tallish with long brown hair, around my age. And I knew her—Casey Jones, the stewardess from the failed airplane bombing attempt during Operation Drug Addict and the failed bombing of the Romanian Embassy attempt during Operation Destruction. Adriana had been right—it was time to go over our Rogue's Gallery and come up with any enemies we'd forgotten about.

"Are they trying to get onto the other cars?" I asked.

"Can't tell," Jeff replied.

Checked my phone. The call had dropped. Whether this meant that Jeff's bellowing had blown it out, we'd just hit a patch of bad reception, or something else, I had no way of guessing.

"Hold onto me." I leaned out of the open doorway as Jeff grabbed the back of my jeans. It was hard to be sure, but I didn't see anyone on the train, and based on the people I could still spot, all eight were still on the concrete.

I nodded and Jeff pulled me back inside. "Now what?" he asked. "I mean other than you once again trying to take years off of my life."

Dialed the phone for Reader. No service. Tried with Chuckie. Same again. Tried to reach Raj. Nada. "I think they've knocked out our telecommunications somehow."

"I'm offline on the laptop, so I think Kitty's right," Christopher said. "But how?"

"Mastermind and/or Langston Whitmore. Figure one of those guns had some kind of pulse thing in it. Just our luck coming through again. Bottom line is that we can't talk to the others and, more importantly, we can't talk to anyone else on the line."

"That's dangerous," Adriana said. "Which I realize we all know. But if we can't advise that we're not stopping, then we can't be sure that there isn't another train on the part of the track we're on."

"Fabulous." Jeff ran his hand through his hair. "Christopher, any luck rebooting the laptop?"

"I've been trying. Nothing."

"The others have to know that they can't reach us by now, wouldn't you think?" I asked.

"Probably a safe assumption, baby. If not yet, one of them will try us soon and then they'll know."

Bruno nudged up against me and squawked quietly. "Good idea."

"What did the bird suggest?" Jeff asked in the voice of a man who's not sure who's crazier, the world around him or himself.

"Time to see if we have Poofs On Board." Looked into my purse. Sure enough, there was a lot of concentrated fluffy cuteness in there. "Poofies, Kitty needs your help."

Poofs poured out and looked up at me in that overwhelmingly cute way of theirs.

Quickly explained the situation. "So, Kitty needs to let the others know what's going on. And then Kitty needs help in being sure that this train doesn't crash into another train or anything else."

Harlie and Poofikins mewed and jumped up and down. They had no problems with the first request. They sent a couple of Poofs off, presumably to share with the Poofs in the other car and give it the old college try for Poof Charades.

However, the Poofs had less of an idea of what to do about our *Runaway Train* situation than I did. Which was, of course, not helpful.

Time to see if Algar was willing to give me some clues. Put my earbuds in.

"Is now really the time for music?" Jeff asked.

"It's always the time for music. And I can still hear you talking with my earbuds in, so you can stop acting like I'm not paying attention to the urgent matters at hand. Tunes help keep me calm and focused."

Turned on the music and waited. Oasis was still playing "Going Nowhere" which was frighteningly true right now. Remembered I'd put the song onto repeat and put it back onto regular play. The next song was "Train" by 3 Doors Down. This indicated I was still on the playlist Kyle had made for me, meaning that it was unlikely that Algar was taking an interest.

Which was, all things considered, odd.

Considered why Algar might not be tossing out the Helpful Hints. Distracted by impending doom? Possible, but if the Superconsciousness Seven or the Black Hole People Police Force were showing up, had a feeling Algar would be letting me know.

Tired of helping me? Unlikely. He claimed I was one of his favorites and I knew he was far too emotionally attached to the A-Cs, both on Earth and Alpha Four, to just ignore what was going on.

Had already given me all that I needed? He'd given me the goggles at the Embassy. But he'd used my purse as a Black Hole Delivery Device during Operation Civil War.

Dug around in my purse, searching for something, anything, that seemed out of place or identified as not being
mine. Was rewarded to find an external flash drive at the
bottom of my purse. I certainly hadn't put it in there.

Handed it to Christopher as ELO's "Last Train to Lon-
don" came on. Barring our barreling into a floater gate, this
was probably part of Kyle's playlist. "Try plugging this into
the laptop."

"What is it and where did you get it?" he asked.

"It's an external flash drive, which I would honestly expect the former Head of Imageering to know, and in my
purse. I think Stryker put it in there," I lied.

"What can it hurt?" Jeff asked.

"Good point." Christopher plugged it into the USB port
in the laptop.

Results were, as they so often were, immediate.

CHAPTER 53

THE LAPTOP SPRANG TO LIFE. Christopher started typing furiously, then he breathed a sigh of relief. "I've reached the main Amtrak control center. Advised them that we were under attack and where, and have requested that we be allowed to go nonstop to Orlando now."

"What did they say?" Adriana asked.

"That they're verifying and will let us know." He shook his head. "We need to thank Stryker for this, Jeff. God alone knows how many lives it just saved, starting with our own."

"He's a prince," Jeff said. "I'll let his continued freeloading be his thanks."

Chose not to argue this because I knew that Stryker had no idea what was on this drive and that him saying so would be the definition of awkward, since I'd be asked who'd put it there if he hadn't.

The laptop beeped. More typing, then Christopher relaxed. "We're cleared through to Savannah, no stops. We need to stop in Savannah, though, due to a variety of factors. The feeling is that we'll have enough fuel and all other trains are being rerouted or delayed. Most already were, since the President was on the train, but this way we shouldn't have any issues."

"We'll definitely have enough fuel," Adriana said.

."Though since we'll be going faster than the norm we might be cutting it close."

"Are you going to be able to handle this for all that time?" Jeff asked her. "We're talking hours."

"I think so." Adriana sounded somewhat doubtful, as the music changed to Aerosmith's "Train Kept A Rollin'." Had no idea if this was a hint or just part of the playlist. Decided to enjoy the sounds of my boys in my ears and not worry about it.

"Adriana, we'll do our best to spell you if we have to. And by we I mean me. But for right now, Jeff, let's search for clues to what happened to the engineer and conductor. They disappeared without a trace."

"And without any signs of violence," Adriana added. "The only damage was to the outer door."

"Which was locked, from the inside, and which damage we caused," Jeff said. "Yeah, okay, baby, why don't you do a better search?"

"Super. Because what we need right now is a locked room mystery, just for grins and giggles. Christopher, while we get our Scooby Doo on, can you see if we can get another train command team sent to us via floater gate?"

"I'm not sure we want to do that," he said. "Right now I'm only on with Amtrak. I don't know if it's a good idea for us to coordinate through them—it's not exactly a secured channel. And Langston Whitmore would have jurisdiction over anything related to the trains."

"Good point," Jeff said. "Kitty, let's see what you find that Christopher and I might have missed." He looked down at Bruno and Ginger. "Put the keen animal senses on it, too."

"Will do. Bruno, Ginger, let's go see what we can see."

There was a door at the back of the cabin that led to one of the smallest bathrooms I'd ever seen. As horrific bathrooms went, I'd seen far more than my share, and this one was definitely in the Top 10 Worst. And there was no ventilation in the ceiling, either.

The animals backed away. Could tell Jeff was trying not to laugh. "Downbound Train" by Bruce Springsteen came on. Had to figure the Boss' downer attitude for this song might have come from seeing a toilet like this.

"This is it? That's all there is to this entire thing? One cramped cabin and one horrifically small toilet area?"

"Yeah," Jeff said. "And there's no gate in here. We already checked." He closed the door. "The rest of what's behind us is what runs the train, baby. So, any ideas?"

"Other than shoving you into that bathroom as punishment for your personal amusement, not really. The door's gone, so we can't verify if it can lock like a regular door, from the outside."

"It can," Adriana said. "Grandmother would say you're trying too hard."

"You think the engineer and conductor got outside and locked the door with the keys they possess and then, what? Jumped for it?"

"They could have been taken by the helicopter," Christopher said. "We didn't notice anything until we heard people landing on the roof."

"Which begs a question we haven't asked yet, or if we have, I don't know the answer: How did the Invisible Commandos get onto the train?"

"The other question is why the engineer and conductor left," Jeff said. "Because that door was strong and this is made of steel, so they should have just locked themselves in and called for help if they were under attack."

"Why take them out of the train at all?" Considered my own question. "Pawns."

"What?" Christopher asked.

"Pawns. Chess. If we think about the three attacks, the Invisible Commandos were here to take over and take hostages. The train can and should arrive in Rocky Mount, right? So that they can show the world how easily the President was captured."

"That makes sense," Adriana said. "What were the Crazy Eights doing?"

"I have no idea, but since they weren't the ones who blew the track, and neither were the Invisible Commandos, that leaves us Club Fifty-One, who've claimed responsibility for it. And said group of wackos are really good at infiltrating at low levels. But it's the low level pawns that can and have set up things effectively to hurt us in the past."

"You think the engineer and conductor were part of Club Fifty-One's plan?" Jeff asked.

"Yes, because if the train was going to derail, I sure wouldn't want to be on it. Why else would they leave? Christopher's right—if they were being attacked, they'd have shared that with someone, and they had the means to do so. They didn't share, there's no sign of violence in here, meaning they weren't killed. So they left of their own accord, meaning they had a reason to leave whenever they did."

"There were plenty of areas where jumping off, even with the train going fast, wouldn't have been too dangerous," Adriana mentioned.

"Yeah, so let's take that as our working hypothesis until we know more."

"The Invisible Commandos have an invisible helicarrier where our people are being held," Jeff said. "My guess is that they also have invisible helicopters. I heard far more than eight people land on the train."

"So, what does this knowledge, or the assumption of knowledge, do for us?" Christopher asked as "Big City Train" by No Doubt came on. Had to hand it to Kyle—he'd really created a cool train-centric playlist. It was also keeping me relaxed and thinking, so a double for the win column.

"It confirms the most important point of this entire day."

CHAPTER 54

"AND THAT IS?" Adriana asked politely after a few moments of silence.

"Sorry, thought you were all following me. The most important point is that the three attacks weren't coordinated."

"Okay," Jeff said. "Don't get mad, baby, but so what?"

"The what of that so is that this raises the key question—why did the Crazy Eights take off earlier when they could easily have caused us a lot of damage and possibly even won? Only to be waiting to shoot all of us at Rocky Mount?"

"Grandmother would say that we need to think like whoever is in charge."

"Okay, Gustav Drax is in charge of the Invisible Commandos and probably Huntress, too. And he appears to want to sell his new tech. That all his crap is a sales pitch seems likely, considering the fact that the commandos weren't really trying to kill us. I mean, they'd have killed some of us if they could have, but considering they had no guns with them and most weren't using their knives, the kill order was clearly not given."

"I agree," Jeff said. "And I also agree that the theory that makes the most sense about the engineer and conductor is that they're part of Club Fifty-One. Even without blowing up the bridge, with no one controlling the train we'd derail or crash somewhere along the way."

"And it sounds like them," Christopher said. "They really shoot for the grandiose plans."

"So, we know that Harvey Gutermuth is in charge of Club Fifty-One, and we can include Farley Pecker and the Church of Hate and Intolerance in there, too. Supposedly they were brokering a deal with the Crazy Eights, but Dier didn't seem to agree. In fact she point blank told me they hadn't sent that message and have no intention of turning themselves in."

"So the Club Fifty-One contingent used the prisoners' escape as an opportunity," Jeff said. "Not the first time that's been done, baby."

"Right, but that means that they aren't the ones who activated the Crazy Eights. Dier seemed more down on them than she is on us, and that's saying a lot."

"The Mastermind is the obvious choice for who activated the Crazy Eights," Adriana said. "He probably activated the Club Fifty-One people, too, but Grandmother feels that it takes almost nothing to stir those people up, so they could have come up with this on their own."

"Oh! I forgot—I saw Casey Jones, she formerly of Club Fifty-One. She's our number eight. She was shooting at us and clearly with the other Crazies."

"She could easily have activated Club Fifty-One then, too," Jeff pointed out.

"She could have. I presume she's our mystery welder. For all we know, she got the engineer and conductor out, too."

"She could have been in here with them when we left," Adriana said. "I doubt the Secret Service checked that bathroom."

"Even if they did, she could have been hiding under here," Christopher shoved open a panel near his feet. "I think it's for storage, but someone could fit in here for a while, rolled into a ball. If the conductor and engineer were in on this, then they wouldn't have said the panel opened and it doesn't look like it should. I kicked it accide... ..., when they were shooting at us, which is the only reason I know it's here."

"So she was working both plans. It's not out of the realm of possibility, especially since she's high ranking in Club Fifty-One."

"Meaning she's taking direction from the Mastermind," Adriana said.

"Aren't they all?" Jeff asked with a sigh, as "Downtown Train" by Rod Stewart hit my airwaves.

"Truly. But that brings us back to the main question then—why were the Crazy Eights sent? All you'd need for the Club Fifty-One plan to work was Casey. She's done this sort of thing before, helicopter escape especially, and was never caught after we saw her during Operation Destruction."

Jeff jerked. "If Stephanie isn't working with them, Casey's probably the one who let the others out of the supermax."

"Somehow. Of course, if whoever let the seven of them out wasn't an A-C, then the 'how' is Casey being helped by some Club Fifty-One infiltration. Again, I might add."

"I can buy it," Jeff said. "But we're still no closer to answering your question. Unless the plan was simply to kill the President and the rest of us. I mean, they were waiting for us at Rocky Mount."

"The Mastermind would know that the President wasn't on the train anymore," Christopher pointed out. "I had the White House hooked in and I know they had other agencies alerted to what was going on."

"So, why try to shoot us at Rocky Mount, then?" Jeff asked. "And don't say to kill us. They had that opportunity already and ran off before they really had to, at least based on what Kitty and Adriana both said."

"Where were the security teams that Mom said would be at Rocky Mount and all the other stops, too? I can understand why we didn't see them at our two uneventful stops, but they should have been trying to get civilians to safety and take the Crazy Eights out, but if they were doing so, then they're as invisible as our commandos."

"Drax or the Crazy Eights took them out," Christopher suggested. "And my money's on Drax, since he'd have been doing his sales pitch at Rocky Mount."

Wished the phones were working. Checked mine. Still no service. Heaved a sigh. Forced to do this without help from Reader, Chuckie, Tim, White, or the girls. Frankly, I'd have really liked to get the entire team's input. But if what I wanted always happened, I'd have a normal life and that apparently wasn't in my particular deck of cards.

"Okay. We've got nothing but time, so let's look at the three plans individually. Club Fifty-One wants us eliminated, so we can absolutely put them into the Terrorist Attack Section. We'll assume that Casey is playing a double game and is activating and directing Club Fifty-One activities, either with Gutermuth's blessing or without his knowing. Their goal was to derail the train."

"Right," Jeff said. "So, we take them out of all of this and then what? The Invisible Commandos were doing a live action sales pitch, right?"

"Right. So we take them out, too. Let's look at the Crazy Eight's plan and try to imagine what would have happened if the other two plans hadn't been active at the same time."

"Pretty much what did happen," Christopher said as "Last Train to Clarksville" by The Monkees came on. "We heard people land on the roof and we flipped into protection mode."

"Per Nerida, they felt that they knew exactly what we'd do based on Dear Sam's input."

Christopher shot Patented Glare #3 out to the world. For once, I was pretty sure he was glaring in a general sense, not at me specifically. Always nice to have a change. "The Secret Service hasn't changed what they do in situations."

"You're sure?"

This time I got Patented Glare #2 just for me. "Yes, I'm sure, Kitty. I've spoken to them about it, more than once. The 'this is how we do things' speech is one they all know. Even Evalyne, Phoebe, Joseph, and Rob cling to that party line. And considering that they're all used to dealing with you and Jeff, you'd think they'd be more open to adaptation, but they're not."

"So, Nerida was right—they absolutely did know what would happen the moment we realized we were under attack."

"Even if the Secret Service had changed things up, the War Room is there for the express purpose of protecting the President and his key staffers in the case of any kind of attack while on Rail Force One," Jeff said. "So they knew we'd herd Vince and the others there."

"We should have been in there, too . . ." Something was nudging at the back of my brain. Something important.

"What?" Jeff asked. "I know that look."

"Not sure yet. Let's say that we let them shove us into the War Room, or that Joseph had been faster than us somehow and kept us in. What, then, would have happened?"

"We'd all have been taken by the Invisible Commandos," Adriana said.

"No. Remember, we're thinking about this as if only the Crazy Eight's plan was in effect. So . . . what would they have done if they'd gotten us, me and Jeff, into the War Room?"

"Taken over?" Christopher asked. "I mean, that's their plan, right? Commandeering the train? Capturing the President?"

"Then why fly off? They couldn't see the Invisible Commandos and they didn't know about the Club Fifty-One plan. I'm sure if Casey was in on both plans that she didn't tell the others about blowing up the tracks. And maybe she wasn't in on that. The engineer and conductor could still be Club Fifty-One and willing to help her out just 'cause."

"You think the goal was to get us all into the War Room?" Jeff asked. "Why? They didn't try to blow it up, and even though they shot the hell out of it, it wasn't breached."

My music switched to "Miss Jackson" by Panic! At the Disco. This had nothing to do with trains or traveling. Focused, because this was likely to be one of Algar's Musical Clues.

"Miss Jackson." Hadn't meant to say that aloud, but whatever.

"Why are you mentioning Lizzie?" Jeff asked.

Because Algar was mentioning Lizzie, at least as far as I could tell. Looked at my phone. I had one bar. "Hang on." Hit speed dial and thanked ACE, Algar, and all the other Powers That Be that he answered.

"Kitty, you guys okay?" Chuckie asked.

"Yes. You were worried about other people being sick earlier. Why?"

One of the many things I loved about Chuckie was that he rarely asked me "why are you asking me that" questions and rolled with my vertigo-inducing conversational shifts without missing a beat. "Because I'm a suspicious person and see conspiracies everywhere."

"And you're normally right. So, who else is sick?"

"Everyone who was in the meeting Jeff was in that he left due to the attack on Cleary. Other than Cliff Goodman."

Algar had said that we had no way of preparing for the real attack. And now I knew why. "Oh. Crap. I know why the Crazy Eights attacked the train. The first time."

CHAPTER 55

"AND THE SECOND time, too," I added, "but that's not as important."

"Putting you on speaker," Chuckie said. "No idea how long we'll hold service. This is the first call I could get or get through to since Rocky Mount."

Talked fast and brought the others up to speed on our situation in the engine as well as the theories. "So," I finished, "I think the Crazy Eights attacked so as to get everyone into a contained room for a significant period of time."

There was silence for a few long moments. Verified that I still had bars. Did. Two now, as a matter of fact. Either we were moving into a better cellular coverage area or whatever the Crazy Eights had hit us with was wearing off.

Chuckie finally broke it. "Your mother, Raj, and Tito were in that room."

"And Malcolm, Evalyne, Phoebe, Joseph, and Rob." Took a deep breath and let it out slowly. None of us could help anyone if we were panicking. "And tons of other people. Lizzie's father came up with a biological weapon. What are the odds someone's finished his work?"

"High," Reader said. "Very high. I can't get calls through but I can text, and I've been texting with Raj. The Planetary Council have arrived. Apparently they were monitoring for when the President hit NASA Base because they arrived shortly after. Once we get into Savannah we need to take a gate to get over there ASAP."

"Kitty, we've been able to reach William and I've put the Embassy onto lockdown," Lorraine said. "No one in, no one out."

"As far as we know, no one in the Embassy has been exposed," Claudia added. "Unless Jeff was."

"I'm not sick," he pointed out. "And those others are."

"Why are Mom and Elaine less sick? At least they sounded less sick."

"I'm texting with Tito," Tim said. "Everyone who was in the War Room car once it went into lockdown is showing symptoms. Including the A-Cs."

"It needs to incubate," Chuckie said. "Whatever this is, it needs a more closed environment to spread."

"That's why the Crazy Eights attacked. To get as many of us as possible into the War Room and locked in it for as long as possible." As always, our enemies found new reasons for me to hate them. They were creative that way.

"Cliff was in the meeting I was called out of," Jeff said. "And you said he's not sick."

"So he released the bioweapon and has already taken the antidote," Chuckie said without missing a beat.

"Meaning that there *is* an antidote," I pointed out. That was me, Susie Sunshine.

"But everyone on this train was exposed," Gower said, bringing things right back down to reality. "And we were in contact with the Crazy Eights and all the Invisible Commandos."

"The commandos in particular," Stryker said. "And they're now at Guantanamo."

"And Falk is with the dead bodies at Dulce, too," Christopher said.

"What are we going to do?" Vance asked.

"First, we're going to verify that this is something more than a mere cold or flu," White said firmly. "I realize that it could indeed be a deadly bioweapon, but cold and flu incubate and pass along in the same way, and half of the people in the War Room were exposed to the President. If he merely caught a bad case of influenza or a terrible cold, it would and could pass as it has."

"Richard's right," Jeff said, Commander Voice on Full. "Until we can verify that this is something more than a bad case of the common cold, we're not going to panic, or panic anyone else."

Wanted to tell White and Gower—who also knew of Algar's existence—that he'd told me to think of Lizzie. But I not only couldn't, because Algar didn't allow us to talk about him with anyone and shielded our thoughts about him, too, but the thought occurred that Algar might have meant something else. Like maybe I should phone home.

"Keep the Embassy in lockdown, just to be on the safe side. I'm going to give Lizzie a call and make sure she's not freaked out by the lockdown and such. And, you know, see if she knows anything about an antidote to whatever horrible thing her father was creating. Just in case and all that."

"Chuck, call me back if you can," Jeff said. "I think Kitty's right to check in."

I hung up and dialed Lizzie as Jeff's phone rang. I had more bars now, and reception was back to what I was used to.

"Hey Kitty, why are we in lockdown?"

"Just a precaution, and not because we have a teenager in the house. How are things there?"

"Fine. Your dad has everyone doing a play."

"Cool."

"Totally not age approps, though. We're doing *Julius Caesar*. And by 'we' I mean all the kids. Even Charlie."

"Wow. Um. I don't think I want to know. Who are you?"

"Brutus. I wanted Marc Antony but he gave that to Raymond."

"I'm going to stop asking. So, does anyone seem like they've caught a cold or anything?"

"Hang on." Heard Lizzie telling my dad she'd be right back, then the sound of a door closing. "What's really going on? Do you think someone's found my dad's formula?" She didn't sound casual and relaxed now—she sounded frightened and angry.

"Why would you assume that?"

"Because you called to ask me if anyone's sick. And I'm the one with the traitor dead parents who were trying to kill everyone using a disease. Makes sense."

Contemplated what to say. Decided that I wasn't going to do what my family had done and lie to her. "You're a smart kid. Yeah, we're concerned. A bunch of people are sick and we just kind of want to be hyper-cautious."

"Who can blame you? Should I tell your dad?"

"No." My Mom was sick. The last person I wanted to share these concerns with was my dad. "I think, if you can, let's just keep it between us."

She snorted. "I'm the adopted daughter of an assassin. I can keep a secret."

"Good point. Just pay attention and let me know right away if anyone starts sniffling or sneezing or anything else."

"Maybe they've just got colds," she said hopefully.

"That's the prevailing optimistic hope. Also, please let your father and the uncles know what we're worried about. And mention to them that we were attacked four times so far on this trip and are wondering if them coming was all an elaborate ruse so they could vacation in Florida."

She laughed. "Will do. We have a way to send coded messages. Is everyone okay?"

"I'm sure you do. And yes, amazingly enough, we're all okay, barring the ones who seem to be sick."

"Good." She sighed. "I miss my dad," she said quietly.

"I'm sure you do. And I'm just as sure that he misses you."

"Really?"

"He wouldn't have adopted you if he didn't want you,

Lizzie. But he wants you safe, and so do we. So stay put and be my eyes and ears in the Embassy."

"Will do, Kitty."

We hung up and Jeff put his arm around my shoulders and gave me a hug. "Good job, baby. You were right to tell her the truth. What?" He laughed at the look I shot him. "Chuck says to tell you to stop being bitter about the past. He and your parents shared what you needed to know when you needed to know it."

"*Sure* they did."

"We have a plan for the rest of the trip," Jeff said as my music came back on and "Good & Bad Times" by INXS came on. Had no idea if this was an Algar or Kyle playlist song and decided not to worry about it.

"I hope it's not going to the bathroom, because I'm never entering that room again."

He grinned. "No. We're going to get Tim and James up here to help Adriana. We found some walkie-talkies and, amazingly enough, most of the food and drink weren't destroyed in the fighting, so they'll bring a walkie and refreshments with them."

"Don't drink anything," I told her. "Trust me."

"I can hold it," she said with a laugh.

"Christopher, you and I are going to go back with the others, at least for right now," Jeff went on. "We want to be sure that the Vice President and his wife are not seen to be driving this train whenever we finally stop."

"I think it would make you look even cooler."

"Chuck thinks it will raise questions we can't really answer," he said. "So, we're going to not be cool."

"Spoilsport. You know it's going to be hard as hell to get up there."

"Paul and Richard are coming to help. We'll be fine."

"Once more onto the roof then. Truly, I cannot wait."

CHAPTER 56

GETTING UP WASN'T as bad as I'd expected, in part because Jeff, Gower, and White were all big men. Reader and Tim had hold of Gower, Gower had hold of White's ankles, White slid down toward me, Jeff lifted me up, White and I grabbed each other's wrists, and up I went.

In deference to all of this, I'd put my phone into my purse, nestled between snoozing Poofs. Had a moment—when Jeff had to sort of toss me up and before White and I caught each other—where I really wanted to ask the Poofs for an assist. However, there was no reason to ask them for help when we didn't need it and, as I was pulled onto the roof, it was clear we didn't need it.

Bruno flew up with Ginger in his claws again. Then Jeff lifted Christopher up. This was harder because Christopher had been steadying him before, but they both made it look easy.

Now it was time to lower Reader and Tim and their supplies. "Are you sure you three shouldn't have an A-C with you?" I asked as we lowered the supplies down to Jeff.

"Yeah, we'll be fine, girlfriend." Reader flashed me the cover boy smile. "Tim and I need to learn how to run one of these things and apparently Adriana's an expert."

"All hail the KGB." Hugged Reader and Tim, then it was time to lower them down. Reader went first, in the reverse move we were all pretty good with by now. Tim was handed down without issue, too.

Jeff had it the hardest because he had to jump up and though Tim was steadying him, there wasn't enough room for Reader to be there, too, and it would take both of them to lift Jeff.

He proved that white men could indeed jump, though, and thankfully White was really good at this sort of thing, because Jeff actually overshot and went up higher than he should have.

White grabbed him around his chest, and I grabbed Jeff's hand and pulled as Christopher dragged Gower backward. In this totally smooth way we got Jeff onto the roof.

"That looks more fun on TV," Jeff said after everyone was upright and as I hugged him and tried not to shake. "I'm okay, baby," he said as he nuzzled my ear. "I promise. And thanks for the assist."

"Any time."

We did the jump down to the next car. It wasn't nearly as bad as the jump up had been, but I wasn't sorry that Jeff had my hand. Abigail had taken the shield down a long time ago now.

We climbed down and went into this car. I was surprised to see everyone there. "We're camping here?"

"It's the least destroyed of all the cars," Lorraine said.

"Well, other than the caboose," Claudia added.

"And it has more amenities than the caboose does," Vance said.

"And it's right by the engine," Chuckie said. "So if we have to detach the other cars for whatever reason, we can."

"God, let's hope we don't have to."

"We cleared out anything else useful," Mahin shared. "And this car has more beds than the others."

"And the least broken windows, too," Gower said. True enough—only two were broken and someone had put what I was pretty sure were floorboards over them. Chose not to ask how that had been achieved—we were a talented group, after all.

"I wanted to stay in Rail Force One," Stryker said, "until I remembered that the President and all the other sick people had stayed there for a couple of hours."

"Good point. We're going to need to decontaminate the entire train. Maybe, I mean. Could just be bad colds."

"Let's hope," Abigail said. "Anyway, we have food, water, other beverages, beds, and a bathroom. We should be good until we reach Savannah."

"Time to rest, then," White said. "Everyone's already overtired. Let's take advantage of the lull we find ourselves in and lie down or sit in a relaxed manner."

"Wise man knows when to take the naps."

Everyone had a snack, we determined our watch and walkie-talkie duty schedule, then we settled into bunks as best we could. Jeff and I were cuddled together with Bruno at our heads and Ginger between our legs. It wasn't the sexy times I'd hoped for on this trip, but we were together and that was what really mattered.

I wasn't given a watch duty, and neither were Mahin or Abigail. The thinking was that the three of us would need to rest and rejuvenate the most, since no one was foolish or naïve enough to think that we'd seen the last of our various enemies.

Despite it being daylight, managed to fall asleep anyway, listening to Chuckie and Reader discussing the finer points of train engineering while Christopher and Tim discussed why the conductor role was also vital. Apparently the guys had all harbored train love that they were just now getting to share. Whatever worked for bonding was my opinion.

Had kind of hoped I'd get a visit from ACE while I was sleeping, or even a hint-filled dream, but all I got was rest. Always the way.

I probably would have slept until we got to Savannah, only my phone went off. Not with a ringtone or an alarm,

eardrum sic activation. "Hurricane" by Lifehouse was
looked around. lume. Algar Hint when it slapped me in my

It was dark out, meaning my purse over my neck, then
White had the walkie meaning it wa be close to Savannah.
one else was waking up, due to my sonic blast atch duty. Every-

"Why is that song shrieking at us?" Christopher asked,
sharing Patented Glare #5 with me.

"It's crooning, and I'm not sure," I lied. Hey, I was human, ergo I was good at lying. Pulled out my earbuds, put
them in my ears, and plugged them in so only I could hear
the melodious sounds. The volume was instantly normal.
Proof again, as if I needed it, that I was again on the Algar
Channel. "I think we might have gone over something."

"No," White said, "we didn't. We're in the midst of the
Savannah National Wildlife Refuge."

Looked out the window. We had a full moon, so it was
relatively easy to see. Saw a lot of what could be swamp or
uld be something else. All of it looked
tell?"

re fully back, Missus Martini, and while
sleep had its own naïve charm, I got

ny core, Mister White."
me to quite a number of fowl, Ameri-
cats."
also home to about a million venomous shakes, too, isn't it?"

"Information does indicate that copperheads and water
moccasins are inhabitants."

"Double hurray. I'll take the bobcats and possibly the
alligators, but the only birds I like are Peregrines." Bruno
nudged up against me to share that I was his favorite, too.

"Hey," Jeff said, sounding hurt, "what about parrots?"

"You mean Bellie, specifically, and ~~~~ me."

~~~~ of her of your avian mistress, so why yo~~~gators," Christopher relatives out here or anywher~~~, we'd have been alligator

"I'll take the parrot ~~~~ said. "Without ACE ~~~~ food."

"Oh, Giga~~~gator and Alliflash were our friends, never doubt it."

"I saw them t~y to eat us," Gower said dryly. "I doubt it, believe m~~."

"I'll still take them over any snake, anywhere, anytime, especially the two Mister White just named. Killers, they are. Vicious, evil killers."

"Phobia much?" Stryker asked.

"She's always been afraid of snakes," Chuckie said, shooting him a "shut up or die" look. "Everyone's irrationally afraid of something."

"There is no irrationalness about this." Wondered why Algar had woken me up. The song's title seemed obvious. "Mister White, can you check with our enthusiastic engineers and see if we have any weather-type stuff ahead of us?"

"I live to serve." He relayed the request to Tim and that I was the one asking.

"Nothing looks off," Tim replied. "Kitty, what are you worried about?"

"No idea. I just have a feeling that something's coming."

"Her music started for no reason," Christopher said as he took the walkie from White. "I think she's just trying to come up with a reason for why she woke all of us up."

The car shook. "What was that?" Lorraine asked.

"I think Kitty's found her reason," Reader said. "That was a gigantic blast of wind."

"There's been no strong wind until this moment," Adriana added.

"We're going to be coming to quite a wide river soon," White said.

"Tim, time to put on the Megalomaniac Capes."

"You think the Crazy Eights are here, don't you?" he asked.

"I do. Lowe is an air bender and Nerida is a water bender. They didn't try to get us at the last river we crossed, but I'm sure that attack gave them some ideas."

The car shook again. "That one was stronger," Reader said.

"Should I put up a shield?" Abigail asked.

"Not yet," Jeff replied. "Wait until we need it. And," he added with a sigh, "I'm sure we're going to need it."

And, as "Tidal Wave" by The Killers came on, I knew he was right.

CHAPTER 57

"HUMANS BATTEN THE hatches and stay inside! Abigail, Mahin, come with me!" With that, I ran for the front door.

I was on the platform before anyone else. Jumped for the ladder on the engine and this time I caught it without issue. Being revved up was always good for me.

The girls were right behind me, which was good as we were hit with another gust of wind and needed to grab each other in order to stay steady.

"What do you think is coming?" Abigail asked once the wind subsided.

"A tidal wave. Or similar. If they can do it right, Lowe and Nerida could work together to create a wall of water strengthened by wind."

Mahin nodded. "They could indeed. I don't know if I can counter that, Kitty. And this isn't me not being confident. Dirt tends to lose to wind and water."

"But not always."

The train was traveling at a fast pace and our hair was whipping around. We were also not wearing goggles, which was a tremendous oversight on my part.

On the other hand, White arrived, goggles on and three pairs in his hand. "I've managed to convince Jeffrey to stay inside."

"You mean you had Paul, Christopher, and Chuckie tackle him." The girls and I put our goggles on quickly.

"That is indeed what I mean, Missus Martini. I have no idea how long they'll be able to keep him down, so I suggest we put whatever plan you have into action with all haste."

There was no wind at the moment and I could hear Jeff bellowing. Pity I had no plan to enact. "Um, we need to block water and wind in some way. Tidal wave level water and hurricane level winds."

As I said this, we were hit with another gust. We dropped flat and held onto each other. However I was watching and saw a variety of birds of all kinds, a small alligator, and a couple of bobcats go flying through the air. The animals that could were screaming in terror.

That was all it took. I flipped into rage faster than I could blink. I didn't care for birds but that didn't mean I wished them ill. And this was a wildlife sanctuary that these horrible people were destroying for the sake of hurting us. It was time to take the fight to them.

I was holding onto Abigail and a shimmering went around each of the animals. "Thanks, Abby."

"Go get them," she said angrily. "I see what you want to do, and I can help."

It was nothing to get into the blocks position from the one I was in. Did so, and took off running. Hurdled off the front of the train and landed on the tracks without issue but definitely with an assist from Abigail. I kept on running.

Couldn't have told how fast the train was going, but I was far faster. I was at the same speed I'd been at during Operation Destruction when I'd run on water to get Tito to try to save Hughes and Walker.

Which was good, because the tracks left the trees that had been surrounding us and were now over water. Could see a wall of water coming toward us, and, thanks to the goggles, I could spot the origination point. Looked like a

sandbar or a tiny island or whatever you called a small land-
mass in the middle of a wide river.

Channeled Johnny Storm—didn't think about it, didn't
hesitate. Went for it and jumped off the tracks.

Splashed a little, but I could tell that Abigail had helped
me again, because I didn't go into the water. Kept on running as the water wall headed toward me and "Wonderwall" by Oasis came on. I was going fast enough that I could
see the individual drops that formed the water wall—they
were small and insignificant and I ran right through and
around them.

Got a little wet, but it didn't stop or slow me and I reached
the sandbar in seconds. Sure enough, Lowe and Nerida were
there, standing next to each other, Bender Stances Activated.

Keeping with my Johnny Storm theme, I didn't slow
down. Instead, I slammed into both of them.

I was going so fast that my momentum carried us to the
end of the sand bar. Didn't bother to see if I'd stopped their
bending—just started beating the crap out of them both.

The moves were flowing like they always did when I was
fully enraged and there was absolutely no one else around
to see them. Went for a multiple attackers form I'd learned
way back when—Tiger Takes on the Poachers. Okay, that's
what we'd called it in class. Its real name was Tiger Greets
the Dawn. But a rose by any other name would still kick the
same amount of butt.

They hit, I blocked, I hit, they didn't block fast enough.
Spinning, leaping, hitting, kicking, sweeping, and definitely
cursing, we were all over the sandbar. Hoped we weren't
destroying precious flora, but had to figure that we were.
Better than every animal around getting tossed about in the
air then getting to die on impact.

"You will not hurt these animals," I shouted while I
back-kicked Lowe in the stomach and hit Nerida with a
chop to the neck. "You people are really the damned lowest

of the low, aren't you?" This was accompanied by a jumping splits kick to both their chests that would have made Jean-Claude Van Damme proud.

Heard the chopper now. Meaning it had to be close. Grabbed Lowe and threw him into the water. "Deal with the alligators on their own terms, you loser!"

Lowe started screaming, in part because there were indeed alligators swimming over as fast as they could. We undoubtedly looked like a lovely buffet.

Grabbed Nerida and threw her at him. She screamed, too, hit Lowe, and they both went under the water.

The chopper turned on its lights now and dropped its handy-dandy ladder but it had to come low to reach them. Decided I'd had enough and I charged again.

Was still going so fast that the only one who could have kept up with me was Christopher. Ran on top of the water, hurdled an alligator, then Lowe and Nerida, then jumped and grabbed the rope ladder.

Climbed up quickly and grabbed the first person I reached, yanked hard on the arm I'd connected with, and tossed them out. Was rewarded to see Kozlow land with a smack in the water. "Enjoy the water moccasins!" I screamed at him.

Reached in again and grabbed another person. This time I got an ankle. No worries. Pulled hard. Whoever I had fell down. All the better to pull again and toss them out.

This time I'd caught Kellogg. Due to how he was leaving the chopper, he was able to grab my legs. But I was at the rage level where he wasn't nearly strong enough to keep my legs together. Knocked them apart and watched him land right on top of Kozlow. Good.

Four down meant four left. Plus I'd been moving so fast that this had taken about three seconds. "Wonderwall" finished and "Fist of Rage" by Kid Rock came on. Clearly Algar approved my course of action.

Pulled myself into the chopper's interior and slammed

my fist into Dier's face. This sent her flying into Wruck's back. Meaning he lost control and the chopper started circling, which tossed everyone around.

Landed on Dier. Gave her an elbow to the head as I scrambled to my feet. Dove and tackled Casey and Dear Sam, knocking both of them down just as they'd started to get up. We rolled around for a bit, but they were humans and I was enhanced. Kicked Dear Sam off me and into Dier, while I punched Casey in the gut.

This gave Wruck time to get the chopper under control and me time to get to my feet. Grabbed Casey with one hand and pulled her up off the floor. Dear Sam ran toward us and I caught him with my other hand. Slammed their heads together, then tossed them out into the river, too.

Dier struggled to her feet. "What the hell?" she asked. "Who the hell are you, really?"

"Devil Without a Cause, bitch." Hey, it was on my personal airwaves now. Kid Rock for the win apparently.

She pulled a gun and pointed it right at me. "Devil going to die now."

CHAPTER 58

DIER WAS FAST but I was faster. Slid toward her like I was trying to steal second while the bullet whizzed over my head and Wruck shouted at her to stop being an idiot. My feet slammed into her legs, which sent her back into the windshield. This knocked the gun out of her hand and it went flying.

Sadly, Wruck caught it. But he didn't turn it on me. Not for lack of trying, but because he couldn't aim and fly at the same time. Clearly he hadn't had Centaurion Division training.

Was able to get the gun away from him. Put it at the back of his head as I hit Dier's head with an excellent side blade kick. Once again, the skills were at optimum and no one was around to be impressed. "You get to choose."

"Choose what?" he asked carefully. He had a slight German accent. If he hadn't been an enemy, it might have been kind of sexy.

Looked out to see all six of those I'd tossed in the water on the sand bar. Bummer. Oh, sure, they were surrounded by alligators, but they were all alive and, as near as I could see, still had possession of all their body parts. Clearly Georgia gators weren't as feisty as their Florida brethren.

"Whether or not you die."

"How would I not die?"

"Tell me the truth."

"There is no Santa Claus."

"Dude, I can't stand any of you. Seriously, one more crack and I pull the trigger. I won't lose any sleep over it, trust me."

"Yes, I believe you—I know who your uncles are."

"Always nice to be infamous. So, what's really going on? As in, why are you Crazy Eights attacking us?"

"Because we got out of prison and want to make the people who put us there pay. Duh."

"Okay, I'll give you that one. Who let you out?"

He was quiet and I nudged his head with the barrel of the gun. "Casey. She has people on the inside."

Nice to be right. "Why did she let you out now as opposed to any other time?"

"If I tell you, you'll kill me."

"No. I keep my word. You tell me what I want to know, you get to live. I find out you've lied to me, then you don't get to live."

"As if you and your people won't try to kill us all the moment you get the chance?"

"Pot calls kettle black, film at eleven. And, let's be clear— I can kill you and Dier right now, then kill all the others, *and then* fly your snazzy chopper off, do some impressive maneuvers before I land it on the top of the train, and all before said train reaches Savannah."

He chuckled. "I'll grant you that one." He looked at Dier. She was still out. "Fine. We're out to cause problems for you with the aliens who are visiting."

"Why did you want everyone locked into the War Room?"

"To have everyone in one place."

"Why?"

"No idea."

Was pretty sure he was lying. "Who sent you and/or gives you your orders?"

He chuckled again. "You know I can't tell you that."

"What else can you tell me?"

"They're going to be eaten alive, you know." Wruck nodded his head toward the sand bar. "The only weapons are inside the helicopter and Annette is still knocked out."

"I care why?"

"Sometimes the enemy of your enemy can be your friend."

"Name the person in your group who's my friend."

"I'd say that I am, but you'd think it to be a lie and you'd kill me."

"Got that right."

"Honestly, none of us are your friends, at least in the sense that you mean it. However, if the situation was reversed, wouldn't you want whoever had your friends and family in this position to show mercy?"

"Yes, I would. I've been in this position a lot, though. No one ever shows us mercy." Looked at Dier. "Starting with that bitch right there."

He'd been waiting for me to be distracted. Discovered this because Wruck spun and grabbed the gun from me before I could react. "And now I have the gun." He pointed it at my stomach. "And what would you tell me to do with it?"

Considered my options. Jumping out was probably my best choice. I could try to get the gun, but he had it in a position where I was pretty sure he'd shoot me before I got the gun back, hyperspeed or no hyperspeed.

"What I'd like rarely enters into my enemies' consideration." My music changed to "Fight for All the Wrong Reasons" by Nickelback. Had no idea what Algar was suggesting, but if this was his goodbye song it lacked a certain something. Like Steven Tyler and Joe Perry and the rest of Aerosmith.

"Annette gave you her word that we wouldn't shoot at any of you earlier when I took her off the train. Which is why we didn't." Wruck handed the gun back to me.

Managed not to let my jaw drop, but it took effort. "I'd like to rescue the others."

"What about her?" Nodded toward Dier.

"I know she's killed people who matter to you. But I'll also tell you that, right now, you don't want to upset the balance of power in this group." He stood up. "Hold the stick a moment, though, please."

Wondering when I was going to wake up, I did as requested. Wruck picked Dier up and tossed her out of the chopper. As he took the stick again I watched Dier hit the water.

"Um . . ."

"Nerida will save her after you threw her out just like you did the others." He flew off toward the train as, sure enough, water lifted Dier up and sort of tossed her to the others on the gator-filled sand bar. So "save" might have been an overstatement. Perhaps "delay being eaten" would be more appropriate wording. "And I'll manage to shove you out over the train just before you kill me."

"Okay." I sat down in the seat next to him, took off the goggles, and put them into my purse. "I'm frankly hella confused right about now."

Took a good look at him. He was a reasonably attractive man, built more like Chuckie than Jeff. Indeterminate age, but older than me and younger than White was my general guess.

"Can you keep a secret?"

"Probably. What's the secret?"

"The enemy of your enemy is your friend." He turned to me as we slowly flew over the tracks behind the train. His eyes glittered. "Your enemies, your true enemies, are mine as well."

"You're in deep cover, aren't you?"

He chuckled again as No Doubt's "Undercover" came on. "Deeper than you can possibly imagine."

"Are you trying to avenge your father's or siblings' deaths, like some of the others are?"

"No."

Considered this and decided to take the Megalomaniac Girl Leap. "You're not actually one of Ronald Yates' offspring, are you?"

He smiled. "No, I'm not."

But he was pretending to be. He'd fooled everyone— Mossad, P.T.C.U., C.I.A., F.B.I., Chuckie, the Crazy Eights, Siler, Buchanan. "Why did you sit in supermax for all this time?"

He shrugged. "I had the time. And I needed to be sure."

"Be sure of what?"

"Who the real enemy is. And I'm sure. My enemies are yours."

"You said that before, and you said the plural both times. We call our main enemy the Mastermind. There's always been a Mastermind, but who he is changes. But he always has two people he relies on."

"One he relies on, one he grooms as his replacement."

I'd have never made this leap if I hadn't met LaRue during Operation Bizarro World and then spent time on Beta Eight during Operation Civil War. But since I had, and since I'd met some other deep cover agents there, my brain was nudging. Especially over him being so casual about sitting in a prison for several years.

"LaRue. Every Mastermind has relied on her. Because she's not human. She's an Ancient. And a Z'porrah spy."

His lips quirked but he didn't say anything.

"She's dead, you know. Esteban Cantu shot her in the head at the end of Operation Destruction."

"So I heard."

"However, she's been cloned. The clone of her I met was a bitchy teenager, but I'm sure she's an adult by now."

"And?"

"And there's also a clone of Leventhal Reid. He was our second Mastermind. The clone's being groomed to take over if the current Mastermind dies."

We were over the caboose. "What does that mean?"

"That we have to find all the clones, all the Mastermind's doomsday and kill switch devices and so on before we kill all of them."

"Correct. Now do you know why I'm in deep cover?"

"Yeah, I think so. It's because you're an Ancient."

CHAPTER 59

WRUCK HADN'T BEEN expecting this answer. At least I figured him losing control of the chopper for a few seconds indicated shock.

He stared at me. "How—"

"Met some other Ancient spies on Planet Colorful when we were visiting the Alpha Centauri system. They were Z'porrah double agents. But you aren't, are you?"

"No," he growled. "The Z'porrah represent all we hate."

"Oh, I'm totally with you on that one." Considered what Bizarro World LaRue had told me. "You were on the crew with LaRue, the crew who came here to see what had happened to the other missionaries who hadn't checked in. On Bizarro World, LaRue murdered her shipmates when they got here. And I'll bet she did the same here. Only . . . you didn't die."

"No, I didn't. The wound she gave me was almost mortal, but not quite. However, I knew how to play dead. Once she left us, I was able to patch myself up and get to safety. And I've been on this planet, in hiding, ever since. It took me years to find where she'd gone, who she'd joined forces with. And even more years to determine how best to stop her, once and for all."

"So, you're trying to protect us?"

"Yes." He sighed. "Doing a rather poor job of it, honestly."

"Oh, I don't know." Looked at the gun I was still holding. "What would you have done if Dier had woken up while you had the gun on me?"

"Figured out how to lose control of it or the helicopter, while also not allowing you to kill her or her to kill you."

"Nice. Difficult to do, but apparently you've had a lot of time to practice."

"I have."

"It's hard to work alone."

"Yes, it is."

"What's the real plan the Mastermind has going?"

"We don't know. He only tells us some things, and only through Annette. Which is why I don't want you to kill her."

"Yet."

"Yet."

Considered things as Algar stuck to a theme and "Undercover Martyn" by Two Door Cinema Club started. "Has the Mastermind released a bioweapon that will kill us?"

"I honestly have no idea. Is that what you think?"

"Right now it's definitely a theory. Everyone in the War Room car is sick. Could be a cold or flu, could be a biological weapon."

"If that's the case, only Annette would know."

"Figures. If that is the case, by the way, we're going to need an antidote."

"Noted. I'll add it to my list of things to do before I die."

"It's nice to know that at least one Ancient has a sense of humor. Is Casey also in the Mastermind's Inner Circle?"

"No, but she's still tight with Club Fifty-One. She uses them as we need."

"Like getting you guys out. Did she know about the attempt to blow up the train tracks?"

"No, she was quite angry when we heard about it. Do you know the engineer and conductor are no longer on board?"

"We do. How did they get out?"

removed them. Casey set it up. She was furious that
told her about the bombing, but they insisted
been informed. I don't think she believed

"In the open...

them and the bomb was"... you, Casey didn't believe

"Interesting. Is Stephanie one of you.. Mastermind wanted."

"No. We haven't seen her since she was released. There's
a lot of bitterness in the group about her. They feel she
could have or should have tried to get them out."

"No honor among terrorists, who'd have thought it? Do
you actually know who the Mastermind is?"

"Yes. But I can't tell you."

"Well, if it's someone other than Cliff Goodman, I'd like
you to share that."

He looked surprised again. "How long have you known?"

"A while now. We all know. We're just not killing him
because of all those doomsday plans and clones and such.
And the fact that we have literally zero proof that he *is* the
Mastermind."

"He's good and he learned from the best."

"Supposedly. I'm just going to say that, ultimately, we're
better."

"I certainly hope so. I've spent a lot of time betting on
that."

"Nice to have the support. What did you guys do with
the Secret Service and other security people we had waiting
for us at Rocky Mount?"

"Nothing, there were none there. We'd expected opposi-
tion, but there was none."

Interesting. That probably meant that they'd been taken
out by Drax's people. Hoped they were all still alive. Though
they probably were—why get rid of bargaining chips when
your sales pitch has gone totally sideways? No point in asking Wruck if he'd seen any Invisible Commandos, either,

though it might be interesting to see how far it. You can't
sarcasm knob went.

"How will I reach you?"

Wruck looked at me with s⸺ ⸺yone about you, or
tell anyone about me. And ⸺
about what you know."⸺se you'd have to tell them about

"Well, you can't⸺
you. Duh."

He laughed. "Good point."

"You don't have to be alone."

He sighed. "Yes, I do. I'm the only one of my kind here."

"So was the Martian Manhunter, but he still had friends
in the Justice League and even went off and got married
and stuff."

"I can't help you if I'm with you. Do you understand
that?"

"Then why tell me who you are?" Other than crushing
loneliness. But I was careful not to say that aloud.

Wruck shook his head. "Honestly? I don't know why I
did, other than that I knew you weren't going to kill me and
I couldn't kill you." He landed the chopper sideways on the
roof of the caboose. "You're who they fear the most. Because you don't fear them."

"Oh, they scare me, especially what they're willing to do.
I'm just not willing to let them win. Ever. So, you know, you
feel the fear and do it anyway." Sales and marketing training had really been helpful in my Centaurion career, as I
thought about it. "What do your friends call you?"

"Rudy."

"Do you like the nickname?"

"It's not my name, my real name, at any rate, but it's
fine."

"What's your real name? In whatever form human ears
can comprehend."

"It would translate to John. Not in meaning but in
sound."

"Really?"

"Really."

So he really was the Martian Manhunter. "Then why not use John?"

"Because I'm undercover."

"Gotcha. Last name isn't really yours, either?"

"We tend not to use last names. My ... wife's name would sound like Ruck, so I chose a human equivalent with Wruck."

"Is your wife still alive?"

He was quiet for a moment. "No."

"I'm sorry."

He nodded. "She died before I was sent to Earth. It was why I volunteered for the mission. In those days, traveling here took much longer than it does now."

"Progress, yay. Your accent is faked?"

"Yes," he said in perfect American English. "It is. I'm a man of many talents, me." This was with a perfect British accent. "It helps me blend in when I need to." Now he sounded Australian.

"I'm impressed. You could have quite the career in the movies. I like the German, by the way, but could get used to any of the others."

"I'll keep it in mind."

"What do you really look like, John?"

"You mean as Ancients? And why are you using my real name?"

"Yes, as an Ancient, what do you look like? And I'm using your real name because we're in the Helicopter of Silence and this is where we tell each other the truth and use our real names and all that jazz."

I didn't really believe that I'd seen what any of the Ancients really looked like, just the acceptable forms they felt the people around them could deal with.

He gave me a small smile. "Got it ... Kitty. And, we don't look like angels or devils or little green men or grays. Well, not in reality. When our people came here long, long ago they took on shapes that helped, ah, soothe or awe the masses."

"Okay and not a surprise. Then what *do* you look like?"

"Get out and onto the roof, and then I'll tell you."

Did as he asked, in part because I had to figure that Jeff was losing his mind with worry. "So, tell me." Had to shout.

"We look like you," he shouted back. "Like all of you on Earth and all of you in the Alpha Centauri system. Only more so."

And with that he flew off.

CHAPTER 60

FORTUNATELY I'D been doing a lot of work on the roofs of trains recently, because the wind from the chopper blades almost knocked me off, even though Wruck sheared off quickly. So I managed to drop onto my stomach and not get blown off. Just barely, but a miss was as good as a mile per some pithy saying.

Contemplated my options as "Devil Inside" by INXS came on and I decided it would be fastest on the roof, especially since we still had a door welded shut along the easy way.

Did the run and jump thing, but my time with Wruck had ensured that my rage levels were back to low, meaning I didn't have anything extra in the tank. Plus I'd used a lot of energy butt-kicking seven out of the eight Crazies.

Had no idea what I was going to tell the others, but figured I'd stick to the same story Wruck was going with—I forced him to take me back and he shoved me out at the last moment and escaped.

I understood why he didn't want me telling anyone else who or what he really was. He was in a position where he couldn't trust anyone. So that he had trusted me was kind of shocking.

Of course, it could all have been a lie and he was just a master at getting me to share vital information with him.

However, I hadn't gotten anything like that from him. On the other hand, if he was a master manipulator, I wouldn't pick it up. Cliff had certainly been able to fool all of us for far too long.

However, my gut, female intuition, or whatever we wanted to call it said he was the real deal. Algar's musical clues were also confirmation. And another reason I couldn't share what I knew about Wruck, because saying that the right songs came on to confirm his status would get me committed at worst or trigger a migraine from the pressure of trying to explain Algar without mentioning anything about him at best, and neither option was a winner.

I was on the middle car when someone else climbed up ahead of me and waited. Reached Jeff and he took my hand as we jumped to the next car. "You know I hate it when you do things like this, baby."

"Yeah. Everyone okay?"

"Yeah. I was able to monitor you."

"I thought your blocks were up."

"They were. Your rage was really strong."

"I'm an animal lover, what can I say? And I hate these people." We jumped onto Rail Force Two. Contemplated suggesting a quickie, but then figured that wasn't appropriate in the current situation.

"Just not all of them."

Stopped running. "What?"

"I could feel your emotions, baby. It's what I do. And I can read your mind, remember? You weren't trying to hide anything from me so it was fairly easy to access you. So I could tell when your emotions switched from overriding rage to confusion, then camaraderie, then sympathy."

"Crap. I'm not supposed to tell anyone that—"

"We have an Ancient on the planet?" He tugged gently at my hand and we started off again.

"Double crap. You got all that?" We jumped to the next car.

"Actually, I was telling everyone else what was going on as it was happening, so we all got it. Chuck guessed, but honestly, most of us were on Beta Eight with you and we all met Usha. That the Ancients have more people out here than we first suspected isn't really that much of a surprise. In the grand scheme of things."

"So, everyone on the train knows?"

"Yeah, all fifteen of us."

"That's a lot of people." We jumped to the War Room roof.

Jeff shrugged. "We'll keep the secret, baby. He's on our side, after all."

"He seems to be."

"I could access him. Not right away, but after a while. If he's representative of the Ancients, I'll be able to read them all now. He's lonely, determined, and on our side."

"I'll take it." The music changed to "Inside" by Vertical Horizon. Apparently Algar wanted us off the roof. We jumped onto Rail Force One. "Let's go the rest of the way inside."

"Fine with me."

Jeff had me climb down first. He jumped down onto the platform as I did and steadied me on the ladder. "Chivalry is not dead."

He grinned. "I wasn't allowed to help you kick butt, baby. Let me pretend you need my help with this."

Leaned up to kiss him. He put his arms around me, pulled me close, kissed me a good long time. As always, his lips and tongue owned mine and as also always I was grinding against him and ready to go, regardless of location of situation.

He ended our kiss, eyes smoldering, with the Jungle Cat About to Eat Me look on his face. I loved this look and was particularly disappointed that I wasn't going to get to enjoy it in all the ways I liked right now.

Jeff chuckled and kissed my forehead. "I'll make it up to you later, baby. I promise."

"I'll hold you to that."

We went inside Rail Force One and moved quickly. "I don't want us exposed to whatever was in here," Jeff said. "But I think we're going to be coming into the station soon and we're safer inside."

No sooner said than the train started to slow down and John Mayer's "Stop This Train" started. We left this car and entered the one with everyone else in time to hear Adriana tell everyone via the walkie to sit somewhere.

The beds were all occupied so Jeff sat in a chair and pulled me onto his lap.

"Good timing," Chuckie said.

"Remind me never to so much as step on an animal's foot in your presence," Vance said.

"Just call me the Animal Avenger."

"We have Field agents in hazmat gear ready to decontaminate the train as soon as we pull into the section of the rail yard we're being sent to," Reader shared over the walkie. "The way things have been going, everyone stay alert and have whatever you need on you, because who knows if we're going to be attacked again or not."

Picked up Bruno and Ginger and held them on my lap while Jeff chuckled. Ignored him. Didn't want to lose my pets in any kind of chaos or turmoil.

But we pulled in and off to a track that wasn't on the main line without issue. My music stopped so I took out the earbuds and put them and my phone securely into my purse. There were no Poofs On Board this time. Interesting.

Would have worried about this but real Secret Service agents were waiting for us—confirmed as such by Tim and Reader—and that didn't seem the time to bring up missing anything, Poofs least of all.

We were quickly escorted into a secured bathroom. Such was the glamorous life we lived. Christopher ensured the calibrations were right for the toilet and one by one we stepped through.

Due to his position, Jeff was not allowed to go last, and neither were Gower or I. Christopher took the caboose slot for a variety of reasons, fastest man alive and former Head of Imageering being the two strongest.

We also had to go in one at a time, though Jeff carried Bruno and Ginger with him. Not because I didn't want to hold them, but because he was concerned I'd squeeze them too much, potentially to death, because of my reactions to gates. Had to figure he wasn't wrong to be concerned.

Jeff stepped through, doing the icky slow fade that always started my nausea revving. Then it was my turn. Closed my eyes and stepped. The feeling of the world rushing past me was still there, but it wasn't as strong when I couldn't see the world rushing past via my peripheral vision.

My foot hit the floor and the nausea stopped. Opened my eyes to find myself happily with the others who'd gone through and where we were actually supposed to be—the receiving area for NASA Base.

The room had been changed quite a lot since my last visit, during Operation Drug Addict, and all changes had been for the better. There was far more security, better access to emergency equipment, and a variety of other safety features.

Of course, there were some things in here I hadn't been expecting.

Like Jeff's parents.

CHAPTER 61

ALFRED AND LUCINDA raced over and hugged me, since they'd just finished hugging Jeff. Then they left me to hug Gower. And on down the list until Christopher stepped through. Everyone, humans included, got parental — or, in the case of White, sibling — hugs.

"We were so worried!" Lucinda said as she hugged everyone again.

"We were fine," Jeff said, but I could tell he was enjoying being fussed over.

"It's okay, Aunt Lucinda," Christopher said as she hugged him a third time. He was also enjoying the fussing.

I would have been, too, but if we had a bioweapon loose, that meant that Alfred and Lucinda had been exposed now, too. Could tell that Chuckie was thinking the same thing, based on the worried look he was wearing when Alfred and Lucinda weren't looking at him.

"Thank goodness you knew how to drive that train," Alfred said to Adriana as she got another hug.

"Have we heard anything from Airborne?" Tim asked, sounding as worried as Lorraine and Claudia looked.

"There have been communiques that went directly to the President that might be about the boys," Alfred said. "I don't know for sure. But I'm sure they're fine and we'll get thing like that." Lucinda hugged him again. "You need to freshen up. The visiting dignitaries are waiting for you. And, ahem, you all look a little worse for wear."

"I'm betting I look like crap, so I can't argue with the need to clean up. However, we probably can't afford to take the time."

"Sure you can," Alfred said heartily. "We anticipated the need and have rooms set up for everyone."

"I'd like to talk to Tito," Chuckie said quietly to me and Jeff as Alfred led us through the NASA Base Rat Maze to wherever we were going to change. "Just to get his medical opinion on what's going on."

"You don't think it's over, do you?" Jeff asked.

"The only logical answer for why the Crazy Eights attacked is Kitty's theory. And that means everyone's been exposed to a bioweapon. Maybe it runs its course if the infected aren't in close quarters with each other. But maybe it adapts after its contagious phase. And if so, then no one's cured, they're just in Phase Two."

With this cheery pronouncement of doom we divided up into changing areas. We were sent to the employee locker rooms, men on one side, women on the other. Refrained from asking if this was to keep me and Jeff from doing the deed because I was pretty sure that it was. Or maybe I was just a little paranoid.

showers, which were he
...hat wasn't great or a relief was that w...
Suits of Those High Up in Politics waiting for us
got out and were dried off, me in particular. Managed
to groan, but it took effort.

"It could be worse, Kitty," Claudia said.

"Yeah." Lorraine laughed. "They could have you in white."

Managed not to point out that they were in the standard
Armani Fatigues for Women, aka a black Armani slim skirt,
white oxford shirt, and low-heeled black pumps, and were
therefore used to and comfortable with what they were
wearing.

"Oh, my standard pretty blue that I still manage to destroy every damn time I step out in it is good enough for the
likes of me."

Adriana was also given an Official Outfit and she wasn't
complaining about it, so I stopped. Out loud.

Checked my purse. Still no Poofs. "Um, does anyone else
have missing Poofs?"

"Yes," Mahin said. "But you know how they are—they
come and go as they please, not as we please."

"True." Decided I had bigger worries right now. Like
what to do with my hair. Decided to go for my favorite
standby—pulled back into a ponytail. Ready for action—
which I fully expected—and still managing to look semi-put
together.

"Kitty," Adriana said once I was done, "do you think
anyone will notice if I'm gone?"

"You mean forever or right now?"

She laughed. "Right now."

"Do you want to leave and go home?"

She shook her head. "I'm learning to think as Grandmother does. And . . . I feel that I need to be on the outside."

"Kitty always says to listen to your gut," Lorraine said.

"And carry a rocket launcher," Claudia added with a grin.

"True enough. Yeah, I think if you can slip out, that would be a good idea. There are so many people here only Len, Kyle, and Malcolm are likely to notice that you're gone and they may not even realize that you came in with us from Savannah. But where are you going? It's a long trip home without a gate."

"Not home, unless that's where the trail leads me. We all know more is going on. I would ask you which is more important—finding our missing pilots or where the Crazy Eights are hiding?"

The rest of the girls and I looked at each other.

"I want to say the pilots," Claudia said, "but I think that's because my husband is one of them."

"If we remove the emotional factor," Mahin said carefully, "I would say that finding the Crazy Eights would be paramount, since Annette Dier seems to have a direct line to the Mastermind at this time."

Lorraine nodded. "Much as I hate to say it, Crazy Eights would be where I think you should start."

"Escaped prisoners it is, then. You sure you're okay doing that alone?"

"I'd ask for Len, Kyle, or Mister Buchanan, but that would be noticed for certain. Otherwise, I know how to stay hidden when I have to."

"I don't doubt your skills." Hugged her. "Choose wherever you want to disappear and we'll cover for anyone who notices. And stay in touch so I know you're okay."

She hugged me back. "I will as I can."

Dressed, coiffed, so to speak, and Mission: Adriana Disappears rolling, we headed out to rejoin the guys. They were all in the Armani Fatigues. Basically, I was the bright spot of color in our group, which was not my preferred option but one I'd gotten used to over the past couple of years.

Onward to the conference center through the Rat Maze I didn't even try to memorize. I was too busy wondering who was coming to visit and what the next thing our enemies were going to throw at us would be.

Adriana had been hanging in the back of the group, so I wasn't surprised when we got into the room to see that she wasn't with us any longer. None of the men mentioned that she wasn't around, probably because they were focused on what was waiting for us.

Was overjoyed to see everyone looking better. Well, not really everyone. The people who'd gotten sick on the train still looked sick, just not that bad. Armstrong, Strauss, and Ariel, however, looked good or at least better than they had. Mom was sort of in the middle in terms of looking okay. She still looked sick but nothing like Strauss or Armstrong had. Thought back—was pretty sure Mom had been in the meeting that Jeff had left. The meeting whose participants were all sick.

Gave Mom a hug. "How are you doing?" I asked softly.

"Pumped full of all the cold and flu crap, chicken soup, orange juice, and whatever else Tito could come up with. I'll be fine, kitten."

Didn't want to consider otherwise, so I didn't argue. Especially since I was also overjoyed to see who had come to visit.

The Planetary Council was pretty much who I'd expected to see, but it's always nice to visit with friends from far away.

In addition to Formerly King and For This Journey Emperor Alexander, Queen Renata, Felicia and Arup, Wrolph, Wahoa and Willem and my Reptilian Soul Sister, Jareen,

were all here, so we had the Not Nearly As Pissed Off Now
Amazons, Cat People, Major Doggies, and Giant Lizards
representing.

Added onto the Council were Rohini and Bettini from
the Shantanu aka Penguin People, King Benny representing
not just the Lecanora but all of Beta Eight—without his
Antlers of Office but still looking like Benedict Cumberbatch to me—Lakin of the Rapacians aka The New Hawk-
man, Misorek from Alpha Six and Haliya from Alpha Five,
who both looked like humans and who I therefore suspected of treason either now or later.

This visit was gigantic news, of course, and we had a tonnage of media of all kinds here, including Oliver, who'd
gated over once we were on site. The princesses were still at
Guantanamo, though.

Hugged everyone, of course, while trying not to worry
that when things went wrong—as they so often did—it
would be blasted to the entire world live, but grabbed King
Benny early on. "It's good to see you. Why aren't there
more of you representing on this trip?"

"Ah, Shealla always asks the right questions. Rohini and
the Matriarchs felt that bringing the katyhoppers or straut-
ruch along would . . . frighten many of your people."

"Possibly." Probably. Big walking otters who looked like
Benedict Cumberbatch and giant, colorful penguins were
cuddly. Giant katydid-grasshopper and Real Life Big Bird
animals were not, necessarily. Plus mind-reading and telekinesis tended to panic humans, too.

He nodded. "Fancy Corzine is unwilling to leave the
planet without leadership protection, Zanell is not, ah, dip-
lomatically minded, and we felt that bringing a representative from each of the Clans would be overwhelming. And
Ronaldo said to tell you that he knows better than to come
to Earth without your express invitation."

"Good thinking on everyone's parts." Ronaldo 2.0's in
particular.

King Benny beamed. "I am honored to be the one who was allowed to visit the Home of the Gods."

"Ah, yeah, I think we'd prefer that you not call it that while you're here. People get a little, um, touchy about that."

He bowed. "What Shealla requests, I will do."

"And call me Kitty here, no Shealla unless we're in private."

"As you wish."

Hugged him then went to Jareen. "Where's Neeraj?"

"At home with Jeenar." Jeenar was their son. "It's time for Jeenar's Young Rites and the father is more vital than the mother for that."

"You're going to run out of names if you have another child."

She grinned the wide Reptilian grin that could look threatening unless you knew better, which I did. "We normally only have two offspring. So if we have another, their name will be Janeer."

"Weird naming on your planet, but who am I to judge?"

"It works for us." She studied me. "You're worried. Is it because Jamie and Charlie aren't here?"

"No. I'll tell you why later." Hoped that aliens were immune to our diseases, but then again, clearly A-Cs weren't, since Manfred and Raj and the other A-Cs that had been in the War Room looked like they still weren't feeling totally well.

After everyone had hugged everyone else—ensuring that if we were indeed dealing with a bioweapon we were all nicely contaminated—we settled down to find out whatever it was the Planetary Council wanted.

Armstrong, Jeff, Strauss, and the Planetary Council members were all on a small stage. Gower, as the Supreme Pontifex was on stage as well. Gideon Cleary was up there, too, looking rather thrilled. Apparently Armstrong wanted to show that there were no partisan issues for this event. The rest of us, me and Elaine included, were in the audience, though Elaine and I were in the front row along with close members of our staffs.

Was impressed with the setup—it was very reminiscent of what we did at the White House, down to microphones and sound system—considering NASA Base rarely hosted this kind of gathering, but there were A-Cs all around, meaning someone had shared what was needed and Centaurion had provided the speedy accomplishment and preparations.

Unsurprisingly to me, Rohini was the speaker. He always deferred to Alexander during his remarks, but it was clear that Rohini was still the Councilor Leonidas of the group. Fine with me—I liked Rohini quite a lot.

As did the press. Cameras were flashing, video was rolling, and reporters were trying to sit still in their seats, with limited success. This was basically Christmas in May for the press.

Rohini spent some time on preamble, but not as much as most Earth politicians would have. "So," he concluded, "we all, from the Annocusal Royal Family to every citizen of every other planet in our system, are here to request that Earth take its place in the Planetary Council as a full member of our Galactic Community."

CHAPTER 62

THERE WAS THE usual excited buzzing you get when gigantic announcements are made and there are a lot of people around to witness them.

I nudged White, who was sitting on my other side. "Who are the Annocusal?" I asked in a low voice.

"We are," he replied in kind. "All of us from Alpha Four. It's our species name, what we call ourselves, based on the gods the majority feel created our system, Anno and Cusal."

"I learn something new every single day."

"It's good to be open to learning, Missus Martini."

"So, that's why you guys call yourselves the A-Cs, isn't it? Not because you're from the Alpha Centauri system, but because of Anno and Cusal."

"Yes. We chose A-Cs once we came here since our religion does not, in actuality, agree with the Anno and Cusal creation stories."

"And sometimes I learn new things every minute of the day."

"I enjoy you taking your time to discover all the intricacies of the people you've married into. It keeps things fresh."

Would have given him a witty comeback but Rohini was speaking again. "And so, we come to you now, to see what you will do."

Armstrong looked pretty pleased, all things considered. Rohini turned to him. "Mister President, while we realize that the United States does not speak for all of Earth, Emperor Alexander would like to ask that we receive your thoughts first."

Lots of press focus on Alexander and Jeff, who was sitting next to him. Not a surprise, really.

Armstrong stood and joined Rohini at the microphone. He smiled for the press. "The United States is pleased to welcome the Planetary Council of the Alpha Centauri System to our world. We're more pleased to accept your offer. Earth is more than ready to join the greater galactic community. And we have our own Earth A-Cs who are welcomed all over the world to prove it."

This was good. Sure, the A-Cs weren't actually accepted all over the world, because Club 51 wasn't the only anti-alien group out there. But this situation would impress many who were on the fence about aliens in general and the A-Cs in particular.

"We would like to meet with other Earth leaders," Rohini said now, "in order to come to a consensus for how many agree with you and, if unanimous, who will be chosen as Earth's representatives."

"We'll organize a meeting at the United Nations," Armstrong said. It was clear he was going to say more, but a scream interrupted him.

One of the reporters was pointing behind Armstrong and Rohini. Looked where she was pointing to see Strauss face down on the floor of the stage.

People leaped into action, with Jeff, Gower, Cleary, and Armstrong all rushing to Strauss. I looked around for where a shooter could possibly be hiding. Other than in the crowd, there weren't a lot of options.

Tito made his way to the stage, along with a couple of Dazzlers who I was pretty sure were medical personnel. Elaine, White, and I followed them. They did a quick examination and tried CPR. But finally they stopped and Tito shook his head. "She's dead. I'm so sorry. There was nothing we could do."

"Was she shot?" I asked quietly.

"No," Tito replied. "She has no external wounds at all that I can see here. We need to get her to an examination room and see if we can determine cause of death."

Ariel and Raj had politely moved Rohini away from the mic, and Ariel was relaying that the Secretary of State appeared to have passed away from causes unknown.

Chuckie was with us now. "Doctor Hernandez, we need to do a full autopsy as quickly as possible."

"She has family," Armstrong said.

"I realize that, and I'm sorry, but I'm insisting on behalf of the C.I.A." Chuckie sounded very official. And very worried.

Made eye contact with him. "It might be a coincidence."

"Let's hope," he said grimly. "Let's truly hope."

CHAPTER 63

STRAUSS'S BODY was taken away on a gurney to the NASA Base medical center. Tito and Chuckie went with it. The conference went on, though there was a lot less jubilance from the participants and the audience.

"We are very sorry that this tragedy has marred our invitation," Alexander said. "It is our hope to bring helpful things to Earth, and to learn from Earth as well. It pains us that you have lost someone important to you within a day of our arrival."

Armstrong nodded. "Thank you. It's a ... hard loss. Monica was a wonderful person and an excellent Secretary of State. She'll be missed and hard to replace." He cleared his throat. "However, death comes to us all, and it's rarely at the time we'd like. So, please, let's continue to write this great chapter in our history. It's what Monica would have wanted."

They continued the discussions, all general We're Cool and So Are You stuff. My phone, which I'd had the foresight to put on mute, buzzed. I heard it because it was rattling against the goggles. Dug it out quickly.

I had a text from Chuckie. *Strauss was a diabetic.*

Is that why she died?

We don't know yet, but it means that her body and immune system are weaker than, say, Tito's.

Lots of people have various diseases. I know what you're worried about.

I'm hoping I'm wrong.

Me too, but I think we need to put everything into finding out if Lizzie's father's formula is out there and, if it is, finding the antidote. Even if this has nothing to do with the killer virus.

There may not be an antidote.

The Mastermind isn't going to release a bioweapon that could kill him. Trust me, if there's a killer virus, there's also an antidote.

Let's hope.

Kept my phone in my hand but went back to paying attention to what was going on onstage. Things were still rah-rah, with Armstrong indeed doing the nonpartisan thing which Cleary was supporting, but Armstrong didn't look too good all of a sudden.

Elaine grabbed my free hand. "Kitty, Vince has mild heart . . . issues," she whispered. "Can we get Doctor Hernandez back? Just in case? I'm worried that losing Monica in this way may be causing him problems."

Sent a fast text to Chuckie asking him to get Tito back here ASAP.

"And now, I'd like to have the man I'm proud to call both my Vice President and my friend say a few words," Armstrong said. "He's the shining example of what our A-C population is and brings into the great mix that is the United States. Please help me welcome Jeff Martini!"

Jeff came forward and flashed his Politician's Smile. It wasn't quite the same as his killer grin, but it worked like magic on every straight woman or gay man he flashed it at. It did pretty well with the lesbian gals and straight men, too.

"Thanks, Vince. It's been my privilege to learn from you how to be the kind of politician who puts the people first. And I'm deeply moved that our nearest galactic neighbors want to welcome us fully into the neighborhood."

The crowd was chuckling at this when Armstrong went pale. Elaine still had hold of my hand, and she gripped it tighter. Jeff was turned toward Rohini and Alexander, so wasn't looking at Armstrong, but even with blocks up, had a feeling he felt panic from both me and Elaine, because he turned back to Armstrong.

Just in time to catch the President's falling body.

CHAPTER 64

ELAINE AND I ran for the stage. I used hyperspeed, but she didn't throw up, presumably because it had been a quick burst and she was far too upset to vomit. We beat the Secret Service there by several seconds.

Jeff was laying Armstrong on the ground as Chuckie and Tito ran up and shoved through the Secret Service agents. Tito didn't hesitate and started CPR immediately.

Meanwhile the rest of Secret Service were putting the room into lockdown, relaying other information, and generally doing their best to keep everyone else from panicking. With limited success.

Tito looked up at Elaine. "I'm so sorry."

She fell to her knees, cradled Armstrong's head in her arms, and sobbed.

Had absolutely no idea what to do. Fortunately, Lucinda was here, and she shoved up onto the stage, put her arms around Elaine, and held the First Lady while she cried.

"Slick is down," one of the Secret Service agents quietly said into his watch. "Repeat, Slick is down. Need full details for Sophistication, Cosmos, and Cyclone."

"We're out of the realm of coincidence," Chuckie said tensely, as a dozen Secret Service agents arrived. They all looked stricken. Couldn't blame them.

"Elaine just told me he had a mild heart condition." Probably sounded more hopeful than I should have. Heard others start crying now, too, many of them on the stage.

"We need to assume the worst," Chuckie said. He looked at Jeff. "I'm sorry, but your first act as President Pro Tem is going to be to institute a quarantine."

Jeff blinked. "What?"

"Quarantine—" Chuckie repeated, but Jeff shook his head.

"Not that. The other thing. What?"

"President Pro Tem. That's what you are now, Jeff. And, you'll be sworn in as fast as we can get a judge here." He turned to Cleary. "Gideon, can you handle that, please? Someone who isn't going to create controversy would be appreciated." Cleary nodded, looking dazed, but he pulled out his phone and stepped away.

Jeff looked far more dazed than Cleary. "But . . . I can't be President. Not now. I haven't . . . I haven't even been a politician for four years. Vince . . . Vince hasn't finished training me . . ." Jeff looked ready to lose it.

This time, though, I knew what to do.

"Jeff." Waited until he looked at me, then made and held eye contact with him. "Jeff, you've been a leader since you were twenty. You led your people for over ten years, and now you just have to man up and lead all your people again. You have more people to lead now, and they aren't all co-operative and they won't like what you do or say and will tell you about it. But that we *have* been dealing with for four years. And you know how to deal with the haters, which is just like you deal with the supporters—fairly and with compassion."

"I'm not ready," he said quietly. "Not for this."

"Good. That proves you're both sane and not power-mad. However, you are ready. And, baby, ready or not, you have no choice. If you abdicate, this country will be thrown into chaos and Earth's chances of really joining the greater galactic community will be harmed if not ruined completely. Now isn't the time to give in to the fear. Now is the time to feel the fear and do it anyway."

Kept eye contact with him and tried to show him emotionally that I had complete faith in him. Finally, he took a deep breath and let it out slowly as he squared his shoulders.

"You're right, Kitty," he said. "Vince wouldn't want me to falter. So . . . I won't." He smiled. "As long as you believe I can do it."

"You know I do, and everyone else here does, too."

Cleary rejoined us. "We're racing a judge over. State Supreme Court Justice Quinn is on her way."

The men started discussing what to tell the crowd as another gurney was brought and Armstrong's body was put on it. Lucinda was still holding Elaine. "I'll go with her," she said to me. "You need to stay with Jeffrey." She reached out and squeezed my shoulder. "You handled that well, Kitty, thank you."

Had no idea what to say so I just nodded. Lucinda, Elaine, Tito, and those handling the gurney headed off. So did a couple of the President's Secret Service agents and all those assigned to the First Lady. Former First Lady really, now.

And then, of course, it hit me. If Jeff was the President, or would be officially in just a little while, then that would make me the First Lady. And therefore it was my turn to feel totally incapable.

White came over to me and put his arm around my shoulders. "I see the full realization of events has hit you."

"Richard, what am I going to do?"

He hugged me. "What you've always done since the first day I met you—handle it."

"I'm not really First Lady material."

"Nor were you diplomatic material, nor Head Ambassador material, nor wife of a Representative material, nor wife of the Vice President material. And yet, here we stand, with you once again set to do what you feel you can't. I, however, have seen your track record and feel that it's quite good. You'll handle this, adapt, and also force the job to adapt to you as well. Because, as we've seen, they can try to take the woman out of the fight, but they've never taken the fight out of the woman."

Leaned my head on his shoulder. Not quite as nice as Jeff's or Reader's, but not a bad shoulder to lean on. "It doesn't seem real yet. None of it. Monica is dead, Vince is dead, Jeff's about to be sworn in as President, and I keep on waiting to wake up."

"I know. But, sadly, this is not a dream or a nightmare. We're all quite awake."

Mom joined us, looking worried. "Kitten, how are you holding up?"

Left White and hugged my mother. She hugged me back, her breath-stopping bear hug. And for whatever reason, all the emotions hit and I started to cry.

Mom held me and rocked me. I knew the media would be eating this up, but I frankly didn't give a damn. Someone who'd started out as our enemy and over time had become our ally and then our friend was dead. And if what Chuckie and I suspected was the reality, then every person in this room, including me, my husband, my in-laws, and my mother, was at risk of death.

Rohini came over as I began to calm down. "Is it inappropriate for us to offer assistance?" he asked me as Mom and I unclenched.

"I don't think so, why?"

"If you recall, my people are the ones who provide the humanitarian assistance to the other planets when they need it. Perhaps we can help in some way." Nice to see that

the universal translator was working well, because I
doubted that Rohini had said the word "humanitarian" in
reality.

"It's certainly worth a shot. I don't know where the medical facilities are, though."

White called Alfred over, and he agreed to escort Rohini
and Bettini to the medical center.

"Where are they going?" a male reporter who'd gotten
close to us asked. Looked around. Most of the press corps,
like everyone else, was crying or looking stricken. Oliver
was talking to Raj and looking like he was only holding it
together because he was forcing himself to.

Mom and White did a fast fade. Clearly it was time for
me to First Lady Up and deal with this without support. Go
team.

Examined this guy. He looked upset. He was also young.
Decided he was probably trying to keep his job. "To see if
they can help."

"Can they raise the dead?" The reporter seemed serious
and rather hopeful.

"No, I don't think so. They're not *E.T.*, they're real people." There were more reporters around us now. Not the
entire press corps, but enough to ensure that whatever I
said was going to be in or on more than one paper or TV
channel.

"They're giant, colorful penguins." Again, he seemed
serious.

"To us. But they're people, just like all of us are. Sentient
beings who feel their calling is a humanitarian one. Sort of
like the Alpha Centauri System's Red Cross."

The reporters around me started talking and I put my
hand up. They shut up. Amazing. If only that move worked
all the time.

"Look, the President of our country and my good friend
has just died in front of us. I'm not really in the mood to
give you sound bites right now, and I can guarantee that no

one else is, either. Please, show some respect and back off. Stop doing your jobs for these few minutes and just act like real people, okay? You'll still have your jobs in the morning, but you'll also still have your humanity."

Then I turned my back on them and headed for Jeff.

CHAPTER 65

JEFF WAS TALKING with Mom, Chuckie, Cleary, Gower, Oliver, Raj, Ariel, White, Christopher, and the remainder of the Planetary Council, though Alexander was more "in" the group and the rest were sort of forming a protective core. Realized they were mostly warriors and that they were grouped around everyone else this way intentionally.

"Justice Quinn is here," Cleary said as I joined them and took Jeff's hand. He gave my hand a squeeze and I squeezed back.

A middle-aged black woman with a cute, short haircut dressed in a navy suit was being escorted in by A-C Field agents and Secret Service. Cleary hadn't been exaggerating about the justice being raced over. Presumed they'd gotten her here via a gate.

Quick introductions were made. "I brought my Bible from home," Justice Quinn said. "Just in case. Is that alright for you?"

Gower, who was on Jeff's other side, nodded. "Your personal Bible is fine. The Bible was used when Jeff was sworn in as a Representative and Vice President."

"Let's get the press assembled then," she said. "It's a terrible tragedy, but I do know that everyone will want to see the pictures and video of this historic event. Not only are you the first President since Johnson to have to be sworn in this way, Mister Martini, but you're also the first President whose lineage is from another planet."

"Our first alien in chief," Oliver said with some pride. "I'll get the rest of the press corps ready." He left the stage and went to his brethren. Hopefully to tell them to behave and act like grown-ups.

Precedent required that the About To Be Former First Lady be present. Mom and White went to get Elaine.

"We need to get a quarantine in place," Jeff said. "Did anyone tell you about that?" he asked Justice Quinn.

She nodded. "Yes, Governor Cleary said that the C.I.A. felt that quarantine was necessary. However, this is, as I said, both necessary and historic. I'll take my chances."

Getting everything and everyone ready took what felt like forever but was, in reality, only about an hour. During that time I sent a text to Dad, asking if Mom had been sick before we'd left for Florida. Because if she had been, then Dad had been exposed and that meant no one in the Embassy was actually safe.

Thankfully, the answer was in the negative. So whether that meant that Mom hadn't been in the room when Cliff had released the bioweapon, or if she hadn't incubated it long enough the first time, I didn't know.

She and Lucinda were literally holding Elaine up. I didn't want to pull my mother away, but I had to. Jeff picked up what I wanted and he went to Elaine and hugged her, effectively holding her up and allowing me to grab Mom.

"When did you start feeling sick?" I asked her as soon as we were relatively alone. Motioned for Chuckie to join us, which he did.

"On the train, why?"

"Chuckie and I are worried that this is the result of a bioweapon. I'm trying to determine if Dad's been exposed or not. Jeff wasn't until the train, at least as far as we can tell."

"We believe that's why we were attacked," Chuckie

added. "So people would be in a confined space while the President and others were still in the contagious phase of the disease."

Mom looked thoughtful. "When do you think it was originally released?"

"In the meeting you all were in regarding the message from the Planetary Council. Chuckie wasn't there because he was shadowing Cleary."

"But you think it was released after Jeff left the room, right?" Mom asked. I nodded. "Huh. I left the room, too. Charles had advised me of what had happened and I stepped out to ensure that all Agencies were put onto higher alert status."

"When did you go back in?" Chuckie asked.

"I didn't actually," Mom said slowly. "Ariel, Fritzy, and Monica relayed information to me while I was out." Fritzy was Fritz Hochberg, the Secretary of Defense. "I have two phones with me at all times, so I was on with them while I was relaying information to the Agencies."

We all had two phones now, too, but that was so we could hide activity from our Secret Service details. That said details hadn't strangled all of us yet was a testament to their dedication to duty.

"So I'm betting the Mastermind released it when he did for two reasons, one being that at least two people he wanted to infect had already left the room. He couldn't delay because more people might take off, too, to do what you were doing but with their own people."

"What's the other reason?" Mom asked.

Looked at the Planetary Council. "So he'd have someone really easy to blame."

Chuckie nodded. "I agree with Kitty, Angela."

"We're still in the realm of speculation," Mom said. "I realize that it looks likely, but since we only have two dead, it's not a definitive pattern."

"Except that we know about the death virus that Lizzie's

traitor father was creating. I'm willing to bet all my Mega-lomaniac Girl Credits that the Conspiracy King and I are right again, Mom. That bioweapon has been created, and the Mastermind has the antidote and has taken it himself. Clearly the disease takes about a week to kill those it's infected."

"Buchanan and I verified that everyone who was in that meeting is sick," Chuckie said. "Including people we'd think would have been given the antidote."

"Like Strauss, honestly. She came on with an emotional overlay, meaning she wasn't on our side. But she's the first casualty, meaning she wasn't given the antidote."

"Neither was Langston Whitmore," Chuckie said. "Unless he's faking it, which is always a possibility."

"We need to get all those people into quarantine and under stringent medical attention." And everyone here, my mother especially.

"That's going to be all of D.C." Mom said. "We're talking about the top movers and shakers in politics."

"The Center for Disease Control is going to need to be involved. Maybe we should call them, pronto. Mom, would that call come from you?"

Chuckie's eyes narrowed. "Now, isn't that interesting?" he said before Mom could reply. Turned to see what he was looking at. Cliff Goodman was in the room, along with the man who headed the Center for Disease Control, Wesley Green.

Green was an average-looking, slender, middle-aged white guy. He didn't have the total politician look, possibly because he was a doctor, but then again, that didn't mean he wasn't a political animal. He was coming in with Cliff, which was suspect. Or it could mean Cliff wanted this guy to get sick and die, too. Considering that Strauss was dead and Whitmore was sick, it was a good bet for both.

"Speak of the devils and they appear."

"Why are they here?" Mom asked.

Looked at the press corps. "The press has undoubtedly already shared that the Secretary of State and the President are dead."

Oliver came over to us, looking ashen. "We just got word—the Speaker of the House has just passed away in a similar manner to the two deaths here."

Mom, Chuckie, and I all looked at each other.

"No more arguing from me," Mom said.

Chuckie nodded. "Meaning we all have less than a week to save anyone who's been infected."

"Yeah." I swallowed hard. "Meaning, for starters, everyone in this room."

CHAPTER 66

"**GUANTANAMO AND DULCE** have to be considered to be infected, too," Chuckie said quietly. "As well as the towns we stopped in."

"What's going on that I've missed?" Oliver asked.

Filled him in on the highlights. "So, the Crazy Eights attacking us at Rocky Mount was actually a good thing." Really wished I'd made Wruck give me a way to contact him. Wondered if he'd suggested the attack for the very reason of keeping us going or if it was just luck. We rarely had luck that worked in our favor, so voted for Wruck doing what he could.

"Apparently so. And Lorraine putting the Embassy on lockdown was also a very good thing." Chuckie rubbed the back of his neck. "This isn't the greatest way for Jeff to start his presidency."

"Fortunately, he's used to handling crises."

Cliff spotted us, of course, waved, and came over. Nudged Chuckie's foot with mine. He needed to get ready to act like Laurence Olivier and Meryl Streep combined.

"We heard the news," Cliff said, as he hugged me. "It's terrible."

"It is," Chuckie said, as he and Cliff did the manly hug-backslap thing and I made sure Cliff didn't have a real knife or a hypodermic needle in his hand. "But what brings you here? Not that it isn't good to see you," he managed to add.

Cliff shrugged as he hugged Mom and I again made sure he wasn't stabbing something into her back. "Jeff's going to be sworn in as President. There's times to take a gate, and this is one of them."

"I'm here," Green said, as Cliff shook Oliver's hand, "because we received a quarantine request from President Martini. I need to know what's going on and who's affected." Interesting that he was saying this in front of a known reporter.

"Not quite President yet," I said. Decided we'd leave the what and who for later. If we got a later.

Cliff smiled at me. "Soon enough, Kitty. Welcome to the rank of the First Lady."

"Thanks. I think."

We all managed a chuckle, forced on my, Mom, and Chuckie's parts, and probably Oliver's, too. But still, we managed.

"How's your head?" Cliff asked Chuckie quietly.

"Holding up. For right now, at least."

"I'm here if you need me, buddy."

"Thanks. You have no idea how much I appreciate that." Chuckie sounded totally truthful. Go Olivier-Streep.

"Can you tell me what's going on that the President feels that we need a quarantine?" Green asked. So apparently we weren't going to be able to leave the whats and wherefores for later. At least Oliver was the only member of the fourth estate present.

"We're suspicious that both Monica and Vince just dropped dead after being sick with what appeared to be a flu for a week," Mom said briskly. "Especially since they seemed better earlier this evening. We have a variety of others who appear to have the same illness, and we were advised that the Speaker of the House, who also appeared to have the flu, has also passed away."

"Who else is sick?" Cliff asked, just as if he honestly didn't know.

"The entire Cabinet and the Joint Chiefs of Staff," Chuckie replied. "Barring a few exceptions. You both seem fine, for example." He sounded relieved, not suspicious. Both Cliff and Chuckie were great actors apparently. A loss for stage and screen both.

Green looked a little worried. "I just started having the sniffles earlier today."

"That's how it starts," Mom said. "I've got it, whatever it is."

Green looked more worried. Cliff did, too, but his eyes opened a little wider for just a moment and not due to shock. He wanted my mother to die, of that I was certain.

Thankfully we were called to get ready for the official swearing in, because I wasn't sure if I could keep up the acting required not to just tackle Cliff to the ground and beat him to death.

Oliver took his place with the rest of the press, and I took mine. Justice Quinn was to my left and Jeff to my right, facing each other, so they were in profile to anyone on stage or in the audience and I was facing the audience, meaning the press corps and everyone who wasn't a visiting dignitary. Elaine was next to Jeff, on his left, so near to me. She wasn't crying right now, but I figured it was a momentary reprieve. Took her hand in mine and she squeezed my hand tightly.

We were essentially in the center of the area between the stage and chairs. For whatever reason, Justice Quinn hadn't wanted us up on stage and no one had argued about this. The Planetary Council were on stage, Rohini and Bettini as well, and presumably Justice Quinn thought that standing next to them would give her and Jeff too much competition for the room's attention or something.

"It's my sad duty to have to swear in a new President of the United States in this manner," Justice Quinn said once everyone was in their seats and had quieted down.

"And my sad duty to accept it in this way," Jeff said.

"However, as leadership passes to you, Jeffrey Martini, please remember the oath you will now give to me and to all of the American people."

Jeff nodded. "I will."

"Then please place your left hand on this Bible, raise your right hand, and repeat after me. I do solemnly swear that I will faithfully execute the Office of President of the United States, and will to the best of my ability, preserve, protect and defend the Constitution of the United States."

Jeff cleared his throat and was quiet for a long moment. Wondered what he was about to say, if he was going to go off script, say that, no matter what, he wasn't going to accept, point at Cliff and shout, "J'accuse!", or something else. Elaine squeezed my hand again and I squeezed back.

Then he took a deep breath, let it out, and spoke.

"I, Jeffrey Stuart Martini, do solemnly swear that I will faithfully execute the Office of President of the United States, and will to the best of my ability, preserve, protect and defend the Constitution of the United States."

Everyone in the room applauded, at least everyone I could see in between camera and cell phone flashes, which was most of them. Could hear the Planetary Council's applause behind us.

And, just like that, Jeff was the President of the United States.

CHAPTER 67

JEFF SHOOK JUSTICE QUINN'S HAND. As she removed the Bible from between us, he stepped over and kissed my cheek. Then he put his arm around Elaine and hugged her.

"Whatever we can do for you, we will," he said. "Just tell me what you need and we'll make it happen."

She nodded. "I . . . it's still too new, Jeff. But, thank you." She still had hold of my hand and pulled me closer. "I heard something—you believe Vince and Monica were murdered?"

"We do," I said. "But we're going to need to do autopsies a soon as possible to have a hope of determining how."

"Whatever you need me to do to expedite that, let me know."

"We'll let Tito know—I think if we can get the bodies to Dulce or get Dulce doctors here, we can speed things up."

"Then we'll make that happen," Elaine said. "I'll go find Doctor Hernandez and ensure that whatever needs to be signed and so forth is."

She went off with her Secret Service detail to grab Tito and do whatever was necessary.

We should have been flying right back to Washington—to reassure Congress and all the citizens that the transfer of power had been done and things were under control, and to actually take some control—and as soon as possible, too. But quarantine made that difficult.

Cliff, of course, was making most of the problems, though he'd set it up to seem like he was trying to help.

Chuckie pulled me aside while everyone was arguing staying here or not. "Because the former First Lady okayed it, we have Dulce medical here. They're processing everything at top speed, which NASA Base is equipped for. Having the Shantanu here is also a help. They have truly advanced medical tech that should mean we have answers sooner as opposed to later."

"This appears to be domestic terrorism. Does that mean you need to give authority of the case to Vander?" Evander Horn was the head of the F.B.I. division that cared about aliens and therefore our go-to in that agency.

"We're going to work together, particularly under the circumstances. But Vander isn't infected, and we need to keep it that way."

"He wasn't in the Aliens Are Coming! meeting?"

"No, he was actually sick and sent someone else in his office to cover. Food poisoning. He's fine now."

"God, I hope so."

"So do we. I told him our concerns, and he's working leads while avoiding as many people as possible, just in case. He's also trying to determine how many people are sick in the D.C. area. And before you suggest it, yes, he's utilizing Centaurion resources to speed things up."

Mahin hurried over to us. "Kitty, I just heard Cliff saying that animals need to be quarantined. I don't know where Bruno and Ginger are, do you?"

Realized I had no freaking idea where they were. Was about to hit my personal panic button when my phone buzzed against the goggles in my purse again. Pulled it out to find a text from Lizzie.

Call me, right now.

Didn't hesitate, I called. "Lizzie, what's wrong?"

"I'm not sure. We have, like, every Poof imaginable here. And somehow your Peregrine and ocellar are back, too. I think some Poofs brought them home. Were they lost?"

"No." Just able to determine that they were about to be used as pawns by our enemies. "But I'm glad they're there. Lizzie, I think we're about to have people try to get into the Zoo and the Embassy to lock up the animals."

Chuckie pulled out his phone. Could tell he was calling Kevin.

"Get to Walter, will you?"

"Sure. Hang on." Could tell she was running, but since she didn't have hyperspeed it took her a couple of minutes. During that time listened to Chuckie advise Kevin that he was to not allow anyone in or out of the Embassy complex regardless of who they said they were.

"I'm with Walter. Want it on speaker?"

"Yes."

"I'm here, Ambassador," Walter said.

"First Lady now, Walter, and that's part of why I'm calling. You need to ensure that no one goes in or out of the Zoo or Embassy. I'm sure people who sound very official will be demanding that you let them come in. You are to refuse and to keep shields up on the highest setting they have. The Embassy complex is American Centaurion soil and we will not allow anyone to leave it or come onto it."

"Roger, Missus First Lady Ambassador."

Decided not to complain about Walter's slavish devotion to titles right now. "Great. Kevin will back you on this, but you guys need to make sure that all the others understand that no one is to come in. And . . . that includes those of us who are part of the Embassy detail and such who aren't there right now."

"Ah, what about those who aren't part of our Embassy detail who are here right now?"

"Well, don't toss my dad out into the street. Obviously."

"He means Olga and all the Romanians," Lizzie said.

"They came over the moment you guys left. Said that their plumbing was backed up and asked to sleep here. They're all in the Zoo."

"God, I love Olga so much. Yes, keep them in with you guys absolutely. Walter, you need to contact the Israeli and Bahraini embassies and advise them that I'm telling them to go into the severest form of lockdown that they can. No interaction with anyone else, make sure anyone who appears to have a cold is put into quarantine. Radio silence if at all possible, and that goes for us, too. Only communications within our own Bases or with the Israelis and Bahrainis if they need us or vice versa."

They were quiet for a few moments. "It's bad, isn't it, Chief?" Walter asked, reverting to the simpler form of address, presumably because he was intelligent and therefore scared. "We heard the news . . . I was hoping it wasn't true."

"It's true. And it's worse than when we brought you onto the team."

"I won't let you down."

"I know you won't, Walter. Lizzie, spend time with Olga, see what you can get out of her that may help us."

"Okay. Um, there's something else."

"What?"

"Do you need Walter anymore?"

"Nope. Walt, do what you do best."

"I will, Ambassador. Security out."

"Okay, I'm in the hall," Lizzie said a couple seconds later.

"So, what's the something else?"

"There are two. One is that I can't reach my dad or the uncles. I mean, my texts get through, I'm pretty sure. But they haven't answered me back. And the other is . . . Jamie's acting weird."

My stomach clenched. "Weird how?"

"She's stopped playing with the other kids, your dad, or me. She's in Charlie's room, surrounded by the Poofs.

Charlie is going to have to sleep with me or your dad, she won't let him in the room. She doesn't want anyone else in there with her."

"Is she eating and drinking?"

"Well, this just started since the last time I talked to you, so yeah, before she was."

"Keep me posted." Had a sinking feeling that Jamie knew exactly what was going on somehow. What she was doing about it was worrisome, especially since she was by the camouflaged but still very functional Z'porrah power cube.

"I will."

"Be sure someone checks on her regularly. Like every fifteen minutes regularly."

"I will."

Remembered that Lizzie was still just a kid. "We'll find your father, and the uncles, I promise."

"They've released the virus my dad created, haven't they? I don't mean Mister Dash and the uncles, I mean the bad guys."

"I'd love to tell you no, but I don't believe in lying to you. So, yes, as far as we can tell. But it appears to be hitting humans harder than A-Cs, at least so far."

"It was made to kill everyone." She took a breath that sounded shuddery. "Mister Dash had my father's notebook. I think he destroyed it. I saw something I thought was it burning when . . . well, when he saved me."

"Praying that he didn't actually destroy the information and that it's in a very safe place somewhere. We're going to need it."

Siler was a trained assassin but he was also more than that—he didn't age like normal people, so he'd been around a long time and was very aware of how the world worked. No scientist worth his doctorate only had one copy of anything, especially not a mad genius working for the bad guys. They always had plenty of backups. Maybe not complete backups, but backups, nonetheless. So other baddies could carry on their evil work when the good guys put a bullet through their brains.

While he might have burned what Lizzie thought was the notebook with her father's formula in it, my bet was that Siler had burned a decoy so that she'd be reassured that the data was destroyed and trust him.

Because I trusted him, I really didn't want to discover that the reason Lizzie couldn't reach Siler was because he'd sold the formula to the Mastermind or one of his lieutenants and he was on a very safe desert island somewhere.

Of course, based on his track record, Siler was, despite his profession, far more on the side of right than he'd ever want to admit. So chances were good that he, the Dingo, and Surly Vic were either deep in something or captured, hurt, infected or dead. Go me, always looking on the bright side.

"You really think he'd have done that?" Lizzie sounded hopeful and worried both.

"Yes. I think he would have realized that it might be needed to create an antidote." Hoped this was reassuring in the right ways. And that I was right.

"You know, my dad told me that he had most of the data in other places, and I know Mister Dash heard him. So, I think you're maybe right, Kitty. That would be good, right?"

"It might mean the difference between us all living or dying, so yeah. We really need to hear from him or the uncles."

"I told him that. In the message I don't think he got."

"You know, text me his number, would you?"

"You don't have it?"

"If I had it, why would I ask you to send it to me?"

"Gotcha. You know I'm not supposed to give his number to anyone."

"And yet, I'm going to demand it."

"Oh, I know this is a special circumstance. I just wanted

you to know that I'm breaking rules. For the greater good and all that sort of stuff."

"Exactly." Cliff and Green were heading toward us. "Gotta go. It'll all work out. I promise. Text me the number, text with updates, but keep them very vague."

"Got it. Kitty?"

"Yeah, Lizzie?"

"I'm kinda scared."

"Me too, Lizzie. Me too."

CHAPTER 68

"I T'LL ALL WORK OUT, THOUGH," I told Lizzie reassuringly.

"You sure?" She didn't sound like she was convinced.

"Things like this always happen to us. And we're still here." This was a lie, though. Algar was right—this wasn't an attack we were prepared for or had any real experience with. "So don't worry. We'll win, I promise."

"Okay. I can't check on Olga and Jamie at the same time."

Managed not to laugh. "That's okay. If my dad is checking on Jamie, you can go to the Zoo."

"Cool, I'll tell him what you want us to do. Thanks, Kitty."

Hung up just as Cliff and Green reached us, Green looking worried as hell, Cliff wearing the Frowny Face of Concern. "Kitty, we may need to take your animals into quarantine," Cliff said. "Just in case whatever this is turns out to be like the Avian Flu."

"Or Ebola," Green said, sounding as worried as he looked. "Or Mad Cow Disease."

"They're all in our Embassy complex, Cliff."

"I heard you had animals with you on this trip. And you all always have Poofs."

"You heard wrong. No animals with us. Including Poofs."

"I'm sorry, but I'm going to have to ask you to prove that."

Opened my purse. Sure enough, no Poofs On Board. "Poofs come to Kitty." Sure, I didn't say that with a lot of enthusiasm, but I said it.

No Poofs appeared.

"See?" I said to Cliff as I shut my purse. "They aren't here."

"Until we know what's causing the illnesses, it seems premature to quarantine animals," Chuckie said mildly.

"I'm more concerned with where we are to go," Mahin interjected, before Cliff could reply. I was all kinds of proud. "We have far too many people who are vital to the running of the government here."

"I agree, Cliff. While I'm sure we're going to have to lock down this facility, Jeff is now the President and can't be kept here like a prisoner. And Elaine needs to be able to cry her eyes out somewhere without a million photographers taking her picture."

He looked like he wanted to argue, but Cliff was, sadly, nothing if not smart. He nodded. "You're right, Kitty. I'm sorry. I'm just kind of freaked out. The Ebola scare we had last year was bad enough. This is a lot to deal with. My big test, in that sense."

Hadn't considered that all the Ebola crap that had ended up being nothing and quickly terminated when the A-Cs came up with the vaccine and got it to affected people around the world had been engineered by Cliff. It had seemed like the Avian Flu and Mad Cow Disease—stuff that happened.

Of course, I was an idiot to not consider that the guys who had Gaultier, Titan, and YatesCorp under their control hadn't created Avian Flu, Mad Cow Disease, and Ebola. It was, frankly, just like them.

However, those weren't our problem right now. "I'm sure you'll do great, Cliff," I said. "You always do."

He smiled. "Thanks, Kitty. Just worried—if the disease is widespread, then FEMA will need to be involved and take over."

What Cliff was doing clicked firmly into place. This was a doomsday plan, only he planned to live through it. Create a disease, release it, make the world sick, kill off everyone you don't like, kill some you do because why not, and then take over the world.

Armstrong and Strauss were dead in just over a week. If the disease worked that fast on everyone, then Cliff would be in charge of the country in less than a month. Without an election, just due to death of political leaders.

Then the institution of martial law to keep the peace would give him complete control, which control he wouldn't give back, for whatever reasons. He was a Sith Lord, after all. And this plan was right out of the Sith Lord Handbook.

Thought about Bizarro World Jamie's messages. She'd told me to be careful on the train. If only I'd realized how careful we were going to need to be. She'd also said she was the key, but that was easy to figure now—either Cliff was after Jamie again, or Jamie was doing something to try to help, and that was why she'd sequestered herself with the Poofs.

But Bizarro World Jamie had also said "he knows." There were so many he's, but, as I thought about what was going on, the obvious one was the Mastermind. So, what did he know?

Considered all of what had happened—the timing of the first bio-attack in particular. Really wanted to talk out loud. Not an option at the moment.

"What about the White House?" Chuckie asked, derailing my train of thought.

"For what?" Cliff seemed confused.

"For where we take everyone who makes sense. It needs to go into quarantine as well, so we might as well take the President, First Lady, Former First Lady, and all the others on their staffs there. That way, we're back in D.C., where we need the President to be, if only to reassure the country that things are somewhat normal."

Chuckie's voice had been extremely pleasant. Not giving an order, merely giving a suggestion. Clearly he'd missed his calling and I should have encouraged him to join the Theater Club in high school.

Cliff seemed to be considering this, but Green responded first. "That sounds like a great plan." Wasn't sure if he liked the plan or just wanted to visit the White House.

Cliff nodded. "Chuck's plans are always good ones, and if you feel that this is the right place for us to quarantine most of these folks, Wes, then let's make it happen."

"What about the press?" Green asked. "Do we keep them here or bring them to the White House, too?" Was glad he'd asked that, because I'd been about to.

"Chuck? Thoughts?" Loved how Cliff was setting it up to be able to say that everything we were doing was Chuckie's idea.

Chuckie shrugged. "Doesn't really matter. I'd say here, honestly. There's a medical facility in case any of them show symptoms and that way we can all have privacy in the White House. You're exposed now, too, Cliff. You're stuck in quarantine with the rest of us."

Cliff looked shocked, and I was pretty sure it wasn't faked. "What?"

"You're exposed," Chuckie said. "Just like the rest of us are. That means you and Wes have to be quarantined just like the rest of us."

Cliff clearly hadn't thought this far ahead. No idea why, other than that he felt success was so assured that he'd gotten careless or was so excited about killing a ton of people that he'd jumped the gun. "But, we have to be out, handling things."

Chuckie snorted a laugh. "That's the answer everyone's going to give, starting with the President and ending with

the greenest cub reporter in the room. But you know how
this works—you're in the room, you're exposed. At least, if
we feel that the theory that this is a biological attack of
some kind is the one we're going with."

"You think it could be something else?" Green asked
rather hopefully.

"There are a lot of ways to kill people," Chuckie said.
"What if this was just an elaborate ruse to kill the President
and make it look like a terrorist attack? The autopsies ar-
en't done. We don't know if someone slipped something
into the water, pricked them with a poisoned pin, and so on.
We've jumped to a conclusion because people have been
sneezing. But we could be wrong. We've been wrong before.
I've been wrong before."

"Rarely, but you're right." Cliff looked at the Planetary
Council. "There are other options for what's going on, you
know."

"You're saying that you think that the Planetary Council
came to kill the Secretary of State and the President? And
somehow also killed the Speaker of the House even though
they were nowhere near him?" Managed not to snarl, but it
took effort.

"They all have hyperspeed, don't they?" Cliff turned
back to me. "And what if they brought others we don't
know about?"

"You're suggesting that the Planetary Council—the
same people who saved us from an alien invasion—came
here to kill our political leaders? Why would they do that?"

Cliff looked at Jeff, who was talking to the press, Gower,
Christopher, and White with him. "To put someone they
prefer into office."

CHAPTER 69

WHAT WAS GOING ON dawned on me—Chuckie and Cliff were playing a live action game of chess right here. And though Cliff had opened himself up and Chuckie had taken advantage of his weakness, Cliff had recovered and just made an excellent move. It was a move we'd expected, sure, but it was still a good one.

He turned back to us. "From what we know, half of the Cabinet and Joint Chiefs of Staff are sick. If it's just that the President had a bad cold that he shared with everyone other than the few of us with really strong immune systems, then we still have a dead President and Secretary of State, as well as Speaker of the House, with no clear answers for what killed them."

"So you like the bioweapon theory?" Chuckie asked him.

"I think we need to follow it through," Cliff replied. "Even though you're right—there are always other options. Frankly, it could be a bioweapon that was released by the Council."

"Okay," I said, "well, if we're going to dissect the bioweapon theory, the Planetary Council wasn't here when we believe those people were infected."

"When do we think the infection happened?" Green asked.

Figured we had to tell them. Cliff already knew, of course, but Green might actually end up an ally.

"The most likely time is during the meeting that was called in response to the Planetary Council's request to visit," Chuckie answered. "And as Kitty's pointed out, none of the Planetary Council were on Earth at the time."

"No, they weren't." Cliff's eyes glittered. "At least as far as we know. However, if you're right, Jeff was in that meeting."

"So were you." The words slipped out without my meaning for them to.

Cliff nodded. "I was. So was your mother. But Jeff isn't sick."

"As far as we know. You're not sick, either."

"Strong immune systems," Cliff said.

"My mother's got a hell of a strong immune system."

"But she's still older," Cliff said. "That alone could make her weaker than you realize."

Lorraine and Claudia entered the room. I hadn't realized they were gone. They spotted me and hurried over, both looking as worried as Green.

"Where have you been?" Cliff asked them before I could.

"Researching what killed the President and Secretary of State," Lorraine said. "I'd like to discuss it with the First Lady. Alone."

"No," Cliff said calmly. "If this is the disease-based threat Chuck and Kitty are thinking it is, then Wes needs to hear what you've found out."

Claudia grimaced. "Not much yet. There appear to be foreign agents in their tissue and blood, but we can't tell what they are yet."

"Rohini wants to run more tests," Lorraine added. "So does Tito."

"Have you determined if it's a disease or, say, a poison?" Cliff asked.

Both girls shook their heads. "Nothing's definitive yet," Claudia said.

"So, what's the medical thought on quarantine?" Green asked. "Do we have a potential epidemic or a murderous conspiracy?"

"Both? Neither?" Lorraine shrugged. "We honestly don't know yet."

"How long do you figure?" Chuckie asked.

"At least twenty-four hours, and that's with people working around the clock," Claudia replied. "Unless we have a breakthrough, and we can't count on that."

"White House Plan it is, then," Cliff said. "We'll get back there, and then if it's not a medical issue, well, we were around to support Elaine and cheer for Jeff and Kitty. And if it is a medical issue, we'll figure out how to deal with it. That's why we have staffs, after all." He grinned. "Get them to do the dirty work."

Managed not to say that this was how Cliff normally did everything. Clearly he was really taken with this particular plan and wanted to ensure he had his many moments in the sun. Just nodded and smiled instead. "Sounds like a party. Girls, you'll stay here, keep on working with Tito and the others on determining cause of death?"

Both of them nodded. "I'd like Mahin to stay, too," Lorraine said, without missing a beat. "And Abigail. They're not as trained as us, but that way we have help without exposing even more of our people."

"Caroline will also want to help," Claudia added. "She's with Tito right now, as a matter of fact."

"Wes, is that okay with you?" I asked.

Green nodded. "That's fine. I don't know that it matters who's where, just that everyone is somewhere already quarantined."

"Super, then we'd better get things rolling. I'm going to ask you and Cliff to deal with the press, if you would. I think it'll be better coming from you than from me or Jeff."

Cliff grimaced. "Not sure that telling them that they're under quarantine and so is the White House is going to be better coming from anyone."

Patted his arm. "I have faith in you."

"I'm going to get Jeff and the Planetary Council ready to leave," Chuckie said. "I don't think you want the C.I.A. lurking behind you for this chat with the press, do you Cliff?"

"No, Wes and I can handle it."

We separated, Chuckie going to who he'd said he would, Cliff and Green heading for the press corps. The four of us grabbed Abigail and headed for the medical area.

"We need a private place," I said quietly to Lorraine, who nodded.

We headed to a woman's restroom far away from the big room we'd been in. As per usual, I had no idea where we were within the Rat Maze. "Talk softly, but we should be good in here," Lorraine said while Claudia checked all the stalls.

"We're alone," Claudia said. "Now, what's really going on?"

"Other than the fact that Adriana was clearly right to leave when she did," Mahin said.

"So many things. We're about to be trapped in the White House, so yay for Adriana for seeing that coming, and we need to ensure that some of us can get out. But first, let me ask you guys something." Told them about what I'd seen from Bizarro World Jamie. "So, what do you think the last message means, 'he knows'?"

They were quiet for a few moments, Dazzler minds all working. Abigail cocked her head at me. "You're sure she meant the Mastermind, right?"

"Pretty sure, yeah."

"Then, what would him knowing cause Jamie to warn you about? I mean, what thing that he might know would be a danger to you?"

"That we know who the hell he is," Lorraine said with a laugh. Then we all stared at each other.

"Oh my God," Claudia whispered. "That's it, isn't it?"

"Yeah, that makes total sense. And also explains why he's rolling this plan now. He's figured out that we know who he is and rather than play games here and there, he's upped the ante. I think he's triggered one of his doomsday plans, but one where he thinks he'll survive and come out on top."

Mahin nodded slowly. "This theory certainly makes sense for what we know is going on."

"That's why he targeted the President," Claudia said. "Vince knew he was the Mastermind and moved Cliff away from us. Once Cliff figured out why he'd been put in charge of FEMA, then killing Vince was a double for him, right? Get rid of the President along with the top guy in charge who's willing to call you a traitor the moment he has a shred of proof."

Heaved a sigh. "Sounds about right."

"And this plan plays right into him being the Head of FEMA, too," Lorraine added. "So that means he's had less time to work on this plan than many others. Hopefully that's going to help us."

"God knows we're going to need all the help we can get. No idea why he's killing his own people, though, but that's truly the Bad Guy Club's Beloved Move, so I'm assuming it's that."

"Drax had better watch himself," Abigail said dryly.

"Yeah, about that. I don't think Drax is in on this."

All the girls stared at me. "Why so?" Lorraine asked, clearly for everyone.

"Because Drax's foiled sales pitch is why we're not all sick as hell and why we're actually able to figure out what's really going on."

"That and Wruck," Claudia said. "As long as you're sure he wasn't lying to you."

"I'm sure. Remember, the Crazy Eights weren't expecting the Invisible Commandos and didn't know about them. And . . . I truly think Cliff was terrified that Huntress was going to kill him. Meaning that Drax isn't his ally." And that if Stephanie was indeed the Huntress she had some unfinished revenge business to take care of. "And Jeff read Wruck, too."

"I think you're right, then," Lorraine said. "So, what are we going to do?"

"We have to find the flyboys—and not just because two of them are your husbands. We need to rescue them and keep them from getting infected. Though they might actually be safer wherever the hell they are than the rest of us."

"That's damning with faint praise," Abigail said, keeping the Team Sarcasm Meter high.

"Yeah, truly. Adriana's after the Crazy Eights, but we also need to find our Friendly Neighborhood Assassins. Lizzie's worried that something's happened to them, and if I were our enemies I'd certainly want to immobilize them. Plus Siler may have Lizzie's father's original notebook hidden somewhere, and if he does, that may be all we have to use to find an antidote."

"And you need to find Wruck," Mahin said. "I believe he'll run from the rest of us, but he chose to bond with you." She smiled. "As all those who see the real story do. Some sooner than later."

Gave her a quick hug. "That was so many Operations ago. And we've always been glad you're with us, Mahin. And you're right—we're going to need him. We also need Stephanie, meaning we need to grab TCC and get him activated, hopefully without infecting him. Oh, and we have a lot less than a week to do this."

"Why do you want Stephanie?" Abigail asked.

"Because I'm hoping that we're going to be able to find

enough evidence to convict Cliff. Not necessarily in a court of law, but in the Court of Public Opinion. One way or the other, due to what's going on now, it's going to be us or him standing at the end of this. I want to ensure that it's us."

"This is going to take teams," Claudia said. "Several of them."

"And we're going to have to work around Cliff, too," Lorraine said.

"Only in terms of escape, because Charles trapped Cliff," Mahin said. "Cliff will be in quarantine with us, too, at the White House. Well, with Kitty. So he'll have to work through intermediaries. The four of us are to stay here at NASA Base, right?"

"Right, because I'm going to want the four of you to sneak out."

"You want Caroline with us or staying here?" Lorraine asked.

"I think staying here. Caro's game, but she's not trained and Tito's going to need someone who isn't vital to determining what the disease is and if it's curable to keep snoopers and such at bay. And Caro's a master at that."

"I think you're right to leave Caroline here as our inside woman, and I'm not against sneaking out, but won't we be missed?" Abigail asked.

"No. I have a plan. And you won't be alone. I and some others are going to sneak out, too."

"Who are you taking, Chuck?" Claudia asked.

"No, he's too visible, honestly." And Jeff was going to need him, especially since my plan couldn't include Jeff in it. The President had to be visible and able to respond to all the crap I knew was coming. "And someone has to be there to ensure that Cliff doesn't kill everyone in the White House while I'm out running errands. I'm hoping to take James, Tim, Richard, and Oliver with me. And, if things go well, Rahmi and Rhee."

"How do you plan for us to get out, let alone you guys?" Lorraine asked. "Seriously, Missus First Lady, how are you going to sneak out anywhere?"

I coughed and sniffled. "I, like the rest of you, am going to be very sick."

CHAPTER 70

BECAUSE WE KNEW that Cliff would be watching me, each girl was assigned one of the four men I'd named and told to tell them that they were to wait for my signal once we were in the White House and then to act incredibly sick.

The girls were going to wait for their own opportunity and take it the moment they could, but definitely before anyone left this facility.

But first we all went to medical so I could tell Tito and Caroline the plan while the girls distracted everyone else in there and so my Dazzlers would be able to truthfully say that we'd gone to medical should Cliff or someone else ask.

Unsurprisingly, Caroline wasn't thrilled with her role. "I'm happy to be the distraction and inside point," she lied, when I explained what was going on. "But I'd rather go with all of you."

"Yeah, I know, Caro, but we need you here. We have to have someone in the know here who isn't trying to find the cure. It's not as exciting, but it's still a vital role."

She hugged me. "Fine, Kit-Kat. I know when I'm beaten. Besides, I'm really enjoying watching Tito, Bettini, and Rohini work. The Shantanu are flat out adorable, kind, and brilliant. Makes me want to visit their planet."

"Yeah? When they get a break, ask them about the

people who live in their oceans." Headed over to share
what was going on with Tito.

My favorite doctor was all for us sneaking out because
he was no more enamored of dying than the rest of us.
"You're right, Kitty—I can't leave, but I can cover for all of
you, especially with Caroline's help. By the way, verify if
Doctor Morin is sick or not when you get to the White
House."

"You think he's in on it?"

"I think it's possible that the Physician to the President
might be a part of either a biological plot or another type
of murder plot. Don't get me wrong, I like Gabe a lot. But
we need to know if he's faking being sick or if he caught
whatever we're dealing with from the late President."

"In which case he's close to death, too, most likely."

"Yeah. This is ugly as hell. I'm not as concerned with
quarantine right now, because if this is a type of plague and
we can't find a cure, then we're all dead, quarantine or no
quarantine."

With this cheery yet accurate pronouncement, the girls
and I hugged everyone goodbye and headed off.

We were somewhere in the Rat Maze when we passed a
door with a window in it and someone banged on the glass.
We stopped and looked. It was Brian.

Went to open the door, but it was locked. "Don't!" he
shouted.

Let go of the doorknob. "Bri, what's up?" Realized that
I hadn't thought about him being here, but he was an astronaut and it made sense that he'd have gone to his job when
we went to Florida.

"I'm on the non-quarantined side, Kitty. Sorry about the
President, congratulations to Jeff." We were standing next
to either side of the door, so it wasn't that hard to hear.
"Didn't you notice I wasn't in the room?"

"Um, thanks? Is that what you wanted to tell me? And
ask me? I figured you were working." This was a lie. I'd

forgotten about Brian. The nature of our relationship, really. Felt bad, but we had a lot more going on than my forgetfulness in regard to former flames, married to a friend of mine or not, so found the will to carry on.

"No. Serene had already told me to stay away from you guys because we were putting various areas under lockdown, which is why I didn't go to the ceremony. I was going to go to the Embassy, but Walter won't let me in."

"Yeah, sorry, no one in or out, just in case."

"No argument, my son is in there. It worked out because Adriana found me, had me help her get a change of clothes, and told me to stay on this side and to see if I was able to help. But she didn't give me any more information than that. I was hoping I'd see someone I knew. Serene is at Dulce, though she's in the part that isn't under quarantine."

"There's parts not under quarantine?"

"Yeah, just like here. Parts of both facilities are considered uncontaminated and we were doing our best to keep it that way. This door is reinforced for chemical leaks, which is the only reason I could get to it and hope to see one of you."

"Good initiative."

"Thanks. From what we heard, the head of the CDC is onsite and is going to stay here until he feels all the quarantine areas are set up correctly."

"And then he's going to the White House?"

"That would be my guess, yeah."

The White House was an easier quarantine, in that sense, similar to the Embassy. No one was to go out or come in, other than those already exposed to whatever the hell we'd been exposed to.

"Are you sure Serene is in an uncontaminated part of the Science Center? I'd have thought she'd have been doing the dissections on the dead bodies."

He shook his head and shot Lorraine and Claudia a commiserating glance. "Melanie and Emily took charge of that." Those were Lorraine and Claudia's respective mothers. Heard both girls breathe in sharply.

"We're going to figure out what's going on before we lose anyone else," I said firmly.

"I hope so," Brian said. "I'm kind of out. I can leave the facility because I'm not considered infected with whatever it is we think we're infected with. However I can't go to the Embassy or Dulce. Serene's concerned that there may be more contagious in Dulce than we realize and I'm expecting her to lock it all down soon, just to be on the safe side."

"Wonderful."

"So, since I can't go home but I can go out, and also since Adriana told me that I'd be needed, what do you want me to do?"

This was good news, in that we had another one of our people free and additionally one unlikely to be on Cliff's radar. On the other hand, Brian was a human not trained by the All-Seeing Oracle and technically not in the military side of either the U.S. Armed Forces or Centaurion Division, so I couldn't give him most of the assignments I needed handled.

However, that didn't mean I couldn't give him something useful to do. "Bri, the Mastermind is aware that we know who he is. I need you to get out of here ASAP and get TCC. Only him, no one else in the family. Keep him with you, keep him safe, and you, too, of course, and I'll contact you whenever I can."

"Okay, will he go with me?"

"You're one of those he considers a god, Bri. Yes, he'll go with you." Operation Civil War had been nothing if not interesting, after all. "If anyone asks why you're going to Alfred and Lucinda's, just explain that you can't go to your normal home options, so are going to stay with the nearest relatives."

We wouldn't even need to clear that with Jeff's parents—it was what they'd expect any or all of us to do, so if they were questioned by Cliff, the answers they'd give would match what we needed.

"Will do, Kitty. Do you want us to stay in their house?"

"Not if you can leave safely. Get out with TCC as soon as you think it's reasonable to assume you'd leave, then stay gone."

"Should we be visible or go into hiding?"

"Good question. I'd say stay hidden if you can. We have enemies everywhere and possibly local Cuban assassins out there, too."

"Beginning to be sorry I volunteered." He grinned. "Don't worry, Kitty, I'll take care of myself and TCC, too."

Brian effectively activated, we headed back again. By the time we finally returned to where the others were, people were already being divided up, with the White House group waiting for their floater gate. Apparently my presence hadn't been missed, though. Felt the love.

Happily, Oliver was in the White House group already, so I wasn't going to have to figure out how to demand he be with me. While he could sneak out with the girls, wanted to have him with me at the White House, for a variety of reasons.

However, Oliver and the other men I wanted on Sneak Out Duty hadn't been advised, though, thankfully, they were all still in the room. So, we split up, with me going to talk to Cliff about whether or not it was safe to let food and such come in and out from Dulce.

"They're on lockdown, too," Cliff said after I'd dragged him off to a corner so we wouldn't be overheard.

"Yes, but I think they're on lockdown in the same way NASA Base is."

"So, not fully contaminated?" Cliff verified.

"As far as I know. I could be wrong, but that was my impression."

"Who'd you talk to?" he asked casually. But I recognized a probing question when the Mastermind phrased it.

"Just heard it when we were in the medical bay. Like I said, I could be wrong."

"Well, hopefully you're not. But if that's the case, I don't think you want anything going back and forth from Dulce to any other areas, just in case. No reason to increase the risk."

"And Guantanamo?"

"That's harder." He grimaced. "Your uncle's there, isn't he?"

Chose not to ask him how he knew that. "Yeah, he is. Cliff, I feel like I'm at risk for losing my entire family."

"Well, your kids are safe, right?"

"As far as we know, yes. I don't think they've been exposed."

He looked very serious. "Kitty, I promise—if something happens to you and Jeff, I'll take care of your kids."

Shocker. The Mastermind was going to take my exceptional children if my husband and I died. On the Surprising Scale from one to ten, this rated about a negative two. Chose not to mention that my father was with my children in relative safety—why give the Mastermind more incentive?

Instead I gave him as tremulous and grateful a smile as I could. "Thanks, Cliff. That really makes me feel better."

Didn't point out that he was apparently quite confident about surviving, but I did find his lack of attention to detail interesting. Either he was trying to lull us into some weird form of security, or he was just so damned confident that he was at the endgame and about to win it all that he just wasn't bothering to sweat the small stuff.

Wondered if he knew that we all knew he was the Mastermind, or if it was only Chuckie who Cliff felt was on to him. Prayed to all the various Powers That Be that Cliff was only aware that Chuckie knew. It wasn't a big advantage, but a sliver was better than nothing.

I'd stalled all I could so we went back to the rest of the crowd. Cliff headed off to talk to Chuckie, probably to try to trigger a mood swing or a migraine. Chuckie was doing really well, all things considered. Which might mean many things, but the likeliest was that we were in an active situation that was requiring a great deal of mental focus from him and he just wasn't allowing himself to falter.

Per our visit to the medical area, Rohini and Bettini were staying at NASA Base to continue to work on autopsies and such. But the rest of the Planetary Council was coming to the White House. Justice Quinn was coming, too.

Jeff wanted Alfred and Lucinda to come to the White House with us. Lucinda agreed, in no small part because Elaine really needed someone good with comforting around her, which both Mom and I were not. Elaine was clinging to Lucinda when she wasn't actively doing something and it was clear she was one breath away from losing it. Could not blame her, at all.

But Alfred felt that he needed to stay at NASA Base for a variety of reasons, it was his job and home turf being the most compelling. Couldn't argue really—I'd seen what the Alfred in Bizarro World had created. Frankly, the best hope we had for a cure could easily come from Alfred.

"I can always just take a gate from one quarantined facility to the others if I need to," he pointed out as Jeff tried to convince his father to come to the White House with us one last time.

"I think you'll be more comfortable with us," Jeff said stubbornly. "I could make it a Presidential order."

Alfred grinned. "I know you want to show off your new house, son." He hugged Jeff tightly. "I'm so proud of you," he said quietly. "But I'm going to do more good here."

"I don't want to show off," Jeff mumbled. "I just want to know my parents are safe."

"Jeff, your dad's right. Elaine really needs Lucinda right

now, but we need to let your dad do as much of his job as he can. He's got everyone here and then some to protect him—he'll be fine."

Alfred hugged me now. "That's my little First Lady."

"One day I might even get used to you calling me that. But I doubt it."

CHAPTER 71

A FLOATER GATE shimmered into view. However, the
way we were going to go through it was very different
from the past.

Jeff's Secret Service detail was going through with him.
I was not, however. In fact, I was held back. By Buchanan.

"We need to chat, Missus Executive Chief," he said quietly, while we waited for the Former First Lady, Lucinda,
and all of Elaine's Secret Service detail to go through.

"Not now or here, Malcolm."

"No, but the moment we're in the White House." Chuckie,
Mom, and the Planetary Council went through now.

Len and Kyle joined us, as well as my Secret Service detail. They all, like Buchanan, were clearly sick. "I'm worried
about all of you."

"Ditto," Buchanan said. He took my arm and the rest of
my security detail surrounded me.

"Cozy. I'm not walking through the White House like
this, you know."

"We'll talk." Buchanan seemed quietly pissed, and I
didn't think it was because he and the others were on the
Potentially Dying Soon List.

Literally everyone else other than me and my detail
were sent through, thankfully Cliff included, before Buchanan let my detail walk me to the gate.

"Why do I get the honor of going last?"

"I want us keeping an eye on you. Everyone will be waiting for us now. As opposed to you getting in the White House and wandering off immediately."

Crap. Buchanan was not cooperating. Not that he knew what he needed to cooperate on. Meaning I was going to have to tell him. Somehow. And ensure he'd let me leave. Somehow.

The girls all noted this, but there wasn't anything they could do, so they waved and headed back to medical, hopefully to put their escape plan into action.

Buchanan put his arm firmly around me and then we all stepped through. Nauseating as always, but not for too long. We landed in the White House, or at least I assumed that's where we were, since I was pretty sure we were in the Diplomatic Reception Room. And Buchanan was right— everyone was there waiting for us.

Jeff shot Buchanan a jealous glare. Always flattering, though under the circumstances being jealous of the guy trying to stop me from saving the day wasn't the right emotion. Buchanan let go of me, I didn't throw up, Jeff stopped glaring. Winning all around.

"Now that everyone's here," Cliff said, "let's take an inventory of who else is in this complex and who isn't, so that we can give that to Wes when he joins us."

"I think people need to rest, though." Everyone looked at me. "I can't speak for anyone else, but it's been a long day for most of us, no one's had dinner, and getting some sleep would be nice, too. It's evening, let's recall."

"I'll get the staff preparing food," Elaine said.

"I'll do that, dear," Lucinda countered. "You just tell whoever to listen to me and I'll handle the rest." Elaine shot her a grateful look.

"Shouldn't Kitty do that now?" Cliff asked.

"No," I said quickly. "I don't care that power has

transferred. This is still Elaine's home, and we're all visiting at this time. Period."

"I agree. We'll sleep in a guestroom," Jeff told Elaine.

"I think . . . I think after I get Lucinda set up, I'd like to go lie down, as opposed to eat, if that's alright. Let me know if you need me. For anything."

Jeff nodded, then the Former First Lady's entourage headed off.

Jeff looked at Cliff. "From now on, and until this situation is resolved one way or the other, no one is to make Elaine feel as if she doesn't belong here." His Commander Voice was on High, and he radiated authority. "Anyone who does so will be sent back to NASA Base. Is that clear?"

Cliff nodded. "Sorry, Jeff. I wasn't thinking."

"Now," Jeff said, "let's get the headcount done as fast as possible. I'd also like anyone who feels even remotely sick to head to White House Medical."

Looked at my security detail. "That's every one of you, and don't even try to lie. Jeff, I'm going to take all of my security folks down. If you need me that's where I'll be."

Mouths opened and I put up my hand. Mouths shut. Wow, that move had worked twice now. Maybe it was my new First Lady Power. I'd take it, however I was getting it.

"Look, you're all sick. I know all of you and I can tell. And, see, I'm going down to see what Doctor Morin has for cold and flu, so you're all going to go down there with me. Mom, that includes you."

My mother gave me a look I was familiar with—her "you did *not* just try that with me" look. However, she didn't argue, just shrugged and joined us.

"You have no idea how to get to medical, do you, kitten?"

"I like to follow your lead, Mom. So, um, lead on."

She rolled her eyes, but did as requested. "I'm wondering how long it's going to take you to learn the layout here."

"Years would be my guess."

"Never would be mine," Buchanan said.

"Blah, blah, blah, I'm ignoring you in that new First Lady way of mine. I know exactly where we are. We're in the Center Hall."

"It's marked." Kyle pointed to the tasteful sign I'd read.

"You're not my favorite anymore."

"So, why are we doing this?" Mom asked as we got away from the crowd and headed down the Center Hall toward the medical offices.

"I want you guys to get some meds."

"Uh *huh*." Mom made a sharp right, which even I knew wasn't taking us to the medical offices. We trotted through another room and reached a stairway. Mom did some hand signal that I didn't get but the others seemed to understand— all the Secret Service muted their devices.

We were midway down the stairs when Mom stopped. "Okay, now, I want to know what you're up to."

"Who says I'm up to anything?" Tried for the Unjustly Accused Look. The Innocent Look never flew for my mother.

This look didn't, either. "I'm your mother, for God's sake. I can tell when you're planning on doing something stupid."

"Thanks for that. And it's not stupid." Heaved a sigh. "Look, we're pretty sure that the Mastermind knows that we know who he really is."

Mom's eyes narrowed. "Who's 'we'?"

"Me, Lorraine, Claudia, Mahin, and Abigail. Tito and Caroline, too. And, um, Brian."

Mom considered this. "Brian's not in lockdown, so you've already sent him off to do something, I assume. Same with Adriana, who disappeared somewhere between you all arriving in Savannah and when you all joined us for the speeches and sudden deaths. My guess is she was inside NASA Base before she left—there was far more security on all of you at the train station than in there. Tito's going to pretend the women are sick, put them into an enclosed room, and they're going to leave NASA Base. Right?"

"Um . . . right?"

She crossed her arms over her chest. "And you think this is a wise course why?"

"Because the Mastermind wants to kill my entire family, starting with my mother, and I don't want to allow that. We have allies on the outside, and we need to find them, and fast. I think Siler may have hidden the notebook he took from Lizzie's father. And if he has, we need it. It's probably our only realistic hope for a vaccine, at least in time."

Mom sighed. "I appreciate you not wanting me to die, kitten, I do. But you're exposed, too, now. And if it's a deadly plague, then you and the others being out means we're spreading it, not containing it."

"Mom, I can tell what he's doing. He's taken the freaking vaccine. So he's going to wait us all out, until we all drop dead. Then he's going to take over the government and rule forever."

"He is a Sith Lord," Len said.

"Len is again my favorite. Look, I get that everyone with me right now wants to protect me. But I'm telling you that I need to protect all of you. You're all sick and infected. Frankly, the biggest risk I've had with this disease so far is being in a confined space with all of you."

"Kitty's right," Evalyne said. "And, speaking as a person, not as the head of the new First Lady's protection detail, I'd like to live. And experience says that Kitty knows what she's doing."

"Sort of," Buchanan said.

"Join Kyle in my no longer favorite group, Malcolm."

"Angela, realize that Kitty's not planning to leave the White House alone," he went on as if I hadn't spoken. "If I were a betting man, I'd be watching Reader, Crawford, White Senior, and Oliver right now."

"Jeez, how did you guess?"

"I saw Lorraine, Claudia, Abigail, and Mahin talking to them while you were distracting the Mastermind. As in, I was doing my job, Missus Executive Chief."

Turned back to the highest ranker here. "Mom, the Mastermind has enacted a doomsday plan he plans to live through. He told me he's going to get my children when we're all dead. Nicely, of course, but still, is that the legacy we want? That your grandchildren were murdered or warped to the teachings of our biggest enemy and a freaking lunatic of the highest order?"

Mom was quiet for a long moment. "No, kitten, that's not what we want." She sighed. "What do you need?"

"Your permission to leave, with the guys Malcolm named. And all of you guys providing the cover we'll need to keep the Mastermind and others believing we're still in this complex. I have to get out—I need to get to people who can help us who also will *only* trust me."

She sighed. "Agreed."

Looked at Buchanan. "But I'd like to change one small aspect of my plan."

CHAPTER 72

THE BIGGEST ISSUE about my and the others' leaving was keeping Cliff in the dark about us being gone. The second biggest was getting Jeff, Chuckie, and Christopher on board in a way that wouldn't raise suspicion.

So, all of us went where I'd planned to go originally anyway, the medical offices. To find Dr. Gabriel Morin and his staff all sick as dogs.

As reassuring as it was to discover that Morin hadn't passed on going on the train because he was in on it with the Mastermind, finding the medical staff sick was definitely not good.

Mom explained the quarantine and what had happened to the President. The medical staff was so ill they hadn't heard the news. So they were all crying as well as being sick.

"We were tending to him every day," Morin said, sounding as if he felt this was all his fault, as opposed to why he and the staff were all ill. "We'd think he'd gotten better and then he would relapse. But it didn't seem life-threatening."

"It's not your fault," Mom said. "But all of you need to be and remain under observation."

"Most White House staff are ill," Phoebe said quietly. Mom had allowed the Secret Service to go off Silent Running Mode once we left the stairway. "Just received confirmation from the A-Cs who did the headcount. Manfred says that they're all in different stages, but most have been sick for about five days."

Meaning we had less than three days to find the cure and save everyone's lives. "We need to keep anyone who isn't sniffling or sneezing yet out of an incubation-like setting."

"How?" Morin asked.

"Camping on the lawn?" This earned me a lot of derisive looks. "I realize that doesn't sound fun but May is a pleasant month, weather-wise, and this disease loves small, enclosed spaces for incubation. Plus air filtration systems would mean that the air can and probably is moving the disease back and around through the complex."

"If it can travel airborne, then us being outside means we're sending it out to the world," Morin pointed out.

"Good points, both," Mom said. "We'll think about it. Gabe, we were given a lot of fluids and home remedy cures when we reached NASA Base and most of us who were just infected felt better. We'll find out what we got and ensure that everyone on staff gets the same."

With that she ushered us out. "Why don't you want people outside?" I asked her quietly, as Len made a call to Tito to get the exact list of what he'd given everyone.

"Because those of you leaving will have a harder time not being spotted. I think Christopher needs to get sick, too."

"I think if he does the Mastermind will be too suspicious."

"And the others you're having get sick he won't suspect?"

Sighed. "I guess. We need to roll Mission: Deathbed soon, Mom."

"Love your choice of names."

"Thanks. Keep Christopher here in reserve. The fastest man alive can afford to wait, and he's probably the only one able to keep Jeff under control if needed, too."

"Cut the chatter," Evalyne said softly. "It's show time."

Sure enough, Cliff was coming out of the Diplomatic Reception Room.

"There you all are. Are you okay?"

"We went to medical," I said, sounding as tired as possible. "They're all really sick, which sucks, because I'm starting to feel crappy, and all of my detail already feels crappy."

"You look okay," he said encouragingly.

"I don't feel okay. I don't want to do First Lady stuff. I don't even want to eat anymore. I just want to take a nap."

"Kitty, stop whining," Mom said, sounding annoyed and tired, too. Had no idea if we were fooling Cliff or not, but we were certainly giving it the old Pueblo Caliente Try.

"Well," Cliff put his arm around my shoulders, "let's get you through what we can and then you can rest, okay?"

"I guess."

He hugged me a little tighter. "Kitty, you need to be prepared, though."

"For what?"

"Ariel . . . he . . ."

Stopped walking and looked up at Cliff. "He what?"

"He just succumbed. He looked like he was doing better and then . . ." Cliff shook his head. "Then he just keeled over while he was talking to Jeff."

"What?" Realized tears were running down my face.

"I'm sorry," Cliff said. "Some of the A-Cs took him down to the bowling alley."

"The bowling alley? What the literal hell?"

"We don't want to risk extra contamination. The bowling alley is far enough away from the main residence area and it's a place we can cool down without affecting everyone else."

"You're expecting to put more bodies in there, aren't you?" Mom asked, managing not to sound accusatory.

Cliff nodded. "I think we are." He reached out and took Mom's hand. "We have word that the Secretary of Homeland Security and the Director of the Central Intelligence

Agency have also passed." He cleared his throat. "And three White House staff, cleaning crew, have died as well."

"Doctor Morin and his staff didn't say anything about that."

"They aren't notified yet. The cleaning staff were found by the A-Cs when they were returning from putting Ariel's body in the bowling alley. The cleaning crew's bodies are there, now, too."

"I don't think we want to bring in anyone to remove them," Mom said, as she gently removed her hand from Cliff's.

Cliff nodded. "I agree, Angela. I think the risk is too great."

"What's the word on everyone else that we think was infected?" Didn't even try to hide the apprehension in my voice.

"Not good. Everyone who was in the meeting where we think original infection happened, other than me, Jeff, and Angela, are all extremely ill. Anyone who they interacted with on a regular, close basis also appears ill. And, frankly, everyone here is starting to show the initial signs." He put the back of his hand onto my forehead. "You feel hot, for example. And from what little we know, this starts like a cold or the flu, so with a fever."

"Fantastic. Any word on what the cause is?"

"Nothing from our people at NASA Base." Cliff dropped his voice. "Kitty, you have to accept the possibility that this was caused by the Planetary Council. There are two of them still at NASA Base supposedly working to identify what's causing this epidemic. But they could just as easily be blocking Tito and the others from finding the truth or a vaccine."

I had to play along, because so many things depended upon it. So I nodded slowly. "You may be right. I'm not saying that you are, Cliff, so don't think that I've agreed. But I agree that we need to consider the possibility."

"Good. That's all I want, you open to whatever possibilities we might have." He smiled at me. "After all, you're the go-to girl for solving these kinds of problems."

Snorted. "Right. I'm not the go-to girl for anything like this. This is a disease that we can't differentiate from cold or flu until it's too late. And even if we think we have an idea of what it is, we have no vaccine for it. I'm totally out of my element here, Cliff, so don't be counting on me for much other than trying not to panic."

He hugged me again. He was hugely into that right now for some reason. Wondered if he was spreading the disease through touch, rather than through the air.

"It'll all work out, Kitty. Now, let's get you back to your husband. He's a little . . . agitated about everything."

CHAPTER 73

WE WENT BACK IN. The room was still packed with people, all of whom looked freaked out or worried in some way. Who could blame them? "Why isn't everyone eating or resting or whatever?"

"Well, aside from Ariel dropping dead in front of us, we've been waiting for you." Cliff brought me over to Jeff. "Found your wife and her entourage. I think Kitty needs to rest, Jeff. The news has upset her."

"I'm not surprised. Where the hell were you?" Jeff snapped. "People we care about are dying left and right and you weren't around."

"I went to the doctor's office, remember?"

"The hell with that, or you lying down. I need you here," Jeff was practically snarling.

I was shocked and I was sure it showed on my face, especially because Chuckie looked shocked, then pissed. "Jeff, I know you're under stress, but don't talk to Kitty that way." Chuckie took me away from Cliff. "Kitty, do you need to lie down?"

"And you think you're going to 'help' her do that?" Jeff growled. It was as if this were four years ago.

Chuckie's eyes narrowed. "If you won't stop to take care of your wife, then, yes, I will."

Jeff stepped closer and got into Chuckie's face. "Try it." He was still growling.

"Um . . ." Honestly had no idea what to say or do. This wasn't something I was used to anymore.

Looked around for help. Cliff was standing back a little, and I could tell he was enjoying this, though he had the Frowny Face of Concern going. Looked over to Christopher, who was directly behind Cliff, for help. He made eye contact with me. Then he winked.

Managed not to say "Oh, duh" aloud, but it took effort. Turned back to Jeff and Chuckie. "Both of you stop it. I feel like crap, and I want to lie down. I'm just managing not to cry about Ariel and everyone else who's just died, and I don't know that I can hold it much longer. I don't care who helps me figure out where in this cavernous complex I'm sleeping, but I want to rest and I want to rest now. You two can have your constant, ridiculous jealousy fight later."

Jeff pulled me away from Chuckie. "I'll handle my own wife, thanks. See if you can manage to get things under control here. Stay here," he snapped at Joseph and Rob. "Try not to drop dead on me before I get back."

With that he stalked off, holding my hand and essentially dragging me out of the room. Shot a grimace at Chuckie which I hoped the other guys in on the Escape Plan would realize was their cue. Then Jeff, I, and my entire entourage, my mother still included, left the room.

"Link up," Jeff said briskly. "If you want to sleep when things are dire, then we'll get you settled in right away and without delay."

Mom took my hand, everyone else linked up, then Jeff hit the hyperspeed. We ended up in his office in the West Wing.

"Nice," Mom said after we stopped and Jeff had closed the door and disabled what I assumed were known surveillance devices.

Jeff grinned then shot me a worried look. "You okay, baby? Was I too rough with you?"

"No, but apparently our entire extended circle should be doing Little Theater in the off hours. What do you guys think is going on?"

"You, James, Tim, Oliver, and Richard are going to sneak out to try to save the day. I assume Lorraine, Claudia, Mahin, and Abigail are already out of NASA Base or about to be, possibly to join Adriana."

"I guess I was wrong in thinking only Len, Kyle, and Malcolm would notice that she'd done a fast fade. But the girls aren't meeting up with Adriana, she's on a solo mission, as is Brian."

"And you want to head out to do a different mission or three." He ran his hand through his hair. "I'd like to go with you, but Chuck was very clear about why I can't."

"Because you're the President now."

"Yeah. I have to be visible, and clearly here, or else the panic that I can guarantee is already starting will only get worse." He sighed. "I don't like it, mind you. Commander in Chief means being on the front lines to me, not behind a desk or hiding out in a bunker."

"I know, Jeff. It's hard on you and probably going to be harder. But if we've ever needed a strong leader, it's right now, and you're that leader. And I'm proud to be your wife, even if my first act as First Lady is to essentially disobey your direct orders."

He laughed. "So, you know, just like when we met and every day thereafter."

"Glad you're rolling with the way things are. I'd check you for fever but we all probably have one by now. Speaking of which, I think Cliff may be spreading the disease through touch. He was hugging me a hell of a lot and went out of his way to hold Mom's hand."

"Have already sent that information to Doctor Hernandez,"

Buchanan said. "And I think you're correct, though I don't know if that's how the disease first was released."

"I'd assume he put something in the water or the air in the conference room," Mom said. "Because Cliff going around the room glad-handing everyone would definitely have been noticed, and since Vince and some others know—knew—who he really is, would have raised all our suspicions. Jeff, check Kitty's forehead."

He did, and looked worried. "You have a fever, baby."

Checked his head while the rest of the room did the same. "You do, too."

"Everyone here feels too hot," Mom said. "So, whether you were infected before or not, we have to work under the assumption that we're all sick."

"Doctor Hernandez wants us to get a blood sample from Goodman," Buchanan said.

"That'll be easy," Mom said, sarcasm knob easily at twelve on the one-to-ten scale.

"Christopher can use hyperspeed," I suggested.

Mom sighed. "It's not that simple, kitten. He could grab a tissue sample with ease, which takes no time and skill. But a blood draw requires an ability to hit the vein and know what you're doing. And it takes time."

Buchanan grunted as he texted away. "Hernandez says it has to be blood. Tissue isn't going to give him enough to work with, if anything."

"Well, to Mom's point, since Lorraine and Claudia are on a mission and Tito's at NASA Base, the only trained medical people with us at the White House are Doctor Morin and his staff."

"They didn't look well enough to administer an aspirin," Phoebe said. "Let alone to draw someone's blood."

"And we'd have to get Cliff to agree to it, too," Jeff said. "Short of a Presidential order, I don't see that happening easily."

"And that gives away whatever element of surprise we may still have," Evalyne added.

"Means what I want to do is that much more vital. How'd you know what we were planning anyway, Jeff?"

"Chuck was watching you. He realized that you'd pulled Cliff away and had him positioned so he couldn't see what the girls were doing. And all they did was talk to those four men. He knows you, I know you—it didn't take a lot of brainpower to make the guess. It's what we both would be doing if we could."

"Malcolm, I hope you're offended."

Jeff nodded to Buchanan. "You figured it out, too?"

"Yes, and I was going to prevent it. But your wife is a lot like her mother, and I was overruled."

"So bitter. We all just want to live past this week, call us crazy sentimentalists. Besides, you're still involved."

Jeff looked relieved. "You'll be going with her?" Buchanan nodded. "What about the jocks?"

"Len and Kyle are humans and so therefore able to lie. They've also still got the football moves in case they have to put them into action. In other words, we need them here, covering for and protecting all of you as needed."

"And we *are* bitter about that," Kyle said.

"Very much so," Len added.

"Also, while Malcolm will be going out with me, Jeff, you have to accept that, right now, you trying to make sure that I've got bodyguards isn't what's important."

"I know what's important. And I'm not arguing about you going, because I had an interesting talk with Cliff when you were off doing whatever you were doing in NASA Base."

"Giving Brian, who was there but not in quarantine, the go order, and telling Tito and Caroline what the plan was so that they can cover for the girls. What did Cliff say to you? He reassured me that he'd take care of our children if we all die."

"Same thing for me." Jeff's eyes flashed. "And I'll let him touch our kids, any of the kids, over my dead body."

"Which is exactly what he wants. How did you and Chuckie have this talk and Cliff missed it?"

Jeff grinned. "We had the talk, which included Christopher and Paul, while you were distracting Cliff and the girls were giving their go messages to the other guys."

"What about your Secret Service detail? Do they think you're a world class jerk now?"

"Joseph and Rob are advised. We *can* function as a well-oiled team, you know. Even without you sometimes."

"Let's hope that Cliff doesn't think so."

CHAPTER 74

"HE DOESN'T," Buchanan said. "There are reasons they always try to separate you from the rest of the team, Missus Executive Chief."

"Operation Destruction being the shining example." My throat felt tight. "When Vince moved from enemy to ally."

Jeff hugged me. "I know. We have to stop this so that we can avenge his murder, and so many others, as well as keep everyone else alive."

"That's the plan."

Jeff's phone buzzed, he pulled it out of his pocket, took a look, and chuckled. "Per Christopher, Cliff is comforting Chuck. He doesn't think he can be overheard, they've stepped away from the others, but Christopher's close enough to catch the conversation."

"Yay for A-C hearing. He's probably ensuring that he's touching Chuckie's skin, by the way. What's the scoop?"

"Cliff's telling Chuck that he doesn't think that you're actually happy with me and are probably looking for any excuse to get a divorce." Jeff shook his head. "What a bastard."

"Yeah. He thinks he's going to get Chuckie thinking that he and I will get to be a couple, even if it's just for a few days. Probably just so he can see me reject Chuckie and you beat the hell out of him. In the dream world Cliff's living in, I mean."

"The jealousy display was very believable," Buchanan said. "Helped by you already glaring at me when we came through the gate."

"That wasn't faked," Jeff said.

"Shocker." Buchanan's sarcasm knob was definitely at eleven.

"Cliff's also saying that it's clear that I'm not ready to handle the stress of the Presidency," Jeff went on as if Buchanan hadn't spoken. Nice to see that it happened to men as well as women.

"Good, that means he fell for the act," I said.

"Yeah, well, Ariel dying in front of me and literally falling into Raj's arms was an easy way to lose emotional control. I just kept it going." Jeff grunted. "Chuck's pretending to have a mood swing because of this news. At least I really hope he's acting. Cliff's helping him into the dining room where we're trying to get people fed. Huh, James and Tim are going with them."

"Possibly to ensure Cliff doesn't murder Chuckie along the way. Are they and MJO starting to say they don't feel well?"

"Richard is, and I think Chuck was doing that as a cover for him. Christopher has to 'help' Richard find a place to rest, so they'll be here shortly."

"Did you coordinate with him, James, Tim, and Mister Joel Oliver?"

"No," Jeff admitted.

Dug out my phone and sent Oliver a text. "Okay, I've told MJO that you and Chuckie are in on the plan. He's going to 'feel faint' shortly. But he says he, James, and Tim did feel that I'd given them the go signal. So, no idea what the other two are planning but they're triggered."

"Good," Mom said. "I assume James will be able to get you floater gates to wherever you need to go?"

"I hope so." Especially because I was fairly sure that most of my team was in the wrong spots for the assignments

I was going to give them and probably all experiencing some level of fever. "I don't think there will be an issue with William and if there is, Serene is at Dulce."

Jeff snorted. "Then everyone will do whatever you want as long as she tells them to in that power-mad way of hers that reminds me so much of you, baby."

"I'm choosing to ignore that. So, where are we going to say everyone is? I mean, you cannot tell Cliff that you put me into your office."

"President's living room," Mom said briskly while she tapped away on her phone. "I've cleared it with Elaine. Everyone who's 'too sick' or supposed to be guarding the sick people will go there."

"Great. Is her Secret Service detail trustworthy?"

Evalyne shook her head. "I have no idea. I want to say yes, but we were infiltrated by someone working directly for the Mastermind, so who's to say they aren't?"

"We have to risk it," Buchanan said. "If we're going, we're going. Besides, the Former First Lady isn't going to leave her quarters, so if any of them leave, you'll know that's the traitor or traitors."

"I agree," Christopher said, as he and White came in. "Kitty, I don't know where or how James, Tim, and Oliver are going to get out. For my dad we could use the 'tired old man' excuse. But those three honestly don't look sick."

"I think I resent that, son."

"You look amazing as always to me, Mister White." Did the forehead check. Sadly, both father and son were too hot, and not in the good way this time. "MJO has a plan, but someone has to bring him to the right location. No idea on James and Tim."

"I'll count on them to ensure it's dramatic," Jeff said.

"Maybe not," Phoebe said. "Too dramatic would draw attention, wouldn't you think? Kitty doing it was one thing. But if others are, too . . ."

Looked at Jeff. "Sounds like you get to go be a jerk again."

Jeff nodded. "Let's use the old 'pressure's getting to me and I'm lashing out at my friends' plan."

"You sound like Kitty far too often." Christopher gave Jeff an Atta Boy shot of Patented Glare #3. Presumably so he'd know the world was still normal.

"I consider that a good thing," Jeff said with a grin.

"Can you do it?" Mom asked.

"Yeah, I'll just tell myself they all want to sleep with my wife."

"Whatever gets you through, Jeff. Okay, so we all need to actually go to the President's Living Room, in part so that Richard and I know where it is, in case we're able to get back before anyone can notice that we're gone."

"And that way we'll be there to take James, Tim, and Mister Joel Oliver with us," White added. "I believe hyperspeed will be, as it so often is, our friend."

"Is there anything else we need to discuss before we do that?" Mom asked. "I'd personally like to know what you're going to be trying to do, kitten."

"Honestly, Mom, I'd prefer not to tell any of you what I'm planning. In no small part because Jeff and Christopher are the worst liars in the world. I know you pulled up how you used to feel about Chuckie for that 'fight,' Jeff. I don't think you can do that for the 'where is your wife going' question."

"I hate to admit it, baby, but you're right on both. I'd like to know, but it's probably better that I don't." He sighed. "And you know how bad it is when I'm letting you do this, without me and without argument."

"Don't worry, Jeff," Christopher said. "Kitty's plan will be something insane and foolhardy that will put her and everyone else on her team in mortal peril. Several times, most likely."

"You don't know me."

"Just be really clear about your location when you call for help."

"You remain not my favorite, Christopher."

He grinned. "Nice to see that Jeff's still number one in your heart."

"And in the bedroom."

"Too much information!" That was said in unison by most of the room.

Jeff just grinned. "Even when we face the potential end of the world, it still sucks to be me."

CHAPTER 75

WE ZIPPED TO the President's Living Room, or what I was thinking of as the Launch Point. As with everything else around here, it was tastefully decorated, huge, and everything in it had a feeling of being very old.

"Is there any chance you have jeans I can change into?" I asked Elaine, who wasn't looking all that great, which wasn't a surprise in any way.

"Maybe. I don't know that we're the same size. But some of my granddaughter's clothes might still be here from her last visit." She led me to a ginormous closet that made ours at the Embassy seem rather average, which, before this moment, I hadn't considered possible. "Just look around, try on anything, take whatever fits."

Hugged her. "Thank you. I work better not all dressed up."

She nodded. "I know. I just . . ." She took a deep breath and let it out slowly. "I just can't look at Vince's clothes right now," she said softly.

Hugged her again, then closed the door behind her. Heaved a sigh. "The Elves, the Elves, my kingdom for the Elves."

I'd been looking toward the end of the vast closet, so I saw the pile of clothes appear out of nowhere. Trotted over. Jeans, Converse, Aerosmith t-shirt, Aerosmith hoodie. All black, even the Converse. Clean underwear, too.

"Thank you, my King of the Elves. You really are the best."

Put the clothes on and dumped my old ones onto the floor. I didn't actually care if they made their way home, though I had a suspicion they would. If it even mattered.

There was something on the floor, under where the shoes had been. A penny, head side up. Figured it had fallen out of Armstrong's pocket somewhere along the way. Picked it up and put it in my pocket. "For good luck. Which we need in the most desperate way."

There was nothing else that seemed out of place or that might be a good luck totem. "Thanks for all the musical memories and those goggles," I said to the closet at large. "Right you were—this isn't something we have any experience with."

No rakish dwarf appeared.

"And . . . if I don't see you again, I get why you're not stopping this, I truly do. I understand the whole Free Will Manifesto. And, much as I want to hate you or resent you for it, I don't. I just have to trust that you somehow know that it's all going to be worth it. Because right now all I see is death and illness and fear. And we already have more than enough of that on this planet."

Waited. Nothing. But then, I hadn't expected anything.

"We'll do our best to stop Cliff and all his evil minions, but I'm saying so long and thanks for all the fish, just in case. You're a jerk, but you're our jerk, and I love you." Headed out of the closet, shutting the door behind me.

I couldn't blame Algar for being himself. He gave me what he'd always promised—clean clothes—and that was going to have to be enough.

Rejoined the others. No one seemed remotely surprised that I'd found clothes that looked a lot like mine in Elaine's closet and I chose not to mention their lack of attention to detail. For all I knew, they were all feeling too crappy to care. No one looked chipper, and if we were at home and not facing an epidemic of biblical proportions, I'd have told every one of them to go take some aspirin or Advil and go have a rest.

"By the way," I said, before anyone noticed that they hadn't noticed my outfit, "we need to protect Gideon at the same level as Jeff and Chuckie."

"Why?" Kyle asked.

"Because he knows enough about the Mastermind to be a liability," Len replied.

"Yep. So, we need to ensure that he's well-guarded."

"Cliff's undoubtedly pawed him by now," Phoebe said.

"I'm betting that Cliff's managed to paw everyone by now."

"We'll handle it," Jeff said.

"You all need to try to get blood samples to Doctor Hernandez," Buchanan said. "Specifically of Goodman, but he wants everyone's blood if we can do it, so that they can determine who is and isn't infected and spot if anyone is naturally creating antibodies."

"We'll handle it," Jeff said for the second time, with a tad more emphasis.

"We should also determine if there's something that Cliff has on him that's helping him spread the disease via touch. There could be an answer to the cure if we can find out what he's using. And by 'we' I mean those of you who are staying in the White House."

"We'll handle it," Jeff said for the third time, sounding annoyed.

"I believe in you."

"I think I resent that, baby."

"What's your plan for protecting Gideon? I'm serious. He's got information that can possibly convict the Mastermind in the court of public opinion if nothing else."

"That he may not be willing to share," Mom reminded me.

"We're facing a plague. I think Gideon might want to try to save the world—not to mention himself and his family—and if that means taking down the Mastermind he's already disavowed, then I'm not seeing the problem."

Mom cocked her head at me. "You're normally far more in tune with motivations."

"I am. And I'm telling you that as far as I can tell, Gideon Cleary wants to die on the side of right. So, let's ensure the right part of that, but not the die."

"Just have him get 'too sick,'" Len suggested. "That way, he's up here. This is where we're going to put all those who don't feel great, right? As in, this is our high-level quarantine area. If he's up here, we can all protect him."

"And possibly get him to give us the information we need," Kyle said. "We do have a very good working relationship with the governor."

Jeff nodded. "That's a very good plan." Both boys looked pleased and a little proud. "We'll get him up here somehow, baby, I promise."

"Great. And if you can't get him up here somehow, keep him under guard."

"We will." Jeff gave me a long, deep kiss. "I know I won't see you for a while, baby," he said softly. "And, if the worst happens and I don't see you again, know that I'll always love you and I'll see you on the other side."

"I'll always love you, too, and I promise the worst won't happen, Jeff. You keep the home fires burning, our friends and family here safe, and our enemy right where you can see him at all times. I'll handle the rest."

"That's my girl."

"Always, Jeff. Always and forever your girl."

One more fantastic kiss and one very long, tight hug, then Christopher and Jeff took off, with an admonition from me to be sure they were bickering loudly when they got to the dining room.

And then we waited. Elaine was filled in at a very high level, Lucinda and Elaine's Secret Service detail far less so. They were all sent off to get sustenance for those coming up here, as well as sleeping bags or linens and whatever. Mom pulled Lucinda aside and asked her not to use hyperspeed, and Lucinda was savvy enough not to ask why.

These briefings were barely over and Lucinda and team sent off on their hopefully time-consuming errand when Oliver came in with Raj. Of the two of them, the one who looked like he really needed the rest was Raj and I said so, while I checked Oliver for fever, which he had.

Raj shrugged. "I'm sick with whatever this is, just like everyone else, Kitty. But I still have a job to do."

"Yeah, and I think you should do it here, while lying down."

"No. Mister Joel Oliver explained what was going on once we were alone."

"Why did you do that?" I asked Oliver.

"Because I could tell that our fine young troubadour knew I was faking. He helped me sell my 'dizzy spell' for our dear Mastermind and I felt he deserved to know what was going on."

"I know you won't let me go with you," Raj said. "But Jeff's going to need me, especially if he's fighting with Charles, so I don't mind staying."

"That was faked, Raj."

He grinned. "I figured, Kitty. However, they're going to have to keep that up for the entire time you're 'up here sick.' They're the distraction for the Mastermind."

"True enough."

"And he's truly enjoying it," Oliver said. "I can tell. The signs are small and hidden, but they're there."

"I don't want to just stop whatever he's doing. I want to end his reign. Here and now."

"No idea how you're going to do that," Mom said with a sigh. "We still have nothing concrete that we can pin on him. And that will include his blood, if we can actually get some, because even if he has the vaccine in his bloodstream, he'll have a believable story for how it got there. And if this is an example of what he can do if he feels like it, then we need to know what all the other doomsday plans are and abort or dismantle them first."

We'd been saying that for years now. And people I cared about kept on dying while we waited. Chose not to get into an argument with my mother, especially because reality said that I might not see her again, since we were all definitely infected. But I knew what I was going to do, and I was going to expose Cliff in any and all ways possible.

More waiting. Finally Christopher came back with Reader and Tim. "Chuck's doing a great job with the faked mood swings, Jeff's doing a great job channeling when he was drugged out of his mind and acting like that again, and I officially want to go with you because I'm somehow stuck in the role of the voice of reason."

"So everyone's having a good time. Awesome." Checked them. Yep, both had fevers. Go Team Sicko.

"I'm glad I was chosen to be 'too sick to stay downstairs,'" Tim said. "Believe me."

"Remember that when we're hanging off of something wondering if we're going to die from falling or being shot, versus this disease," Reader said with a grin.

"I'll resent that later, James. Now, back you go, Christopher and Raj. Ensure that Cliff doesn't sleep alone and that he's not bunking with Chuckie only. Try not to let Cliff touch anyone, not that I think that's going to be easily accomplished. Try to help Jeff figure out how to get a sample of Cliff's blood and good luck with that. If someone has to sell how sick we are, let that someone be Raj or my mother."

"Or me," Elaine said. "I can do it, and anything I can do to help you right now I will."

"Got it," Christopher said.

"Do you want us downstairs or up here?" Len asked.

"Here," Christopher said. "In case someone tries to get in to 'see' the sick people. Unless we need you for muscle or as a way to get Cleary up here, in which case, one of us will call or text."

"Roger that," Kyle said.

"Love you guys, be safe." Hugged Christopher and Raj, then they left us.

"I hope this works," Elaine said. "Or we won't care in another, what, week? Week and a half?"

"No idea yet," Mom said. "Based on what we know, if you're healthy, maybe more than a week. If you're not, then probably not."

"Ariel was healthy as far as I ever knew," Elaine said, clearly trying to keep her voice steady, with limited success. "And Doctor Morin and his team, who sound close to death right now, were all very healthy."

Reader's phone beeped and he drew his breath in.

"What?" I asked with trepidation.

"Chuck says the entire medical staff other than Morin just died. Morin called for help about a minute ago. All medical staff other than the doctor are confirmed dead and being taken to the bowling alley. Morin appears very close to death himself."

I was prescient. Great. And everyone who'd gone to the medical offices with me was now more exposed. Or something. And this also meant we only had one person on site who had a hope of taking a useable blood sample from Cliff, and that man was close to death. For all I knew, Jeff would get the perfect plan to take Cliff's blood in place and Morin would die before he could perform the act.

"This has to stop," Elaine said, now not even trying to hide how distraught she was. She was also presciently saying what I was thinking. Maybe this illness made you telepathic. But probably not.

Went to Elaine and hugged her tightly. "I'm going to stop him," I whispered to her. "I swear to you I'm going to make him pay for what he's done."

She hugged me back. "The best way out is through the basement. Mister Joel Oliver will know where to go."

Oliver nodded. "I know where the secret exit is."

"There's only one?"

He smiled. "There are several, but I believe the one our First Lady is referring to is the one that will let us out at a decent distance from the White House Complex yet not so far that we can't catch public transportation."

"Former First Lady," Elaine corrected. "And you're right. Now, all of you, go save this country and possibly the world from the plague released by a madman."

Hugged everyone and told them I loved them, Mom especially, before we left. Then we linked up and, Oliver steering and White providing the hyperspeed, took off for the great outdoors.

CHAPTER 76

OF COURSE, we had to go down two floors, skulk around in a dark basement, follow a rather sterile tunnel, go down some stairs into a far less sterile tunnel, up some stairs, and into another tunnel that wasn't as nice as the first and not as bad as the second, one more set of stairs up, to end up in a small building. Then, once we found our way through that and found the right door, there we were, in the outdoors.

Was incredibly glad we'd done it all at hyperspeed.

Looked around. The little building at the end of this tunnel turned out to be at the far side of Lafayette Square. Saw no rioting in the streets. So that was good. Didn't expect this quiet to last.

There were park benches very nearby, so we went and sat down while I sent texts to Brian and the girls, Buchanan, White, and Oliver keeping a lookout.

"So, what's the plan?" Reader asked.

"Hang on." Brian replied that he had TCC with him but they were still in Alfred's home, mostly because there was indeed panic in the area around NASA Base and he wanted to be sure he could actually get both of them wherever I needed them to go. They were hunkered in the basement, hanging out with the gate. So everyone was having fun tonight.

On the plus side, Brian and TCC showed no symptoms of this disease. So far, at any rate. Who knew what would happen when they left the safety of the Martini Mansion Complex?

"So glad we're out to save the day by sitting around," Tim said.

"You wound me." The girls were out of the quarantined side of NASA Base and were waiting at a gate for where I wanted them to go. They all had fevers, though they felt mild. Tito had taken blood samples from them, then pumped them full of water and chicken soup before they left, so they insisted they felt okay.

Adriana hadn't replied yet—hoped I hadn't blown her mission but assumed she had her phone on Silent Running. "Okay, we have a lot of targets, and a short time to find them all, so we're going to split up."

"I figured," Buchanan said. "And I already know I'm not going with you, Missus Executive Chief, based on what you told our new President."

"Let's chill with the titles right now, Malcolm, just in case anyone's around to hear us. First off, do you know how to get in touch with Camilla?"

"Why?"

Heaved a sigh. "Because we're literally facing the end of the world and I know she's deep undercover somewhere and I'm just praying that it's somewhere that can help us in this situation and for God's sake, dude, we need her help. Is there some other freaking test I need to pass to get her freaking number?"

"No, just curious." Buchanan pulled out a phone. Not his regular phone. Like the rest of us he was using a second one. But this looked like a burner phone to me. He dialed. "I'd like to know if you'd like a subscription to the Times."

"What the literal hell?" I said quietly to Tim.

"I think it's spy code," he replied in kind. "Let's listen and learn."

"We have a great deal for you," Buchanan said, continuing his sales pitch.

"You brought him why?" Reader asked.

"For the laughs."

"Okay, well, if you change your mind, give us a call." He hung up.

"You didn't leave a number," I pointed out.

"Nothing gets past you, does it?" Buchanan asked, as a different phone rang. "Hello? Great, we have a situation. Handing you off to Cyclone." He gave the phone to me.

"Hilarious. Is this the party to whom I am speaking?"

"I'd have thought you were too young for that show," Camilla said, sarcasm knob already turned to eleven.

"TV Land saves the day and I'm married to an old shows junkie. We have a situation." Filled her in fast on what was going on. "So, I'm really hoping you're in deep somewhere that could help us."

"I am, actually," she said. "But I need muscle to get what I think you'll want."

"Want to tell me who, what, or where you're entrenched?"

"Nope. Want to tell me who I can access for backup?"

"Can you tell me who or what you're going after, so that I can, perhaps, send the right backup to the right place?"

"Nope. Who's got the easiest way out of wherever they are?"

Pondered. I needed the guys with me for various missions. I needed the girls for other missions. Said missions might overlap with Camilla's, but hopefully Buchanan would give us a hint in that way.

So, who else did we have? Really only had two options, who were together and who I'd hoped to get out and into the action anyway. "Rahmi and Rhee are probably the easiest, if you can call getting them out of a cell in Guantanamo where they're terrorizing a bunch of commandos easy."

"I can and do. You'll need to give them the order."

"What order?"

She heaved a sigh. "The order to come with me if they want to live."

"When did you go all *Terminator* on me?"

"I know what speaks to you."

"Whatever. Okay, I'll let them know. How soon should they be ready to leave and should James send a floater gate for them?"

"In five minutes and no. Where's the meet point?"

"Um . . ." Hadn't given this any thought. Chose to think quickly right now. Meet up point would need to be in Florida or D.C. Cliff was in D.C. however, so that was the winner. But where in D.C.? My phone beeped. Adriana returning my text. Fortuitously. "The Romanian Embassy."

"Excuse me?"

"Nice to surprise you for a change. The Romanian Embassy. It's empty, they're all in our Embassy complex because Olga—"

"Isn't stupid and saw this or something similar coming. Got it. Works for me. Don't text or call me. I'll contact you."

"What if I'm in the middle of a mission?"

"Then either mute your phone or figure the disturbance will help you save the day."

"Love your optimism on that last one."

"Love how late you called me in."

"Is that why you're bitter? This is the first chance I've had."

"I'll accept your lousy excuse and apology."

"You know, I'm the First Lady now."

"God help us all."

"I'd be offended but it's like you read my mind."

She laughed. "You'll do fine, Kitty. Roll whatever, we'll get our side of things taken care of."

"What exactly is—" She hung up. "Your side of things?" Sighed and hung up myself, then handed the phone back to Buchanan. "Sometimes I like her."

"And sometimes she's busy and we disturb her at inopportune times." Buchanan shrugged. "It's part of the job."

"Whatevs." Sent Rahmi and Rhee a group text with high-level information and the request that they do what Camilla said, short of trying to kill anyone they knew for certain was an ally.

Thankfully, Rhee replied right away. They were still in the cell but would be ready to do whatever, whenever, that Camilla needed. They had no fevers, and neither did any of the Invisible Commandos.

Who were, apparently, becoming visible. What the princesses had learned was that the invisibility irradiation was a cumulative thing. The first big treatments didn't make you invisible forever, just for about twenty-four hours. The thinking was that the more irradiation a person had, the longer the invisibility would last. So the princesses felt secure in leaving, because all the commandos were coming more into focus for those without the special goggles.

"Okay, the princesses are activated and ready." Shared what Rhee had told me with the guys.

"Don't know what them not being sick means," Reader said.

"That they weren't near the main source of infection long enough is my guess," Oliver said. "I assume I'm ill because Cliff Goodman shook my hand at NASA Base."

"Or because you were around people who were very ill, or in the contagious stage, or both," Reader said. "Really, we have no idea how this disease transfers, so any option could be the right one or ones."

My phone beeped—it was Adriana. She had a bead on the Crazy Eights but wasn't in a position to take them down because she didn't want to spook Wruck and also felt she was outnumbered. Told her to sit tight and that we'd be there as soon as we could. The Crazy Eights were in Florida, which was convenient, though I didn't ask where, specifically, since they weren't our primary target yet. Adriana also didn't have a fever.

"And Adriana's on the case and fine, so the NASA Base handshake theory seems quite sound. As does the NASA Base Surrounded By The Sick And Dying theory. So we're good there. Malcolm, I'm going to outline who's doing what and then I really want you to tell me if we have overlap with whatever the hell Camilla's planning."

"We'll see."

Rolled my eyes and resisted the urge to strangle him. "Fine. Okay, Malcolm and Mister Joel Oliver, I need you two to find Colonel Hamlin, get him to gather all his evidence against our Mastermind, and get him to the safe house, which is the Romanian Embassy."

Male mouths opened.

"If one of you says that you already figured that out I'm going to take out all the pent up energy I used not killing Cliff for the past few hours and not strangling Malcolm for the last ten minutes and expend it on you."

Male mouths closed.

"Good. MJO, any questions?"

"No, just concerns. The colonel is not going to want to come out."

"Explain the damn situation to him and I guarantee he's going to have a reason to risk it. We need him. He's the one with the comprehensive information. Send out the carrier pigeons and get him on board and ready."

"Fine," Oliver said with a sigh. "We'll do our best."

"Super-duper. Adriana is after the Crazy Eights and has them located but can't take action yet. However, we know where they are which is a huge win. Mahin and Abigail are after Stephanie aka Huntress. Lorraine and Claudia are trying to find the flyboys. Yes, we realize that their missions may overlap each other, which is why they're still together and waiting to see if we have any idea where their quarries are."

"What are you going to be doing?" Buchanan asked.

"I have two missions. I need to find Siler, the Dingo, and

Surly Vic and determine where Siler has, please God let it still exist, hidden Lizzie's father's notebook. Then I need to find another ally. This will overlap with what Adriana is doing, at least I hope. I'm going to take James, Tim, and Richard with me because I know I'm going to need help."

Buchanan didn't look happy. "You should take me with you for the assassins."

"I know they're your best buds forever. The thing is, Hamlin trusts exactly two of us—you and MJO. And this situation is probably going to require both of you. He's more important to the end game, you go after him."

"Where are we heading to search?" Reader asked. "It's a big world and we don't have a lot of time."

"See, that's where being Megalomaniac Girl comes in so handy. Oh sure, two of our teams are in the places the other team should be, but that's what gates are for, am I right?"

"You think the flyboys are around here somewhere?" Tim asked.

"Yes, because Drax was doing a sales pitch. He might have been selling along the way to Florida, but he planned to close the deal here."

"And the assassins are in Florida?" Tim didn't sound convinced.

"Remember my visit to Bizarro World? Well, in that world Luis Sanchez and Julio Lopez are Cuban assassins. Well, they were. They're dead there now and no loss to that universe."

"And?" Reader asked.

"And, per Mom and Chuckie, they exist in this world, too. Per Team Assassination, dear Luis and Julio are raving loons and our guys expected them to be lying in wait for us in Orlando. We never made it to Orlando, and therefore instead of having a great time at Disney World we are instead stuck once more having to save the entire world. But I think Team Assassination made it there and, since they were not representing during our frolicsome train ride, nor can Lizzie reach any of them, I think they've been captured."

"Hopefully captured, not killed," White said.

Reader shook his head. "Their relationship with Kitty is well known. They'll be used as bargaining chips, I'd think, before they'd be killed."

"So, we'll have the girls gate here and we'll go there. But I kind of wish I'd let Len and Kyle come with us."

"Why so?" Buchanan asked.

"Because I have a last mission and I can't spare anyone to do it."

"And that is?" Reader asked.

"Someone needs to get to Langston Whitmore, keep him alive, and convince him to share what he knows about the Mastermind with us and the world."

"Ah," Buchanan said. "I'd suggest that you put Lorraine and Claudia on that one."

CHAPTER 77

"SO, CAMILLA'S** in deep with Drax? How the hell is that when he's come out of nowhere?"

"She's not in with Drax."

Tim nudged me. "She's in with Titan."

"I thought she'd been going in deep at Gaultier."

"She did," Reader said. "But Chuck said something a couple of years ago about moving her around. I think, based on what Buchanan here is and isn't saying, that he moved her to Titan."

"Super. So, we'll assume that she's somehow magically going to know what we need her to do?"

Buchanan shrugged. "You told her what was going on, including about the Invisible Commandos and the flyboys being captured." He checked his burner phone. "She has the princesses with her and they're going after Drax's helicarrier."

"I don't even want to know at this point."

"Good, because we can't tell you."

"Can't or won't?"

"Take your pick. Anyway, reassign the others, would you?"

Shot him a glare I hoped was channeling Christopher, then sent a group text to Lorraine, Claudia, Mahin, and Abigail. Wherever Drax was, it was likely Stephanie was, too.

Told Abigail and Mahin to do their best to connect up with Camilla via the princesses and to stay in touch with Brian, since he and TCC would need to meet up with them once they had Stephanie corralled, while I reassigned Lorraine and Claudia to Whitmore. To their great credit, none of the girls complained about this. Too much.

"The girls have been in touch with Serene, so they have a floater gate waiting to take them wherever they need to go. Dulce has floaters ready to go for us, too."

"We won't need one," Buchanan said. Oliver nodded.

"Nice to know Hammie's still sticking close to home and you're going to show him that you're not revealing his hiding place to anyone else. Okay, you two head off. Contact Serene if you need or want a gate. We'll see you at the Romanian Embassy, and if not, we'll try to let you know where we are."

"Be careful." Buchanan looked worried. "You know they're going to kill you if they can."

"Malcolm, we killed these guys in Bizarro World. I'll be fine." He didn't look convinced, but he nodded, then he and Oliver turned to go. "Oh, one last thing, just in case?" They both turned back. "Love you guys."

They both smiled. "We'll all be back," Oliver said. "Never fear." Then he and Buchanan walked off down the street.

"Hurray for team efficiency and fond farewells," Reader said. "Where are we going, Kitty? Orlando is a big town. And if you say Disney World I'm taking you back to the White House."

Considered this for a moment, in no small part because Reader was right. But it also occurred to me that there might be a simple way to find out where Siler was—by asking him.

"Hang on." Sent a text to Siler, since I actually had a number for him thanks to Lizzie. Didn't try to code it, just said that I needed to know where he was.

Got a reply very quickly. *Go to the roof.*
Can't. Have to come to you.

Got a return text with an address. Sure enough, it was in Florida.

"Okay, we have a location and we're going in hot."

"You suspect a trap?" White asked.

"Very much so. Siler hasn't responded to Lizzie's coded messages, but he was Johnny on the Spot with the reply to me for where he was. They expect us to come to him, so that's where we're going."

Reader called Serene, gave her the location, then asked for the gate to deposit us nearby but not at the location. "It's nice to see that others have learned from our experience, Missus Martini."

"Warms the heart, doesn't it, Mister White?"

"James and I are going to vomit all over both of you if you're not careful," Tim said.

"Megalomaniac Lad, you wound me. I kept the best with me."

Tim grinned. "That's better."

Looked at the texts again. "Mister White?"

"Yes?"

"It's likely that Siler knows what's going on, right?"

"Even captured I'd assume the news of the President's death, as well as the Secretary of State and Speaker of the House, has reached them."

"Their captors are probably cheering about it," Tim added.

"Yeah . . . so, why would they tell me to go to the roof?"

"No idea," Reader said. "Because he was trying to give you a clue? I mean, I assume that it's not Siler who's replied to your texts, since he didn't respond to his daughter."

"Right. Lizzie was sending coded messages, so it would be easy to pretend they were nothing. I sent a very straightforward 'it's me and I need you now' message . . ."

"What are you thinking that we're not?" White asked.

"The Dingo always tells me to go to the roof of the Embassy if I need him. Siler does, now, too."

"So you think it's really Siler answering?" Reader didn't sound convinced.

"I think his captors told him I was texting and insisted he give them a reply I'd believe."

"Why use the obvious code, then?" Tim asked. "That's both telling our enemies where Siler and the others expect you to go and also useless."

"Or it's a code you're not catching," Reader said.

"Or he said it was a countersign so you'd know it was he who was calling," White suggested.

"Unless James was right the first time and it's neither useless nor code nor a countersign." Called Lizzie.

"Kitty, I still haven't heard from my dad."

"I think I have, and I need you to do something for me."

"Sure."

"Great. Tell Walter that you have to go to the roof, with my permission. I want him to ensure that you can actually walk on the roof while still keeping the Embassy complex shielded, or if he can't, that he's watching to turn the shields off and on again fast."

"Okay. Why am I going to the roof?"

"Take a strong flashlight with you and search every inch of the roof. You're looking for your father's notebook or something similar. Maybe even a flash drive. Something that can store data. The Secret Service already searched the roof, so whatever's up there is well hidden."

She was quiet for a few moments. "You think Mister Dash hid my father's notebook on the Embassy roof?" It was interesting—when she wasn't talking about her real parents, she called Siler her father. But the moment we were talking about her parents he became Mr. Dash. Couldn't argue—whatever got her through the horror was okay with me. Especially now.

"Yeah, I do."

"Why?"

"Because he has an interesting sense of humor, and he'd consider our roof one of the safest places in the world."

"He did tell me that he was putting me in the safest place he could think of."

"There you go. We need you to be Quick Girl with this, by the way, because unshielded means tremendously vulnerable and if the information is indeed on our roof, you need to get it to my dad and start deciphering it beyond fast."

"Will do, Kitty." She sounded far more alert and efficient—less teenager and more superhero sidekick. Clearly being Quick Girl gave her confidence. Again, couldn't argue—being Megalomaniac Girl certainly helped me.

"Be sure to look absolutely anywhere and everywhere on the roof. You know Mister Dash—think about where he'd hide something and search there first. Figure he anticipated someone looking for this, so try to think like he would have. Whatever you find, take it to my dad immediately. I'll check in with you when I can."

"You got, it Commander." Yep, she was definitely more official and ready for action as Quick Girl. "Quick Girl out and on the case."

"So, if we know where the notebook is, why are we going to Florida?" Reader asked as I hung up.

"Because we don't know for sure that I'm right and our allies are captured and probably being tortured and we don't leave our people behind."

Tim chuckled. "Nice to know you'll move heaven and earth for anyone on your side, Kitty."

"It's what we do," White said. "All of us, even if you two want to pretend you don't want to go."

"I don't want to go," Reader said. "We didn't weapon up before we left, meaning all we have is whatever bullets Tim and I have loaded and whatever's in Kitty's purse."

"Hey, my purse tends to come through."

"Because you put everything you find into it, girlfriend."
Reader flashed me the cover boy grin. "Not that I'm complaining."

"Could have fooled me, James."

As the floater gate shimmered into view, Reader grabbed my hand and Tim's, White took my free hand. Then we walked through, me truly doing my best not to throw up. I hadn't had food or rest in far too long and my stomach was tired of running on empty.

Which turned out okay, considering where we landed.

CHAPTER 78

WELL, WE LANDED in a bathroom, of course. Because even when the fate of the world was at stake, aliens were weird. However, when we stepped out, after verifying that no one was around or looking in our direction, it turned out we were in a Wendy's.

"Awesome." Went to the counter and ordered a chocolate Frosty.

"Is now really the time?" Reader asked.

"I'm starving, so yeah, it is." Got my Frosty and started spooning it into my mouth as fast as possible, though at human speed.

People were in here, talking about the President's death and worrying that there was a disease out there. Heard the word "Ebola" more than a few times. But no one was running crazed through the streets. Yet. However it felt like that was imminent and just one thing would set off the powder keg.

"Interesting," White said, looking at his phone while I scarfed.

"What is?" I asked between mouthfuls.

"We appear to be at the closest fast food restaurant to the Amtrak station. We're also quite close to the Orlando Regional Medical Center."

"Being near where we'd have disembarked makes sense.

Are you saying that we're heading to the medical center?"

"No. We appear to be heading into the industrial area on the opposite side of the main street next to the train station. To a metal recycling plant to be specific."

"That bodes."

"As if this entire situation doesn't?" Reader shook his head, took my empty Frosty cup, and threw it away. He returned to our table. "Are you ready to rock and roll now?"

"Now that I won't faint from hunger at an inopportune time, yes I am."

"I'm willing to wait for Kitty to get a burger and fries, if need be," Tim said.

Reader rolled his eyes. "I swear you guys weren't this much work when Jeff and Christopher were in charge."

"Sure we were, you were just on our side then, boss man."

"True enough. Let's get back into our old mode, then, girlfriend, and kick it like it's hot."

"You really are so gangsta, James."

We headed out of the Wendy's and walked down the street. "Huh," White said, again looking at his phone.

"What now, Mister White?"

He held his phone so we could all watch Cliff Goodman and Wesley Green giving a joint statement to the press. Clearly they'd done this when we were all at NASA Base because I recognized the location and the people in the background.

Green was saying that we potentially had an epidemic on our hands. Cliff was reassuring that, if so, FEMA would step in to support the CDC.

"Why is that only running now?" Tim asked. "They did that a while ago now."

"This is on a loop," White said. "Wait for it."

Sure enough, we got a reporter sharing that they had newer information now. We saw Cliff again, clearly inside the White House, though this time none of our people were around though clearly some press were, press we hadn't brought over with us from NASA Base. He was confirming an epidemic and listing the names of the dead—which included names of people I didn't know but assumed worked in the White House or with those who'd been infected first. This was a move that would absolutely cause panic, which was, I was sure, the goal.

Cliff then urged the populace to go to FEMA emergency units that were being set up in most major cities to get vaccinated for flu and bubonic plague. "We don't know if the vaccines will work on this Alien Flu, but we can but hope and try to save as many as we can."

"Oh. My dear God. Cliff's lit the match. He's got the disease all set and ready to go, doesn't he?"

"Lit the match?" Reader asked.

"The current situation is commonly referred to as a powder keg, James," White answered for me.

"Oh. Should have caught that."

"We're all tense, James." I was certainly tense now.

"Alien Flu?" Tim asked angrily. "Since when?"

"That's who he wants to blame it on, us or the Planetary Council or both."

"I'd say both," White said.

"That would be my bet," Reader agreed, voice tight.

"Jeff must have tried to get his blood. That would explain him stepping things up."

"Or this is just the next step in his timeline," Reader said. "And based on this video it looks like he has both the President's approval and that the President is nowhere around, too. It's perfect. Tell the people to panic, blame aliens, get them to your facilities, give them the plague, tell them that the symptoms are just a reaction to the vaccine, let them infect everyone who didn't come to see you."

"And then let them all die." Tim's voice shook. "Why is he going to kill everyone if he plans to survive?"

"It won't kill everyone," White said. "No disease is a hundred percent effective. Those who survive will be too lost to argue with the changes in leadership. The republic will go down."

"And the Nation of Cliff will go up. And when it does, any aliens left alive will be hunted and killed, blamed for this plague. And then, anyone who's accused of being an alien, or an alien supporter is killed, too. Or rounded up into death camps."

"Yes," White said quietly. "This does sound much like the beginning of World War Two."

"Then let's do what the U.S. did in that war, get into that metal recycling factory, and get our allies out. By the way— I no longer care about Cliff's kill switch plans, or even where the clones of Reid and LaRue are. Or if he has a million clones waiting. I want him, the Original Cliff, dead before this is over."

"I'm with you, girlfriend, but what we want and what we get aren't always the same things."

Pulled my phone out and called Serene. "You're on speaker and have you seen the news?" I asked before she even said hello.

"Yes, I have. I don't trust those vaccines, Kitty."

"Neither do we. And Cliff has us all under quarantine, doesn't he?"

"He does."

"Well, we've risked more for less. I need you to send teams to wherever FEMA's setting up. They need to grab those vaccines and bring them to Dulce for analysis. Then we need to supply something safer for them to inject into all the unsuspecting citizenry."

She was quiet for a few moments.

"What?" Reader asked.

"I'm just wondering ... He knows our playbook, you guys. Isn't this exactly what we'd do? The chess move we'd make? Maybe this is all a ruse to get us to have the killer drug in our possession, so that he can blame us for everything. He's already calling it the Alien Flu, after all."

We all looked at each other. "Very possible," White said. "We are reacting just as expected."

"So, does that mean he thinks we're out, or that he thinks we're trying to circumvent from inside the White House?" Hoped he thought we were in, but didn't count on it.

Tim was texting. "Christopher says that he thinks Cliff believes we're all upstairs."

Nice to have a tiny bit of luck go our way. "It's the order we'd give from inside or out, though. The question is—does he know that the rest of us know who he really is, or does he think it's only Chuckie's who's figured it out?"

"There's no way to be sure," Reader said.

My brain nudged. Bizarro World Jamie had said "he knows" and she'd said that to me. Besides, it was always best to assume the worst. And him telling me and Jeff he was going to take our children was much more of a direct threat if he knew that we knew he was the Mastermind. Meaning he definitely knew and was just playing with his prey. Well, screw that. I was the cat in this game.

"Cliff knows we all know."

"You sound pretty certain all of a sudden," Tim said.

"I am because it makes the most sense and the time for wishful thinking is probably well past. So I think Serene's right—this is potentially a trap for us. At the same time, we can't allow him to infect God knows how many people."

"We could remove the vaccines," Serene said. "But if we're caught, it's the same thing as everyone finding us holding the death drug—it looks like we're trying to hurt everyone."

"And you know we'll be caught," Tim said. "Because that would be part of the overall plan."

Was staring at my phone, so I saw the song alert flash

onto the screen. "Countdown to Armageddon" by Public Enemy. Nice to know Algar was sending me the extra pressure needed to either collapse or turn into a diamond.

Another song flashed. "Irresponsible Hate Anthem" by Marilyn Manson. Then the Public Enemy song flashed again. Then the Marilyn Manson one.

"What's up with your phone?" Tim asked. "Is it low on battery right now? Because that would just figure."

"Don't know." Stared at the songs flashing alternately. Algar wanted me to think, because we were running out of time.

"Is that one song the theme song for our favorite church?" Reader asked with a bitter laugh. "Because that would also make so much sense. Though in that case, Public Enemy should be the group recording 'Irresponsible Hate Anthem.'"

"I love you, James. Serene, we need to figure out how to get a message to Club Fifty-One and the Church of Hate and Intolerance."

"Uh, why in the world would we want to do that?"

"Well, we don't want to call them straight out. But we need to ensure that they firmly believe that everything going on in the various FEMA centers and wherever is all A-C run. And that the A-Cs created the vaccine."

Didn't want to have to point blank ask her to assign her A-C C.I.A. team to this, but sincerely hoped she'd get my unspoken message. Pity none of us were psychic.

"Oh," Serene said, sounding like a total dingbat. Which meant she'd figured out what I wanted and didn't want the guys to catch on. Maybe she was psychic after all. I was getting to the point where I sort of figured there was nothing Serene couldn't do. "I think I know exactly how to do that, Kitty. And . . . that's brilliant."

"You're going to try to get our enemies to destroy the very thing they want to have happen?" Reader asked.

"That's the plan. They're just stupid enough to fall for it."

Cliff wasn't, of course, but he wasn't who I hoped Serene's team would be contacting.

"Let's hope," Serene said. "I'm going to get off. I'll contact you when I have news."

"Don't call us, we'll call you, Serene. We're about to go hunting wabbits."

"Gotcha."

"Really?"

"Really. Raj has us all watching a lot of TV shows so we'll learn how you think."

"Oh good. I think."

"It's a compliment. Hang in there, Kitty. We'll get this rolling."

"I know I can count on you, Serene. And, just in case, we love you."

"We love you, too. But we're not saying goodbye forever, okay? Someone I really respect taught me to never give up and never surrender. And also that if we were going down, we were going down fighting. So, I'm planning to do what you taught me, and I suggest you do the same."

We hung up and the men looked at me. "She has a point. So let's show these Cuban assassins just how we do things downtown, Dingo Style."

CHAPTER 79

"DINGO STYLE?" Reader asked.

"Don't question, she's rolling," Tim said.

"I'm ignoring both of you. Mister White, what are your thoughts about how many unfriendlies we're about to meet?"

"I sincerely believe that it would take far more than two people to capture our three friends."

"My thinking as well."

"Mine, too," Reader said. "Hence why I wish we had more weapons than what we have on us."

Looked at him, shook my head, and sighed. Then started walking again, while I sent a text to William. Text sent, grabbed White's hand, he grabbed Tim, I grabbed Reader, and we took off at hyperspeed. Oh, sure it was literally just across the street, but why be a good citizen when we were faster than the cars?

Though I realized that I was only faster than the cars because I was holding onto White.

We did a cursory run around the building and the area. It was your basic industrial area, with a lot of piles of scrap metal, buildings and machines that did whatever they did to scrap metal, old train cars, smooshed cars, and the like. There were other related businesses like welding and glass and such that seemed to share the same yard, rail cars off the main tracks that might or might not be ready for scrap, and no one around since it was after normal business hours. There were also no night watchmen or guard dogs. In other words, it was the perfect Bad Guy Lair area.

We stopped at the side of the building that wasn't on the street, behind a big pile of scrap metal.

"Guys, I think my hyperspeed is failing."

They all looked concerned. "I don't feel a hundred percent," White said, "but I'm having no issues other than the fatigue I'd associate with fever."

"So that means it hits humans harder than A-Cs," Reader said. "That's not what I thought it would do, based on what Lizzie told you."

"The original goal of this disease may have changed," Tim pointed out. "Or it was made at such high strength that those without regeneration are going down faster."

"I'm not fully human anymore," I reminded them.

"Which is why you're losing hyperspeed versus feeling terrible," Reader said. "Unfortunately, it's only a matter of time. For all of us. So, let's keep moving."

"You're right." Sent the go text to William. Guns and clips appeared at our feet. "Look," I whispered. "It's like magic!"

"I hate you," Reader muttered. "Fine, yeah, I wasn't thinking. Tell whoever sent this thanks."

"William says he lives to serve. So, let's weapon up, boys."

We all grabbed semiautomatics and a ton of clips. Grabbed extra clips for my Glock and dropped them in my purse while Tim and Reader slung rocket launchers over their backs. Put a semiautomatic rifle over my back.

Dug my Glock out of my purse and as I did my hand hit the case I carried that contained the adrenaline I periodically needed to slam into Jeff's hearts. Had a pang of worry—what if Jeff got sick or overstressed while I was gone? Sure, Dr. Morin was there, but he might die before he could administer the adrenaline. And could we trust anything there anyway?

"What is it?" White asked.

"I just . . ." I pulled out the adrenaline case. "I've got this and Jeff doesn't."

"He'll be fine, girlfriend," Reader said gently. "You need to focus on kicking butt."

"And administering that to me should I die from first the anticipation of life-threatening activity and then the boredom of us not actually doing anything," Tim added.

"Tim, I love you." Dumped the adrenaline back into my purse and called Mom.

"What's your status?" she asked without so much as a hello. Knew where I got it from. She didn't sound as good as when we'd left, though.

"Get all the adrenaline you can—have Serene send it to you from Dulce because I think anything in the White House is suspect by now."

"And you want me to do this why?"

"Because it occurred to me that adrenaline both starts hearts and opens lungs. And more people than Jeff can use it."

"You think it will keep those near death alive. It's possible, though I'd prefer to ask a doctor about it. But for how long?"

"Hopefully long enough, and ask Doctor Morin, who might be very willing to be a test case. Or call Tito, who may have already thought of it and be administering doses as we speak. As it is, most of us are feeling a lot better than I'd have expected." Decided not to tell Mom that my hyperspeed was leaving me. Why make her worry more?

"Yes. As to that . . ."

"What? Is someone dead?"

"No. But I've spoken to your father. You need to hurry, kitten. With whatever you're doing."

"Why?"

"Because your father thinks that Jamie is ... doing something to keep us all ... protected."

"Huh. Does Dad know what?"

"No, only that the Poofs and other animals won't let him into the room she's in. They did, however, let Patrick in. And then, shortly after, the rest of the Embassy hybrid children. Lizzie, Raymond, and Rachel are the only Embassy children not in the room. They're with your father, feeling quite left out."

"Oh, fantastic." Jamie had used her powers to protect us before. As had ACE. What they could do together, especially with Patrick and the other hybrids adding in, was potentially limitless. But it was also draining, of that I was sure. And while they were powerful, they were still little children. "Is Charlie in with her?"

"No, apparently baby brothers are not allowed in this particular club."

"Good, I hope."

Whatever they were doing had another negative in addition to the kids overstraining themselves dangerously — it would undoubtedly be noticed on the Superconsciousness Radar. And that would be bad for ACE, Algar, and the rest of us. If any of us were alive to worry about it, of course.

"What? Oh, Vance and Stryker both are insisting that I say hi to you for them. God alone knows why. They've joined us because Jeff and Cliff are having a shouting match with each other."

"Really? About what?"

"Cliff creating panic in the streets without Jeff's approval. Which started because Cliff used Jeff's suggestion that everyone have blood drawn to help determine who is and isn't sick as his excuse to declare a total epidemic."

"Huh. I think Jeff needs people down there watching his back."

"Which is why I sent Len and Kyle down. On the plus

side, Lizzie has apparently found something on your roof. Your father appears to be in his element."

"Did he say if it was her father's notes?"

"No, just that he had to get back to it, is working on it with Lizzie, and I should encourage you to speed up whatever you're doing when next we spoke."

"Wow. Dad's either got understatement down to an art form or he's really unclear on what's going on."

"I'm voting for the latter, since he said he'd turned off the news because it was upsetting everyone."

"Fantastic. How are things in the Sick Suite?"

"Boring, but the kind of boredom you have when you're wondering how long you're going to live." Mom's sarcasm knob went well past eleven.

"Got it, I just thought I'd share my potentially life-extending brainstorm with you in order to ensure everyone's lives get extended."

"Duly noted, kitten. I'll call Serene."

"Please text Lorraine and Claudia, too. Text not call, just in case. They may need the adrenaline idea for their assignment."

"Do I want to know?"

"Probably not."

"So, business as usual."

"Yep. Love you, Mom."

"Love you, too, but stop saying 'goodbye' to everyone and get moving. And that's an order."

We hung up. "Jeez, you'd think people would appreciate being told that they're loved."

"I live for it," Tim said. "So, are we, you know, going to raid this beast now or are we going to make more phone calls? Just curious."

"Raid," White said. "While you were chatting I did an interior search."

"Did not even notice that you were gone, Mister White, you silver fox, you."

"I live for the flattery, Missus Martini, so thank you. Skills are still in top form, too, so we can rest easy for the moment."

"What did you find?" Reader asked.

"There are far more than just a few Cuban assassins in the metal recycling building—at least I assume the gentlemen who look like they're from all over Cuba and are also armed even more heavily than we now are happen to be assassins as opposed to night watchmen. There were rooms I couldn't access, however. Naturally fortified and hard to reach due to the number of armed men around them."

"Naturally." Made sure I had a clip in my Glock and that the safety was off. Totally unsurprisingly, the safety hadn't been on and the gun was loaded. Go me, Gun Handler of the Year.

"Going in guns blazing, blow the building up, or stealth?" Tim asked.

"I have to figure that this is someone's legitimate business and not every business like this is Mob-owned, plus we have hostages we're trying to save, so I think stealth is the right answer."

Contemplated my options and decided to keep doing what worked for me, whether Algar was paying attention or not. Put my earbuds in, slid my phone into my back pocket, and hit play, keeping the sound low so it wouldn't carry to our enemies.

The Killers' "Battle Born" came onto the airwaves. Check. Algar was on the case and reminding me that, powers or not, I'd had what it took before and still did.

"Shoot to kill unless we know who they are," I said. "Mister White, are you comfortable taking point?"

"I am indeed, Missus Martini."

"Great, you first, me, then James, and Tim, you bring up the rear. Let's lock and load."

CHAPTER 80

WE LINKED UP to make it inside at hyperspeed without being seen or anyone noticing the door opening and closing.

White zipped us through the facility as well, so we could see what he'd already told us—there were a lot of guys with guns, knives, and hand grenades, and no sign of the three dudes we were looking for. They were definitely speaking Spanish to each other, too.

In Bizarro World, Cliff had had strong ties to the Cuban Mob. Presumed he did in this world as well. Meaning we had at least one Cuban hit squad here. Maybe three of them, considering the numbers. We were definitely in solid double digits.

The interior was exactly what I'd expected a scrap metal company's insides to look like. A big rectangle with absolutely no frills, filled with lots of big pots for melting metal, many iron catwalks and such, lots of machinery, ropes and pulleys, and things I couldn't easily identify. It was like being in the final fight scene of the first *Terminator* movie. Tried not to worry, but only Sarah Connor had made it out of that place alive.

On the plus side, it was night and the place wasn't well lit. Presumably so the bad guys could remain in shadow and see us coming and all that.

There were a couple of rooms that were closed and, as he'd said, White hadn't felt it wise to verify if the door was locked due to the number of dudes with guns around them. Meaning they were the likely place or places where our hostages were being held.

Who I didn't see, however, were the two Cuban assassins I'd expected, Sanchez and Lopez. Was sure they were here somewhere, or at least involved, but if they were, they were inside one of the two rooms or they were supervising from somewhere else.

We went into stealth mode once White got us behind a particularly large bin of scrap that was near a back wall where, amazingly enough, there was no catwalk overhead. Put the hood of my jacket on to hide my hair while ignoring the silent snickers I got from Reader and Tim.

Gave the guys hand signals to indicate that we should split up and see if we could each get into one of the well-guarded rooms. This only took about ten tries, but I was somewhat confident that, after a lot of exasperated expressions and hand motions, they knew what I wanted to do.

My hyperspeed might be running down, but I was confident that the regeneration wasn't, since I still only felt slightly feverish, so I took point with Tim behind me and Reader went after White. We edged out of either side of the bin.

Tim and I headed for the room that was on what would have been the second story if this building had bothered to put in a real floor between the ground and the roof. They hadn't—that was part of what the catwalks were there for.

I'd headed us here because it had the least amount of guards in the area. Even so, neither Tim nor I were gigantic people, and while not all of the Cubans were big, they all looked dangerous and we only needed one to sound an alarm.

We were under the room, and also under the catwalk and stairs that allowed someone to get to the room, when the door opened.

"We'll let you sit here a while longer," a woman said. "Eventually you'll get tired of trying to protect people who couldn't care less about you and would arrest you if they had half a chance."

Tim and I looked at each other. It was a familiar voice — Annette Dier was in the house.

Which, as I thought about it, made total sense. Raul had been out of Cuba, she'd been his woman, so that would mean she had Cuban ties, too, even if she wasn't Cuban originally. The Crazy Eights, like the rest of the Assassination Squads, had figured we'd end up here, in Orlando.

Meaning Adriana was somewhere around. Wished I'd figured that out before we'd gone in, but oh well. Our team was nothing if not resourceful, especially when we screwed up.

Resisted the urge to shoot Dier. Mostly because it would draw immediate attention and I couldn't be sure I'd hit her through the catwalk's grating. And a bullet ricocheting would naturally hit me or Tim or one of the others. Or all of us. Because we were just lucky that way.

Dier wasn't alone. As she walked away from us on the catwalk, seven pairs of feet followed her. So they weren't leaving anyone in there with our hostages. Or there were ten guys with guns in there. Gave it far better odds for the latter.

The other room, the one White and Reader were heading for, was on the ground. It looked like Dier and the rest of the Crazy Eights were heading there, too. Happily, it was far enough away—on the other side of the building—and we were in enough shadow that they were unlikely to spot us.

Was about to go when my music changed to "Shoot Speed/Kill Light" by Primal Scream. There were a lot of ways I could take this cue, but I figured that Algar was telling me to kill the lights and shoot adrenaline.

Opened my purse and pulled the adrenaline case out of my purse. Tim's eyes opened wide.

Took off my hoodie—no reason to stretch out the sleeves of a piece of Aerosmith clothing. On rare occasions I'd been able to give Jeff the adrenaline somewhere other than in his hearts. Upper arm was the best—least pain, less loss of mobility.

Took out a needle and handed it to Tim. He did the "me too?" sign. I felt his head. He felt a lot hotter than he had before, and he looked crappy. Nodded, but indicated I was first, just in case. He nodded, then gave me the shot.

Results were instantaneous. I felt as if something was flowing through my veins, something that made me feel faster, stronger, and infinitely better. Got the next needle out as Tim rolled up his sleeve. Had to give it to him in his forearm, just due to how he was dressed.

Could tell the adrenaline hit him the same way, because he stopped looking sick. Truly doubted this was the real cure, but as a standby, I'd take it. I had eight more hypodermics left, so if we needed to jump-start anyone, we were set. I sincerely hoped.

Put my hoodie back on and put the hood on again, too. Handed Tim one of the spent needles and kept the other one with me. We didn't have a lot of silent weapons with us, but these would work really well. Had a feeling Team Assassination would approve, too.

Looked around and realized that we were by the power box. So we wouldn't have to shoot out the lights, and instead could just turn them off, which was a lot stealthier. The win column was filling up.

Waited until Dier and the others were going down, then flipped the main switch. The lights all went out, right on cue, and Tim and I started up the stairs that led up to the room above us. We were both shaking but it didn't matter because we were going so fast. I still had to hold onto him for him to go at hyperspeed, but we were upstairs in a split second.

Couldn't tell if it was the adrenaline or not, but my eyes adjusted quickly to the darkness. We had that full moon out tonight and this place had windows up high, so while it was dark, it certainly wasn't pitch black.

As we reached the door, I let go of Tim and we each took two of the four guards there. Breaking their necks was easy, as was laying them down onto the ground so that their bodies didn't make noise when they dropped. Heard plenty of other voices—people were shouting to get the lights back on, among other things.

The door wasn't locked, which was nice, but right now I could have ripped it off its hinges if I'd had to. However, that would have let everyone outside know where we were, let alone those in the room.

Got to see that I'd been wrong—there weren't ten guys in here. There were a dozen, all armed to the teeth. Happily, twelve guys still unaware that we were here. Shut the door behind Tim—we were inside in less time than it took someone to blink.

There was only one person not armed in here—Siler. He was stripped to the waist, tied to a metal chair that sat next to a small table that had a candle burning on it. It also had wax and a few other nasty things, which lined up since Siler showed signs of torture. Which pissed me off, which was good, because I flipped from adrenaline-fueled to adrenaline-fueled and enraged, which was, all things considered, better. At least for what we needed to do.

My music changed, clearly in honor of this being me and Tim fighting together—The Beastie Boys came on, sharing that, once again, "(You Gotta) Fight For Your Right (To Party)." Message received.

Tim and I were a speedy wrecking machine. I knocked them down with an impressive arm bar to their throats, he knocked them out once they were on the ground. Then I knocked them out again, only a lot harder. A few of them might live, but I wasn't overly concerned.

We had everyone knocked out in about ten seconds and

all of them down and out for good or for a good long time in less than a minute. Hyperspeed, as always, rocked.

Got over to Siler. He didn't look great. Had to figure they'd infected him, and he also looked even more worked over close up than he had when we got into the room.

Didn't have a lot of time to think about it. Looked at Siler as if he was Jeff. And I knew what to do when Jeff was at death's door.

Dropped my Glock into my purse, pulled out another adrenaline harpoon and, as Tim held Siler's head and torso steady, slammed it into his hearts.

Unlike Jeff, he didn't bellow. Like Jeff, he thrashed. Enough to break his bonds, which were leather straps.

Watched his body repair itself in front of us. "Maybe I should have named you Wolverine, not Nightcrawler."

He gave me a weak grin. "Nah, I'm used to Nightcrawler. It's really good to see you."

"You, too. Are you aware of what's going on?"

"Did you figure out what I was trying to tell you?"

"That Lizzie's dead father's notes were hidden on my roof of all places? Yes."

"Then yeah, I'm aware of what's going on."

"Good fail-safe."

"Yeah. Hope she doesn't hate me for doing it." He looked worried.

"No, I think she understands. She's a smart little cookie. And she's safe in the Embassy, which is on lockdown and has no one infected that we know of."

"She is. And . . . thank you."

"You're welcome. How did they infect you, by touch?"

"No, they injected me with the disease."

Tim went and collected the weapons that were on the dead or unconscious guys in the room. "There's a lot more than we can carry. Even if Richard and James were up here with us."

"Adriana's here, by the way."

Tim nodded. "Yeah, I figured that out when I saw the Crazy Eights. No idea where she is, though."

"Haven't seen her," Siler said as he selected what he wanted, then took the rounds out of the guns at hyperspeed. The knives he held onto. All of the knives. "However, I don't think she's captured. I'm sure they'd have tried to use her to make us talk."

"What are they trying to find out?" Tim asked.

"How to get into your Embassy and the Dulce Science Center."

"And just when I thought my hatred of these people couldn't get any deeper. Are Luis Sanchez and Julio Lopez involved?"

"Yeah, but you won't find them here. They were sent off on another mission about an hour ago. No idea what the mission is, by the way. They didn't talk about it much in front of me, nor did they use a code name for the target or the operation."

"Figures. Where are the Dingo and Surly Vic?"

"I don't know. I also don't know if they're still alive." He cleared his throat. "They were given the disease, too—that happened the moment we were captured. Then we were separated. I wasn't sure that I'd survive another round of what they were doing to me. And they don't have my regeneration."

"Let's go find out. If they've killed my uncles or hurt a hair on James or Richard's heads, they're going to pay."

CHAPTER 81

WE LINKED UP, mostly to use Siler's blending when we might need to. Then we took off, with me providing the hyperspeed.

Raced us across the catwalk—knocking assassins off as we went by—and went down the same stairs that Dier and the others had.

Felt the tingling that meant we were blending as we slowed down. Had to slow down because there was a lot of ruckus going on down here and we didn't want to hit the wrong people.

White and Reader were back-to-back and surrounded. On the plus side, there were so many assassins here that no one was shooting. On the not plus side, there were a lot of assassins here, and they were all happy to fight as a group.

Looked up at the other catwalks. That no shooting rule wasn't going to last. These guys were hitmen and lots were up on good vantage points. By now, everyone's eyes would have adjusted to the dark. Meaning we had snipers.

"Taking care of the peanut gallery," I said to Tim and Siler. Let go of their hands and body-slammed through the nearest assassins, got to a ladder on the other side of the room and ran up.

My music changed to "Extraordinary" by Liz Phair, presumably because Algar was giving me an Atta Girl.

There were three main catwalks. One that ran along the long back wall—which was what Siler, Tim, and I had already been on—one that ran along the long front wall, which I was on now, and one that ran along the middle. There were shorter catwalks that connected these to each other, but they didn't go all the way across.

The shorter catwalks were to allow workers to get to big vats and bins or other things hanging from the ceiling. If you knew what you were doing, this setup probably made a lot of sense.

For me, it was like I'd been dropped into the new video-game, *Uncharted: Mastermind*, in the Orlando Factory Level, complete with enemy fire and a maze that looked simple but would turn out to be really complex to survive and which I had to work correctly in order to finish this part of the level. Only I sucked at mazes, in this game there were absolutely no do-overs, and my friends and I weren't going to heal up just by my waiting out a fictional clock.

Took off down the catwalk and knocked the guys on it over the side. So far, so very easy. Fully expected the difficulty level to increase exponentially.

Which was good, because it did. While I'd distracted the snipers from shooting at the people on the ground, they'd all seen their buddies fall off both catwalks, and the smarter among them had figured out that someone was probably on the side where the bodies were currently falling.

The smarter snipers started shooting at me, or at least where they thought I was. The dumber ones caught on and did the same. Technically I was at the speed where I should be able to dodge bullets. But it was dark, there were a hell of a lot of bullets, and I wasn't willing to bet that every bullet was going to miss me.

I was near one of the perpendicular catwalks, so I ran across it in a crouch, which was a first for me and hyperspeed. Clearly I was going to need to discuss Christopher's training oversight with him. Presuming I lived to do so.

There were two guys on this shorter catwalk and I was able to knock them down before they hit me. Of course, this alerted the rest to where I was, and also of course this catwalk dead-ended at a large metal tub. Decided not to find out what was in it—it was warm and I was willing to bet that whatever was inside wasn't going to be good for me to swim in.

As I spun around, still in a crouch, I slipped. Thankfully I didn't fall off, because as I went flat onto my face I got a good look at what was on the floor below. A big pot of molten metal was under me. Oh goody.

Naturally there were vats of molten metal and bins filled with sharp metal objects and all other manner of Deadly Things To Drop Into down below. And also naturally absolutely none of the Cuban snipers we'd knocked off the catwalks had landed in any of them. Some of them weren't moving, but far too many apparently had catlike reflexes, because there were more up and aiming for me than down and not moving. Always the way.

The issue with a body at rest is that hyperspeed is meaningless. I was in all black, but they were all looking where I was, and my face, which was on the latticed catwalk, wasn't covered.

Bullets started flying at me from the catwalks and the ground. Pulled up into the blocks position and took off.

Ran onto the front side catwalk and headed for where the others were. Only there were now more snipers up there. This really was a videogame level. Once again, time "wasted" in college was going to come through for me. Hurray.

Made a sharp left and was on a shorter section that connected me with the center long catwalk. There was one sniper on this section and he was standing next to a big vat that was hanging on my right. Ran up to the sniper.

The problem with adrenaline is that, after the first huge rush, it wears off. For me, the problem was that the adrenaline wore off now. Maybe it would have lasted longer if I

hadn't been doing everything at hyperspeed, but hindsight
was always crystal clear.

Just like that I was back to tired, feverish, and now kind
of feeling like I was a little stuffed up and going to sneeze.
Which I did. Right in the sniper's face.

The element of surprise is a wonderful thing. Surprise
combined with something that grossed most people out—
someone else's sneeze and snot—was an even better thing.
Chose to take advantage of my stunning the guy in front of
me by slamming him against the vat he was standing by.

The back of his head slammed into the vat, hard, and he
went down. One down. So very many to go. Time to use the
guns.

Pulled the rifle off of my back and took a look around.
My back was protected by the vat I was next to, meaning
that I couldn't see two-thirds of the room. I could see where
I'd been, both the first short catwalk, part of all three long
catwalks, and the room where Siler had been.

Spotted two guys on the front wall catwalk, one on the
middle, and two on the back wall catwalk. Didn't waste
time—I might have five targets, but they only had one.

The guy on the center catwalk was closest to me.
Dropped onto one knee to make myself a smaller target
and also to get some extra stability. Aimed, made sure he
wasn't someone I knew, and fired.

Winged him because I was still shaking from the adrenaline even though the main positive effects were gone.
Didn't let it throw me. Aimed and shot again, even as he
shot at me and missed, and winged him again. Got him on
my third try as bullets hit the vat behind me.

Reminded myself that I had a semiautomatic for a reason and decided to stop trying to be fancy and precise and
just channel *Scarface*. Even more fitting here than it had
been on Planet Colorful, because all these guys actually
were Cubans.

Stood back up, pointed the rifle in the general direction of the guys on my left, and let loose with a barrage of bullets in the sweeping pattern so beloved by gangsters and people on a rampage everywhere. Didn't scream out anything about my "little friend" because I wasn't feeling anywhere near confident enough to risk giving the cosmos a chance to really play a joke on me.

This was effective in that I hit both of them and they went down. It wasn't, perhaps, my best choice, because I ran out of ammo fast and it encouraged the rest of them to follow suit.

Hit the catwalk as a tonnage of bullets headed toward me. Then they stopped. Looked up and around. The two other guys were down. And certainly not from my gunfire.

Guns were still going off and it was clear that a gunfight was going on around where I'd left the others. But around here, I appeared to be alone. Looked about some more and stood up slowly. Nope, just me. Considered what I knew and looked way up. A hand waved from the crawlspace between the top of the room that Siler had been in and the roof.

Adriana was in a really good spot. She was hard to see and harder to hit. So one of us was smart.

Left my empty gun and took the one from the guy I'd knocked out. It was a gun I could shoot one-handed. Got my Glock into my other hand. Then looked back at Adriana.

She held up three fingers then pointed to my right, her left. Two fingers and pointed to my left, her right. Two fingers and pointed to the middle. Then two and one, and made a chopping motion. Then one and one and a chopping motion.

It was easy to understand her signals, at least for me. Had no idea if White, Reader, and Tim would have gotten them, based on my experience from a little earlier, but I was clear.

Pointed to my right and nodded as "Afraid to Shoot Strangers" by Iron Maiden came on. Hopefully my signal was clear—I was going to head down the middle catwalk.

Meaning I'd be a moving target for, if I'd counted Adriana's signals correctly, twelve snipers.

Or, as we called it, routine.

CHAPTER 82

NATURALLY, the vat I was next to was in the middle of the catwalk. Tried looking carefully around it—couldn't see any targets. Always the way.

Took a deep breath and ran to the middle catwalk and made a right. Saw two guys ahead of me, one closer, one farther. Assessed that they were not anyone I cared about, and started shooting.

They started shooting, too, of course. As did the two guys on the catwalk to my left, though those two had vats on either side of their catwalk they could use for protection.

The vat I'd just left provided a bit of protection from those on my right, aka the front wall catwalk, and the two vats on the left-hand short catwalk blocked me from those on the left long catwalk. But that still left five guys shooting at me, because there was also a catwalk on the right, a little farther away than the one on the left, and there was someone on that, too, and he had a clear shot at me.

The positive about being a moving target was that I was hard to hit, and I ensured that I was bobbing and weaving as much as I could.

The negative was that it was hard to shoot accurately while bobbing and weaving, let alone running, and they didn't have to move to shoot at me.

Which worked out as the two in front of me went down.

Then the one on the catwalk to my right. Adriana was a great shot, for which I thanked God and Olga.

Reached the left catwalk, ran onto it shooting like I was at the O.K. Corral. Meaning lots of bullets and not a lot of hitting anything. From the two guys there and me. So, at least we were all consistent.

Body-slammed the guy on my left and sent him against the side of that vat. Shot my Glock at the guy on my right. Winged him. Hit the guy on my left with an elbow to the face as he bounced off the vat. Shot him with the rifle as he went down.

As the guy I'd winged aimed for me, told myself I was my mother's daughter and if I could hit an A-C running— and I could—then I could damn well hit a Cuban assassin basically just standing there.

Aimed and fired, using the rapid-fire technique I'd learned. Fortunately for me I shot him in the head with the first bullet, because that was actually my last bullet in the clip.

Had a moment without someone shooting at me, so dropped the rifle and reloaded my Glock. Shoved extra clips into my front jeans pockets.

Considered grabbing another rifle from the guys I'd just taken out and decided I was probably better off with my Glock. I was more used to it and I wasn't really hitting brilliantly with the rifles.

I was still between the vats so I couldn't see Adriana from here. Based on what I could remember, the next short catwalk was only accessible from the left-hand long catwalk. So, after taking a look and, as per usual, not being able to see any targets, ducked low and headed for the next part of this gauntlet.

There were three guys in front of me, but they were close together—they'd had time to get closer to the action. For whatever reason, me bounding in front of them seemed to shock them. Guessed they weren't used to suicide missions.

Which gave me time to unload my entire clip into the three of them. The one in front was down fast, the one behind him dodged, and the guy in the rear took the rest of the bullets. While I ducked to avoid the last guy's shots, I dropped the used clip, reloaded, and, still crouched down, put that clip into him.

Reloaded on the run. Still heard gunfire and the sounds of fighting elsewhere. Could see the guy on the last catwalk on the side. He could see me, too. Ducked low so that he had a harder shot.

Which was wise. He was sending a steady stream of bullets at chest height for me. Rounded the corner onto the catwalk and flipped into a somersault. Had learned this years ago in kung fu and still had what it took. Rolled three times, and came up shooting. Was rewarded to see the guy look really surprised as he died.

There were suddenly a lot of bullets coming toward me again, even though I was blocked by the vat that was this catwalk's dead end. Looked to my left to see Adriana do a spinning leap off of her perch and land perfectly on the catwalk. Couldn't see her for a bit, then she came running down the catwalk bent low.

Grabbed the dead guy's rifle and shot wildly around the vat. Wasn't sure if I was hitting anyone or helping, but gave it the old college try. Adriana made it to me and I pulled back.

"Are you hit?"

She shook her head. "The Crazy Eights are on the catwalk that lines the opposite wall. Lowe sent gusts of air at me, so I figured I'd better get down and get to you."

"You were amazing as always. Did you see the others?"

"Thank you, and I believe they're still on the lower level. Wruck is here."

"Let's try really hard not to kill him."

Adriana reloaded her rifle. I had no idea where it had come from and chose not to ask. She also took the dead guy's gun from me. "I think I'm better with these than you are."

"No argument at all."

"Can you shoot a pistol with both hands?"

"Yes." Well, I'd managed with a rifle and a Glock, so my answer was yes.

She pulled another Glock from her back and handed to me. "The clip is full and the safety is now off. You ready?"

"Fight Till Death" from Slayer came on my airwaves. "I'm ready, Sundance."

She grinned. "Grandmother loves that movie. Let's do it, Butch."

"Out and then where?"

"To the left. We need to cross over to the middle in order to get the others."

"So, we're running right at the Crazy Eights?"

"Yes."

"Wow. We really are Butch Cassidy and the Sundance Kid, aren't we? Let's hope we get a better ending."

CHAPTER 83

WE RAN OUT hunched over again, which was a move I was getting used to in the same way that you get used to braces—something really uncomfortable you're dealing with in order to get a hoped for better result.

It was a little harder to be less easy to hit, since we were next to each other. And we had to run and shoot, so we were sort of bobbing up to shoot then ducking down again to keep on shooting. However two of us spraying bullets at the bad guys was definitely a plus. Most of them ran for cover, meaning they headed for the other catwalks that had vats by them.

We made it to the catwalk with the two vats on both sides of it and the two dead guys in the middle. We were able to pause while Adriana took the clips out of their guns.

"Over to the left. Don't go right at the first bridge we come to," she said as she reloaded. "Head for the last bridge on the right. There are two vats there that will provide cover."

"I suck at mazes and while this isn't all that hard of one, I'd swear that catwalk bridge dead-ends into a vat."

"It does. That means they can only come at us one way."

"That also means we can only get away one way."

"There was at least one sniper there, and if he remains, we can clear everyone else out and he can still kill us."

"I hate it when you're logical."

"We could split up again."

"Just when I was enjoying the company. But yeah, that makes the most sense. I have no hyperspeed right now." Considered shooting up, but figured we were going to need it for the others.

"I can tell. I'll take the far bridge, the dead end. You take the first one and see what you can do. But keep in mind that you're going to be heading right for them."

"Yeah, I guess I'm prone to the extreme displays of stupidity."

"See you on the other side."

"Let's hope."

We took off again similarly to how we had before. Fewer bullets were coming at us, though, so we were able to turn left on the middle catwalk and run for the cross-sections we'd assigned ourselves.

I turned right first. This section had a vat on my left, centered between the middle and front wall catwalks. Meaning it was useless to me as protection from half of this room, and the Crazy Eights were, naturally, on the far side now, massing to shoot the hell out of me.

Hurdled over the dead body that had one bullet hole in the head. Clearly this was one of Adriana's hits. Mine rarely looked that professional.

Reached the front wall catwalk in record time and decided getting to the others might be the better part of valor. As I turned left, realized I was heading straight for Wruck.

This wasn't good, because I couldn't shoot him now. On the other hand, I could be shot in the back at any moment. In fact, I was sure of it, as Motörhead's "Shoot You in the Back" came on. Algar was nothing if not literal at times.

Flipped into another somersault as bullets whizzed by. Wruck was shooting, too, but not at me.

Well, technically, I was sure he was going to say that he'd

been shooting at me and I'd just fooled him with my clever rolling move. But he was spraying bullets well over where I was.

Rolled three times and was next to him. Jumped up and leaped behind him. "Do I take you hostage now?"

"Please."

Grabbed him with a modified choke and put a gun to his head. "Stop shooting or I'll kill him!" I bellowed as loudly as I could. I wasn't up to Jeff's standards—no one was, really—but I was pretty good. The sounds of gunfire slowed down. "I mean it! Stop shooting or I kill him!" Moved us so that my back was to the wall, so that, hopefully, Wruck was working as a shield for me from the front and sides, at least as much as possible.

"Kitty," Reader called. "We have the lower level cleared. It's only whoever's up there with you."

"So much for the Cuban hit squads," I said quietly as my music changed to "Last Chance on the Stairway" by Duran Duran.

"They have done their damage already," Wruck said just as quietly. Was pretty sure he was doing his best not to move his mouth.

"Kitty!" This was Adriana. "They're escaping!"

Looked down my catwalk. Sure enough, the rest of the Crazy Eights were climbing out a window. It was high, but Lowe was using his air bending to lift them and himself up high enough to grab the bottom of the window and flip themselves over.

"He's gotten really good," I mentioned, while I shot at them and missed every single one. It was harder to shoot around my "hostage" than I'd have thought. Adriana was shooting and missing, too. Maybe Lowe was using his bending to keep the bullets away. That was going to be my story and I was going to stick with it.

"He has. Prison is an excellent place to practice."

"Duly noted. I'm going to keep this fiction up, just in case. Adriana," I called in a louder voice, "do we have any more unfriendlies upstairs?"

She ran over to us. "No. I just checked all the areas. No one is still breathing."

"I don't think everyone Tim and I took out in the upstairs room is dead. Ditto the first guy on the catwalk I dealt with but didn't knock over the railing."

As I said this, Wruck wrenched the gun out of my left hand, aimed it at Adriana, and fired several times.

Only he wasn't actually aiming at her, but at the guy I'd just mentioned—the one I'd knocked out but not killed. Said guy was dead now, though.

"Thank you," Adriana said, voice shaking just a little.

"You're welcome. Someone needs to check on those you think might still be alive. And kill them."

Adriana nodded and took off, back through the catwalks while I let go of Wruck. "Thanks, John."

He turned to me and smiled. "You're welcome, Kitty." His smile faded. "Though you may not feel pleased shortly." He nodded toward the stairs. "You will want to get into that room as soon as possible. There's a reason it was heavily guarded."

Headed down, Wruck behind me. White and Siler were pulling the door open, but I could tell that the adrenaline had worn off for Siler and that White was starting to feel the effects of infection, because they were having trouble.

Wruck waded in. "Allow me." He shifted into a much bigger creature, one I'd never seen. At best, it looked like a Bigfoot, but without hair. He wrenched the door open easily, then went back to what I'd become used to.

"Meet the Martian Manhunter, everyone. He's on our side despite how things may have looked for, oh, the last several years." With that I went into the room, "Flesh and Bone" by the Killers now on my soundsystem.

That the Dingo and Surly Vic were in here wasn't the

surprise. How crappy they looked wasn't a surprise, either. Siler hadn't been kidding—they'd been worked over badly. As with Siler, their upper bodies were naked and the signs of torture were clear and rather horrific.

That they were both somehow still alive was the surprise.

But alive they were. "My Miss Katt," the Dingo said, voice basically a croak. "I apologize for our failure."

Hurried over to him and kissed his forehead. "It's okay, Uncle Peter. Sometimes I get to save you, remember?" Dropped my Glock back in my purse and pulled out the adrenaline. "Not sure if this will help much, but it's all we've got with us. Going straight into your heart. On the plus side, I'm really freaking good at this by now."

Tim held the Dingo's head and chest as he had with Siler, and I slammed the needle in. As with Siler, he didn't make noise but he did thrash. Because he was human, he didn't break his bonds, which was okay, because White and Reader were getting them off for him.

Siler supported the Dingo while I moved to Surly Vic. "Don't let the Sith win," he said to me. He sounded worse than the Dingo had.

"We won't." Kissed his forehead, too. "It's okay, Uncle Victor. We'll get it all taken care of. This sucks, but it helps."

Tim and I did the drill all over again. Surly Vic shouted in pain, but didn't thrash. Interesting differences that Tito probably would have been interested in. For me, it just meant I was hurting people who, frankly, I loved by now. But, Surly Vic seemed a little better, and that was what mattered.

Adriana rejoined us while Tim put all the used needles into my purse. "Upstairs is all clear, and I rechecked down here, too. All the Cubans are dead. While we may have hit the other Crazy Eights, none of them were here."

"All seven made it out," Wruck said. "I should go after them."

"No, you're our 'prisoner' now. Get used to hanging with the good guys, John."

White and Reader got Surly Vic untied, then they helped him up, putting his arms around their shoulders. Siler and I did the same for the Dingo.

"We're going to get you both to NASA Base. Tito's there and he'll get you fixed up. Since they infected all of you with the disease we need to get you to medical and that's a quarantine area already."

"Whatever you say, Miss Katt," the Dingo said.

"Caroline's there, too. I know she'll be glad to see you." It was potentially a lie, but I knew he still liked her and, after losing Michael, she might want to see him and, if not rekindle the flame, at least say hello.

"I will appreciate seeing her again." He chuckled weakly. "Raul's woman said you would never come for us. But we knew she was wrong."

"Annette Dier?"

"Yes. She was our torturer."

"Only her?"

"The Cubans worked us over," Siler said. "But the torture? Yeah, that was all her. To his credit," he nodded his head at Wruck, who was with Adriana and Tim, pretending to be their prisoner, just in case, "he kept on telling her that torture wasn't the answer. But she didn't care. She likes it."

"Yeah, she's an evil bitch." Saliva's "The Enemy" came on. Fitting. Dier was definitely an enemy I wanted to get rid of.

"And the only real link to your Mastermind," Wruck said. "Which is why she's still alive."

"I don't have a phone signal in here," Tim said. "So we can't call for a gate. We're going to have to get outside to do that."

"Then let's get outside and out of here fast."

Siler and I took the lead with the Dingo, and Tim, Adriana, and Wruck were in the rear. We couldn't move as fast as any of us wanted to—Team Assassination was far too injured.

"We did gather information," the Dingo told me as we

walked slowly around dead bodies. "The disease is alien in nature. Its core is from another planet, and not one in this or the Alpha Centauri system."

"You're sure?"

"Yes. Raul's woman was gloating, explaining that even if we could be saved by someone, we would all die, since there was no cure."

"There's always a cure."

"Yes, but most cures take time to discover. And the world does not have the time."

"Why did they escalate now, did they tell you?"

"They told me," Siler said. "The Mastermind knows that he's discovered, and he's angry that your side has been playing him like he's played you all this time."

"Our side."

Both men chuckled as we stepped outside. "Yes, but grant us the fiction that we are lone wolves, my Miss Katt."

"You're my wolves, so not lone."

"Not for long." Dier stepped out from behind a pile of scrap, gun pointed straight at me. "Say goodbye for good, bitch."

Then she pulled the trigger.

CHAPTER 84

WHAT HAPPENED NEXT was one of those slow-motion experiences I knew I'd end up reliving over and over again, usually in the middle of a deep sleep.

As Dier pulled the trigger it dawned on me that Algar had been giving me a warning with the Saliva song.

At the same time, the Dingo shouted, "No!" Then wrenched out of my and Siler's hold and flung himself in front of me. Siler grabbed me and pulled me down.

The bullet's impact meant the Dingo fell back and down into my arms.

Dier aimed again, but Surly Vic had already gotten free from White and Reader. He leaped over us, making me wonder if he'd been a hurdler way back when, and slammed into Dier. Which meant he took the next bullet in the gut but landed both of them against the scrap metal.

I'd been angry before, many times, really. But there were only a few times when the rage was so overwhelming that I was seeing red. This was one of those times. I put the Dingo gently on the ground. His eyes fluttered. "Never . . . let them . . . change you," he gasped out. The shot was to his heart.

"I won't, Uncle Peter. I promise."

He smiled. "Always be My Miss Katt . . . with her nine

lives." He was still smiling, but I saw the light go out of his eyes.

Stood up and turned around. Dier had gotten out from under Surly Vic's body. Whether he was alive or not I couldn't tell. But she was still alive. Scratched up from the scrap metal, but alive. And everything I was seeing was still red.

My music changed to The Cure's "Fight." Okey dokey.

"You killed Fuzzball," I said as I walked toward her.

She fired, but the gun just clicked. Surly Vic rolled over— he had the clip in his hand. He raised it up in his fist. "Jedi forever."

"I promise to keep the faith and use the Force, Uncle Victor."

His arm dropped, though the clip was still tight in his fist. His eyes were open and glassy, though I wasn't close enough to see their light go out.

Looked back at Dier. "You killed Michael." Walked closer. "You're part of the reason Gladys and Naomi are dead."

"You killed Raul."

"And now you've killed my uncles."

She smirked. "Just like I'm going to kill all of your family, starting with your mother and ending with your brats."

"No," I said calmly. "You're not." I was close to her, just out of arm's reach. "Because you end now."

Her eyes narrowed and she smiled a particularly evil smile. "I'll end you in five seconds."

"Yeah? You know what we say in Pueblo Caliente when someone says that? We say, bring it, bitch."

She lunged for me, but I was ready and so was my music. "Prize Fighter" by the Killers was back, and I agreed that this was a title bout and I was ready for it. The rage was flowing and so were the moves. I wasn't at hyperspeed, but I was definitely going for double black belt right now.

We traded hits for a while, sweeps the other jumped over, impressive kicks the other dodged or blocked, and so on. We weren't talking, we were just trying to kill each other. And I was now listening to "Killer Queen" by Queen.

I'd moved her away from the others. Wasn't really paying attention to where the other Crazy Eights might or might not be. That was what the rest of my team was for. I was only interested in getting Dier into just the right place.

Well, I was interested in one other thing. "So, you seem all confident that you're going to outlive everyone."

Dier smirked again. Definitely one of her fave expressions. "Some of us have been given the actual vaccine."

"Good to know."

We were now near a scrap pile with a particularly sharp and nasty-looking piece of rusty metal sticking quite far out. My music changed to Panic! At the Disco's "Let's Kill Tonight." Totally agreed with the sentiment.

Dier punched with her right, I blocked with my left and slammed a palm heel strike into her face. Followed this with a knee to her sternum that knocked her back. She was winded and I didn't hesitate. Kicked her knee out, hard, and sent my other knee into her chin.

Grabbed Dier as she went down and threw her toward the extended metal, and, as she was going back, I did a double kick that sent her back even harder.

The metal went through her chest. She stared at me, mouth open. But she was still alive. Barely, but more than the Dingo and Surly Vic were.

Pulled out my Glock and walked up to her. "Did you know that a person doesn't have to be alive for someone to get a sample of their blood?" Put the gun between her eyes. "Which is good for me. Because this is the part where you die and go to hell, you murderous cunt." Then I pulled the trigger.

My clip wasn't empty.

CHAPTER 85

"KITTY?" Reader asked quietly from behind me. "Are you hurt?"

"Not really."

He put his arm around my shoulders and gently backed me up and away from Dier's dead body. "Okay. Emptying your clip into her face was an, uh, interesting touch."

"I wish I could do it again. At least five more times."

"But dead is dead, girlfriend. And before others we care about die, we need to do something with your uncles' bodies."

That snapped me out of it. "What do you mean?" Realized my music had stopped. Left my earbuds in, just in case.

"Siler says that you're going to be a lot safer if no one can prove that they're dead. I think he's right."

"Um, okay. What do you suggest?"

He grimaced. "Well, we're at a place where they melt metal."

"Oh, so the Darth Vader funeral pyre? Surly Vic would appreciate that, I'm sure."

"You need to cry?"

"No. Not right now. I'll cry later. Possibly for a really long time. But not right now. Right now we need to dispose of my uncles' bodies and then go try to save the rest of our friends and families and the world."

"So," he said, as he kissed my forehead, "routine."

Leaned against his shoulder. As always, a nice place to be. Reader took the hood off my head and stroked my hair. "Is it wrong that I'm as upset and angry about her killing the Dingo and Surly Vic as I was when she killed Michael?"

"No, it's not wrong. They may have been top assassins, but they respected and then ultimately loved you. That you loved them back isn't wrong, Kitty. It's part of what makes you the person who can flip a bad guy to our side. Like Jeff says, you see the best in people."

"There was no best in Dier."

"No, there really wasn't."

"But now we've lost the link to the Mastermind."

"Oh well."

Looked up at him. "You're not upset with me for that?"

"Babe, I'm glad she's dead. Dead she can't hurt anyone anymore. I also want to burn her body. Not to hide that she'd dead but so that there's no DNA around to make a clone of her."

"Presuming they haven't already."

He shook his head. "From what I've gotten, they're kind of selfish with the cloning. Cliff, Reid, and LaRue, and that seems to be it. Other than the two clones we found on Beta Eight, that is. And they were cloned for usefulness, which is what I think they'd clone Dier for. Hence why I want her gone."

"Yeah. Do we have to touch Dier's body? I ask because I don't think I can without rending her limb from limb."

"No. I called in Field teams. They'll do the cleanup. The other Crazy Eights were here, by the way. Lowe, Nerida, Casey, Kellogg, and Kozlow escaped—they ran the moment it was clear you were going to take Dier and only got away because Lowe held us off with his talent. Wruck is with us. Sam's dead. Adriana shot him."

"That's my girl. We burning Dear Sam's body, too?"

"Sure. Funeral pyres for all."

"Oh, speaking of Dier DNA, though, we need to get some of her blood to Tito ASAP. She felt that she'd been given the vaccine."

"On it."

Reader had a Dazzler team come and take several samples of Dier's blood, then head off to Tito. While Field teams came and helped moved the bodies, I put a new clip into my Glock and we discussed the little intel we'd gotten.

"What Dier said about the disease is worrying," White said. "If it's alien in nature, and not from our two solar systems, we may have no way of finding a cure."

"Let's see what Tito and Rohini have found. After all, Dier's blood could be the cure." Called Caroline. She answered right away and got Tito. "You're on speaker. How are things?"

"Okay, speaker here, too, we're alone. Your adrenaline idea was a good one. The problem is, it doesn't last, but it's definitely keeping the most sick alive."

"Yeah, we learned that firsthand."

"Lorraine's checked in," Caroline said. "They have Whitmore and the adrenaline's working on him. So are she and Claudia. They have him ready and willing to make a public confession, because he's clear that Cliff's set him up to die, too."

"He feels that there is a vaccine," Tito added. "But he doesn't have it. He expected to be given the vaccine before Cliff launched this offensive, and has been waiting for said vaccine every day. Cliff isn't returning his calls. Ergo . . ."

"He's finally flipped allegiance. At least somewhat. Not sure if what he has is enough, but it'll be better than nothing. How are people at the White House?"

Tito heaved a sigh. "Adrenaline helped Gabe, but only for a little while. As soon as it wore off, he expired. He had an existing health condition, by the way, so that probably contributed."

"Fabulous. Everyone else?"

"Still alive and still dealing with Cliff from what we can gather," Caroline said. "Do you want me to go to the White House and run interference?"

"No, Caro. Running interference for Tito and the Shantanu is far more important."

"We need to get back there, though," Tim said. "I have a really bad feeling about our leaving the Mastermind in the White House."

"Oh, he's not in the White House anymore," Reader said, looking at his phone. "He's left to, and I quote, 'calm the populace since the new President is infected and can't leave the White House complex.' Meaning Tim's right—we need to get back."

"Interesting," Tito said. "He was supposed to be coming here to give me a blood sample. Jeff has had everyone in the White House gate back and forth to do that, by the way, starting the moment Gabe died. They've come over one at a time. Cliff insisted on going last, but supposedly he was coming to us. We paused this process to take your call, but last I heard Cliff was waiting to come here."

"What about Annette Dier's blood that we sent to you? What have you found?"

Tito sighed. "Nothing, Kitty, I'm sorry. She may have thought she'd been given a vaccine but there was nothing in her blood to indicate it. Her blood is healthy, but it also doesn't contain anything that would indicate that she'd had a vaccine for this illness. And before you ask, the Shantanu have verified this in ways we aren't able to. Dier's blood is a dead end."

Heard some noises. "Listen, do you guys hear something? Tito, is that by you?"

"I don't think so, Kitty."

"No," White said slowly. "I believe it's coming from that way." He pointed toward the Amtrak station and the hospital complex. "And it sounds like rioting."

"Ah, are you guys near a hospital?" Tito asked.

"We are."

"Don't go any nearer to it," Caroline said quickly.

"Um, why not?"

"Apparently FEMA sent vaccines—which I already know we assume are actually the infection—to a lot of major hospitals," Tito replied. "If you're in Orlando, they sent a big shipment to the Arnold Palmer Hospital for Children. However, it's being attacked by Club Fifty-One people, claiming that the vaccine is, in fact, an alien flu."

"Serene really has what it takes, doesn't she? Good to know."

"This is happening all over, though, Kitty," Tito said. "Club Fifty-One, and of course our favorite religious sect, are causing havoc. Though that started before the time I think we can say Cliff left the White House, since he was confirmed as in line to come over about fifteen minutes ago."

"How the hell did he get out?" Tim asked. "He was in a quarantine he approved himself. And if he was using a gate to get to NASA Base he should have exited exactly where everyone else did."

"No idea," Tito said. "Walked out the front door? Took a gate calibrated to somewhere else? Him not being there or on his way here is news to me just like it is to you."

Pondered for a moment, then remembered the other reason why we'd called. "Tito, we were told that the virus has an alien component, and that it's not from either our or the A-C system."

"That aligns with what your father told me."

"Dad's checked in?"

"Yeah, sorry, he has, but I didn't lead with that because while what he gave us was helpful, we're still stuck."

"How so?"

"He and Lizzie feel confident they've deciphered her father's notes—she'd been taught the code, so it wasn't as hard as it could have been. They gave us the formula, and

what you just said—that there's an alien component—
seems clear from that formula. But we can't figure out what
his symbol for that component is, other than that he used L
as its designation."

"Cliff's calling it an alien flu. So that's accurate?"

"Sadly, yeah. This is definitely a form of influenza, but it's
more than that. It's a super virus mixing in malaria, measles,
and tuberculosis as well. But there's something extra in it,
that L-factor, and that's what's causing the real problems. We
could combat this by creating a super vaccine that fought all
four diseases, but without that one component, it's unlikely
to work."

"Wow, they left out hepatitis and all the poxes? Slack-
ers."

"Yeah. There's something odd about one of the cells
we've isolated. It keeps on shifting without actually altering
or splitting. Bettini says it's similar to blood samples we took
from Queen Renata, but not a close match. Rohini feels that
it's our L-factor, and what's making this disease kill so
quickly, but without knowing what it is, we can't determine
what will combat it. Adrenaline makes that cell normalize
and stop shifting, by the way, but it doesn't last too long."

"When did you take Renata's blood?" Reader asked.

"We had the Planetary Council come back here to give
us blood samples just like everyone else at the White House.
We've taken samples from those at NASA Base, too, including Rohini and Bettini. We have human, A-C, and A-C hybrid blood samples already."

"I donated to the cause," Caroline said.

"That's my girl." Considered telling her about the Dingo,
but decided that would be better done in person. Also felt
like I should make a connection here, but my brain didn't
want to cooperate. My phone showed a text alert—Brian
asking what our status was. "Tito, Caro, let me call you back."

"Okay, only call if you have something new for us," Tito
said. "Otherwise, don't worry about it."

"Check." Hung up. "James, I think we want to bring Brian and TCC here."

"I'll set it up." He sent some texts while I did the same, telling Brian to get ready for them to travel. Less than a minute later there was a shimmering by us, then Brian and TCC stepped through.

"Are you guys okay?" Brian asked, sounding worried. "I haven't heard word one from Abigail or Mahin and there's rioting everywhere it seems like. And you kind of look like you've been in one."

"We were in a fight but we're okay. Clarence, it's good to see you. I'd hug you, but we're all infected."

TCC looked disappointed, but he nodded. "I understand. Are you feeling sick, Kitty?"

"Kind of." I was. My internal adrenaline had worn off and I felt limp. Saw TCC looking at Wruck and Siler. "Oh, sorry. Clarence, this is Benjamin Siler, he's a friend of ours. And this is Rudolph Wruck, whose close friends get to call him John, but only in private like we are now."

"Nice to meet you both. Where are you from?"

Siler blinked. "Ah, Earth."

TCC looked expectantly at Wruck. Who shifted uncomfortably but didn't offer the lie of being from Germany.

"John's from far, far away, Clarence."

"Oh! Do you know LaRue?" he asked Wruck happily.

"Excuse me?" Wruck sounded freaked out.

"Sorry," TCC said apologetically. "She always said she was from far, far away. No offense meant."

"None taken," Wruck lied, while I congratulated myself on bringing TCC here and finally figuring out the connection.

"I didn't mean to scare you," TCC said, sounding very sorry and worried.

"Don't be upset, Clarence. John is frightened because he's an Ancient."

Wruck drew his breath in. Brian looked shocked, Siler

looked like he'd figured this out when Wruck had shifted to open the locked door.

"Oh, sorry, John. My husband was reading me the entire time we were talking in the Helicopter of Silence. Most everyone here knew before this conversation. And none of us will tell people we can't trust about you, even those who just found out. However, I think you're going to be telling a few more people about yourself shortly."

"What do you mean?" Wruck asked suspiciously.

"I know what the L-factor is. LaRue's blood is in the alien flu. Meaning your blood might be the cure."

CHAPTER 86

EVERYONE STARED AT ME, but Reader nodded. "It makes sense."

"Especially because LaRue's been the brains behind every Mastermind, and has affected the other Brains Behind people since she landed here."

"So, we're all going to NASA Base then?" Tim asked, as the Field agents came to tell Reader the bodies were ready to be dumped into a vat.

"No. First we're attending a funeral."

We all went back inside. All the Cubans and their weapons had been dumped into one of the big vats on the lower level. Reader nodded and they dumped Dear Sam and Dier into the same vat. Watched them be engulfed and burn up. It happened pretty quickly. Wished Gower and Abigail and their parents could have watched with us or at least see it somehow, but videotaping this event wasn't a wise move.

I insisted that the Dingo and Surly Vic be interred in a different vat and no one argued with me. Played Elton John's "Funeral for a Friend" as their bodies were lowered together into their Final Resting Place.

"Ashes to ashes," White said. He held one of my hands and Reader held the other. "Dust to dust. Go with our love. We consign you to your god."

"Nice sermon, Mister White."

"It's what we do under standard circumstances, Missus Martini."

The bodies were fully consumed by the time "Love Lies Bleeding" came on. Let Sir Elton's voice soothe me as much as it could. Didn't cry. Didn't think the Dingo and Surly Vic would want me to cry in public. I'd cry in private, hopefully sooner as opposed to later.

But as soon as that song ended, "Freedom Fighter" by Aerosmith came on and I knew that Algar was telling me that it was time to go.

We left the building and I sent a text to Abigail. She replied back quickly. "Stephanie's gone to ground. The girls have had no luck finding her. As far as Abby knows, the other team is on Drax's trail, but Huntress isn't with him as far as they can tell, which is why they split up."

"I'd offer to try to flush her out," Siler said, "but I honestly don't think I'm in any condition to do so." As he said this, "Fight the Frequency" by American Hi-Fi came on. Nice to know that Algar and I were in sync.

"Yeah. But that gives me an idea. But first, let's get you and John to NASA Base."

"Are you sure?" Wruck sounded very much less than sure.

"John, you helped us, and I know you researched us. What do you think we're going to do to you?"

"Take all my blood?"

I laughed. "I'm sure that Tito's going to take some. But we have really good medical and science facilities, right there, as a matter of fact. They'll replicate your blood for the cure, if your blood even *is* the cure. The idea is just me spitballing, but it would be great if we can smoke it over the plate at a hundred."

"I don't understand you," Wruck said.

Heaved a sigh. "So few ever do. We don't want you dead,

or locked up for medical experiments. We want you alive
and working alongside us. You know, just like the Martian
Manhunter is part of the Justice League."

"You're Wonder Woman?" he asked. Nice to know he
knew his comics.

"Not in this universe. In this universe I'm Wolverine
With Boobs."

Wruck stared at me for a moment, then he started to
laugh. "Okay. Count me in. I'm blown with those I know on
the Mastermind's side anyway, at least as myself. But, I can
always infiltrate in another form."

"If we need you to. Right now, let's just save as much of
the world as we can."

"Who's taking them in?" Reader asked.

"You and Tim. And take some of the Field teams for
backup." Just in case. "Richard, Adriana, and I will meet the
others at the rendezvous point. You guys can join us there or
meet up with us wherever we happen to be when you're
ready. But get going." Hugged all of them, including Wruck.
"I'm getting grief for telling people I love them, but I do love
all of you, so get Nightcrawler to our doctor and John to our
Shantanu Medicine Men."

Wruck brightened up. "Oh, the Shantanu are here?
That's good, and a relief. Their medicine is far more advanced than yours."

"We feel the love, John."

He smiled. "Let's hope, Kitty."

"What are we going to be doing, Missus Martini?" White
asked, as the team going to NASA Base stepped through
their floater gate and "The Masterplan" by Oasis came on.
Algar wanted me to focus and I planned to. Sent Abigail,
Mahin, Serene, and William a group text.

"We're going to be escorting Brian and Clarence around
to every riot location that has television camera crews and
ensuring we get on camera."

"We are?" Adriana asked, sounding less than thrilled with this plan.

"I echo Miss Dalca's unspoken concerns."

"Everyone's a critic. And, well, when I say 'we,' I mean Clarence. We're going to make sure that Clarence absolutely gets his fifteen minutes of fame."

CHAPTER 87

"ARE YOU SURE this is a good idea?" Brian shouted to me. He had to shout. We were in the middle of a riot and that made it hard to hear.

"Yes! Just do what I told you to!"

My plan was to flush Stephanie out. Going to ground was one thing, but there was no way she was without access to a television. There was too much going on, much of which she'd been intimately involved with, for me to believe that she wasn't somewhere watching the world burn. Whether she wanted it to burn or not might be the question, but until we could find her, we wouldn't know the answer.

What channel she was watching, however, and when, were the things I had no guess for. So, in order to cover all the bases, we were covering all the bases.

Media, social and otherwise, were advising the population of what riots were going on where. Serene picked our location, William sent a floater gate, we stepped through, and the team got TCC up in front of as many cameras as we could. Then it was just lather, rinse, repeat.

Mahin and Abigail had joined us in Orlando at the children's hospital, so we had plenty of muscle, in that sense. The goal wasn't to get TCC a speaking part—just to have him seen, in the background.

Once we felt he was seen, or it was too dangerous to stay,

we used hyperspeed—which Abigail, Mahin, and White still
had going—to get out of the crowd and through a floater
gate that would take us to our next location.

I didn't have music on—I was on the phone with William, so that he could tell me where we were going and
where our floater gate was located.

We were on our eleventh stop and, other than getting
banged up a lot, the plan was working smoothly, despite all
of us wanting to call in Field agents from around the world
to stop the riots.

But we didn't. In part because we didn't want them to get
infected. And in other part because that very possibly was
what Cliff wanted.

I'd asked Serene for one thing when she was choosing—
to ensure, after Orlando's hospital, that we hit towns that
spelled Stephanie's name in order. Just in case.

So, we'd hit Savannah, Tacoma, East Pittsburgh, which
was a double, Houston, Anaheim, Nashville, Indianapolis,
and Escondido. Now we were in Stephenville, Texas, because there were no towns named Stephanie that Serene
could find. It wasn't a gigantic crowd, but it was representing in terms of panic and riots.

We were about to go when a reporter focused on TCC.
"Sir," she said in a Texas drawl, "can you tell us what you're
hoping to do here?"

"I'm just trying to find my eldest daughter," TCC said.
"She's lost and we're worried about her."

The reporter was jostled and lost interest in TCC. Mahin
grabbed him and the rest of us linked up and we zipped off
out of the area.

"That was picked up," William said. "And Imageering
Main is ensuring that it's sent out as fast as possible to all
news outlets."

"Awesome, then send us back to D.C. Walter Reed, if it's
got riots."

"It does," Serene said. "Everywhere does. Where you

just were doesn't even have vaccines yet, but they have frightened people and Club Fifty-One members and that seems to be enough."

"It's probably why Clarence got his interview, so I'm not going to complain." A floater gate shimmered into view. I could tell I was losing my A-C Extras—I could barely see the shimmering.

"Step through now," William said.

We linked up and stepped out near Walter Reed. Did our usual hyperspeed push and shove to get near reporters. Only this time, the person who was spotted wasn't TCC, but was me.

"It's the First Lady!" someone with a microphone and camera crew shouted, and we were surrounded fast. The questions started coming even faster.

"What are you doing here?" "We heard the White House was under quarantine." "Is the new President dead already?" "Is this your new boyfriend?" "Did your people cause this epidemic?" "Why aren't you saving everyone?" "Why aren't you doing something?" "Why aren't you saving us?"

TCC was right next to me, so presumably he was the new boyfriend that had been referred to. The rest of our group was bunched up behind us. A quick look over my shoulder shared that we were cut off and essentially trapped. No way to use hyperspeed right now, not after I'd been recognized.

Reporters were still shouting questions and crowding us.

"Kitty, you're on every news station," William said.

"And I'm not stopping it," Serene added. "I don't know if you prepared a speech, but now's the best hope you have for getting the nation's attention."

So, basically, I wasn't all dressed up or ready, and God alone knew what my hair looked like, but I was on the national news and whatever I said was going to be used for or against us for the rest of our lives. Always the way. And also routine. And also sucky.

The phone clicked off, which was sort of panic inducing,

since now I had no link to Serene and William. But music started. "The World is Watching" by Two Door Cinema Club.

So, scratch national news and replace with international news! I definitely wasn't ready for my close-up. However my close-up was ready for me and apparently Algar was at the musical controls. There was probably never going to be a better time.

Cleared my throat. Some of the reporters stopped shrieking at me. Not all, but some, so it was a start.

Decided to go with what TCC had said in Texas. "We're here looking for one of my nieces. His daughter." Indicated TCC. If Stephanie was watching, maybe this would bring her out. Or cause her to try to kill me. Maybe both.

"Why are you risking everyone to come out of quarantine for one of your family members?" a male reporter snarled.

"Because we haven't heard from her, our family is worried, everyone's at risk, and quarantine isn't going to work."

"Why not?" another reporter shouted.

Oh well. Now or never. Might as well go out in a blaze of glory. "Because the vaccine that Clifford Goodman is telling all of you is the cure is actually the disease."

"Because you created it?" a female reporter asked.

"No. Cliff Goodman created it. He's the reason President Armstrong is dead. And he's the reason so many others are dead already or going to be very soon."

"You're saying there is no cure for this alien flu?" Couldn't keep which reporter was shouting which question. Decided not to care.

"No. I'm saying that the so-called alien flu was created by Cliff Goodman and his cronies in order to take control of this country."

"As opposed to it being brought by all those alien animals you house, or by those aliens who came to take over our country yesterday?" This was from a reporter I vaguely recognized. Knew he was anti-alien, so this question coming from him wasn't a shock.

"Correct. I'm saying that this so-called alien flu was created by a human being, Clifford Goodman, the current head of FEMA. Intentionally. To kill as many of us as possible. And by 'us' I mean humans, A-Cs, and visiting aliens."

The music changed to "My Only Enemy" by American Hi-Fi. So, what happened next didn't come as a complete surprise.

"That's one hell of an accusation," Cliff said. He walked over, surrounded by reporters, but they moved a bit, so that it was like he and I were in the outline of a figure eight. "But, since you have absolutely no proof, it's just yet another example of how you and the rest of those aligned with the A-Cs have deceived us for all these years."

"You're the deceiver." Just managed not to say Decepticon. Score one for diplomatic experience. "You pretended to care about this country and its people, but all you care about is lining your own pockets and power. You're in with the Cuban Mob and you've been behind half a dozen murderous conspiracies in the last five years alone."

The Cuban Mob was a guess, based on Bizarro World, but it struck home. For whatever reason, Cliff hadn't been prepared for me to say it, and he jerked. And looked up over his shoulder.

Followed his gaze. Was pretty sure I saw figures on the roof of the hospital. Meaning where Sanchez and Lopez had gone was to support Cliff's takeover bid. Figured I didn't have long to live.

On the plus side, the reporters were silent and, because they'd shut up and there was clearly something going on with bright lights shining, the mob began to form around us. But it was far less unruly, presumably because the people in the mob wanted to hear what was being said.

Cliff recovered. He shook his head sadly. "It makes me sad to see how you're trying to blame me for what you and your people have done. All to put your husband in the White House." This earned some nasty sounds from the crowd.

"My husband is probably the only politician on this planet who doesn't want to be a politician at all. But he's accepted what he has to do in order to serve the country that took his people in, and he does it. But kill people to get there? No. Kill innocent people to get more power? No. That's not Jeff's thing. But it's sure yours, Cliff."

"See, Kitty, the problem with accusations you can't back up is that you just sound like a sad little girl, grasping at a conspiracy theory to hide behind."

"Oh," a voice boomed out, "she has proof. And lots of it."

CHAPTER 88

MISTER JOEL OLIVER was on the scene, and he wasn't alone. Colonel Hamlin was with him. Didn't see Buchanan anywhere, though. However, "Caught, Can We Get A Witness?" by Public Enemy was now on my airwaves.

"I've just done an exclusive interview with Colonel Marvin Hamlin," Oliver said, voice still booming. He had a full camera crew with them, too, and extra lighting. "It's streaming live right now. And in that interview, Colonel Hamlin, Clifford Goodman's former direct superior, explains just why he had to fake his own death and go into hiding, to avoid being murdered by this man." Oliver pointed at Cliff.

Cliff honestly looked shocked out of his mind to see Hamlin standing there. "Did you clone him?" he blurted out.

"No," I said quickly. "Because the only people doing cloning of actual human beings are you and your cronies."

"They've done more than that!" Gideon Cleary shoved through, with Cameron Maurer and Bruce Jenkins.

Why Jenkins was here was easy—he was a reporter, this was the news event of possibly the decade, and he knew both Cleary and Maurer. How he'd convinced Walter to let him out of the Embassy was the big question, followed by the question of how he'd gotten Cleary out of the White House, though I suspected Jeff had probably had something to do with both of those.

Maurer being here, on the other hand, was a surprise, albeit a pleasant one.

Maurer had been turned into an unwilling android during Operation Defection Election. We'd saved him, but I honestly hadn't realized that Cleary was in any form of contact with Maurer, since Cleary had known Maurer was an android well before we'd discovered it. And now we were friends with Cleary and it appeared that he and Maurer had buried the hatchet. Politics, it was an amazing thing. As Armstrong had loved to tell me, it made for strange bedfellows. Shoved down the pang thinking about Armstrong gave me—I needed to focus all my attention on the current situation.

"They turned Cameron into an android," Cleary said. "Cliff and his people did that, not the A-Cs or their friends."

Maurer was in a t-shirt. He took it off and opened his chest. To show the interior workings of an android. There were a lot of screams from the crowd. Couldn't blame them. The first time I'd seen it I'd been pretty horrified, too.

Maurer closed his chest up and put his shirt back on. "Cliff Goodman did this to me," he said calmly. "So that he'd have an army of androids to do his bidding."

"You can't prove it!" Goodman shouted. Realized I'd never seen him lose his cool before. "This is all innuendo and lies from a bunch of lunatics who are trying to use me to further their political careers."

"We have proof," Claudia shouted, as she and Lorraine helped Langston Whitmore into the spotlight. It was getting hella crowded on this very public stage. Was amazed the girls were getting through, then realized Field agents were moving people at hyperspeed. I couldn't see it anymore, but as the crowd parted, I could tell that they had to be there.

Whitmore looked horrible. "I'm dying," he said. "From the alien flu."

Cliff looked relieved. "See? The Secretary of Transportation knows who's responsible."

"I do," Whitmore said. "And it's you, Cliff. You promised I wouldn't get sick, and you lied. Then you told me you'd give me the cure, and you lied again. You told me you'd be President and I'd be your right-hand man, but that was a lie, too. But unlike the others you've killed or had murdered, I'm not going to take your secrets to my grave. I've already sent copies of all the documentation I've been keeping on you for years to every major news outlet in the world. As well as to the F.B.I. and C.I.A."

Cliff looked wild-eyed. It was nice, and I hoped Chuckie was watching, but this all wasn't enough.

"It doesn't matter," I said.

Everyone, including Cliff, turned to me. Even Cliff looked shocked.

"It doesn't matter because the supervirus that Cliff created does indeed have an alien element to it. Unfortunately, it's not an alien element from our Earth A-Cs, nor from any other species in the Alpha Centauri system. The element is from a planet very far away from us."

"Does that mean you think we're all going to die?" one of the reporters asked me.

"No," a man's deep voice said as "Magic Man" by Heart hit my airwaves. "Not on my watch."

"Oh, my God," one of the people in the crowd squealed. "It's the new President!"

CHAPTER 89

SURE ENOUGH, JEFF, flanked by Christopher, Chuckie, Gower, Reader, Tim, and Raj, strode into what had become the public square, crowd control being provided again, I was sure, by Field agents I couldn't see. Yeah, we were amassed in the hospital's Emergency entrance area with overflow out onto Palmer Road, but right now, it was doing public square duty.

They were walking with purpose, but proving that I wasn't at death's door yet, I saw them moving in slow motion, like the heroes always did in every Michael Bay film. If they'd been shirtless, I'd have compared to *Magic Mike*, but since they had the nerve to be showing decorum during a national disaster, I'd have to make do. Always the way.

Had no idea where the Secret Service was, but they weren't here as far as I could see. Didn't matter. Unless Wruck's blood held the secret to the cure, we were all dead anyway.

The guys all looked sick, because they were, but Jeff still radiated leadership and confidence. How anyone could look at him and not see The Leader of the Free World was beyond me, but then, I was slightly biased.

"I can feel the emotions of everyone here," Jeff said to the crowd. "I know you're frightened, angry, worried, and wondering just what the hell's happened to your country. But I promise you that it's going to be alright."

"You really do feel their pain," Cliff said sarcastically.

"I do. Clifford Goodman," Jeff said, voice projecting, "I'm arresting you for treason for the murder of President Vincent Armstrong, and so many others."

"See what lengths they'll go to?" Cliff wasn't shouting to the reporters anymore, but to the crowd around us. "These aliens want to control us, to take our resources, our lives, and," he pointed to me, "our women!"

Couldn't help it, the Inner Hyena released in a big way. I was laughing so hard I couldn't speak for a few seconds. I was laughing so loudly that no one else tried to talk over me. Oliver having a portable microphone that he was holding near me probably helped with this.

"Oh, my God, dude, your blah, blah, blah is amazing," I said as I caught my breath. "You're making this sound like *Mars Needs Women Two: The Martians Take Manhattan*." This earned some laughs from a few of the reporters—all the female ones—and some of the crowd, as well. "They didn't come here to steal our fine bitches. Though, I think that all the gals in the audience will take one good look at the A-Cs and agree with me that if that packaging thinks I'm a total hottie, sign me up for interspecies marriage."

There were some female whoops from the crowd. Good. We might all be close to dying for real, but not so close that looking at some of the hottest dudes around wasn't giving many the will to go on.

Ensured my sarcasm knob was turned well past eleven as I pointed to Lorraine and Claudia, Abigail and Mahin. "And I'm sure that all the guys out there would, you know, actually rather die than get to mate with and potentially marry women who look like them." Now there were some male wolf whistles.

"But right now, the only chance we all have to marry

anyone and have lives and all that awesome jazz depends on one human doctor, a lot of A-C scientists, and two aliens who look like giant penguins."

Knew without asking that Wruck wouldn't want me to mention him, particularly to the entire world. We'd been there, not that long ago, so I knew why he felt he had to hide. Maybe someday, if any of us got a someday, he'd be able to come out of this particular closet and share who he really was. And maybe on that day, we'd be, as a world, ready to accept and understand it. But that day wasn't tonight.

Raj nodded and stepped forward. One of the reporters shoved a mic near him, and rather nicely set it to broadcast to the crowd. "The First Lady is correct." Raj had his Troubadour Tones set to Somberly Soothe and Reassure. "We have scientists working to find a cure. If we'll find it in time . . ." Raj spread his hands. "We don't know if we'll find the cure in time for all of us here to survive. But we do know that many people have bravely fought to protect you, and not just our people."

My music changed to "Flip the Switch" by the Rolling Stones. Hoped Algar wasn't telling me to do something, because I had no clue as to what I should be doing. Prepped myself for anything.

Raj looked around. I followed where his glance paused. On people in the crowd with anti-alien signs. "The Office of the President would like to thank the brave members of Club Fifty-One, who have been risking their lives all over the country to try to prevent any uninfected civilians from receiving the supposed vaccines that are, in fact, the killer virus created by Clifford Goodman."

There was audible gasping from the reporters and the crowd. My bet was that the loudest gasps were from the Club 51 people themselves. The only reason I hadn't reacted was Algar's musical clue. Cliff looked furious. Good.

Raj went on without missing a beat. "The President will

preside over a ceremony thanking you for your service once we're able to coordinate it, after the loss of life due to this homegrown terrorist's biological attack is assessed."

Cliff was now in the middle of a set of circles. We were around him, the reporters were around us, and the crowd was around the reporters. There was a lot less shoving and such, undoubtedly due to the Troubadour Influence.

Jenkins had his phone to his ear, and went over to a reporter I recognized as being one of the biggies on one of the major networks. The reporter nodded and then their feed was on Jenkins.

"I'm Bruce Jenkins, and I've got Tom Curran, the Director of the Federal Bureau of Investigation, on the phone. For those of you watching at home, you'll see him on split screen. For those here, Director Curran has requested, due to the amount of substantial and substantiated evidence his office has received over the past week, that Clifford Goodman be arrested immediately under the charges of treason, terrorism, and premeditated murder."

"Confirmed," the reporter nearest to me said. The other reporters were getting the same information from their news desks as well.

Heard the sound of a large motorcycle I was sure was a Harley at the same time as Foreigner's "Woman in Black" came on my airwaves. Knew who was coming. Just wasn't sure if she was coming to praise Cliff or to bury him.

The crowd parted for Huntress to come in, because most of us were trained to let people in leather riding Harleys do what they wanted as opposed to getting our butts kicked by said Harley riders. She parked the bike and dismounted. Had to hand it to her—she looked pretty badass.

She was dressed as I'd seen her before, all in black leather, with the mask on and her crossbow on her back. Cliff stared at her and, for the first time tonight, he looked afraid. And, as when Huntress had almost killed him and me both, I was sure he wasn't faking.

"Stephanie?" TCC asked.

Almost told him to be quiet but she spun toward him. "Who do you think I am?" She sounded angry. And a lot like I remembered Stephanie sounding. Made eye contact with Jeff. He nodded. So, it was her.

"My eldest daughter," TCC said.

"How would you know?" She sounded angry. Yep, definitely Stephanie.

He shrugged. "A father always knows his daughter, even when she's disguised."

She stared at him for a few long second, then turned back to Cliff. "All these others aren't the only ones who have dirt on you."

He'd recovered from his fear, or at least was back to hiding it. He smirked. "What could *you* possibly have on me?"

She stalked up to him and got right in his face. "You know that saying they have about a woman scorned? You should have never let me find out that you were sleeping with LaRue and Annette. You should have never told each of them that you loved them. You should never have picked anyone over me. But you did. Or you picked none of us and just lied to us all. I don't care. I have the data on everything you have and everywhere you have it. And I have copies stashed all over. Who do you think sent that information to the F.B.I. a week ago?"

"Oh, well done, and now you've come to kill me?" Cliff asked snidely.

She shook her head. "No. And I didn't come to rescue you, either." She turned to TCC. "I came because my father was looking for me."

Stephanie took a step toward us and, as she did, Cliff looked up on the roof and did the throat-slash hand signal that, in this case, clearly meant Kill Them Now.

Most of us saw it, because he wasn't even trying to hide that he'd done it. So results were, as was so often the case, immediate.

TCC leaped to tackle Stephanie and shield her with his body. Reader and Chuckie grabbed Jeff and pulled him down and did the same thing, while Tim and Christopher had Gower down and were covering him.

Those who had witnesses with them did the same thing — got those witnesses down and shielded them with their own bodies.

White was the one who got me down, which was ironic because I was thinking I needed to cover him. Which Brian did, which was nice in that sense. However, ducked and covered or not, I still had a view of the roof and the area around us.

Heard a lot of screaming, because when someone makes the "kill them" signal and prominent people are being shielded by the people around them, the natural tendency is to scream. But what I didn't hear were gunshots and what I didn't see were people dropping or bullets hitting.

American Hi-Fi's "The Everlasting Fall" came on. That didn't sound like a hint to duck and cover. "We need to stand up, guys. Now."

"If you insist, Missus Martini."

"I do."

"Kitty, you're making yourself a target," Brian said, but he stood up and helped White up, who in turned helped me stand. White held onto my hand and Brian's, clearly ready to use hyperspeed to get us out of range.

"No worries, Bri, you can complain to Jeff, Chuckie, James, and all the others. Later. Right now, I think something's going wrong with our Mastermind's Masterplan."

Cliff made the signal again and looked rather annoyed and beyond impatient. But his expression changed as something came hurtling down from the roof. Two somethings.

The bodies of Luis Sanchez and Julio Lopez landed at Cliff's feet. The very dead bodies. Nice to know exactly where Buchanan, and possibly Siler, had gone.

"Those are two highly wanted Cuban assassins who work for the Cuban Mob," I said, doing my best to project my voice, as I let go of White's hand and moved closer to Cliff. But not too close. "As I said earlier, you have deep ties to the Cuban Mob, meaning you were also planning to assassinate the current President of the United States, seeing as he hadn't dropped dead from your supervirus like President Armstrong did."

Cliff gaped at me.

Chuckie stood up. "Oh, and one other thing, *buddy*."

Cliff turned to him and for the first time the hatred showed on his face. It warped him from a normal, nice-looking guy into what I assumed his soul was—pure ugliness. "What's that?" Cliff snarled.

Chuckie smiled very slowly. "Checkmate. You lose. Again."

CHAPTER 90

CLIFF REACHED INTO his pocket as my music changed to "Pennies on the Floor" by The Little Willies. Had no freaking idea what Algar meant by this, but fortunately my memory nudged. I'd picked up a penny off of the floor of the Armstrong's closet.

Dug into my pocket. It was still there. Pulled it out as Cliff pulled out what he was scrambling for as well.

He was holding a cube that glittered as if it was a white and golden Rubik's cube. In other words, Cliff had the last Z'porrah power cube. How he'd had something that bulky in his pocket without it showing was beyond me, but I knew what the power cubes looked like, and he was definitely holding one. Meaning he was going to use it to get away.

Had no idea what a penny was going to do in this situation, and less than no idea of what to do with said penny, but my motto was, when in doubt, go with your gut and the crazy. Threw the penny at Cliff.

As it sailed through the air, the penny changed shape and became a cage made of thin copper wire. It opened like a mouth and snapped over the cube. Cliff just managed to get his fingers out.

The copper cage with its sparkly prize fell to the ground. No one needed to tell me that we wanted that picked up. Cliff and I both lunged for it. But it was gone.

Christopher was back by Jeff and the others, only he had the cage in his hand. He grinned at me and I laughed.

But I was now close to Cliff and he took the opportunity to do the only thing he hadn't tried yet—grabbing a hostage. Namely, me.

If I hadn't been infected I'd have been able to get away from him. But infected I was, and the "high" of my latest adrenaline rush was starting to crash. Meaning I had very little in the tank.

Cliff produced a gun and put it at my temple. "I will happily kill her," he said to Chuckie, not Jeff. "So you're going to let me go, or I'll blow her brains out in front of you."

People around us all raised their hands, but Reader, Tim, Christopher, and Raj literally dragged Jeff, Gower, and Chuckie back.

Knew without asking that Buchanan and Siler, if he was up there, wouldn't have a safe enough shot to take it. Meaning I was on my own right now, because, as First Lady, no one was going to risk shooting near me.

The crowd was parting again, as Cliff headed us for Stephanie's motorcycle. "We're going to take a ride now."

Couldn't speak for anyone else in the crowd but I wasn't scared. I was pissed. Didn't have the She-Hulk Rage thing going for me, but Wolverine could work up a good Berserker Rage when he needed to, and I focused on that. Well, that and my other motto—keep 'em monologuing.

"Wow, Cliff, you're really going for the whole Cackling Mastermind Is Revealed On International Television thing, aren't you?"

"Well, when someone takes your anonymity away, you have to improvise. Take off the earphones and dump your phone."

"Yeah, you're the master of that, aren't you? Mister Mastermind." Did as he told me, though I managed to put my earbuds into my purse. My phone I tossed toward Jeff. Well, I tossed the phone that I'd been listening to music on over. The other phone, the one that the Secret Service, and therefore Cliff, didn't know about? That one was still in my purse.

"How long have you known?" he asked as we got awkwardly onto the Harley. It's really hard to get two people on a Harley at the same time, especially when one is wrapped around the other and a gun to the head is involved. But we managed. No one laughed, though I had to figure some people watching probably wanted to. We had to look ridiculous.

"For a lot longer than you've known that we knew. You're lucky I know how to ride one of these."

"You're not going to stay lucky."

"Oh, see now, Cliff, if you just plan to kill me anyway, I'm going to give the kill order and go out in a heroic blaze of glory. Don't be stupid. You know you're going to let me live."

"Why would I do that?"

"Because you like the game."

He chuckled as I started the bike and he wrapped one arm tightly around my waist, keeping the gun at my head. "That's true. It's been a good game."

Had to pay attention to get the bike turned around and out of the crowd. Did my best to send Jeff an emotional signal that told him not to worry and not to come after me himself. Had no idea if I was doing that well or not.

"So, how did you infect everyone?"

"Gaseous release mostly. And the 'vaccine,' as you guessed."

"Yeah, that seems obvious. But you were pawing all of us a lot."

He laughed. "You caught that? I'm impressed. Yes, I have a stronger form of the virus in my pocket. Skin-to-skin contact ensures complete infection for those who weren't dying quickly enough. And it's helpful to spread the disease to those who weren't exposed to the gas or those who were in the contagious stage."

"Wasn't that a risk for you? I mean touching the disease over and over again."

"No. The cure is very final. Either you die or you get the vaccine and the vaccine is, if I do say so myself, a brilliant bit of medical engineering. Once vaccinated you can never get the Alien Flu again."

Well, anything that could be engineered could be reverse engineered, so I didn't lose hope. Actively chose not to mention that the brilliance of this disease and, most likely, its cure had far less to do with Cliff and far more to do with Lizzie's dead father. Also actively didn't point out that there was no such thing as a vaccine that worked a hundred percent of the time and forever. The best vaccines came close, but nothing was a foolproof cure. However, I wasn't in any position to get cocky, so I kept all of this to myself.

Headed off slowly, mostly because I didn't want him to get any ideas and shoot into the crowd. No musical clues from Algar now. Just me and the Mastermind, riding off into the sunset. Well, sunrise, really. Refused to consider how long it had been since I'd slept, in part because a gun to your head makes you very wide awake. Couldn't hear Poison's "Ride the Wind" for real, but I was listening to it in my mind. On repeat. 'Cause that was how I rolled.

"Take the Three-Fifty-Five to the Beltway, then get on the Ninety-Five," he said. "And speed it up."

"You got it. Can I put sunglasses on, or do you want me blinded so we get to be organ donors?"

"Fine, get your sunglasses out. Try anything, though, and I'll pull the trigger."

"Blah, blah, blah. It's going to take me longer than normal since I have to use my left hand." Or I'd have to let go of the throttle and that wasn't in anyone's best interests, especially mine.

Moved my purse onto the tank in front of me. Pretended I was having trouble and dug through for my Glock as well as my sunglasses. Felt the used hypodermics Tim had dumped in there and carefully moved them to the top of my purse, just in case.

Because of how he was holding me, Cliff couldn't really look down into my purse, because it would mean he'd have to lean over and move the gun from my head. Nestled the Glock next to the needles, then put my sunglasses on.

"Done, and thanks. We'll be a lot safer this way."

"Oh, good. I'm so glad we're being road safe and law abiding."

Chose not to reply. Revved the bike and headed us out as directed.

Couldn't really talk now, and couldn't go as fast as I wanted until we were on the 355. But once we were, I focused on speed, though I was going to have to wait for the Beltway to make my move.

Sure, Christopher could catch us, but the problem was that Cliff *wanted* to kill me, so if any of the others gave him the slightest provocation, he'd pull the trigger. No, I needed to get him away from everyone, let him think he was safe, and then make my move.

Zipped up the 355 and got onto the Beltway in short order. Presumed he'd want to go south on the 95, because I knew without asking that he wanted to get to Cuba. So I went east on the Beltway.

"You're going the wrong way," he shouted.

"You said you wanted the Ninety-Five!"

"I do, going south, you idiot." Always nice to be right.

"Sharing directions is helpful, you know. It's the Beltway, we'll go in a circle." And then I really cranked the throttle.

We were moving fast in short order. If my days weren't completely jumbled up, it was a workday. There were certainly enough cars on the road at this time of day to indicate that, killer epidemic or not, most people were headed in to their jobs.

I weaved us in and out of cars as I went faster and faster.

We went past the exit for Andrews Air Force Base. Wasn't ready to go for it.

"Slow down!" Cliff shouted.

I went faster. We flew past the 95 interchange. "Whoops! We'll have to catch it next go 'round."

"Slow down or I'll shoot you," he snarled in my ear.

"Go ahead. At this speed, if you shoot me, this bike goes down and you'll die for sure. We're not in gear, so it's not going to be pretty for either one of us. But me, I think I've got a good shot. I'm an athlete, I'm the one driving, and I'll have all the medical attention from the top doctors in the world. You, on the other hand, are not an athlete, are not the one driving, and are going to get dead before you ever reach a hospital." And then we could get his blood, too. Crashing was definitely one of my Win-Win Options. Oh sure, not Option #1 but definitely up there in the Options List.

My hair was flying around, but mostly in his face. Hoped it was hurting and blinding him both. Was pretty sure I had the Harley at top speed, but wasn't willing to take my eyes off the road to find out. Though the road was a lot less crowded.

Risked a look in the rearview mirror. Not a lot of cars behind us, either. Assumed that law enforcement was getting people off this road so that I could pretend I was starring in *Speed* with a bit more safety.

We went on, him snarling at me to slow down and me ignoring him completely. "Oh, by the way? Annette Dier's dead, so if you're expecting to meet up with her or that she's going to save your bacon, you're in for some real disappointment."

"Whatever. She was going to be dead soon anyway."

"Yeah, you didn't give her the real vaccine, did you?"

He laughed again. "No, I didn't."

Saw a helicopter. Several. They were hovering over parts of the Beltway. Probably news helicopters watching the

First Lady ride a Harley with the Domestic Terrorist Supreme. Hoped Dad still had the TVs turned off at the Embassy.

"Annette loved you, though."

"So did Stephanie. And so what? Chuck loves you—but that didn't change anything for you, did it?"

Had to make a move before the Harley ran out of gas. Had no idea how much gas was in the bike before we'd gotten on it, but even with a full tank, I couldn't go like this forever. And the likelihood that I was working with a full tank was slim.

"Not in this world, no."

"Right. Because it takes the right person."

"True enough. And at the right time."

"Exactly. You know, Kitty, you and I could make a really good team."

Managed not to let the Inner Hyena out again. Also managed not to say the first several replies that came to mind. "Oh yeah?" was the only safe reply I could give, so I gave it.

"Yeah. Come down to Cuba with me. You know you deserve a man who can keep up with you intellectually."

"Wow, I'm used to my enemies telling me I'm an idiot."

"Just because other men haven't respected you doesn't mean I'm like that."

Cliff had apparently had some real good luck with lines like this. Possibly they worked on LaRue. Certainly they'd worked on Stephanie, and probably Dier, too. That he thought he had more to offer than my husband and presumed other options was amazingly conceited. But then again, that was his fatal flaw—he was awfully pleased with himself.

"So, what could you offer me that my current husband can't?" One of the helicopters was flying toward us and getting lower at the same time. It looked much beefier than the other choppers that were higher up and clearly news choppers. Military. And black. Could be coming for me, could be coming for Cliff, could just be trying to get a really good shot for the morning news shows. Had no bet either way.

"Wealth, power, all the things women like."

"I'll bet you want me to bring my kids, too, don't you?"

"Well, of course. I'd never want to separate you from your children, Kitty. What kind of man would I be to do that?"

Managed to refrain from comment, but it took real effort.

There was another helicopter, also flying low, also military grade, but this one was grayish. Was pretty sure it was coming from Andrews. But it was well behind the closer one. Which had a rope ladder hanging down.

Tried to figure out how long it would take to fly a helicopter from Orlando to D.C. Had no clue, but it was doubtful that the remaining Crazy Eights were in that chopper.

On the other hand, who said clones couldn't learn to fly?

CHAPTER 91

MY SUSPICIONS WERE confirmed as I saw someone leaning out of the chopper, one arm hooked through the strap that would keep him in, holding what looked like a very impressive gun.

"I see your other ride's here."

"Right on time."

"You had this escape planned?" I found that doubtful.

"No, but I always have contingency plans in place."

"True. You are the current Mastermind, after all."

"The only Mastermind, now."

"You're not going to let Reid take over when you're an old man?"

"No."

"Does *he* know that?"

"If I said no, would you tell him?"

"No, because of the two of you, despite everything you've done, I still like you better." This was perhaps my finest Damning With Faint Praise statement ever.

Cliff laughed. "I'm flattered. You can come with us, still, you know."

"Would you give me the cure? The real one, not the one you gave Annette?"

"Of course. And your children, too. Why would I bring you along if I didn't intend to save you?"

Wanted to say that he'd do that to get my children, possibly give them the real vaccine, definitely give me the fake vaccine, and then watch me die while he and the others laughed. Knew better than to say this out loud, however.

"Good point."

"So, are you coming with me, then? No extradition from Cuba. We can live there like a king and queen."

"Oh, you know how it is. I don't want to ruin whatever weird relationship you and whatever clone version of LaRue is flying the chopper happen to have this week. And while it'd be just loads of fun to reunite with Leventhal Reid, I'm going to pass."

"Suit yourself. You're choosing to die, you know."

"Not really. There is no way on God's Green Earth you're getting off this hog and onto the rope ladder with that gun in your hand. And until you're safely on the ladder and off the bike, Reid isn't going to shoot."

Oh, sure, the moment Cliff *was* considered safe, then they'd all be shooting at me. But not until then. Slowed the bike down just a bit.

Cliff didn't argue, but the gun went away from my temple. "Keep the bike steady," he said to me as he began to move to stand on the seat.

"Oh, to be sure."

I actually *had* to keep the bike steady and not let Cliff become roadkill, despite my desire to get a blood sample from him. But other than crashing, I didn't see any workable options and due to his team being right here, the likelihood that they'd save Cliff before he died on the asphalt was high. The other chopper, the one I really hoped was coming for me, was still too far away. And if I dumped Cliff and managed to keep the bike upright, Reid would fill me full of lead, of that I was certain.

So, pretending that we were trained stunt people, Cliff shifted and slipped and climbed, and held onto me to keep himself steady and managed to get his feet up on the seat as we reached the chopper with the rope ladder. It was a good thing we were on a nice, heavy Harley, because a crotch rocket would have probably dumped due to the shaking and jerking Cliff was doing to me and the bike.

Risked it anyway and took my left hand off the handlebars, reached into my purse, and grabbed the hypodermics.

Cliff grabbed the rope ladder and the moment he did, I slammed the hypos into the part of his body currently closest to me—his butt. Cliff screamed in pain, and Reid pointed his gun right at me. I gunned the bike and swerved under the chopper at the same time, just getting my hand back on the handlebars in time.

Now I wanted a crotch rocket, because I'd be able to get away faster and more nimbly. But I wasn't able to change iron horses in midstream, so I just kept the Harley at its top speed and rolled in a serpentine manner toward the other chopper.

Saw bullets hitting the road in front of and around me. Ignored them. Either I was heading for help or being herded toward an enemy, but stopping was no longer an option. Checked my rearview—Cliff was still on the rope ladder, hypos still in his butt, but he was almost inside. And the chopper was after me, coming up fast.

Pulled my Glock out of my purse. It wasn't going to be easy to shoot, let alone left-handed, and steer the bike at the same time, but I was going to have to give it the old Pueblo Caliente try.

The chopper pulled up next to me, still flying very low. Pointed the Glock at the chopper and did rapid fire.

Heard a man shout but didn't look to see if I'd hit anyone. Because the other chopper was closing in on my other side.

The nice thing about military helicopters was that you could be on either side to get on or off. I cared about this because the chopper I really hoped was coming to save me was flying low on my right, coming at me, while Cliff's chopper was flying low on my left and going with my flow, so to speak.

Because there were two choppers now trying to act like commuters on the Beltway, neither one could get all that close to me. This also meant that my Glock probably wasn't going to have a chance of hitting again. Dumped it back into my purse and happily put my left hand back onto the handlebars.

More gunfire, but this time no one was shooting at me. Reid was shooting at the other chopper. Said chopper swerved away and, as I caught a glimpse of who was in this chopper, realized why the pilot had swerved to avoid being hit—Jeff was in there.

So much for him not coming for me. Then again, right now, I was all over him coming for me. We could have the old "you're the POTUS and need to be careful" chat later.

Jeff's chopper swung around and came up fast on my right, but this time going along in the same direction I was.

A quick check of my rearview shared that there were two guys hanging out of the right hand side—Jeff and Siler. Siler, like Reid, had his arm hooked through the safety strap, had a rifle, and he was shooting at Cliff's chopper, meaning he was keeping Reid occupied.

Jeff had hold of another safety strap, but he wasn't shooting. He was leaning out. Far out.

The chopper dipped even lower and I figured it was now or never. Jeff reached down for me. "Come on, baby!"

Stood up, feet still on the pegs. "On three! One . . ." Left foot onto the seat. Technically, this was my starting blocks position—left leg in front, right leg providing the starting power.

"Two . . ." Left hand off the handlebars. Jeff tried, and so did I, but he couldn't reach me. Yet.

"Three!"

I let go with my right hand and pushed off with my right foot while Jeff leaned really far out, one foot on the skid, holding onto the security strap with one hand and, as the bike fell over and started sliding down the highway, he caught my left wrist. And Siler fired his gun.

The chopper went up fast and veered to the left. For a long second I thought Jeff was going to lose his hold and I was, if I was really lucky, going to land on the skid and hope like hell to hang on.

But Jeff didn't lose his hold and managed to drag me into the belly of the chopper.

Then he got me into his arms and held me and I buried my face in his chest and we didn't talk. We just held onto each other for dear life.

CHAPTER 92

OUR REUNION WASN'T LONG. Heard a man curse. "They're going out of range," Buchanan shouted. "That chopper has more power than we do. Mister President, do we pursue?"

"No, absolutely not," Jeff said. "Get us back to the White House. Let Andrews take it from here."

Jeff sort of loosened his hold on me and I looked around. Just the three of them in here. "Where's everyone else?"

"Probably still trying to tell me that they're better equipped to rescue my wife than I am." Jeff hugged me again. "I think you took years off my life with this, baby."

"Since we may only have days, I'm not going to feel guilty. How did you get this chopper?"

"I ran to Andrews," Jeff said. "With them." He nodded his head toward Buchanan and Siler. "I may be sick, but I still have hyperspeed."

"By the time you were actually on the bike and leaving, Malcolm and I were down on the street level with everyone else." Siler shrugged. "We knew what your husband was going to do. Malcolm grabbed him as he took off, I caught up, we ran for Andrews, grabbed a chopper, and came after you."

"They just had one warmed up and ready for you?"

"They did," Siler said, with a glance toward Buchanan. "We called ahead."

"Go team."

"Thanks. I hit Reid. No idea if it was fatal or not, but he's hit."

"Hurray. And really nice to see you. I thought you weren't up to action."

"Adrenaline's really great."

"Yeah, I think mine's all used up and then some. It's weird hearing Malcolm call you Mister President, Jeff."

"Yeah, well, let's worry about that when we're back on the ground."

"How did you find me? Tracking via my other phone?"

Jeff stared at me. "No. I followed your emotional trail."

"Oh. Duh. But I'd have thought your blocks would be up."

"Uh, not when my wife was kidnapped by our most bitter enemy, no."

"Well, I appreciate your dedication to my safety."

"Do you? I'm sure I'm not the only one who can't tell."

"I'm ignoring that. Are you feeling okay?"

"Yeah, actually. Maybe it's because of the disease. It could be sapping my talent. But even though I can feel all the emotions, they aren't bothering me as much."

It didn't take us too long to get to the White House. Buchanan set us down on the nice helipad and turned the chopper off. Then he came back to join us. "Missus Executive Chief, let me be the first to ask you to never do anything like that again."

"Hey, all of this wasn't my fault! I didn't take myself hostage."

"It's never your fault, baby," Jeff said, as he hugged me again. "But I'm with Buchanan. Let's not repeat this performance. Ever."

"I doubt we'll need to in the next three days."

"I think we have longer," Siler said. "The Shantanu were really excited about Wruck when I was there."

The chopper's blades slowed down. "We ever getting out of this bird?" I asked Buchanan.

"Once a security team is here, yes."

"Oh my God, really?"

"Yes," he said flatly. "Really. But impressive shooting while driving a motorcycle. You hit their chopper and I think you winged Reid."

"Then it's a good day."

Secret Service people were literally running toward us. Had to figure we'd just earned the Worst Presidential Couple to Protect Award and didn't look forward to the tongue lashings.

Since they were coming, though, Buchanan and Siler got out, then helped Jeff out, who then lifted me out. Jeff kept his arm around me, Siler and Buchanan flanked us, and we headed to meet the Secret Service.

Evalyne reached us first, grabbed me away from Jeff, and hugged me. "We thought we were going to watch you die."

Hugged her back. "Nah. Per someone who would know, I have nine lives."

Phoebe grabbed me next. "I'm going to put a tracking anklet on you," she said as she hugged me and I hugged back.

"Oh, why make life that dull?"

The Secret Service got us back inside the White House and into the good old Diplomatic Reception Room, which was packed with people. There were a lot of hugs, a lot of reprimands, and a lot of talking. And then it was time to catch up on what I'd missed while I was racing around with Cliff.

Pretty much everyone who'd been here the whole time or had been on missions with us was down here, with a few exceptions. While TCC was here, Stephanie wasn't. She'd hugged him and told him she'd see him again, but then had run off. Because everyone was focused on me and Cliff, she'd been able to escape.

No one had heard from Rahmi or Rhee, and the flyboys were still considered MIA, as were all those who'd been on assigned security detail at Rocky Mount. Buchanan had gotten one short, cryptic message from Camilla: *Staying longer on Spring Break, getting lots of souvenirs.*

The general assumption was that the flyboys and the others were not nearby as previously assumed, but this wasn't a great comfort, especially to Lorraine and Claudia, who were understandably worried about their husbands, or Tim, who was understandably worried about his team.

The decision had been made to tell Tito that we hadn't heard from Rahmi after he'd finished hopefully creating the cure. Not wise to distract one of the guys most likely to save everyone's life.

On the other hand, no one had heard from Drax, either, and we still had all of his commandos in custody at Guantanamo, so the expectation was that the sales pitch had been put on hold, due to the change in government. I refused to think the worst, in part because at least I knew the flyboys weren't infected, so they might outlive the rest of us.

Abigail was at NASA Base because Tito needed a hybrid to test his vaccine on, and she was looking a little worse than Mahin. Adriana was with her, because he also needed to test the vaccine on a human who was probably infected but wasn't showing symptoms. Jeff had sent Len and Kyle along with them for protection, as well as all the A-Cs on my security detail. Brian had also gone with them, since he felt he'd been exposed to the virus by now anyway. Justice Quinn had gone as well, giving Tito humans at various stages of exposure to the virus to test the vaccine on.

Christopher still had the Z'porrah cube and the weird cage that now held it, but I took it from him and put it into my purse. Had a feeling Algar was going to want it.

"How did Cliff get out of quarantine?" I asked Chuckie.

"We think he used the Z'porrah cube. One minute he was here, fighting with Jeff, then agreeing to go to NASA Base and give Tito a sample of his blood, the next, we went to look for him and he was gone. Where did you find that cage?"

"Honestly? I saw the shiny thing and picked it up. It was

just the easiest thing at hand to throw at Cliff." Sort of true, sort of a lie, but he didn't push it. "I'm sorry they got away."

He hugged me. "I'm just relieved you're still alive and unhurt."

"Me too, if you can count us probably dying from the alien flu alive and unhurt."

All I really wanted to do was to get home to Jamie and Charlie, and I knew that's how the others with family in the Embassy or other Safe Zone locations felt, too, but we still weren't allowed into the Embassy or anywhere else because we were still infected. Unfortunately, the bowling alley had more bodies in it than when I'd left. But, other than two Secret Service agents who'd been on Armstrong's detail, no one else who'd been in the Sick Suite was among them.

Mom wasn't looking great, though. I sat with her and put my arm around her shoulders and let her lean into me. That way we just looked cozy and she wouldn't look weak in front of her subordinates.

"Despite the complaints, you did great, kitten. I'm very proud of you." She sounded exhausted and very sick. Tried to think of a time I'd seen her this ill and came up blank.

"Thanks, Mom. I just tried to do what you'd do."

"You sound tense. Put in your headphones. It'll relax you, and I'm used to talking to you like that." Did as she suggested. Hey, when your mother gives you a pass to listen to tunes while you're talking to her, you take the pass. "James told me about the Dingo and his cousin," she said as I got my earbuds in and my phone out. "I'm sorry. I know they meant a lot to you."

"Yeah, they did. They died to protect me, Mom. The two top assassins in the world died to save me, and yet there are probably more people who think Cliff's an okay guy than would think they were good people."

"It's all in the perspective, kitten."

Our discussion of The Study of Comparative Bad Guys was interrupted by Jeff getting a phone call.

"Yes? Yes. Yes. Right away. Yes. Good. Thank you. All of you." He hung up and turned to us. The room went still. "That was Tito. Doctor Hernandez for any who don't know, who's in charge of the team working on the cure."

"How bad is it?" Tim asked quietly.

"They just gave the vaccine to Manfred, Abigail, Len, Caroline, Adriana, Brian, and a Field team from Sydney Base who were not exposed to the virus, along with a human astronaut who was also not exposed."

The room was so quiet you could hear a Poof walking. Couldn't take the pressure and hit play. "Far Too Young To Die" by Panic! At the Disco came on. So much for music relaxing me—this was a song about the death of loved ones.

Jeff grinned. "Those who had the virus are showing immediate signs of recovery. Those who were not showing symptoms or who had no exposure to the virus are showing signs that the vaccine is working as it should, as a preventative and a protection. The vaccine is being replicated at NASA Base, the Dulce Science Center, and Caliente Base. We should have enough to supply the entire country in two days."

Everyone cheered. Everyone but me and Mom. Mom didn't look like she had two days and neither did Elaine.

Jeff looked straight at me. "We have enough doses right now for those who are sickest to get vaccinated. Tito's on his way over to administer the cure."

Hugged Mom. "It's going to be okay."

Wanted to cry with relief but didn't because I wasn't sure that we were out of the woods and I had too much to cry about right now and didn't want to be bawling my head off for the foreseeable future. I'd experienced life without my mother in Bizarro World. I wasn't ready to experience that in my own world. But that wasn't going to be up to me.

"Thanks for worrying, kitten." Mom leaned her head on my shoulder. "But I'll be fine." Then she sighed and closed her eyes.

CHAPTER 93

WE WERE BACK IN the Embassy after the funeral.

We were supposed to be in the White House now, seeing as it had been a week since the big attack, but Jeff refused to rush Elaine out. We were also supposed to do some kind of inauguration party, but Jeff really didn't want to do that.

Had no energy to argue about these things one way or the other. Plus I was jumpy and nervous and generally out of sorts. Understandably, but still, it didn't make being First Lady any easier.

Cliff, Reid, and LaRue had gotten away. Their helicopter had been faster than the jets Andrews had scrambled. Maybe they were in Titan tech, maybe Drax's, maybe someone else's. We'd find out, but for now, they, and the five remaining Crazy Eights, were at large and were all on every nation's most wanted lists.

A new Vice President needed to be selected and approved as well as a host of Cabinet members and some of the Joint Chiefs. Probably more. But right now, we were too busy mourning.

Pierre had provided his usual Funeral Feast and people were eating, even Elaine and her family, who'd come back with us.

Dad was carrying Charlie and Jeff had Jamie. Jamie

hadn't been herself this week because, as far as I could tell, she'd come dangerously close to draining all her power trying to keep everyone she could alive. The other kids who'd been helping her were all quiet, too, which was worrisome.

But I'd spoken to ACE while Jamie was asleep, and he'd reassured me that all the children were and would be fine, and that ACE was also fine and still on the case, protecting Earth and its inhabitants in the ways he could, just as Algar and Naomi protected us in the ways they could.

Fine or not, all the kids were clingy, Lizzie included. She hadn't let Siler out of her sight and on the rare occasions when he went to the bathroom, she was sticking as close to me and Jeff as she could manage without asking us to carry her around like the little kids.

Camilla, Rahmi, Rhee, the flyboys, and the Rocky Mount security teams were still MIA, there was no sign of Stephanie the Huntress, and Drax had made no moves. It felt like the eye of the hurricane to me—the calm in between the two big storms.

Buchanan came over to me. "Nothing's going to be the same now, Missus Executive Chief."

"Yeah. So many decisions need to be made. I know I'm supposed to be excited, but now that it's all over, or at least we're getting a small chance to catch our breath, all I feel is sad. It's a brave new world I don't think I'm ready for."

"Oh, I think you're going to find out that the more things change, the more they stay the same, kitten," Mom said as she joined us, snacking on one of Lucinda's brownies. "State funerals are the worst. State funerals combined with additional funerals that cause the state funeral to last three days? Beyond the worst."

"I was just getting used to living here." Looked around the Embassy. "It's finally become home and now we have to move."

Mom snorted. "You managed to get out of moving into the Vice President's residence, so you dodged that bullet for a year and a half. And it's not as if you're moving down in the world."

"Speaking of moving, I need to talk to a couple people, since apparently you're telling me to pull up the big girl panties and get on with things."

Mom laughed and kissed my cheek. "I am. While you do that I'll go relieve your husband and play with my grand-daughter. And stop worrying—it'll be fine."

"Hope so." Wandered toward Doreen, who was talking with Vance, Guy, Lillian, Abner, Nathalie, and Vander. "Can I join this illustrious party?"

"Absolutely," Lillian said. "We were just telling Doreen to get ready."

"I don't know for what," Doreen said.

Rolled my eyes. "I'm the First Lady now. I cannot be the American Centaurion Ambassador anymore. But the person who should have been doing the job all these years can be. And that's you, Doreen. So, get used to it."

"I agree," Jeff said as he joined us. "My mother-in-law has stolen our daughter," he said to me.

"I thought Mom was going to die. I'm fine with her monopolizing anything she wants, Jamie and Charlie especially."

Jeff sighed. "I told you we had enough to cure all those who were near death. Angela wasn't even in the closest to death group. But I had Tito give her the vaccine first, since you were so freaked out."

"Blah, blah, blah."

"Speaking of those who almost died, how's Langston doing?" Nathalie asked.

"Recovering slowly, but recovering," Vance answered. Wasn't shocked at all that he knew. "Lorraine and Claudia got to him just in time. Guy's going to be fine, too, thanks for asking." Gadoire grinned. "My nerves are shot forever, though. Next time you suggest riding on the train, Kitty, I'm saying no."

"Oh, you say that now, but I know it's not true."

Raj came over and it was clear he was trying not to laugh. "We just had an interesting call."

"Oh yeah? What?"

"A major entertainment conglomerate would like to create a movie franchise."

"Thrilling. Why are they calling us?"

"Well, they were actually calling for you, Kitty. I just took the call. They'd like to create a series based on you."

Stared at him. "Someone's high."

Raj gave in to his Inner Hyena. "No," he said when he stopped laughing. "They think that *Code Name: First Lady* has the potential to be a huge action hit."

The others began talking excitedly about this. Put up my hand. They stopped talking. Clearly, once you were First Lady you had the Power of the Paw at your disposal.

"I think they're punking us, Raj."

"No, they're not. I'm having contracts sent over, just as an exploratory thing. I'll make sure Charles reviews them, too."

"Unreal. Okay, since I can't drink alcohol I'm going to go get a Coke and chug it as if it were whiskey and pretend this isn't happening. Doreen, as the new American Centaurion Ambassador, just remember that these lobbyists and politicians are a sneaky bunch. Be sneakier."

Left this group, still talking about Hollywood calling. Jeff came with me. "I think you'd make a great action star, baby."

"We are so done with that conversation, Jeff. I think we need to have Siler and Lizzie move into the Embassy or onto our staff."

"Yeah? Why so?"

"You don't sound like you disagree."

"I don't. I just want to know why you think they should come in out of the cold."

"Because, with the uncles dead, they both have lost tremendous protection, just as we have. Lizzie's made enemies, so she can't go back to her cushy boarding school. Siler's made the same enemies in the Cuban Mob we have now, and I think he's rethinking his career. And Buchanan's coming to the White House with us. I think having someone hella sneaky and willing to break necks if he has to on staff will be a huge help, especially since Mom's pulling Kevin off as the Defense Attaché."

"Promotions cause changes as much as deaths do."

"So, you agree?"

"Yeah, I do. You'll talk to them about it?"

"Yeah, I will. I'll run it by Doreen first, too." Grabbed a Coke, chugged it, tossed the bottle into the trash, got another. This one I planned to sip. "Com on."

"Yes, Chief First Lady?"

"Not the Chief anymore, Walt. That's going to be Doreen. I think you could call me Kitty now."

"No, ma'am. Missus First Lady it is. What can I do for you?"

"Let's put on some music, Walt. As my last act as Ambassador."

"Will do."

Thusly fortified and now hearing the Killers' "Spaceman" wafting quietly from our speakers, went to the Planetary Council folks. They were staying in the Embassy guest rooms because, realistically, in the entire time they'd been here we really hadn't dealt with their issues.

Alexander seemed unfazed by this. What he seemed to be, though, was enjoying himself, at least when we weren't being solemn and crying at gravesides and such.

Queen Renata wasn't willing to leave with her daughters unaccounted for, and I couldn't blame her for that at all. Besides, it was nice to have them visiting. It made things more chaotic, but also a little more fun.

Jeff, Alexander, and Renata started talking about some protocol issues and my ears turned off. Jareen grinned at me and pulled me aside. "The politics never stops does it?"

"Not that I can tell."

"How're you doing?" she asked.

"Oh, okay. I'll deal with this new world order. I always do."

She snorted. "That is not what I'm talking about."

"Oh. That. I don't know yet. Worried, I guess."

Caroline and Adriana came over and joined us. "I know we know what's coming, but I'm still excited," Caroline said.

"It's nice to have something to celebrate," Adriana added.

Didn't want to point out all the things that could go wrong, so I just nodded.

Jeff jerked, then got a big grin on his face. So I wasn't totally surprised to see Melanie and Emily come into the room at hyperspeed. I had all my A-C Extras back, so I could actually see them. Lorraine and Claudia were behind their mothers. All four women were smiling.

"Rebecca Ann Gaultier-White has officially arrived," Melanie said. "And she's perfect. Mother and baby are doing great."

"Christopher, on the other hand, is a blubbering mess," Emily said. "I'm not supposed to tell anyone about that, though."

"His father is with him and is handling it, Jeff," Melanie added. "So don't feel that you have to race down to help him. I think Amy wants a little more time with just them."

"Well, them and your parents." Emily laughed. "Your mother is kind of hogging Becky."

"I'm not surprised," Jeff said. "I'm just surprised Amy's letting her."

"It's a family love fest down there," Melanie said. "So, give it about ten minutes, and then go join in."

Lorraine and Claudia came over to us. "So far, it doesn't look like Amy's mutated," Lorraine said. "Tito, Magdalena, Rohini, and Bettini are still with her and Becky, though, and still doing tests."

"She had a totally normal delivery," Claudia shared. "It was fast, but not bad."

"So, thankfully, nothing like when I gave birth to Jamie."

"Nope," Claudia said cheerfully. "More like how it was for you with Charlie."

The worry I'd had all day disappeared. "Thank goodness."

"Immortals" from Fall Out Boy started. Fitting enough, under the circumstances. Sent a mental thank you to our own special immortals—ACE, Algar, Naomi, and any and all other Powers That Be who might be listening.

Lorraine sighed. "Now, we just need to find our husbands and the rest of our missing friends and life'll be back to normal."

Thought about what Mom and Buchanan had said while I watched the President of the United States happily tell our daughter that her new best friend was waiting to meet her while he held her and her brother in his arms.

"No. Constant change, upheaval, and danger *is* our normal. But, just like everything else—starting with finding the flyboys and the princesses and ending with hunting down Cliff and his cronies—we can handle it."

Somehow, I was about to move into the biggest house in the world. But I'd made a deathbed promise to never change who I was. So I wouldn't. Megalomaniacs of the galaxy and whoever has my friends held hostage beware. Code Name: First Lady is coming for you.

Available May 2016,
the thirteenth novel in the *Alien* series
from Gini Koch:

CAMP ALIEN

Read on for a sneak preview

"EXCUSE ME, President Martini, but we have a situation. It seems the Planetary Council is requesting foodstuffs that, ah, we don't actually have on hand."

This whispered, worried statement was coming from the head of the White House's household, the Chief Usher, Antoinette Reilly.

She was an attractive black woman a few years older than either Jeff or I, wearing a constantly worried expression for the past week. I'd met her before this, when the now late President Armstrong was the man in charge, and she'd never seemed this ready to request immediate leave as she had been in the week and a half since his death.

And she wasn't the only one. We were already clearly stressing the staff of the White House out beyond their obvious expectations, and we hadn't even officially moved in yet.

"What could they possibly want that we don't have?" Jeff asked just as quietly.

"It's, ah, considered a delicacy. Apparently. Only we would need to import it from, ah, the Alpha Centauri system, and even if we could do so easily, Chef is flat out refusing to make it. And," Antoinette looked over to me, "ah, I can't blame him."

Took the leap. "Oh my God, Alexander wants to have the horrid Alpha Four boiled tapeworms dish, doesn't he?"

Antoinette nodded. "Madam First Lady, could you please help?"

"The formality of this new stage of my life is literally going to kill me. Can I order you and the rest of the staff to call me Kitty and have a hope of it sticking?"

Antoinette smiled. It was the first smile I'd seen her crack in a week, so go me. "Possibly in private. But right now, we need your help. Formally."

Nodded, and turned to look down the long conference table. "Excuse me, Alex?"

Emperor Alexander, Ruler of the Entire Alpha Centauri System—at least as far as anyone on Earth other than those of us who actually knew the political system over there knew—nodded his head toward me in a regal manner. "Yes, Kitty?"

"Dude, you're asking for food that makes humans literally want to barf their guts out. It's a no go. And anyone else requesting personal country or planetary specialties, up to and definitely including haggis, need to run those requests through me. So that I can say no in the nicest possible way."

"That wasn't what we were going for," Antoinette said quietly.

"No problem, Kitty. But they're really delicious," Alexander said, sounding far more like what he really was—Jeff's and his cousin, Christopher White's, younger relative who we'd put onto the throne of Alpha Four—than the Ruler of the Free Alpha Centauri Worlds.

"Dude, gag me. Seriously. Never speak of those things again in my or any other human's presence and we'll continue to love you." Turned back to Antoinette. "Learn this now—I may have been forced to be the American Centaurion Ambassador, but don't for one moment think I enjoyed the job. I get far better results by living by the cat motto of asking for exactly what I want. And that includes being the

FLOTUS. By the way, FLOTUS really makes me feel like I'm co-starring in a *Finding Nemo* spin off as the chipper strip of seaweed that helps the gang save the day."

Antoinette was now clearly trying not to laugh. Or cry. Possibly both. Gave it even odds either way. "Duly noted, Madam First Lady."

"The less said about what movie that title makes me think I'm starring in, the better."

"*Best Little Whorehouse in Texas*?" Tim Crawford, the Head of Airborne for Centaurion Division, aka the guy doing what remained my favorite job on my entire resume, asked with a quiet snicker.

"Got it in one."

Antoinette heaved a sigh. Had to figure I was going to generate that in her for the foreseeable future. She was a nice, smart, competent, capable woman, and I felt bad about stressing her out. However, we were still in Major Crisis Mode, and therefore me not being me wasn't in our best interests.

"So, now that we've had an entire week to collect ourselves, what do we do?" It was the day after the third day of State Funerals, otherwise known as the day we buried our friend and the late President of the United States, Vincent Armstrong, and this question was coming from, of all people, his widow, Elaine.

The Former First Lady wasn't normally included in matters of state, but we were possibly the most unconventional politicians the world had ever known, the former unwilling Vice President and even more unwilling President also known as my husband, Jeff Martini, wanted her input, and the man who'd murdered her husband and so many others was still at large. As such, Elaine had joined Team Megalomaniac with gusto.

Frankly, the Current First Lady wasn't normally included in this stuff, but—under the variety of circumstances that had, in just over six short years, moved me from a happy-go-lucky marketing manager into being a superbeing exterminator, the Head of Airborne, the Co- then Head Ambassador for American Centaurion, and now the wife of the President of the United States—my husband valued my input and so my input would be inputted. This was a fast path career track that college had definitely not prepared me for.

"Jeff needs to assign a variety of Cabinet posts and then some," Charles Reynolds said. He was the Head of the C.I.A.'s Extra-Terrestrial Division. He was also my best guy friend since 9th grade. He'd been the focus of the Mastermind's insanity, and since Clifford Goodman and his Goon Squad had escaped after Operation Epidemic, that meant we needed to keep Chuckie very safe while listening carefully and acting on his input.

"Starting with Vice President," my mother said. She wasn't saying this as my mother, of course, but as the Head of the Presidential Terrorism Control Unit. Yeah, my friends and family were definitely representing in the higher levels of government.

"Angela's right as always and we need to assign Embassy staff as well," Doreen Coleman-Weisman said. She'd been raised in the American Centaurion Diplomatic Corps and was now our Ambassador, since I couldn't do the job any longer. "I realize you're going to say that you want me to choose, but under the circumstances, I want your input, Jeff, as well as Kitty's. And everyone else's, too, Chuck's and Angela's in particular."

"I think we're avoiding a key issue," Evander Horn said. He was a handsome black man in his late fifties and the Director of the F.B.I.'s Alien Affairs Division. "And not just because Doreen doesn't want my input specifically." He grinned at her and she laughed.

"What's that, Vander?" Jeff asked.

Horn pointed to the end of the table where Alexander and the rest of the Planetary Council were sitting. "The people who accidentally triggered the Mastermind's doomsday attempt. They came here for a reason and we're not even sure what that reason is."

Alexander nodded. "Yes, I suppose everything has been rather . . . jumbled. Rohini, if you would?"

This was directed to one of the two Shantanu, meaning one of the two giant, colorful penguin-people in attendance. I'd liked Rohini from the moment we'd met him during Operation Civil War, and that he was functioning as Planetary Team Spokesbird wasn't a surprise. He reminded me very much of Alpha Four's version of Winston Churchill, Councilor Leyton Leonidas, and our own Stealth Diplomat, Top Field Agent, and All Around Ladies' Man, the Former Supreme Pontifex of our Earth A-Cs, Richard White.

White was sitting next to Rohini, meaning he was far down the table from me, but of those in the room other than Alexander, he had the closest ties to the Alpha Centauri system, since he'd been born on Alpha Four.

Rohini put his flippers onto the table. "Our earlier stated intent to ask Earth to join the greater galactic community is the main reason we are here. However, we want Earth to join with us because we fear two things—repeated Z'porrah attacks and contact with other alien life from systems far from both of ours."

The Z'porrah were an ancient race of dinobirds who had a deep-seated hatred of the Ancients, who were an ancient race of shapeshifters. Both races had meddled around with Earth and the inhabited Alpha Centauri planets, with the Ancients winning the overall war. However, we'd found Ancient turncoats working for the Z'porrah on several planets, including Earth. So the concern about the Z'porrah wasn't surprising.

"What indication do you have about other sentient races contacting you or us?" Chuckie asked, covering the surprising portion.

"Since our solar system repelled the Z'porrah so

forcefully, we have received numerous transmissions from planets around the galaxy. Apparently the Z'porrah are very unpopular."

"Shocker." Could tell by the expressions of several White House staffers in the room that I wasn't the one who was supposed to be speaking right now. Oh well, they might as well learn how we rolled right now. "So, while we can appreciate the need to show a united front, honestly, we have bigger issues at home that we need to fix first."

"I agree with Kitty," Jeff said. "Not that we want to insinuate that the concerns of the Planetary Council aren't important to us. They are. But if there is no immediate threat, we need to get our own house in order. There's going to be tremendous fallout from the situation Cliff Goodman's insanity put us in."

Alexander nodded. "We agree and understand. And, with your permission, we will stay as long as we are able to assist you in any way, up to and including proving that we weren't responsible in any way for the so-called Alien Virus our mutual enemy released on your unsuspecting populace."

Alexander had gotten really good at the political speak. Nice to know he'd been spending his time learning, not being a jerk, not that this was a big surprise.

"So, since I'm reassured that we aren't offending the Planetary Council or not paying attention to an imminent threat, who are you thinking of for Vice President, Jeff?" Vander asked.

Jeff looked down the table at Senator McMillan. He was the senior senator from Arizona, a good friend, and one of the few honest politicians we knew. "Don?" Jeff asked hopefully.

McMillan shook his head. "I'm tempted, Jeff, don't get me wrong. But honestly, if I'd wanted to be Vice President, I'd have been Vince's running mate instead of you. And as the President Pro Tempore of the Senate, I can do a lot more good for your presidency by staying put."

This wasn't a new statement. Jeff had been trying to harangue McMillan to take the Vice Presidential position for the past several days. McMillan standing firm was in keeping with his personality and beliefs, so couldn't really argue. Even though his wife, Kelly, was an alumna from the same sorority as me and I really liked her, meaning I'd have a pal in the White House.

"You need to ensure that whoever you put into the position is either an existing politician or high enough up in a government agency to be a name the public would know," Nathalie Gagnon-Brewer said. She would know—she'd been the wife of a Representative who'd become our good friend, Edmund Brewer. He'd been murdered by Cliff's people during Operation Sherlock. And the fact that two out of the three men who'd been mentoring Jeff in how to be a good politician were dead at our enemy's hands wasn't lost on me. I'd assigned extra guards to McMillan during Operation Epidemic and had insisted they remain indefinitely.

"What about you, Nathalie?" Jeff asked, clearly not joking.

She shook her head. "I'm a naturalized American, Jeff. I cannot become President and, sadly, as we have just seen, the Vice President is truly a heartbeat away from the Presidency."

Jeff looked at Vander who shook his head with a grin. "I know that look, Jeff, so let me say no on behalf of myself and Chuck, too. We're both not high enough up in our respective agencies to take the job."

"Oh, I wasn't thinking of Chuck for Vice President," Jeff said.

Everyone at the table stared at him, some with their mouths open. James Reader, the Head of Field for Centaurion Division and my other best guy friend since I'd joined up with the gang from Alpha Four, found his voice first. "Why the hell not?"

Jeff grinned at Chuckie's hurt look. "Because I already have a job that Chuck's by far the best qualified to do. Due to Goodman's virus, we have an opening—I want Chuck to take over the C.I.A."

"I'm already the Head of the E-T Division, Jeff," Chuckie said, sounding confused, which was a rarity along the lines of a blue moon.

Jeff shook his head. "I want you in charge of it all, Chuck. As of right now, you're the Director of the Central Intelligence Agency."

Gini Koch lives in Hell's Orientation Area (aka Phoenix, Arizona), works her butt off (sadly, not literally) by day, and writes by night with the rest of the beautiful people. She lives with her awesome husband, three dogs (aka The Canine Death Squad), and two cats (aka The Killer Kitties). She has one very wonderful and spoiled daughter, who will still tell you she's not as spoiled as the pets (and she'd be right).

When she's not writing, Gini spends her time cracking wise, staring at pictures of good looking leading men for "inspiration," teaching her pets to "bring it," and driving her husband insane asking, "Have I told you about this story idea yet?" She listens to every kind of music 24/7 (from Lifehouse to Pitbull and everything in between, particularly Aerosmith and Smash Mouth) and is a proud comics geek-girl willing to discuss at any time why Wolverine is the best superhero ever (even if Deadpool does get all the best lines).

You can reach Gini via her website (www.ginikoch.com), email (gini@ginikoch.com), Facebook (facebook.com/Gini .Koch), Facebook Fan Page: Hairspray and Rock 'n' Roll (facebook.com/GiniKochAuthor), Pinterest page (pinter est.com/ginikoch), Twitter (@GiniKoch), or her Official Fan Site, the Alien Collective Virtual HQ (thealiencollectivevir tualhq.blogspot.com).

Gini Koch
The Alien *Novels*

"Gini Koch's Kitty Katt series is a great example of the lighter side of science fiction. Told with clever wit and non-stop pacing, this series follows the exploits of the country's top alien exterminators in the American Centaurion Diplomatic Corps. It blends diplomacy, action, and sense of humor into a memorable reading experience." —*Kirkus*

"Amusing and interesting...a hilarious romp in the vein of 'Men in Black' or 'Ghostbusters'." —*VOYA*

To Order Call: 1-800-788-6262
www.dawbooks.com